HONOR

SKY RIDGE HOTSHOTS

HONOR

DANIELLE BAKER

PAN BOOKS

First published 2026 by Slowburn
an imprint of Zando
First published in the UK 2026 by Pan Books
an imprint of Pan Macmillan
The Smithson, 6 Briset Street, London EC1M 5NR
EU representative: Macmillan Publishers Ireland Ltd, 1st Floor,
The Liffey Trust Centre, 117–126 Sheriff Street Upper,
Dublin 1 D01 YC43
Associated companies throughout the world

ISBN 978-1-0350-9316-8

Pan Macmillan does not have any control over, or any responsibility for,
any author or third-party websites (including, without limitation, URLs,
emails and QR codes) referred to in or on this book.

9 8 7 6 5 4 3 2

A CIP catalogue record for this book is available from the British Library.

Text design by Neuwirth & Associates, Inc.

Printed and bound in the UK using 100% Renewable Electricity by CPI Group (UK) Ltd

Visit **www.panmacmillan.com** to read more about
all our books and to buy them.

To those out in the world, on their own paths, setting little fires.
You have the power to create the life you desire.

'We are the warriors of the people, who stand on the front line
facing Mother Nature's fury; running in when everyone else is
running out. We are facing fear, death and hell's wrath to protect
souls we may never know, breaking through the devastation of
flames. We honor those that came before us and the souls we fight
valiantly with side by side. We are firefighters.'
~author unknown~

A special thank you to the brave men and women that call
themselves Wildland Firefighters – Interagency Hotshot Crews.
Thank you for your services.

AUTHOR'S NOTE

TROPES

Firefighter romance, angst, small town romance, forced proximity, friends to lovers, widow, love after loss, single mom, brother's best friend, curvy FMC.

TRIGGERS

This book contains mentions of parental death, mentions of spousal death, PTSD/anxiety and emergency home birth.

If you are triggered by any of these situations, please skip this one.

CONTENT WARNINGS

This book contains profane language and explicit, consensual sexual content.

SUPPORT WILDLAND FIREFIGHTERS

I won't call them heroes because they'd hate that, but I could not write this book without acknowledging the real wildland firefighters who perform these hazardous duties every fire season. They work long hours in treacherous conditions, facing extreme heat, smoke and inhospitable terrain – oftentimes without receiving an adequate living wage and while sacrificing time with their loved ones. The challenges they face are beyond what most of us can imagine, taking a toll on their physical, mental and emotional resilience. Their dedication to protect our communities, landscapes and natural resources deserves our deepest appreciation and support.

Grassroots Wildland Firefighters advocate for proper classification, pay, benefits and comprehensive well-being for federal wildland firefighters by providing solutions and support through policy reform.

If you would like to contribute monetarily, please consider donating at givebutter.com/GRWF.

HONOR PLAYLIST

APPLE MUSIC

SPOTIFY

1. Gettin' Warmed Up – Jason Aldean
2. If I Die Before You – Chris Lane
3. Wildfire – Austin Snell
4. World on Fire – Nate Smith
5. Lies Lies Lies – Morgan Wallen
6. Bulletproof – Nate Smith
7. Somebody's Problem – Morgan Wallen
8. You Look Like You Love Me – Ella Langley and Riley Green
9. In Case You Didn't Know – Brett Young
10. To the Men That Love Women After Heartbreak – Kelsea Ballerini
11. Scared to Live Without You – Morgan Wallen
12. Spin You Around – Morgan Wallen
13. Come Back . . . Be Here – Taylor Swift
14. Stand by Me – Lil Durk and Morgan Wallen
15. I'm Gonna Love You – Cody Johnson and Carrie Underwood
16. Bring That Fire – WAR*HALL

ORGANIZATION FLOW CHART

There are thousands of people from various command teams involved with wildland fire operations, but for the sake of keeping it simple, we are only listing the roles mentioned in the Sky Ridge Hotshots series.

```
                    INCIDENT COMMANDER

                       OPERATIONS

                        DIVISION

  VARIOUS ENGINES      SKY RIDGE      HELICOPTER
                       HOTSHOTS      (WITH CREW)

                    SUPERINTENDENT

                        CAPTAIN

    SQUAD BOSS                      SQUAD BOSS

     SAW TEAM                        SAW TEAM

  CREW MEMBERS                    CREW MEMBERS
```

PROLOGUE

XANDER

"Thank you for coming."

My voice sounds hollow even to my own ears. I've repeated the same sentence so many times it's started to sound less like real words and more like a foreign language that I'm not fluent in.

The room around me is bustling though subdued. Small groupings of attendees all waiting to head into the parlor, waiting to pay their respects to my dad.

Superintendent Garrett Macomb, lost in action.

I can see through the dark wood double doors left open wide to the front of the funeral home, to the solitary pedestal in the center of the dais. Flanked by a large, framed photograph on one side, and a folded American flag secure in its shadowbox for safekeeping on the other. His Pulaski—a tool that combines an ax and an adze hoe—is propped up, and his yellow helmet is balanced atop it. Sprays of ferns and a few peace lilies are scattered along the floor as a backdrop. A stage light illuminates the metal urn sitting on the pedestal, the burnished red flaring like flames. I can just make out the metallic gold Maltese Cross of the firefighter emblem on the front of the urn.

I hate the sight of that urn; it's there simply for show. My dad's ashes are out on that mountain where he'd laid down his life to get his team out alive.

My mom is standing just to the left of the large photograph, staring at the man pictured there in the standard yellow wildland fire shirt with his helmet pulled over his graying brows. His eyes are crinkled in the corners, face hastily scrubbed of soot and dirt, but a wide grin splits his face. It's a candid photo; I remember the day it was taken. Though the photo is cropped to show only him, I know that his arm is thrown across my shoulders. We were posing for the picture after fighting a fire in Arizona that had lasted over a month. We were exhausted and hungry and desperate for showers . . . but damn. That was a good day.

Mom's black-clad back is to me, to the still-empty room behind her. Alone in her grief, mourning the man she'd loved and lost nearly thirty years ago, only to lose him all over again now. My throat closes with unshed tears as her shoulders shake, and she reaches out one hand to draw her fingers over my dad's cheek in the photo. She'd requested a few minutes alone with him, so my brothers and I had made ourselves scarce.

I look up when a shadow appears next to me, and I reach out to hug my younger brother Zach. He's a structure firefighter back home in Michigan, and he's garbed in his dress blues. My mom, Zach, and our youngest brother, Joel, had flown into Sky Ridge, Washington, from Michigan to attend. Michigan had been home for the first twenty-five years of my life, but I'd followed Dad to Sky Ridge, much to my mom's disappointment. Followed in the career that had taken my dad from her all those years ago, and the career that had now taken his life.

We all know the risks of the job. He knew. I know. We're hotshots—wildland firefighters—and the risk of not coming home is always high, no matter how well trained and meticulous we are in the field.

My mom had given Dad an ultimatum all those years ago. God, I could still hear the argument, the crying, the begging. She'd begged him not to go, not to leave us again. Told him if he walked out the door, he wasn't welcome back. That we needed him home more than his crew needed him out here. I was eleven, Zach was eight, and Joel was six. She said we needed him home, that growing boys need their father home. She wasn't wrong . . . but neither was he.

I love my mom, truly I do. And I grieve for her more than she knows. She lost the love of her life to the love of *his* life—the job. But she doesn't understand that these men and women are family too. That the job we do, the lives we save . . . it's important. And to those of us who are in it, it's hard to explain to others who aren't.

So Dad had kissed my mom one last time, and then he'd left, because his crew—his brothers—needed him. And when I was twenty-five, I'd made the decision to leave the safety of home, our little slice of heaven in northern Michigan, and join him in Washington. Because this was where my heart was. I'd joined the fire department at nineteen, but my heart wasn't in fighting structure fires. I was born to be a hotshot. I knew it; my parents knew it. Even back then.

I hadn't looked back. Not in all the years since.

We'd worked side by side, year after year. He was a fair but demanding superintendent. He gave as much of himself as he demanded from any member of his crew.

Zach brings me back to the present, slapping my back and then squeezing my shoulder. Taking a deep breath in, I run my palm down my chest, over the front of my own standard-issue yellow wildland fire shirt. It's clean—mostly—and the olive-green Nomex pants I have on are the cleanest ones I own. My boots are scuffed and work-worn, but I'd cleaned those the best I could too. I'm fairly certain Mom almost had an aneurysm when I'd arrived wearing my gear; she had urged me to go back home and put on a black suit, but I'd said no.

XANDER

Our gear is like a badge of honor—this is how we choose to show respect to those whom we've lost.

Zach pulls a silver flask out of the inner pocket of his dress blues and uncaps it, handing it over to me. We share a small smile before I tip it up and take a healthy swig; our dad's favorite whiskey burns my tongue and throat as I swallow. Handing the flask back to Zach, he does the same before pocketing it again.

"Superintendent."

I stiffen at the title and turn, nodding at the man who spoke. Mack Treynor, superintendent of Colorado's Vantage Hotshot crew, a man who'd worked alongside my father for most of their careers. His hazel eyes are solemn, his face stoic as he glances between me and Zach.

"I know how awful that must sound to you right now," my dad's friend says gently, reaching out to grip my shoulder hard in his hand. His grasp is tight, grounding me. "Your dad was a great man, and you've got big boots to fill, son. He was so proud to know you were stepping in behind him. I'm sorry he didn't make it to retirement."

My gut clenches. Twelve weeks. *Twelve fucking weeks and he'd have been retired. He wouldn't have even been on that goddamn call, wouldn't have died on that fucking mountain.*

Mack clears his throat, his own emotions making it difficult for him to speak. His eyes go to Zach then. "He was so damn proud of all of his boys, for following in his steps."

My brothers are both firefighters back home in Michigan. We'd all been on the same crew when I still lived there, before I moved. Joel had only just joined when I left. Zach is now married and has the two cutest girls I've ever seen—*not that I'm biased as their uncle, or anything*—with another on the way. I have no idea what Joel is up to these days, other than being a giant pain in my mom's ass.

Zach nods. "Thank you, Mack. He loved this job more than anything."

But Mack shakes his head, his eyes growing sadder, and he slides his gaze over to my mother, still weeping in front of my dad's photo in the parlor. "Not more than anything."

With one more squeeze to my shoulder, he turns and walks away, leaving the two of us alone. We're not alone for long, because through the plate-glass doors leading outside, I see a group of men, dressed in mostly clean wildland fire gear, making their way across the parking lot.

My brothers, my crew, eighteen of them in total. A force to be reckoned with, and some of the bravest motherfuckers I've ever met.

Callahan Woods, my newly appointed captain, leads the pack. He's followed closely by Jacob Taylor and Rowan Kingsley—King, as we call him—two of our newest recruits. They're young, can't be more than twenty-two, but damn they're hard workers. Jack Taylor—my dad's right-hand guy and Jacob's father—walks several paces behind the others. He's been our squad leader for as long as I can remember. He's retiring at the end of the season, having decided to move his own retirement up, but he wants to work one season with his son, Jacob.

Losing my dad hit him hard and it opened all of our eyes to the risks of this career. He has a family, a wife . . . and he's choosing to step away to focus on them. I can't fault him for it, in the light of what we're doing here today. Jack's wife and their daughter, Violette—Jacob's twin—follow the group in from the parking lot, coming to pay their respects to my dad too. We're all family. Especially on days like today.

Jack walks beside Dixon, one of my crew, who is slowed by a set of crutches and a heavy cast on his right leg. My heart hammers in my chest, the fear and anxiety barreling through me all over again, much like it had in those terrifying moments on the mountain. I had nearly lost most of them, and that memory will haunt me forever. The bravery and leadership that had been my father's Roman Empire had saved them, and I know he would gladly have given his life a hundred times over to save the lives of his outfit, just as he'd done until his dying breath.

The doors open and my team walks through, a somber group today, so unlike the rowdy hell-raisers that I'm used to. Here to pay their respects to the man who had led them through so many fire calls, the man who had been a boss, a friend, a father to every single one of them.

Cal stops in front of me and we shake hands, his eyes darker than usual as he nods to me. I know he's suffering. He was the last man out of that fire, heard the snap of the snag that had come down; he was the one who had seen firsthand my dad's final moments. Knowing there was nothing he could do to save my dad had broken something inside of him. I clasp his shoulder tight and he grips my elbow hard, our conversation silent, before moving inside.

Rowan and Jacob both step forward then, shaking my hand and then Zach's, before moving into the room with Cal as the rest of my crew files through, shaking our hands and offering gruff words of solace and respect. I'm barely conscious of saying something to King about how proud my dad was of him and Jacob this season. I just feel so damn disconnected from everything. Like I'm here, but not.

My chest aches by the time the last of them filter through, that burning, twisting agony back full force. Jack squeezes my shoulder as he comes through the door last. I nod once in acknowledgment, my throat too tight to speak.

The minister from the local church steps over to us then, letting us know that it's time, and Zach makes the announcement to please take a seat inside. Those in attendance wander through the doors, filling the rows and rows of chairs.

My crew takes up two rows by themselves. I stride to the front and take my mom by the shoulders gently, leading her to the front row. Zach and Joel sit on either side of her, each in their dress blues, clasping her hands in theirs. I step to the very front of the room, turning to those assembled in front of me. I clear my throat.

"On behalf of my family, I would like to begin by thanking everyone who is here today and for those who have sent their condolences. The outpouring of love and support have been both comforting during this time and a reminder of the impact that my dad had on so many others. On behalf of my crew, we thank you for the support of the community, while so many others are grieving too."

I clear my throat, swallowing down the emotion that clogs it, and continue. "My dad loved this job, the work he did, the lives and homes and forests he saved, year after year. "All people are created equal, only a few become firefighters," he'd told me once, and it stuck. He died doing what he loved: fighting for those who couldn't and protecting those whom he could. We will honor his sacrifice, honor his bravery in life and his heroic death." I bow my head, clearing my throat again as unmanly tears fill my eyes. "Thank you."

I take my seat to the left of Zach, and my mother reaches across Zach's lap to clutch my hand in her own. My eyes collide with hers, those blue eyes that are so much like mine rimmed with tears, her lips wobbling.

"He loved you boys—loved this—so much. This is how he would have wanted to go."

And finally, the tears slide down my own cheeks as I see in those eyes the thing she won't say—that she wishes he had loved *her* that much. Wishes that he had loved her enough to stay.

I vow to honor my dad, his bravery, and his sacrifice to the best of my ability.

Because honor is all I have in the wake of my grief.

XANDER

1

XANDER

PRESENT

That was too fucking close.

My stride is steady as I exit Bakersfield Hospital, but my shoulders are tense, my mind heavy.

Scrubbing my hand over my face, I exhale as I step out into the warm May sunlight, crossing the parking lot to my truck. I reach up and spin the brim of my ball cap around on my head so that the brim is shading my eyes.

Goddamn, these motherfuckers are making me go prematurely gray.

We all know the risks of this job, but damn it, it doesn't make seeing it with our own eyes any less terrifying. To watch your crewmate, your brother, writhing in pain or hooked up to machines and bandaged head to toe . . . it's sobering. That Skykomish fire was brutal, and it will be a long time before I get the vision of King stuck in that ash pit out of my head.

Reminds us all that we're not invincible, and that the beasts we fight out there are stronger than we are, more ruthless, and far more diabolical.

King will be fine, though, even if he has some healing to do yet. Pulling out of the parking lot, I snort a laugh. If Violette Taylor has anything to say about it, that man will be just fine. She's too stubborn to let him be anything less than okay, and King is too head over heels for the woman to disappoint her. Even if neither of them realizes it yet. They're both whipped.

My phone buzzes in my pocket, so I fish it out and slide my finger across the screen to answer. "Yeah?" I'm not a man of many words. Sue me.

"Lunch at Shifty's?" Callahan, my captain, asks without preamble.

I glance at the clock on the dashboard. It's still early afternoon, but why not. Fuck it, I could use a drink after seeing King in the hospital. "Sure."

"Ten minutes?" he asks.

"Yep."

Twenty minutes later we're seated shoulder to shoulder at Shifty's, our local watering hole that I'm a little ashamed to admit has become somewhat of a second home. We each have a beer and a platter of hot wings in front of us, and we're quiet while we eat. He's my brother in every sense of the word except for biologically, and we've been working on the same crew together for years.

"How's King today?" he asks around a bite of chicken.

"He's fine. Getting discharged later," I answer, taking a swig of beer. I rest my forearms against the edge of the bar and stare down at my plate. "Fucker is lucky."

Cal sighs, licking the sauce off his fingers, and nods. "Yeah, I know. Scared the shit out of all of us, man. It was like Jacob all over again."

I nod without saying anything, because that's exactly what it felt like.

Lou, our bartender, slides a couple fresh beers in front of us and we nod in thanks.

XANDER

"Hey, thanks again for helping me get Teddy and the kids moved in," he says then, tearing off a chunk of meat with his teeth and chewing. "It's a whole lot easier checking in on her now that she's not forty-five minutes away."

I nod, popping a carrot stick in my mouth. "She doing all right?"

Cal snorts, shrugging and shaking his head at the same time. "She's surviving, I guess?" he says, and my gut clenches as he continues. "I hate that I'm not here to help more. I can't imagine what she's going through—losing Logan, being pregnant. I worry about being out on a call now that she's so close to her due date. But at least she's got Scottie here while I'm gone. And I'm grateful that you're right next door when we are home."

I nod again, taking a long pull off my beer. Cal's sister, Teddy, lost her husband about six months ago after finding out they were expecting their third baby together. Being the protective big brother, Cal had insisted that she move closer to him and his girlfriend so they could help. But it's hard when we're gone as often as we are. It helps that she's my new neighbor though.

"You know I'll keep an eye out," I offer gruffly. "She's not alone, Cal."

"I appreciate that more than you know," he says quietly. "I, uhh . . . I know you watch out for her, Xander."

I swallow hard around a drink of my beer but keep my eyes trained ahead. We don't talk about this. Not out loud, anyway.

"Always, man," I admit on a gruff whisper, and he nods.

Because he knows, even if I've never said the words, and possibly never will.

2

Teddy

Braxton-Hicks contractions are the most useless and annoying things in the universe, I've decided.

Bracing my palms against the sides of my rounded belly, I sigh heavily. They're not painful, necessarily, but they're not all cupcakes and rainbows, either.

"You okay, Mom?"

I smile into the rearview mirror at my eight-year-old son, Dalton. "Yeah, I'm fine, bud. You all buckled in?"

He nods, his chocolate-brown eyes finding mine in the mirror from the back seat. "Penny dropped her cup, but I grabbed it for her."

"You're the best helper," I say to him with another smile as I put my minivan in reverse and back out of the parking spot at the grocery store. We did a huge grocery haul in preparation for the new baby's arrival in the next couple weeks, and the back end of the van is loaded down with grocery bags.

I'm already dreading carrying them all inside.

My back hurts, my feet are swollen—not that I can see them at this point anyway—and these stupid false contractions are *just* uncomfortable enough to make me more emotional than usual. I know Dalton will help me carry some of the bags in, my little helper, but the heavier bags are all mine.

The drive home is short, and by the time I'm pulling into the driveway, Penny, my four-year-old, is chomping at the bit to get out of her car seat. Dalton helps her unbuckle while I slowly slide out of the driver's seat and grab my purse. The baby stretches, and I press a hand to where I can feel her rump pressing just below my ribs, and I smile.

"Almost there, baby girl," I whisper, then laugh when I feel a kick. My heart aches, seizing my chest even as I smile. This pregnancy has been bittersweet to say the least.

I never thought I'd be doing all of this alone. Going to appointments, seeing the ultrasounds, hearing that whooshing thump of her heartbeat on the monitor, all of it without Logan.

It wasn't supposed to be like this. I wasn't supposed to be doing this alone.

I wasn't supposed to be a widow at thirty-one with two—*almost three*—kids. Logan was supposed to be here. My sweet, loving, goofy Logan. My high school sweetheart and the best daddy ever. The man with a heart of gold and a giving nature . . . but it had cost him his life, and now I'm left here alone. So alone and tired and scared all the time. I hate it.

But now, with Logan gone, I *have* to do it alone. I can't imagine getting involved with anyone else. It's safe this way. Because I can't imagine *losing* someone again.

Thank God for my brother and his girlfriend, Scottie, and Logan's parents. My new friend Vi has been a godsend too. We met about a month ago, after I moved to Sky Ridge to be closer to Cal and Scottie, and her friendship has been exactly what I needed. I honestly don't know how I would have survived the last six months without them all.

Dalton clicks the button to open the slider door and he hops out, then helps Penny climb down. We make our way to the back of the van and I open the hatch. Thank modern mechanics for hands-free liftgates, because bending over is pretty much not happening at this point.

"I can carry some," Dalton says, looking up at me. I smile, ruffling the hair on the top of his head. He ducks away but grins.

"How about you take these two bags," I say, taking some of the lighter ones, handing one to Penny and one to Dalton. "And take Penny inside while I grab some more?"

"Okay!" they say in unison, taking hold of the plastic handles, and then they're off. I contemplate just loading up my arms with as many bags as I can physically carry, but decide against it, just taking a few and following my kids up the paved pathway to our front door. It's a single-story, split townhouse with duplex apartments on either side. It's not big, but we have enough space for just us.

And it's less than ten minutes away from Cal and Scottie.

Glancing over at the door that matches ours on the other side of a bricked partition, I sigh. Pretty sure Cal had insisted on *this* house because his boss—who also happens to be his best friend—lives next door and can help keep an eye on us too.

While I appreciate the sentiment and the fact that my brother just wants to make sure we're all okay . . . did we have to move into an apartment directly next to Xander?

His side of the driveway is empty, his black pickup truck not in its usual spot, and I can't help but feel relieved.

The man makes me nervous.

Not in a bad way . . . but in a "good Lord this man is outrageously attractive and the way he watches me makes me blush" kind of way.

I've known Xander Macomb for years, first as my brother's co-worker, then best friend, and most recently, as his boss. Pretty sure he, Logan, and Cal had all gotten drunk together playing beer pong at a family barbecue a couple years ago. He's come with Cal to Dalton's baseball games and had sent a teddy bear to Penny after she'd had her tonsils removed earlier this year.

He had come with Cal to Logan's funeral.

I honestly don't remember much of that day. I know he'd been there, but I was so numb with grief I simply don't remember many details from that entire week, let alone the day itself.

After I lift the bags onto the counter, I get Penny situated in the living room with her tablet to keep her occupied, and then Dalton and I head back outside to get more groceries. Leaning in awkwardly to reach a bag that's rolled to the back, I groan when I hear the familiar rumble of Xander's truck as he pulls into his side of the driveway. *Why now?*

"Hey, Xander!" Dalton calls to him across the yard, and then I hear the door of his truck shut with a clang. A particularly brutal Braxton-Hicks contraction tightens my belly and I hiss out a breath between my teeth as I straighten, pressing a palm to my stomach.

"Teddy?"

His deep voice is laced with concern as he reaches us, and I blow out a breath as the false contraction eases. Bracing myself, I raise my eyes to his. He's got the most incredible eyes I've ever seen, and they never fail to stun me. The icy sky-blue irises are ringed with darker blue and flecked with gray near the pupils—framed by dark, annoyingly long lashes. His face and arms are tanned, like he works out in the sun shirtless a lot, and his lower face is darkened with a close-trimmed beard.

He's wearing a pair of jeans that fit way too well, and an ancient-looking Petoskey Fire Department T-shirt that molds to his upper body. His dark hair is thick and just a tad too long; the ends are curled slightly beneath the brim of his Detroit Tigers baseball hat.

"You all right?" he asks gently, stepping close. His gaze travels over me completely, from head to toe, and I can't help the heat that spreads across my cheeks in embarrassment.

I nod, dropping my hand from my belly. Baby does another stretch; she doesn't like the false contractions either. I give him a small smile, though I can still feel the heat of the blush on my cheeks. *Why does he have to be here to witness this?* "Just a little false contraction. I've been getting them a lot this week."

"Should you be heading to the hospital?" he asks, his dark brows furrowing over those eyes.

Shaking my head, I laugh. "No, it's okay. They're normal, and not anything to be concerned about. I had them for two months before I went into labor with this one," I chuckle, draping my arm over Dalton's shoulders.

"Mom," Dalton groans, shrugging out from under my arm. "You're embarrassing me."

Xander laughs, and the sound does something to me. It's low and deep and soothing. I miss the sound of a man's laugh.

"Hey, champ," he says, holding out his fist to my son. Dalton bumps his knuckles to Xander's and grins. "What do you say we grab the rest of these bags for your mom?"

"Xander, I can carry my own groceries—" I protest, but he pins me with that blue stare. My words trail off.

"Absolutely not," he says quietly. "Your brother would never forgive me if he knew I let you carry all this in by yourself. You go inside and sit down, Dalton and I can handle this."

"Xander—"

"Teddy." His tone stops my protest. Deep and husky and laced with just a little bit of heat.

My cheeks bloom with more heat as he stares at me.

"Let me help you."

TEDDY

He doesn't pose it as a question, and I know arguing won't do any good, so I nod. "Okay. Thank you."

I move to pick up a couple bags and the man growls at me. Full-on *growls*. "Don't touch those bags, Teddy. I'm warning you."

Dalton giggles and I roll my eyes. "You're being ridiculous."

Xander places his hands on my shoulders and gently moves me away from the van and the pile of groceries, then turns me toward the townhouse. "I said go sit down. Dalton and I have this under control, right, champ?"

"Right!" Dalton exclaims.

I shake my head again but do as he says.

Penny requests that I sit next to her on the couch when I come through the door, so I sink slowly into the cushions and let her snuggle into my side as Dalton and Xander make the several trips in with the remaining groceries. His gaze takes in the space and I scrunch my face up in mortification. Penny's toys are all over the living room floor that I didn't take the time to clean up earlier, and there're dishes in the sink from lunch that should probably be rinsed and put in the dishwasher.

When I make to stand, Xander glares at me, pointing one finger at me. "Don't move. We've got this, remember?" Turning to Dalton, he asks, "Can you help me put these away?"

"Yeah!" he says, grinning, and I can't help the smile that pulls at my own mouth. He's missed having a guy around.

Grief seizes me then. I miss my husband. So much. It's strange having another man in my space, even if he's only here to help because of his loyalty to my brother.

It doesn't take long before the two have all of my groceries unbagged, sorted, and put away. Xander had to ask where to put a few items, and I directed him with a grin from my spot on the couch.

Bunching up the plastic bags, Xander stores them in the "bag of bags" Dalton shows him under the sink, and then they're finished.

Dalton looks so darn proud of himself, and Xander offers him his knuckles for another fist bump. "Good work, champ. Thanks for the help."

Scooting to the edge of the couch, I brace my hand on the arm of the sofa to push myself up awkwardly, but before I can, Xander is in front of me with his hands outstretched.

I laugh, feeling the heat rising in my cheeks, and roll my eyes. What a sight I must be. I've never been small, but being at the tail end of my third pregnancy has me feeling like a beached whale. Placing my hands in both of his, I allow him to help me up from my seat on the couch. God, I can't wait for this baby to get here. These last few weeks have been torture and hard on my body this go-around.

He steadies me, taking a step back so that my stomach doesn't bump into his. His body is hard all over, heavily muscled and tanned. Every part of me is soft and big, especially now, and it makes me self-conscious being this close to a man built like a damn god. It's unfair.

"Thank you," I murmur, ducking my head and dropping my hands from his to smooth my shirt out over my belly. My leggings are soft and cling to every inch of my legs, and I'm thankful the top I'm wearing is flowy and covers my butt. "And thank you for doing all of that. You didn't have to."

"You don't have to do all of this alone, Teddy," he says gently, but takes several steps back. "I'm right next door if you need anything."

I laugh then, crossing my arms over my stomach as we make our way toward the door. I feel bad that he and Cal feel that they have to babysit me. I try so hard to hide away my grief and be superwoman so they don't worry, but that's clearly failing on my end. "You're home once every two weeks, Xander."

"Well, if I'm home and you need anything, you come get me, okay? You have my number," he says, staring down at me.

TEDDY

I laugh again. "Yes, I have your number. Cal made sure I have it for emergencies . . . though I think that's what nine-one-one is for too. They might get here quicker than you most times."

He laughs, nodding sheepishly. "Well, we both feel better knowing you have someone else looking out for you and the kids. At least when we're home, I'm just a few feet away."

"We're fine," I assure him, my chest tightening. He's such a kind man. I just wish he didn't make me so damn nervous. Why couldn't I have a nice elderly neighbor that doesn't look like Xander? That doesn't look at me the way Xander does . . . I shake my head to clear the thought before another blush can tinge my cheeks. "Logan's parents check in regularly. And I have Scottie nearby too."

He nods. "I mean it, Teddy," he urges as he steps out the door. "If you need anything. Day or night. You come get me. Okay?"

"Okay," I whisper, nodding.

"Try to relax a little, all right? No lifting anything heavy."

I snort a laugh and roll my eyes at him. We both know he's being ridiculous, but I'll let him if it makes him feel better. "Okay."

He stares at me from my front patio. "Good night, Teddy."

"Good night, Xander," I whisper before closing the door.

His heavy footfalls fade into silence as he walks away, and I'm once again alone with my kids.

3

XANDER

It's been almost a week since I've been home last. We just pulled back in from a fire in Wyoming. Running a man short with King still out hasn't been peaches either, but I'd rather he be back here recovering properly than out with us.

The rigs are unpacked and cleaned, and most of the guys are headed down to Shifty's for a celebratory beer or two. Cal checked on Teddy on our drive into town, and he gave me a thumbs-up, the signal that she's all good at home. Shoving my fingers up through my hair, I grimace at the dust and grime caked there. I'm desperate for a hot shower, and though I could shower at the base, I'd rather use my own.

And it gives me an excuse to check on Teddy too.

The sun is hanging low in the sky, the horizon darkening when I pull into the driveway, and I'm happy to see her minivan parked across the lawn on her side. I can see the TV on in the living room and a light glowing in the kitchen as I grab my pack from the passenger seat of my truck and climb out.

I can't wait for a hot shower, food, and sleep.

Shower is first up though, so I drop my pack in the center of my bed and disappear into the bathroom to turn the taps on. I strip out of my filthy Nomex gear and shower quickly, scrubbing off the dirt and soot and grime of the last week until the water runs clear. Dunking my head under the spray of water, I freeze and pull back when a sound from next door alarms me. I strain my ears but hear nothing further. Must be imagining things.

Turning off the water, I step out and reach for a towel, scrubbing it over my body and hair haphazardly. Padding into the bedroom, I pull on a pair of underwear and jeans, then pull a T-shirt out of the drawer and slide it over my head.

Barefoot, I head out to the kitchen and snag a beer from the fridge, bringing it to my lips and taking a long pull.

A timid knock sounds on the front door and I lower the beer bottle away from my lips. A second knock follows, then the sound of a pained cry through the walls of the duplex has me moving on instinct, my heart in my throat.

Opening the door, I stop in my tracks, nearly bowling over Dalton in my rush. His young face is pale, fear stamped across it, his chin wobbling with emotion. Something wet and pink has stained the knees of his khaki pants. I drop to my knees in front of him, taking his shoulders in my hands.

"Hey, what's going on? Are you hurt?"

He shakes his head and swallows, then points toward the other side of the townhouse. Another pain-filled cry drifts to me through the darkness. I already know what he's about to say.

"Mom. She's—"

I stand, shoving my feet into sneakers. Taking him by the hand, together we rush around the partition toward their front door. Pushing the door open, I stop Dalton at the threshold and say softly, "I want you to take your sister into the bedroom and close the door, okay? Do you have a TV in there? A tablet to keep her busy?"

Dalton nods, his eyes flashing toward the back bedroom as another sob meets our ears. Timed apart, she doesn't have long to go, I realize with a grimace.

"Okay, champ, I'm going to help your mom. You can be brave for her, right?" I ask.

He nods. Penny is crying, so I scoop her up into my arms and stride down the hallway, following Dalton. He stops in front of the bedroom door and I set down Penny, crouching to ask her, "Where's your teddy bear? Can you get it and hold on to it for me?"

She sniffles and nods, taking hold of Dalton's hand tightly.

I stand and offer him my fist, which he fist-bumps. "You got this, champ."

He closes the door and I continue down the hallway.

"Da-Dalton?" I hear Teddy call weakly, and my stomach clenches. "Buddy, did you find my phone?"

"Teddy?" I call softly. "Is it okay if I come in?"

"O-okay." I hear the breathless reply, hear the briefest of hesitation in that voice, and I push the door open.

She's standing in the doorway to the bathroom, a towel on the floor at her feet that she's attempting to use to clean up the mess her water breaking had made on the tile floor. Her hand grips the door handle so tightly her knuckles turn white as she folds in on herself, and I can see the way her rounded stomach contracts and tightens beneath the material of her shirt. God that looks painful. She grits her teeth and pants as her body relaxes.

"I'm sorry," she mumbles, glancing over at me. "I didn't know Dalton went to find you. I asked him to find my phone so I could call an ambulance."

I step closer to her and smile gently. "He did exactly what he should have, Teddy. I'll get an ambulance on the way, or I can drive you, or call Cal—"

XANDER

She starts to shake and tips her head back as another contraction takes over, and I don't hesitate another second, stepping forward and easing myself around her so that I'm standing at her back. Her pained sob as it fades eats away at my armor. Her forehead is dotted with sweat, her T-shirt is loose but sweat makes it cling to her. The pair of leggings she has on are wet from her water breaking.

"May I?" I ask before touching her. She nods jerkily, her body sagging as the contraction fades. I slide my arms around her, under her arms, and slide my palms under the swell of her very pregnant belly. She leans back against my chest, her head falling against my shoulder as I gently lift, relieving some of the pressure and weight. "How long since your water broke?"

She breathes in and out through her mouth, slowly, methodically. "Maybe ten minutes ago? I was fine, and then it just came out of nowhere. I came back here to get my bag and that's when my water broke. Dalton tried to help me clean up, but I told him to go find my phone—"

With my hands supporting her stomach and her back leaning heavily into my chest, I can feel the contraction start beneath my palms. She grits her teeth again and another agonized cry escapes her. She's trembling violently and tears stain her cheeks.

I murmur soothingly into her ear. "That's it, there's another one. I'm going to let go for just a second so I can grab my phone out of my pocket."

She nods again, and I pull my arm back, digging into my back pocket for my cell phone. I dial 911 and turn on the speaker feature, then set it down on the bathroom counter. Two rings, and a familiar voice answers. "Nine-one-one, what is your emergency?"

"Hey, Laurel, this is Xander Macomb. I have a woman who is in active labor, contractions seem to be timed less than a minute apart, and her water has broken. Can you send an ambulance our way, please?"

"Of course, what's your location, Superintendent?"

I wince at the title, something I'm still not entirely used to even six years later, but another contraction starts and I make sure I'm supporting Teddy fully again. Her shaking has intensified, remaining even when the contraction ends. I rattle off the address and Laurel assures us that she'll get an ambulance headed our way immediately. I request that she stay on the line.

"Sweetheart, what's your name?" Laurel asks.

"T-Teddy Hansen," she manages to say before another pained cry escapes her lips. I hold on as tightly as I dare, fear that I might somehow hurt her tempering my hold slightly.

"Hansen?" Laurel asks, and I sense the surprise in her tone, and understand why. Logan might not have been an EMT in this district, but word travels, especially in small, close-knit towns like Sky Ridge and Cedar Valley.

I glance down at Teddy, watching a tear slip down her cheek as she squeezes her eyes shut. My eyes land on her left hand and the wedding ring set on her third finger that she hasn't taken off yet. Not that I blame her.

"She has two other kids here in the residence," I tell Laurel after the contraction subsides again, forcing my brain to focus. Then, speaking directly to her, I murmur, "Teddy, sweetheart, do you want me to call Cal?"

She shakes her head. "I didn't even know you guys were back in town. Lo-Logan's parents are in Cedar Valley."

My chest constricts painfully, listening to the sadness in her voice, the despair and hopelessness in her tone. I hate that she's here alone, having buried her husband six months ago. My gut clenches. Fucking hell. I hold on to her tighter, letting her lean her weight into me.

"I'm right here," I whisper, my throat closing with emotion, knowing it means little to the woman I'm holding right now, but hoping it helps even just the slightest. "Lean into me, Teddy."

XANDER

A pitiful, keening sound escapes her through fiercely clenched teeth, her legs trembling, and then she sobs, "I can't, can't wait—I need—" She scrabbles weakly at the hem of her shirt, her fingers reaching for the waistline of her leggings. As gently as I can, I help her, peeling the leggings and her underwear down her legs. Her fingers tighten around my forearms where she's clutching them.

"Teddy, I'm going to lower you down to the floor, okay?"

She nods again, and I get her lowered to the floor. Reaching over to the rack next to the shower, I grab a handful of the fluffy terry cloth towels. I position one beneath her head and then stand, rushing to the sink to wash my hands hastily.

"Laurel, ETA?" I ask toward the phone's speaker.

"Looks like they're about five minutes out," Laurel's voice comes through.

I swear and glance over at Teddy, keeping my gaze on her face. "They're not going to make it in time," I mutter, and then sink to my knees in front of Teddy. "Hey, you're doing so great."

She shakes her head with a sob.

"Look at me, Teddy. Sweetheart—"

She raises her eyes that look like silver pools as I position myself between her raised knees. I place a folded towel beneath her bottom and another one next to us, then smile at her. I can see the baby's head already.

"We're going to deliver this baby, okay? I haven't done this in a really long time, but I do have training, all right? Trust me?"

"I can't do this—" she cries on a whisper, rolling her head on the towel tucked beneath it. Her eyes are squeezed tightly shut, though tears continue to track down her cheeks where they disappear into her dark blond hair. "He was supposed to be here."

I take her hand in mine and squeeze gently. "Teddy. Listen to me; you *can* do this. You've done so good. We're going to get this baby here and then we're going to get you into the hospital, okay? On the next contraction, I want you to push. Can you do that?"

She shakes her head no, but seconds later the next contraction is on her, and while I'm kneeling before her, she bears down on instinct.

"There you go. Teddy, one more and this baby is here. One more. Here we go—"

A hoarse cry rips from her lips, and then I'm catching the squirming, tiny baby in the towel I prepared. I swipe my finger into the baby's mouth to clear the airways, then flip the baby over and thump her on the back. The longest heartbeat of my life passes and then a gusty wail erupts from the baby's mouth. Teddy sobs out a laugh as I pass the baby over to her, setting the baby girl on her mother's chest.

"You did it," I praise quietly, leaning over to brush the hair away from Teddy's face. She's flushed and sweaty, and unshed tears make her eyes look luminous as she stares up at me. I'm lost in those eyes. Lost . . . and completely helpless to pull my way out of them. "You're a badass."

I watch as she swallows hard, her throat working with the motion, and she opens her mouth to speak—

A knock at the front of the house pulls my eyes from hers to the bathroom door. I can hear the front door opening and a man's voice call out, "Superintendent Macomb?"

"We're in the back bathroom," I reply, cautious not to shout too loudly in deference to the tiny babe in her mother's arms. I listen to the telltale rattle of the stretcher as it's guided through the living room and down the narrow hallway. "EMS is here, Teddy. We're going to get you loaded up and take you two girls to the hospital."

"What about my kids?" she whispers, her gray eyes wide and bouncing between mine. "I can't leave them—"

"We'll be right behind you," I assure her gently, clasping my hand over hers, where it's curved around the baby's towel-covered back.

XANDER

I raise my eyes to the two uniformed EMTs that have just popped in through the bedroom door. I can't help but breathe a sigh of relief. I'm glad Prescott—Cal's girlfriend, Scottie—is one of the first responders Laurel sent. I shift out of the way, just to Teddy's side to allow Scottie room. Teddy's fingers squeeze around mine, like she doesn't want to let go of my hand either.

"Hey there, sis," Scottie murmurs as she kneels next to Teddy, who lets out a soft sob at seeing the familiar, friendly face.

Emotion burns in my throat.

Beaming a smile down at Teddy, Scottie whispers reverently, "Look at what you did!"

"Can you call Cal? And Lo-Logan's parents, so one of them can help with Dalton and Penny—" Teddy stammers, her words breaking through the tears, and I clasp her hand tight in my own. She swings her eyes from Scottie's to mine.

"Hey, sweetheart, we've got this, okay? We'll be right behind you," I repeat quietly, my gaze firm on hers, stalling the rapid fire of words that are tumbling out of her mouth. I squeeze her hand again. "Teddy, I know this is all scary and you've had to do this all by yourself, but you're not alone now, okay?"

Tears shimmer in her eyes as she nods, just slightly. Her lips are pulled tight, and I can see the pain etched there, now that some of the adrenaline has started to wear off.

I nod once to Scottie and her partner Matthew, then return my attention to Teddy. "You're not alone, sweetheart. We're right here."

I want to comfort her in some way. Hold her. Make her realize she's *not* alone. Because I'm right here. Fuck, am I glad I came home instead of heading down to Shifty's. I squeeze Teddy's hand once more and then lose the inner battle with myself and lean down to press a kiss to the top of her blond hair. I squeeze my eyes shut tight for a second before opening them as I lean back.

"I'm so damn proud of you, Teddy," I murmur gently. Smiling down at her, my fucking heart is thumping wildly in my chest for this incredible, brave woman. "You did so good, sweetheart. So damn good."

4

Teddy

The events from a week ago are both a blur and painfully clear in my brain. Xander drove Dalton and Penny to the hospital in my minivan, following myself and the baby in the ambulance, and hung out in the waiting room with my kids until Cal showed up to take over.

Logan's parents arrived at the hospital shortly after Cal, and Colleen, my mother-in-law, is staying with us for two weeks to help out. She left to run a few errands earlier when Violette got here to let us have some girl time and to let the kids play.

Vi was my savior today; she brought Dalton and Penny Happy Meals earlier and let me eat my own carton of deliciously salty fries while they were still hot. She took the opportunity to snuggle on Bea, who is already somehow a week old. She and her daughter Hollie left just a few minutes ago. Ugh, I owe them all so much. I couldn't do this without Colleen or Vi.

Cal had called the morning after my emergency home birth to say that they had gotten a roll out back to Wyoming to a sister fire that had broken out, so they've been gone for the last week. It hasn't stopped my brother from texting every day and requesting new baby pictures to share, of course. Vi mentioned that the crew is getting back tonight according to Rowan, who is apparently jonesing to get back to work after his accident.

I haven't seen Xander since the night Bea was born, which is totally fine with me. I might never be able to look the man in the eyes again after that night. As much as I would love a little amnesia to take over and save me from the waves of mortification that keep swallowing me whole every time I remember the events of that night, it hasn't happened yet.

"Oh god," I groan, dropping my face into my hand. The man is fine with a capital *F*, and he not only witnessed, but assisted, in birthing my newborn. *Was all up in there.* Fantastic. Poor man is probably scarred for life.

I may or may not be watching out the window for a black pickup truck to appear in the driveway so I can avoid my stupidly hot neighbor for the rest of my life.

"I see the way you look at him. I think it was fate for him to be the one to come to your rescue."

Now Violette's words from our conversation earlier are on replay in my head. Dammit, Vi. I don't look at him any certain way.

I don't.

Not *really*, anyway.

He's just nice to look at. And really kind and gentle and obnoxiously good with my kids. *And* it's probably just my stupid postpartum emotions doing their thing making me all sensitive and super emotional.

Right?

Scooping my newborn up just to feel her tiny body against mine, I snuggle her up on my chest as I walk around the kitchen, all seven pounds, two ounces of her. She has the same light brown hair as Dalton and Penny and the same dark eyes.

TEDDY

I press my lips to the top of her head, breathing in her baby smell as tears well in my eyes. Pushing my glasses back up the bridge of my nose, I swipe at the wetness on my cheek.

Logan made sure I had him with me. In all of our kids. All three of them have his hair and chocolate-brown eyes.

It's like my genetics didn't even try.

I snort a laugh and then wince at the slight pull of pain in my midsection. Taking Bea with me, I lower myself slowly into the corner of the couch and prop my feet up. I am happy to announce that I once again have ankles and toes that don't look like sausages. Small win, but a win just the same. I'll take it.

I haven't let myself look at my naked body in the mirror yet, not quite ready for that hit to my self-esteem. My body is just built differently, always has been.

Don't get me wrong, I've grown to appreciate everything this body has done for me. It carried and birthed three beautiful, healthy babies. But I'm pretty sure this mom pooch will forever be with me. *Yay*.

The telltale rumble of a truck engine perks my ears and I slink down on the couch as if that will somehow make me less visible to the man in that truck, like he has X-ray vision and can see through the walls or something. I hear the metallic thunk of his truck door closing, and then the quiet snick of his front door.

It's quiet for a while, Penny zonked out after her playdate with Hollie, and Dalton is in his bedroom. With Bea asleep on my chest, I almost doze off, but startle awake when a knock sounds on the door.

Pulling myself and Bea to a stand slowly, I make my way to the door and pull it open. Xander is standing on the porch, a bouquet of flowers and a paper sack in his hands. He looks like he just stepped out of a shower, his hair damp and curling slightly at the ends, and he's wearing a pair of clean jeans and a T-shirt that looks like it's seen better days.

He's gorgeous, of course.

And I'm painfully aware of the fact that I didn't put any makeup on after my shower earlier and my hair is piled up on the top of my head in the messiest of buns. I'm wearing a loose-fitting pair of pajama pants and an oversized sweatshirt. My glasses have a smudge on one corner of the lens that I was too tired to worry about. Mom couture at its finest. I almost snort another laugh. *Yikes*.

"There's the two prettiest girls in Sky Ridge," he says quietly, his eyes dropping to the baby snuggled against my chest.

I blush and roll my eyes. He's ridiculous. "Hi, Xander," I murmur, smoothing my hand over Bea's back.

"How are you?" he asks, gesturing with his chin to the baby in my arms. "Are you all right? I didn't do anything to hurt you or the baby, right?"

I smile and shake my head, moving to the side slightly. "We're both great, thank you. I wouldn't have known what to do without your help. Would you like to come in?"

He steps inside, closing the door behind him. He follows me into the kitchen and sets the bouquet of flowers down on the counter, along with the white paper bag. "My mom always says the best thing to bring a new mom is a home-cooked meal. Best I could do was a deli sandwich from Leo's. Cal said it's your favorite."

"With a pickle spear?" I ask, grinning.

He nods, smiling too. The corners of his eyes crinkle when he smiles, and a little dimple appears in one cheek, partially hidden beneath his dark beard. My heart flutters just a bit, little butterflies that aren't quite ready to take flight yet.

"Would you like to hold her?"

His eyes drop from mine to the top of Bea's head, which is resting beneath my chin, and then he nods. Scooping my baby into my hands, I gently spin her and place her in Xander's arms. She looks so tiny in comparison to his muscled arms and large hands, and tears prick my eyes again as he leans in close and croons to her quietly.

She won't know what it's like to have a dad.

Swiping at the tear that threatens to slip down my cheek, I spin so that I'm facing away from him. I don't want Xander to see me break down. I need to be strong. For my kids at the very least. If he and Cal think I can't take care of myself or my kids, they'll never give me any peace.

"Want to dig into that sandwich while I hold her?" he asks my back.

I nod, moving toward the counter and pulling the thick deli sandwich out of the bag.

"Sit down, Teddy. You don't have to eat standing up."

Moving the sandwich and the plastic-wrapped pickle spear to the other side of the kitchen counter, I pull myself up into one of the barstools. I wince at the tightness in my lower abdomen and hiss out a breath.

Xander is there in a heartbeat, one of his hands dropping to my back, Bea cradled securely in his other arm. "What is it? Are you hurting?"

"Just a little sore still," I whisper, embarrassment heating my cheeks as I settle into the chair. My eyes find his, but I drop my gaze quickly, shyly. "I'm fine, I promise. Just moved a little quicker than I should have. I'll be moving around like normal by this time next week."

Xander moves back to the other side of the counter so that he's once again standing in the kitchen, his body swaying slightly as he holds Bea. I dig into the sandwich, moaning at the fluffiness of the fresh bread and deli sauce as it hits my tongue. He chuckles lightly and I blush again. Dammit.

"This is delicious, thank you," I say. "And your mom is right, this was a great idea."

"You're welcome. I needed an excuse to come see how this little one was doing. And to see how you're doing," he says, his eyes on me. "You sure you're all right? I was so worried I did something to hurt you—"

I shake my head again, wiping the corner of my mouth with a napkin. "I promise, we're fine. You did everything right. You don't need to worry about me, Xander."

He swallows hard, his eyes still on mine. "Yeah, I do."

I blink at him several times, the quiet huskiness of his words short-circuiting my brain.

Warning bells go off in my head. This is dangerous territory. My heart is not available. Like, ever again. He must know that, right? I internally shake my head; I'm being ridiculous now. He's just being polite. As my neighbor. And my brother's best friend.

Swallowing another bite, I send up a silent prayer of thanks when Bea starts to fuss in his arms. Standing, I round the counter and take her from him.

"Umm, she's probably hungry," I whisper lamely, keeping my eyes lowered from his. "Thank you for the sandwich, and the flowers."

"If you need anything—"

"I know," I whisper, raising my eyes to his as he backs away. "Thank you, Xander."

He moves forward then, swiping his knuckle across Bea's cheek once, and I squeeze my eyes shut when he drops a kiss to the top of my head, tears threatening again. *Oh shit*. I need him to go. I need him to go so I can fortify these walls around my very fragile and hyper-emotional heart. That's all this is. Clearly, my postpartum hormones are on overdrive.

Besides, I have a promise to keep to myself, and to my kids.

"Teddy."

I shake my head, stepping back. Whatever he's going to say, I can't hear it. Swallowing around the tightness in my throat and blinking

TEDDY

back the tears, I whisper almost desperately, "I need to feed her, you should probably go . . ."

"Okay," he murmurs softly, almost hesitantly, and then he disappears out the door.

When the door closes behind him, I let my head fall back to my shoulders so I can blink up at the ceiling, sucking in deep, shuddering breaths.

My husband has been dead for only six months . . . I focus on remembering Logan's sweet, kind face. How his coffee-brown eyes would sparkle when he'd look at me, how loving and passionate he was when he'd make love to me . . .

But his face keeps getting further and further from my memory as time passes. That face that I had once known like the back of my own hand is now blurred. Like trying to focus on him through a fogged-up window, he always drifts away from me like tendrils of smoke. I keep his pictures up throughout the house, for me, and for Dalton and Penny. Dalton has a picture of Logan in a frame next to his bed, from the last baseball game Logan had made it to. Dalton had hit a home run, his first, and we'd celebrated with a picture and ice cream after. Dalton was missing one front tooth, but his grin was wide and happy as he held up the home run ball in his hand. Logan's arm was draped over his shoulder, and the wide, proud smile on his face said all it needed to of how much he loved his kids.

I sink into the corner of the couch and lay Bea on her back just long enough to pull the sweatshirt over my head and toss it aside. Lowering one side of my tank top, I lift her back into my arms and guide her searching mouth to my breast. When she latches, I sigh, closing my eyes.

Opening my eyes, I find our wedding picture across the room where it sits on the TV stand. We were such babies, so young and carefree and without a single idea of what this world was about to bring our way. How little time we would actually have.

Despite the ten years of marriage, our ridiculous naïveté, and the sometimes-hard times, it hadn't been enough. I wanted more time, and I hated the cruelty of fate that had taken that away. Taken him away from us. From Dalton, Penny, and Bea.

They would grow up without their dad. And I'm to blame.

Well, I blame myself, even if no one else does. A freak accident, something no one could have predicted, or stopped. Just cruel fate.

Just like how cruel fate would dangle the gorgeous and infinitely kind Xander at me, knowing full well I'll never take the bait. That harsh reminder of what I'll never have again.

I'll never date again, *period*. A vow I made the day we'd buried Logan. My kids had lost one dad; I wouldn't subject them to ever having to lose another father figure. I won't ever allow them to feel this heartbreak again. Even if it means I'll be single until I'm old and withered and the loneliness in my soul has faded everything else into shades of gray. My kids would be my joy, my light. It would have to be enough. I'd *make* it be enough. I have to.

Fate didn't bring Xander as my rescuer, Vi, I think to myself. *Fate* has made sure Xander is out of reach entirely. By my own self-imposed law.

Because Xander is a career Sky Ridge Hotshot; a wildfire firefighter.

And I'll never be with another man with a dangerous job.

TEDDY

5

Teddy

THREE MONTHS LATER

Fumbling the heavy car seat onto my forearm, the bottle of liquid gold—my hard-earned, hand-pumped breast milk—is jostled out of the diaper bag. I watch as it rolls beneath the running boards of my minivan and disappears out of sight.

Pinching my eyes shut, I take a deep, steadying breath in and then let it out just as slowly.

"Don't worry, Mom, I can reach it," Dalton says softly. Dropping to his hands and knees, he fishes it out from beneath the van from where it's rolled behind the right rear tire. Thank heaven above, the safety top has stayed on, which means the bottle nipple is safe from dirt and grime. I don't have to toss the whole bottle down the drain when we get inside.

I might just cry if I have to toss any more of that hard-won nutrition down the sink today.

Hiking Bea's car seat up my forearm so that it rests in the crook of my elbow, I sling the diaper bag higher over my other shoulder. Dalton slides the bottle back into the side pocket and I smile down at him as I huff out, "Thanks, Bud. Can you take Penny's hand?"

"I don' need to hold Dalfon's hand," Penny grumbles. Crossing her arms over her chest, she stuffs her hands under her armpits and glares at her big brother. "I a big girl, Mommy."

I sigh, rubbing the spot between my eyes with my middle and index fingers. I have a headache from hell. But momming never stops.

Especially single momming to three kids under nine.

"Do you promise not to run off toward the creek?" I ask, staring down into the wide, chocolate-brown eyes of my daughter, giving her the best *mom glare* I can muster. I shift Bea's car seat up my arm again. Good grief, she's heavy.

"I pwomise."

I sigh again and turn back toward the paved walkway that leads to our side of the duplex townhouse. I glower at the too-long grass in our front yard, then sigh. I really need to mow. And weed-whip. *Ugh.*

I'm just stepping up onto the small paved patio to our front door when Penny squeals out a high-pitched giggle and bolts.

"Penny!" I shout, dropping the diaper bag from my shoulder in a heap. I set the car seat down on the patio and start running after my preschooler. "Dalton, stay with Bea!"

Fuck, I'm out of shape, I groan as I hustle around the side of the townhouse. Her little legs are pumping as fast as they can toward the creek and a tiny shed that stands near it, her new favorite spot the last few weeks. The creek is shallow enough most of the time, but one side of it gets deeper when the rain hits—not that we've had any of that in weeks—but it still makes my mom heart nervous as hell for her to get too close.

"*Penelope Louise!*" I shout again, putting on a burst of speed. Just as she's about to hit the water, a form steps out from behind the shed and snatches her around the waist, hauling her away from the water and into the air.

TEDDY

I come to an embarrassingly awkward stop, panting. Bending over, I rest my hands on my knees as I huff for breath. Cheesus above, this is so humiliating.

"Well, this isn't what I was fishing for, but I guess it'll do."

My hair has started falling out of its messy topknot, and I blow a loose tendril away from my face as I straighten, raising my eyes to the man standing ten feet away. *God, why did he have to be here today of all days?* Looking like *that*?

Xander holds Penny aloft with one ridiculously muscled arm like a sack of potatoes. She giggles shrilly when he reaches up and tickles the exposed flesh of her belly. Her head is dangling in front of his chest, her feet kicking wildly above his head. I shake mine. Dammit, Penny.

"You know, I just might let you cook her," I grumble, stepping forward the last several feet. I'm achingly aware that my plum-purple biking shorts have hiked their way up my thick thighs, and the loose-fitting Lainey Wilson band tee is clinging to my chest and the residual soft roundness of my stomach, my least favorite souvenir from birthing my babies. I push my glasses back up the bridge of my nose and shake my head.

"No! I don' wanna be cook'ded!" Penny wails, flailing wildly again.

The chuckle that rumbles out of Xander's chest is deep and light. His dark beard is scruffy today, slightly longer than normal. He's wearing a pair of jeans that fit way too well, and an old, worn-looking Sky Ridge Hotshot T-shirt that has the arms cut off. His dark hair is thick and just a tad too long, like he's overdue for a haircut. He's stupidly handsome.

Not that I've noticed. Nuh-uh. Nope.

He's one thousand percent off-limits. The caution-taped, neon-signs-blazing, foghorns-blaring kind of off-limits. Especially when he looks at me like *that*.

I swing my attention back to Penny, who is still frantically kicking her feet above Xander's head. "Well, then I guess you shouldn't have run off after you *promised* not to. We've had this talk, miss ma'am."

Reaching up, I snag my wriggling preschooler around the waist and he lowers her into my arms. His hand gets caught between Penny's stomach and my chest and I probably flush eight shades of red. *Oh God, am I sweaty? Of course I'm sweaty, it's like ninety degrees out. Can he feel it? Ugh, I hope not.*

It's obscenely hot out today, the late summer heat brutal, and my little sprint around the house didn't help, I'm sure.

He pulls his hand from between my still-wiggling child and my body, and I force back a sigh of relief when he steps back slightly. He nods toward the back side of the duplex. "You've really got your hands full with this one."

I groan as I lug Penny up against my chest, still hanging upside down. She laughs again and I can't help the grin that tugs at my lips or the roll of my eyes. We start our way back toward the townhouse.

"Full hands, full heart," I laugh cheekily, my go-to response. Because that's what everyone says when they see me with my kids. We round the corner and I spot Dalton sitting on the patio steps, rocking Bea's car seat back and forth. He's playing a game of peek-a-boo, making her coo, which she's just started doing. My heart melts. He's the best big brother.

Xander clears his throat and says quietly, "If you ever need anything, please don't hesitate to ask."

That weight settles on my shoulders again, like it always does. I itch to fidget with the band of my wedding ring on my left hand, but I don't. I swallow around the lump in my throat. "Xander, we're okay, just like the last time you asked. Cal, Scottie, and the Hansens come around to check on us."

TEDDY

Those incredible eyes of his do that thing where he stares into mine for what feels like a small eternity, as if he's trying to see clear into my soul, and I can't help the flush that erupts over my chest and cheeks. He's just so ungodly good-looking I can't help but stare back. Even if my heart has shriveled up inside my chest, and I have this self-imposed no-dating-ever-again rule, my eyeballs can still appreciate a gorgeous hunk of man.

"Thanks for hog-tying my escapee back there," I say lamely, my voice coming out in a weird, husky croak thing. I blush again and drop my gaze from his. "I swear she lives up to the middle-child stereotype."

He chuckles again, tucking his hands into the front pockets of his jeans as I twist Penny in my arms so that she's right side up again, and I set her down, keeping a firm grip on her hand. "Well, the offer still stands, just like every other time."

Glancing down at Bea in her car seat, her cheeks finally filling out, I can't help but feel so incredibly grateful for the man that lives next door, even if I'd rather the ground open up and swallow me whole than to *ever* talk about that night again. Or to admit that I may or may not have a *teeny tiny* crush. It's pointless, anyway.

"Th-thanks," I mutter, my voice shaking as I drop my eyes again. "Umm, anyway, I should get them inside—"

He nods, then holds out his fist to Dalton, who fist-bumps him, a wide grin spreading across his face as he stares up at Xander. I watch, fascinated as always, as he winks down at my son, then points a finger at Penny and says gently, "Quit running off on your mama. I know she's told you to stay away from that creek. You could get hurt down there."

Penny nods, her big brown eyes wide.

He hunkers down in front of Bea's car seat—and I swear my long-shriveled-up ovaries just about burst as I watch him—as he grins at my infant. She waves her little arms like crazy, a wide, toothless smile scrunching up her tiny face.

"Good gravy, Miss Bea, look how big you're getting!"

From where he's hunkered down in front of her, he turns his head to glance up at me, that same wide grin still stretching his face. His teeth are perfectly white and straight, another punch to the gut. Why is he so obnoxiously handsome?

"You did good, Teddy."

God, the sound of my name on his lips is intoxicating. That low, gravelly rumble of his voice does something to my insides, turns my heart to thrumming and parts of me that haven't been acknowledged in almost a year to awakening. I haven't heard a man say my name in that husky, low tone in so long . . . Some days I forget my name is something other than some variation of *Mom*.

Flustered with my internal thoughts and praying he can't read them on my foolishly heating face, all I can do is nod and produce a shaky half-smile that feels more forced than anything. He straightens, standing to his full height again. I barely come up to his shoulder and have to tilt my head back to look at him, especially from this close. He nods once more, and then his tall frame disappears around the center partition that separates his half of the townhouse from ours, the muscles in his back and shoulders easily visible thanks to the DIY cut job on his T-shirt.

"Umm, Mom. I'm really sorry, I didn't notice it until after you had run around the house to get Penny."

Dalton's voice brings me back, and I glance down at him curiously.

He holds up the diaper bag. "The top came off when the bottle fell out, and it went in the dirt."

I sigh and pat his cheek gently. "It's okay, bud. It happens."

I lug Bea in her car seat into the house behind Dalton and Penny and try not to burst into tears as I dump the six ounces of contaminated breast milk down the sink after all.

TEDDY

6

Teddy

Peeking into the bedroom, I let the light from the hallway illuminate a sliver of Dalton's room. His sandy-brown hair is tousled, but he's sleeping peacefully. Closing the door as quietly as I'd opened it, I pad down to the door to the room that Penny and Bea share—though most nights Bea ends up in the bassinet next to my bed anyway. Penny is zonked out, lying diagonally across her new big-girl bed that my brother helped me put together last week. She'd picked out her new sheets and comforter—rainbow dinosaurs, of course—and is sleeping better, finally.

I'm sleeping better finally, too, having gotten her out of *my* bed and into her own again.

Bea will wake in another couple hours for her middle-of-the-night feed, but for now, I'm content to let her sleep in her crib. Maybe I can sneak a cool shower and wash off the sweat and grime from the day.

Sky Ridge, Washington, has had record-high temps this week, with no relief in sight, according to the meteorologist.

Stepping into the bathroom, I set the baby monitor on the bathroom sink, then turn the shower on, setting it to lukewarm. I strip, tossing my sweaty and wrinkled clothes in the laundry basket in the corner. It's overflowing, but I'm too exhausted to care tonight. Laundry with three kids—*how do newborns go through so many outfits in a day?*—is never-ending.

If there is a hell, it's comprised of nothing but mountains of tiny human laundry for eternity, I'm sure.

Standing in front of the mirror, I can't help but critique all the ways my body has changed since I had Dalton. I have wide-set hips and more junk in the trunk than I'd like. Thick thighs that are dimpled with cellulite when I sit, but with a little self-tanner they look soft and smooth. I run my hands over my rib cage and over my stomach, the "mom pooch" I still have ever the bane of my existence. I trace one of the more noticeable stretch marks on the right side of my belly button. Penny had given that one to me and it never went away, along with the myriad new ones I acquired while carrying Bea earlier this year. My breasts are normally fairly small, but breastfeeding has made them fuller and heavy. I sigh, closing my eyes.

I shake myself out of the funk, taking off my clear-rimmed glasses and setting them on the counter next to the baby monitor. I step into the shower, letting the lukewarm water cool me from the heat of the day.

Ugh. What a day.

Some days are easy and I lull myself into a false sense of security that I can do this on my own . . . and other days, my kids are uncivilized heathens. Those days I usually cry myself to sleep, because dammit, this is *hard*.

I stare down at the simple white-gold band that still sits on my left ring finger, the water dripping from my hands. I took my engagement ring off two months ago, placing it in the jewelry box on my

TEDDY

dresser, but I can't bring myself to take off my wedding band. Not yet. It feels so final, like if I take it off, I *have* to admit that he's gone. That he's not going to walk through the front door, no matter how many times I wish for it to happen.

7

XANDER

I can hear her crying through the wall.

I lean back and let the back of my head thump against the wall that separates my bathroom from what I know is her bathroom. The sound of the shower running is muted, an almost imperceptible thrum through the thin walls. The deep, wracking sobs are more pronounced and make my chest ache.

She doesn't let herself cry for long though. She never does. Mere minutes later the worst of it subsides and then quiets altogether. The water shuts off, and I force my mind away from the thought of my best friend's younger sister stepping out of the shower, naked and wet, just on the other side.

I blow out a heavy exhale and let my chin fall forward so that I'm staring at the floor between my feet, my hands shoved into the front pockets of my jeans. I will my body not to react to the thought of her naked, but I know it's a lost cause, even if the self-loathing that accompanies it is soul crushing.

She'd looked so damn pretty today—honey-blond hair messily tied up on top of her head, her glasses sliding down the ridge of her nose, cheeks flushed from the summer heat. The dark purple biker shorts she favors delineated every delicious, thick curve of her body, all soft and grabbable. Her tee was paper-thin and clung to her body, the wide neckline slipping off one sun-kissed shoulder as she'd bolted after her escapee preschooler. The outline of her sports bra had been visible through the thin material, and one strap had cut across her shoulder when the tee had slipped.

As much as I know I shouldn't, I look forward to the times that I can run into her. Like a fiend, I hope for it on the days that I *am* at the townhouse and not on a call or bunking at base.

I'd inherited my half of the townhouse after my dad died six years ago, and I had every intention of selling back then. But, admittedly, every once in a while, it's nice to have a place to go away from the rowdiness of base. So I'd held on to it, splitting my time between base and here.

The previous renter of Teddy's side had retired and moved to Florida—why the hell anyone would go to that croc-infested hell-hole is beyond me—and four months ago Cal and I had helped his heavily pregnant, newly widowed younger sister move in with her two kids. I spend a helluva lot more time here than I used to, now that she's next door.

I can't seem to stay away.

I curse, then strip, turning the water on in the shower. I turn the taps down until it's just above frigid and step in, hissing between my teeth as the cold water makes contact with my skin. After the heat of the day, it's welcome, though it does take a few minutes to get used to.

It's been a crazy summer of constant fires, and we've been gone more than usual. Normally, I'd be loving it; I've always been happiest when I'm out in the field with my crew, but I hate knowing Teddy is here alone.

The guys razzed me mercilessly for weeks after the night I helped Teddy deliver Bea, teasing me about my new offseason career, doula services. Though I knew it was all in good fun, I felt extraordinarily protective—and concerningly possessive—over the single mom, and admittedly, that feeling hasn't diminished at all in the months since.

When I step out of the shower just a few minutes later, all is quiet through the wall that separates my apartment from Teddy's. Toweling off lazily, I chuck the towel into the hamper and cross the room to the dresser to pull on a pair of boxer briefs and a set of loose athletic shorts. I shove my head and arms through another old, ratty T-shirt with the arms cut out of it and pad through the rapidly darkening house to the kitchen, where I snag a beer from the fridge.

I'm not on call tonight, which is why I'm even here at all. I used to sleep exclusively at base in one of the several tiny bunks we offer to our out-of-town crew members. But apparently, my weakness is a single mom with honey-blond hair and curves for days. So, here I am.

I step out the back slider door that leads to my partitioned-off patio, taking my beer with me. Teddy has the same patio setup on her side of the townhouse, though I've never wandered over toward it, except for today, when we'd walked back around the house after stopping Penny-the-Runaway. I'd just gotten glimpses of it, not wanting to seem like I was spying on her space. A small patio table surrounded by four chairs, a miniature wooden picnic table littered with an array of outdoor toys, a baseball bat, a glove, and a small bucket of baseballs. Colorful sidewalk chalk art covers the concrete patio floor.

Mine looks sad and boring compared to hers. One single folding chair and an overturned, ancient milk crate that serves as a little table next to it. A propane gas grill sits off to the side. My dad had rarely stayed here when he was alive, choosing to bunk at base most nights when we weren't on location for a fire. He was only ever here for offseason, but the man hadn't known how to relax in the slightest, so he'd always been off on other projects.

I sink down into the sun-faded, weather-worn folding chair, the metal legs creaking as it absorbs my weight. Another reminder of my age. At almost forty-three, I can still outrun most of the guys on my crew decked with full gear and can confidently say I'm in prime physical shape. But I can recognize that my body is starting to slow and change. The once-defined, heavy muscles in my arms, shoulders, and back have started to soften slightly. I'm not in the same physical condition as I was in my twenties. I snort a laugh as I take a long swallow of my beer. Fuck, that was a long time ago. Cal loves to remind me of my "advanced age," the fucker.

The sun has faded beyond the front of the house as dusk approaches, the velvety periwinkle sky bleeding into the darker navy on the edge of the horizon, casting the backyard into pale shadows.

I lift the beer to my lips again when a movement to my right catches my eye and I have to force myself not to jump upright. I hadn't even heard her patio door slide open, but through the pale dusky light I see Teddy wandering over from her side of the town-house. Her hair is loose around her shoulders, curling slightly as it dries in the still cloyingly hot and humid air. The blond strands seem to shine blue in the rapidly fading dusk. There's no trace of the tears on her face from earlier, and her eyes seem bright in the twilight that surrounds us.

I shift in my seat slightly, willing my dick not to rise at the sight of her wearing what looks like a thin, soft robe that doesn't quite reach her knees. It's tied closed around her waist, and her arms are crossed over her stomach as she walks closer. She's barefoot, and her legs are completely bare up to the hem of her robe. Her skin looks tanned and smooth and so fucking soft I ache to run my hands over every inch. To run my palms up and over the swell of her thighs and hips as she straddles me—

"Hi," I call out gruffly across the fifteen feet or so that separates us. My voice is rough and husky from my wayward thoughts.

She waves awkwardly, stopping, though I can see her eyes darting over me. My dick notices and wonders if she likes what she sees. *Dammit, down, boy.*

"I heard your patio door open and just wanted to come say thank you again for stopping Penny today," she says softly. She points one hand toward her side of the apartment. "I don't know what to do with her some days. I think she was sent here by Satan himself to test me."

I can't help the barking laugh that escapes my chest. Her laughter is light and self-deprecating. "I think that's the middle child in her. Or maybe that's the Woods genes coming out."

Her throat tips back as she laughs again, and the sound wraps around my insides . . . and my cock. I'm sporting a chubby that's now straining the material of my boxer briefs. Christ, how long has it been since I got laid? I keep my arm and beer braced in my lap to hide my erection, though I doubt she can see much in the fading light.

She wanders a few steps closer and I shift in my seat again, sitting forward so that I can lean my elbows on my spread knees in the hopes that maybe that will make it less visible.

"That's so true. She is definitely like a mini Cal. She's so much like her dad too, always running headfirst into the fray without a second thought," she mutters, shaking her head. I can see it as she physically straightens herself, as if a puppeteer just yanked hard on a string connected to the top of her head, pulling her spine stiff. She forces a little head shake, as if to clear it, and lifts her lips in a half smile. Fuck, she's so beautiful. "Anyway, I just wanted to thank you. I'm so . . . well—" She waves one hand at herself and her body, gesturing to her ample curves, then smiles ruefully over at me again before continuing. "I wouldn't have caught up to her before she hit the water."

My brows lower over my eyes in a glower as I stare at her hard. "Teddy."

"What?" she asks, her voice shaking slightly at the hardness of my tone. Her arms are banded around herself again, that damn self-conscious instinct to hide as much of herself as possible making its presence known.

I fucking hate it. I want to see all of her. And I hate that too. I soften the gruffness of my voice but none of the intensity as I tell her, "Don't ever let me hear you talk about yourself like that, do you understand? You're perfect just like this."

Her brows shoot up and those pink lips that I've fantasized about tasting too many times to count open in an *O* of surprise.

8

Teddy

Like the coward I am, I mumble a hasty "good night" to Xander and run like the hounds of hell are nipping at my heels back to the safety of my duplex. I slide the patio door closed and flip the lock, more out of habit than any real fear that the man on the other side of the partition would follow . . .

My breathing is ragged, I'm fairly panting, and my heart is beating out of my chest.

I'm still trying to wrap my head around the husky, intense words he'd said, and *the way* he'd said them. Even in the pale blue twilight, I could see his eyes as he'd watched me. His gaze hadn't left mine, just stared at me with all that intensity arcing between us.

A very long, very dead part of me has awakened recently, much to my dismay. I haven't let myself feel anything, don't give myself time to think or feel or do anything other than survive day to day.

The attraction I feel for Xander is always accompanied swiftly by a wave of guilt. All I can think about at night is what those warm, sun-kissed muscles might feel like beneath my palms, my fingers.

What that mouth might feel like as it presses to mine, what it might feel like to feel his weight on top of me . . .

No, I remind myself, pacing through the kitchen, the glow of the bulb over the stove the only light. I'm just horny and lonely. This will pass. Hopefully.

Even if I wanted to date—which I don't, despite the many nudges that I've gotten from Vi lately—Xander is strictly off-limits.

He's my brother's boss. And his best friend.

And he's a hotshot.

Despite the walls I've built around my heart where my sexy-as-sin neighbor is concerned, I can't help but worry about him whenever he and Cal leave for a fire. I tell myself it's because he's my brother's best friend and because I care about him *as a friend and neighbor.* Nothing more than that.

I groan, letting my head drop back so that I'm staring at the ceiling. I'm lying to myself. At least a little.

Because I do care about Xander. A lot. As a friend and neighbor . . . but *more* too. This stupid crush that I've been fighting for the last several months is silly, especially knowing that I'm never going to allow myself to act on it anyway.

I can look. I just can't touch.

Well. I can't touch *him*, at least.

I do, however, touch myself at night . . . when I let myself pretend for just a little while that I'm not alone in my bed with a silicone toy in hand.

Again. I'm just horny and lonely.

It's pathetic, to be honest. I'm a hot mess on good days.

Leaning my hips against the counter in the kitchen, I fan myself. I can't even blame the August heat; this is all because of Xander and the way his deep, growly words and impossibly intense gaze affect me.

Stealing a glance out the patio door into the darkness that's shrouded the outside world, I bite my lip. Fuck it.

Slipping quietly down the hall, I close my bedroom door and slide into bed before reaching for the drawer of my nightstand and pull out ol' faithful.

Turning the toy on, I slide it and my hand beneath the folds of my robe, letting my thighs drop open.

"Oh shit," I whisper into the dark as the vibrator buzzes along my skin. Circling it over my clit, I let my mind wander to Xander . . .

9

XANDER

Dropping my head back against the metal frame of the folding chair, I close my eyes as Teddy disappears around the partition, back to the safety of her duplex. The way that robe clings to her skin is damn near my undoing, and I'm apparently too much of a masochist to look away from her ass as she walks away. Pressing my palm against my dick, I will my erection to go down.

Draining the last of my beer, I push to my feet, groaning at the way my joints and muscles ache. Once inside, I toss the empty beer bottle into the recycle bin and head down the hallway. These duplexes are mirror images of each other, with my bedroom and connected bathroom sharing a wall with Teddy's. Some nights I can hear Bea fussing through the wall, but it never lasts long.

Climbing into bed, I lay on my back, one arm bent beneath the back of my head as I stare up at the ceiling. I'm still half hard, thinking about Teddy in that sanity-stealing robe.

And then I hear it.

It's quiet, muffled through the wall.

Muted buzzing, and fucking Christ—a quiet moan that turns into a louder one, one that sounds suspiciously like my fucking name. And I know exactly what Teddy is doing on her side of the wall.

I've never been more grateful for thin walls than I am in this moment.

I'm rock-hard in an instant, her quiet, muffled moans while she plays with herself heating my blood to a fucking boil. Shoving my shorts down my hips, I wrap my fingers around my cock and glide my palm up and down, from root to tip. Squeezing the base of it, I strangle my dick and strain my ears for more of her sounds. I'm ravenous for more.

I should be ashamed of myself, but I'm not. Not when she's doing the same thing, thinking about me.

"*Xander*," I hear through the wall, and there's no question that it's my name this time. I pump my fist over myself, my hips bucking into my hand in time with her sounds. My spine tingles and my balls draw up tight, my impending orgasm barreling through me swiftly as I come in long spurts, my release painting my abdomen. I hear her come and I groan through my own orgasm, my mouth dropping open, my chest heaving.

Fuck. What I wouldn't do to witness that with my own eyes. Feel it with my fingers, my tongue, my dick.

Shame does wash through me then, because I *am* an asshole. Despite the feelings I've secretly harbored for Teddy, I know there's nothing that will ever happen between us. I can't give her what she undoubtedly deserves.

So, as I clean myself up, I remind myself of all the reasons my feelings for her need to remain in the dark. Just like this.

XANDER

10

Teddy

I huff out a groan, hiking Bea's car seat up my arm again, all the while never letting go of Penny's hand as we walk up the sidewalk toward the Nook, an adorable little coffee and dessert shop, one of the only coffee shops in Sky Ridge. Of course, the sidewalk parking is packed though, so we had to park half a block away.

I remind myself that the coffee is worth it, as is the absolutely ginormous orange-cranberry muffin I'm going to let myself indulge in during Penny's weekly playdate with her little bestie, Hollie.

Vi's a nurse at Bakersfield Hospital in the burn unit, but we try to make sure to meet up once a week so the girls can play. And if I'm totally honest, I need the adult time so badly I could cry. I love my kids, but sometimes a girl just needs to have an adult conversation, you know? Something that doesn't involve fart noises, the words *Look what I can do* on repeat, or baby spit-up.

Ugh. I'd kill for a girls' night free of kids. I almost laugh at the absurdity of the thought though. Maybe I'll ask Violette if she and Hollie want to come over soon, even if it's just to let all the kids play while we have a glass of wine . . . It wouldn't be the most *relaxing* girls' night ever, but it would mean adult conversation. I know I can always ask Scottie to come over, but she works long hours as an EMT, so getting us all together is tricky sometimes.

Dalton pulls the door to the Nook open, holding it for me. I huff out a breathy, "Thank you, bud," and direct Penny in front of me, hiking Bea's car seat up my arm again. There's a short line in front of us waiting to place orders, and I smile. *Speaking of Scottie . . .*

We stop behind a woman with ginger hair that's pulled up into a sleek ponytail. She's shorter than me by several inches, her body thin in that athletic-build type of way that mine will never be.

Navy blue tactical pants cover her legs, and a white, short-sleeved polo shirt in that lightweight, sweat-wicking material is stretched over her shoulders and back—the standard uniform of an EMT. She's scrolling away on her phone while we all wait, oblivious to our presence and the noise around us.

"Auntie!" Penny shrieks in excitement as she recognizes who is in front of us, launching herself away from me and into the back of Scottie's legs. Startled, she spins, taking my preschooler with her.

"Hey, you!" she laughs, glancing down and behind her at Penny, who has her arms wrapped around her thighs in a bear hug. "How's my girl? Hey, Dalton." She holds out her fist, and he bumps it, grinning widely.

"Hey, Aunt Scottie," he says, leaning in for a hug. He's tall for his age and stands nearly to her chin already. She hugs him around the shoulders.

"Ugh, you're so tall," she grumbles, eyeing him with a glower, and he grins again.

"I'm pretty sure we're in another growth spurt," I mutter, though I wink at him. "I swear he's outgrown half of his clothes already this summer."

I shake my head and shift Bea's car seat on my arm again, the handle cutting off the circulation below my elbow. I considered unpacking the stroller, but it had seemed like too much of a hassle for such a quick errand. I'm regretting that now. I blow out a breath and focus my gaze on the handwritten chalkboard over the counter, scanning the daily specials.

"Can we get cake pops?" Dalton asks, looking up at me. I side-eye him.

"Cake pops for breakfast?" I deadpan.

He grins and shrugs his narrow shoulders. Penny yanks on Scottie's hand, jumping up and down excitedly.

I roll my eyes. "Ugh. Fine. Only because today is our freebie day and now that Penny heard you, she'll be a terror if we don't get them."

"Cake pops are under the Mom Freebie clause. If they facilitate a no-meltdown day, it's a win," Scottie mutters out of the corner of her mouth, winking at me.

I laugh out loud, grinning while I nod. "Cake pops for breakfast it is then," I laugh, shaking my head. Dalton does a little victory fist pump and Penny dances in place.

The barista calls out to Scottie quietly to get her attention. Scottie holds up one finger and then spins toward the counter. She steps forward as the person in front of her slides out of the way. My eyes go back to the menu board, trying to decide what I want as she orders, and then pays. My eyes drop when she spins to face us, two chocolate-frosted cake pops dusted in colorful sprinkles clutched in her fingers.

"I got your usual, too, by the way," she says, smiling at me. She grins at me as I protest, but then hands one cake pop first to Penny, then to Dalton.

I squeeze Penny's hand and eye Dalton with my best mom glare, focusing on what's in front of me. "Guys, we have manners, what do we say—"

"Tank you so much!" Penny exclaims, her brown eyes round as saucers as she gazes at the cake pop in her hand.

Dalton grins. "Thank you."

"You're most welcome. Try not to be heathens for your mom today, okay?" she says, laughing. She winks at me again.

I'm so lucky to have a *hopefully* soon-to-be sister-in-law as amazing as Scottie. I never liked my brother's ex, Molly. Good riddance to the awful woman that broke my brother's heart. She and her douchey husband, Dave, deserve each other.

Scottie ducks again and coos to Bea, who babbles animatedly up at her. "You're just too precious." Glancing up at me as she straightens again, she murmurs gently, "You did so good, Teddy."

"Thank you," I murmur awkwardly. That's the second time in a week someone has said that to me, and it reminds me of the way Xander's eyes had done that deep, heated thing as he'd stared up at me. I shiver. I blame it on the AC blasting directly above us.

She grins once more and then steps aside to wait for her order at the other end of the counter. We step forward as one hot-mess grouping so I can order two waters with lids and straws and the orange-cranberry muffin I've been dreaming about for the last two days.

Scottie still has Penny by the hand—she knows the way this child can Houdini her way out of anywhere—and I'm grateful she's here as I struggle to grab my wallet out of the bottom of the diaper bag slung over my shoulder. I'm paying as Scottie's drink is ready along with the iced coffee with caramel sweet cream she'd ordered for me. She stands with us while we wait.

I jostle the paper-wrapped and bagged muffin the barista hands me, stuffing it into the wide-open pocket of the diaper bag as we shuffle down the counter to wait for the rest of our order.

"Are you headed out to a play date with Vi and Hollie?" Scottie asks as I sidle my way over to her. Penny's hand is still clutched in hers, and she's swinging their arms back and forth while Penny finishes the cake pop. "That is today, right?"

TEDDY

"Yes, we're heading there as soon as we're done here," I murmur, hiking Bea's car seat back up my arm. I'm going to have welts in the crease of my elbow by the time we leave here.

The barista smiles kindly at me as she places the two waters on the counter in front of me. "Thank you so much. Here, Penny, here's your water," I say, reaching for one of the clear plastic cups, the lid and straw already in place—bless the barista's heart—and hand it to her. I hand Dalton the other one, then grab the iced coffee that has been waiting for me. "Okay, guys, head to the door. Penny, you stay close to me and Dalton and Aunt Scottie—"

My left arm still cradling Bea's car seat handle, I shift my iced coffee into that hand, holding it aloft over Bea as we make our way toward the door. I'm sure we're a sight. Dalton pushes the door open, and Penny sees her chance, yanking her hand out of Scottie's and darting out the door into the blinding sunlight.

"*Oh for the love of—*" I growl, lunging forward. *You've got to be fucking kidding me.* This child. The sun blinds me momentarily and then I hear Penny's shrill scream, and my heart stops as I rush forward.

"Do I need to get a leash for you? I know we talked about this a few days ago, Miss Penny."

My heart thunders back to life with a vengeance as I recognize that voice. I step out onto the sidewalk and shake my head. Xander has Penny lifted in his arms—upright this time instead of hanging upside down—but those intense blue eyes of his aren't on my runaway daughter, they're on me.

I glance over at Scottie, who is standing behind Xander, and she winks, grinning widely, before waving bye to the kids and stepping over to where my brother is climbing out of the passenger seat of Xander's truck parked nearby. He waves briefly, but then his attention is on his lady as she stops in front of him. His mouth drops to hers as she steps up on her tiptoes to meet him. I blush and look away, my gaze colliding with Xander's again.

His gaze runs from my head down to my toes and back, taking in all of me, before they come back to mine. My breath stalls in my throat at the intensity in his eyes as he stares at me. Heat settles low in my belly and I blush, remembering what I'd been imagining him doing to me just last night . . .

Blinking, I drop my gaze shyly, and then mentally take stock of my outfit; Violette has been daring me to wear outfits way outside my comfort zone and I'd been brave this morning while dressing, but now, with Xander's eyes on me, I'm freaking the fuck out.

The skintight, square-neck tank top–style bodysuit she'd talked me into buying is sucking my gut in and snatching my waist like a paid actor, and also pushing my tits up like crazy. White and ribbed, I hadn't even worn a bra underneath—brave of me, I know—the stretch and compression top-notch in this contraption. The bodysuit is tucked into a pair of high-waisted, light-wash cutoff jean shorts that leave little to the imagination, but Vi said they make my ass look amazing. I reapplied my sunless tanner on my legs, so at least they don't look pale, and my toes are painted Funny Bunny white, peeking out of my flip flops.

My hair is down and curled in slight waves around my shoulders, a small claw clip securing it half up and away from my face. I'd even managed to put on makeup today, which I'm extremely thankful for now, with Xander still staring at me with that intense heat in his gaze. He's just so unfairly attractive.

One of his well-muscled forearms is banded beneath Penny's bottom like a seat, his large hand spanned wide across her leg to hold her up. I huff out a heavy breath as I move toward him and Penny, who is looking properly contrite. This child is going to be the death of me.

TEDDY

My mouth opens to scold Penny for taking off *again*. Before I can make a sound though, he takes me completely by surprise when he steps forward, straight into my bubble, and reaches for the handle of Bea's car seat without a word. My hands move without any conscious thought from my sluggish brain at having him so close, and I move my iced coffee from that hand to my free hand, allowing him to slide the handle off my arm. The crease of my elbow has deep red marks on it now from holding the handle for so long, and instinctively I straighten my arm down at my side to try to return some blood flow to my numb arm.

I watch as his fingers grip the handle of her car seat tightly, holding her down at his other side, making sure to angle her away from the sun. His eyes never leave my face, which makes me blush hotly and I drop my gaze from his.

Ugh, but his body is just as nice to look at as his face though, covered in army-green tactical cargo pants that fit his thighs and hips, and a tightly fitted black T-shirt with the Sky Ridge Hotshot emblem on his left pec. His usual baseball hat is on his head, shielding the upper portion of his face from the midmorning sun as I peek back up at him shyly.

He nods to Dalton. "Hey, champ, why don't you take that diaper bag from your mom so she doesn't have to carry everything on her own? We should always help out when we can."

Dalton nods, eyes wide, but I murmur, "No, that's okay, I've got it—"

"Hey." His eyes laser-focus on mine, stopping my stammering words. "Let us help you, Mama."

I hear variations of *Mom* and *Mommy* all day long, every day. But this?

Mama. The way he says it in that husky, intimate rasp has completely short-circuited my brain. All I can do is stare up at him dumbly before nodding.

I drag the diaper bag over my shoulder and hold it out to Dalton, and he places it on his shoulder. His body dips slightly with the weight, and I instinctively reach for it again, but Dalton just assures me with a grin, "I've got it, Mom!"

I swallow hard, letting my hand drop to my side. I feel naked now, with no diaper bag, car seat, or preschooler attached to me as usual. I'm left feeling incredibly self-conscious and fully second-guessing my outfit choice now that I don't have my built-in shields up. So I smile gratefully down at him, even if my lips tremble just the slightest. "Thank you, bud."

"Now you can take a drink of your coffee before it starts to melt," Xander says quietly, gesturing to the drink in my hand.

I laugh nervously. What must that be like? To drink an iced coffee before it melts or a hot coffee before it gets cold?

He chuckles then, the sound deep and soothing, his eyes crinkling at the corners with his smile. "Teddy, I can see your brain buffering because it's such a foreign concept to you. Take a drink. Where are you parked? I'll walk you."

I dutifully take a sip of my coffee, the caramel sweet cream lighting up my tongue. Gosh, it's good when it's fresh and not all melted. Some of the cream sticks to my upper lip and I lick it away quickly, daring a glance up at Xander again.

But those eyes of his are no longer on mine; no, they're on my mouth, and the heat in that gaze is enough to scorch me alive.

TEDDY

11

XANDER

*J*esus fuck.

The tip of her pink tongue flicking out to lap up that frothy cream from her top lip is damn near my undoing. Especially after the way my mind had conjured up what that mouth could do to something else . . .

I swallow reflexively, and I can physically feel the knot in my throat bob at how difficult it is to swallow around. My mouth is bone-dry, though I panic momentarily that I might actually be drooling. I'm acutely aware of the fact that her brother is standing ten feet away.

The second I saw her walk out of the coffee shop, my brain—and all my good intentions about staying away from her—went straight to hell. That damn tank top thing she's wearing should be illegal. It's cock-teasingly tight and the way it cinches in her waist and pushes up her tits . . . I can imagine the soft, stretchy material being pulled down when she has to nurse Bea, who is babbling and cooing from the car seat suspended in my hand. *Fuck me.*

And those shorts. High-waisted, which only accentuates the narrowness of her waist and the wide curve of her hips. The jean material's frayed edges play against those tanned, smooth, grabbable thighs.

I'm a fucking pervert. And a terrible friend and boss.

A breeze sends the blond ends of her hair flipping around her shoulders, tendrils loosening from the little clip that's holding half of it up at the back of her head, away from her face. Her clear-rimmed glasses are shielding her eyes from me, but only barely, as she keeps looking up at me. Then blushing, looking away. Only for those eyes to come back to mine again moments later.

Like she can't help herself from staring at me, either.

My male vanity beats at my chest all caveman as her eyes swing to mine again. We start down the sidewalk, Penny in one arm and Bea's car seat at my side. I peek down to make sure she's not angled toward the sun.

Cal stares at me over the top of Scottie's head as I walk away, raising one eyebrow, a smirk tugging at the corner of his mouth. I tip my head in acknowledgment and he chuckles lightly, crossing his arms around Scottie's shoulders as we pass them.

He's going to give me fucking hell when I get back, but the bastard can wait.

I spot Teddy's white Chrysler Pacifica minivan ahead. Shit, she'd walked all this way to the coffee shop carrying Bea and a diaper bag and probably corralling Penny too? No wonder her skin is still sporting those angry red lines in the crook of her elbow. The woman is a goddamn superhero.

"Was there not any closer parking?" I ask, nodding toward her vehicle.

She shrugs. "No, but it's okay. I've gotten pretty good at all this on my own."

XANDER

I hate that. I hate that she has to do this all on her own. Logan's death had sent shockwaves through the area last winter. A reminder that no matter how long you've been in the field, how well trained you are . . . accidents happen that are simply beyond our control.

She stops Dalton, smiling down at him, and he beams up at her as he slides the diaper bag over his head and hands it back to her. She digs into one of the smaller front pockets, clicking the fob to unlock the doors. Sliding it open, he climbs between the bucket seats in the middle row to the back bench seat, settling himself in. Teddy opens the front passenger door and sets the diaper bag in the seat, then leans forward to place her coffee in the center console.

She stretches forward, one leg kicking out slightly as she reaches in. As she bends over the seat, I can't keep my eyes off the wide fullness of her ass in the cutoff jean shorts that leave the backs of her thighs bare to just below the delectable curve of that ass. My dick is half hard in my pants already. Her flip-flop pops against her heel as she straightens, turning with a smile as she glances up at me.

"Who do you want first?" I ask, my voice coming out far gruffer than I expected. I clear my throat. Fuck, the chokehold this woman has on me . . .

"Penny," she says, holding her hands out to the girl. I lower her down into Teddy's waiting arms, but my hand and arm get caught between Penny's little body and Teddy's front, and we linger for just a heartbeat too long for it to be accidental.

I also may or may not allow my arm to *accidentally* slide across the softness of her chest as I remove it from between her and Penny. The heavy weight of her breasts grazing the back of my forearm will haunt my every waking moment for the next week, I'm sure. As will the way her lips drop open, a soft, stuttering breath escaping those lips as I move away slightly. Goddamn, she's so fucking pretty.

She swallows hard, her eyes bouncing between mine before she spins, turning to the open slider door. Setting Penny on her feet inside the car, she instructs her to climb into her car seat, and then Dalton is leaning forward to help her buckle.

I notice the way Teddy's hand shakes as she turns back toward me, her fingers tucking that stray strand of hair behind her ear. I heft Bea's infant seat up, curling my bicep—hoping she notices the way my muscles bunch as I do—and she wraps her hands around the handle, our fingers grazing.

She doesn't hesitate this time, though, turning immediately to snap the infant seat into the stationary base secured in the seat closest to us. She clicks a couple of buttons to make the handle fold backward, then she pushes the retractable baby shade down. A tiny mirror is attached to the headrest of the seat, and I assume it's so she can see Bea while driving.

Teddy takes a few seconds to adjust everything, and it's easy to see that the safety of her kids is a high priority. Speaking to Penny, she says, "I'll come around and check your buckles, Pen. Dalton, seat belt, bud."

Before she can slide the door closed, I lean in, bracing one hand on the top of the van and the other on the edge of the door. "Thanks for your help, champ."

Dalton grins widely, then nods. "Yeah, no problem."

I offer him my knuckles, and he fist-bumps mine lightly. I grin. The kid has got a lot on his young shoulders. Turning my attention to Penny, I say, "Miss Penny, are you going to start behaving for your mom?"

She nods, kicking her little legs in front of her. "Yes. I pwomise."

Teddy coughs lightly behind me, as if covering a laugh. I fight my own grin. We both know this isn't the last time that Penny is going to try to escape, but we can pretend just for this moment. The tiny terror has me wrapped around her probably crossed little fingers.

Bea is happily sucking on one of her fists, gnawing on the knuckles. Drool is dribbling down her little hand, and it's a good thing she's wearing a pretty, floral drool bib over her clothed chest, because it's soaked. I laugh, shaking my head.

"See you later, little one." She flashes a toothless grin up at me, her big, brown eyes wide and fringed with long dark lashes. Dammit, she's cute.

I lean away and Teddy touches the button that slides the door shut automatically. She rounds the back of the van and opens the sliding door beside Penny's seat, leaning in to double-check the latches and straps of Penny's car seat. When she's satisfied, she closes the door. I followed her around the car, standing between her and the cars that are driving down the road just feet beyond us. It's a downtown street, so the speed limit is slow, but this protective instinct in me is becoming harder to ignore.

She glances up at me as I lean around her and open her door. She smiles, shaking her head lightly. "You don't have to do all this, Xander."

"I know, but I want to. Come on, hop in," I murmur, notching my chin toward the empty driver's seat.

She climbs in and I close the door gently. Starting the ignition, she presses the button to roll the window down. Reaching up, I flip my ball cap around so the brim is facing backward, then lean my forearms against the window frame as she buckles her own seat belt. I'm drawn to her like a fucking idiot moth to a flame. I can't seem to help myself.

There's a smattering of freckles across the bridge of her nose and across her cheeks that I can see now that we're this close, and I itch to trace them with my fingers. They're half hidden behind the clear acrylic frames of her glasses. I'd always thought her eyes were a dusty blue, but from this close, I know that they're a stunning, silvery slate gray. And I'm transfixed, totally and irrevocably caught in her gaze.

As always when I'm around her.

"Thank you," she whispers, those eyes bouncing between mine.

Against my own better judgment, I reach one hand inside and tuck that damn stray strand of hair that keeps falling into her face behind her ear. "You don't ever have to thank me."

She nods, ducking her head as a blush creeps up her neck and over her cheeks. Fuck, she's adorable when she gets flustered. I wonder if any of her blushes today are because of what she'd done the other night and the fact that she'd been thinking about me while she did it. I fucking hope so. I want all of her blushes, all of those sexy fucking sounds that no one else gets to hear.

Grinning, I wink at her when she looks back at me. Before she can look away again, I murmur, my voice husky, "I'll see you soon, Mama."

I fucking love the way her eyes dilate and those pink lips part when I say that. I noticed it earlier, and I wasn't going to let her leave without seeing that reaction again.

Her teeth dig into the plushness of her bottom lip, and I wink again, slapping one hand onto the window frame as I straighten. I waggle my fingers at Penny and Dalton as I step around the hood of the minivan and back onto the sidewalk. Teddy pulls out of the parking spot and I watch her vehicle disappear down the street as I make my way up the sidewalk, back toward Cal, who is now alone and leaning against the side of my truck.

He does, however, have a coffee in one hand and another sitting on the hood of the truck. I must have been gone with Teddy long enough for him to run inside and get our coffees. *Whoops.* He grabs the one on the hood and hands it to me as I reach him. His brown eyes are shaded by darkly tinted sunglasses, but the shit-eating grin on his face says everything it needs to.

"Shut the fuck up," I grumble as I step around the hood of my truck. His answering chuckle is devious and makes me roll my eyes. Payback is a bitch. And I gave him *a lot* of shit about Scottie when they first got together. Dammit, this is going to suck. Have

XANDER

I mentioned Teddy is his younger sister? And I'm his boss? *Fuck my life.*

I climb into the driver's seat and he slides into the passenger side. I flip my cap around again, so that the brim is once again facing forward, shading my eyes marginally from his scrutiny. I can feel his gaze on the side of my face, but I refuse to look over at him.

My truck rumbles to life and I pull us away from the curb, heading us toward base. Cal takes a sip of his coffee and then drapes his left arm across the back of the bench seat that stretches between us. The truck was my dad's; it's a '93 box-style Dodge Ram that's seen a few too many winters. The black paint isn't shiny anymore, and there's some rust over the wheel hubs, but it's reliable and handles the Washington winter roads well.

"So, is this why you haven't been staying at base? You got a thing for my sister?" Cal asks, grinning over at me.

I grunt. Guess we're finally talking about this. Cal knows me better than just about anybody. He knows, even if I don't say it out loud.

He knocks his knuckles into my arm, bringing my attention around to him. He's flipped his sunglasses up to the top of his head, and he's staring at me, his face drawn and his eyes solemn. "Be careful with her, Xander. She's been through enough. If you do something to hurt her, I'm gonna have to kick your ass on principle."

I shift in my seat, tightening my fingers around the steering wheel until my knuckles turn white. "I know," is my gruff response.

He harrumphs then, leaning back in his seat and taking a long draw of his coffee. "The bigger they are, the harder they fall."

I shift in my seat as my heart skitters in my chest painfully.

Shit.

The fucker isn't wrong.

12

Teddy

"Umm, hello, hot mama!"

My cheeks heat and I offer Violette a grateful, timid smile as I push Bea's stroller toward where she is sitting beneath a shady maple tree. Penny spots Hollie in the sand surrounding the playground equipment and takes off with a squeal toward her little bestie. Dalton has his baseball bat and bucket of baseballs clutched in his hands, and he heads over to the field beyond the playground after asking for permission. It's still early, and we're blessedly the only ones here.

I sink down onto the wooden bench next to Vi and heave a sigh as I angle Bea's stroller toward us both, adjusting the shade over her to make sure none of the already hot summer sun's rays get to her. She fell asleep on the drive over and will be good until she wakes up for a feeding.

"Did you need this?" Vi asks, holding up a bottle of children's sunscreen. I shake my head.

"Already loaded both kids up," I laugh, blowing out a breath.

She nods, dropping the bottle back into her own bag next to her.

"Can we talk about the 'fit? *Holy hotness*," Vi says, fanning herself as she side-eyes me. Her thick, light-brown hair is pulled into a ponytail, the waves waterfalling down her back. She's dressed for the heat in a sage-green tank top tucked into cut-off jean shorts and low-top chucks. "Am I allowed to say 'I told you so'? Because ma'am, that outfit is—" She kisses the tips of her fingers and holds them aloft in the pantomime of a chef's kiss.

I laugh out loud, grinning over at her as I pluck my half-empty iced coffee out of the cup holder built into the handle of the stroller. Vi lifts her iced chai to her lips, her hazel eyes coming back to mine.

"Did you get hit on?"

I choke on my coffee and splutter slightly, coughing. "Violette!"

"Oh, come on. There's no way not one hot-blooded male *didn't* hit on you looking that smokin'."

"I was wrangling my three feral children while trying to get my coffee," I deadpan, shaking my head. I can't stop the blush that creeps up my neck at the memory of the way Xander's eyes had lingered on me though. "I'm a hot mess on a good day."

"Hot mess still qualifies as hot," Vi chuckles, tipping her chai toward me in a salute.

I laugh again and she narrows her hazel eyes on me.

"You totally got hit on. Who was it?"

"I wouldn't call it getting hit on—" I hesitate awkwardly, and she waggles her eyebrows at me expectantly.

I heave a sigh and cross my legs, angling toward her slightly. "Penny did her Penny thing and ran out the door of the Nook as we opened it, and Xander was there to stop her from running into the street."

Vi bobbles her eyebrows again, nodding. "I still can't believe he's your neighbor. *And* that he helped deliver Bea."

I groan. I really won't ever live that down. "Can't forget that he's my older brother's boss and best friend," I grumble around a drink of my iced coffee. *Or the center of my late-night fantasies . . .* I don't add.

She grins, nodding, and I worry for a heartbeat that I said it out loud.

Vi and I met a month before I had Bea, and then she'd started dating Rowan Kingsley, her high school crush turned enemy, who also happened to be one of Cal's co-workers and Xander's hotshots. I remember Cal telling me about all of them years ago, but I can't remember if I'd ever actually met her before our first playdate with the girls.

"Okay, so keep going. What happened next?" she asks, her eyes leaving mine to sweep over the girls. Penny is about a year older than Hollie, and she's currently got the younger girl by the hand, leading her up the wide rubber-coated steps of the play structure toward a small suspension bridge.

"Well, other than stopping my runaway child from becoming a splat on the road, he insisted on taking Bea's car seat from me, convinced Dalton to carry the diaper bag, and then carried both Bea and Penny back to the van for me."

Vi's eyebrows go up and it's like she can't help the smirk that tips at her lips.

"He helped me get them all loaded up. Escorted me around the car and made sure I got in safely." I chew on my bottom lip and hesitate, then decide to just go for it. "He called me *Mama.* But like, Vi. *The way he said it . . .*"

She's practically dancing in her seat as she giggles, throwing her head back to stare up into the branches of the maple above us. "God, yessss, queen! Please tell me you flirted back."

I can't help the scoffing laugh that escapes me as I shake my head in bewilderment. "That was *not* him flirting with me!"

TEDDY

"Oh, yes, it most definitely was," she laughs, using one finger to point at me and she waggles that finger. "I've known him since I was a kid, and he's this grumpy, no-nonsense, silent-type dude. Well, except with Rowan and Cal, I guess, because they're all super close, but you know that. He's polite but stoic when I've been around him. I'm sure you've seen a different side of him, with Cal being your brother, and since he's your neighbor. I mean, I can't say *for certain* that that's his version of flirting, but he's definitely sweet on you."

I throw my head back and laugh out loud. "*Sweet on me?* What is this, the 1950s? He's not asking me to go to a sock hop with him, Vi! And just because we're neighbors doesn't mean we, like, hang out or anything. He's still gone a lot. When Cal and Scottie come over, it's just them. He seems to stick to himself."

"Did he stare at you? He seems like an intense starer."

I laugh again, though another blush heats my cheeks at the memory of just how hard he had been staring at me.

"Is *starer* even a real word?"

She mean-mugs me and I roll my eyes as I continue.

"I mean, yeah I guess you could say he was staring, but it doesn't mean he liked what he was staring *at*—"

"You're *the most* ridiculous human being," Vi grumbles on a laugh, shaking her head. "You are stunning, Teddy. I can guarantee that he liked what he was looking at. Especially in this—" she says, waving at me in general. "That bodysuit is hot as shit on you, and you know it. Otherwise, you wouldn't have left the house wearing it today. Right?"

I give her the stink eye, but it lasts for only a moment before I smile. "I do feel really great in it. Like, did you see my waist? I have *a waist.*"

"Umm, did you see your *boobs*?" Vi asks, her eyes wide. "I'm a dick girl through and through, but I'd motorboat the shit out of you in this."

I laugh fully this time, smiling over at her gratefully, and knock my shoulder into hers. "You're the best."

"Well, yeah, so don't forget it," she teases, bumping her shoulder into mine too. "Are you getting any sleep?"

Inhaling deeply and then letting it out slowly, I glance over at Bea, who is still snoozing away in the stroller. I'm exhausted from putting on a brave face all the damn time. I wonder if Vi can tell how tired I am. Being strong for my kids is one thing, and I try my best to hide my grief away. Especially around Vi, Cal, and Scottie by trying to appear bubbly and happy, even if it's just on the outside. I don't want them to worry about me constantly.

Sometimes I think I'm hiding it well, and other times, I swear they can see right through me to every broken part. Like now.

"Honestly, not much. I think she's teething; she's been drooling like crazy." I look over at Penny and Hollie. "I did finally get Penny back into her own bed though, so that's been a big help."

"Is Dalton still having bad dreams?" she asks, her voice quiet.

I nod and lift one shoulder. "They seem to be getting less frequent. I know he misses Logan." We watch my almost nine-year-old as he tosses baseballs up in the air and hits them across the open field before grabbing the bucket and heading out to pick them all back up and start again. "All these 'firsts' without him have been hard. Dalton's birthday is next month and I don't know how to make it easier for him, not having his dad here." Tears burn my nose and fill my eyes and I blink them away quickly. "The way Dalton's eyes lit up having Xander talk to him today . . . I know he needs a dad figure, but the thought of dating again is—" My words halt and I groan, letting my shoulders slump and my head tip back so I can stare up at the branches above us. The light breeze flutters the leaves and sunlight trickles through in dancing rays. "The thought of dating again is literally my worst nightmare, Vi."

TEDDY

"I get it," Vi sighs, leaning back against the bench and kicking her legs out in front of her, crossing her feet at the ankles. "After my divorce from Troy, I was so burnt-out and exhausted. I had just moved, just started at the hospital, working twelve-hour shifts there and picking up moonlight shifts at the bar, trying to do everything on my own and single-momming on top of it all. And then, enter Rowan fucking Kingsley." She shakes her head, but she smiles over at me wryly. "It happens when we least expect it though, right? I never thought I'd fall all over again for Rowan after he broke my heart."

I nudge her shoulder and smile. "And here you are, all lovey and smitten and happy."

"Meh, he's all right," she jokes, but I know she's only teasing. She's crazy about Rowan, and from what I've seen, he's just as dopey over her too.

"How is Hollie doing with custody time with Troy?" I ask. I know her ex-husband comes to see Hollie almost every Saturday. After they were separated for a year, Violette had moved back home to Sky Ridge to be closer to her family and to take the job at the hospital.

"She seems to be doing well. I think she can sense that I'm at peace here," Vi says, casting her gaze over to her daughter. "She is just loving that she gets to see my parents more now that we're here. And don't get me started on how much she loves Rowan . . ."

"How is Rowan's leg healing?" I ask. He had gotten injured in a fire earlier this season, falling into an ash pit and coming out with moderate burns on his leg. He ended up in the same hospital where Vi works as a burn unit nurse, and, well, the rest was history.

"It's good, actually," she says, nodding. "It still bothers him a bit here and there, but other than that, it looks great. Healing really well. And it's not like it slowed him down at all."

We look over to the girls just in time to see Hollie trip in the sand, face-planting. Penny is there in a heartbeat, helping her stand. Hollie's face tips down as she cries, and Violette grimaces as she stands and walks over toward the two. She hunkers down in front of her daughter and wipes the sand from her cheeks and arms. Little blond pigtails bob as she nods, answering a question Vi asks her that I can't hear. Penny stands close by, her hand on Hollie's back.

A wiggle out of the corner of my eye brings my head around in time to see Bea wake, and within a heartbeat her little face has contorted into an angry pout. She lets out a disgruntled cry as I stand and reach into the stroller to pull her out. I settle back on the bench and grab the lightweight blanket I keep at hand.

We're still the only ones at the park, but I quickly adjust the top of my tank top, and within seconds she's settled in to nurse. I drape the lightweight blanket over her, but she flails her arms and drags it down off of my shoulder. I lift it again, adjusting it to cover her, but she kicks her legs at the same time as flailing her arm wildly again, dragging it completely off herself and my shoulder, and I shake my head as I stare down at her.

"Bea, you tell your momma, *Mom, it's too hot under there*," Vi coos as she comes back to sit down. Thank God for mom friends who don't judge, honestly. I don't know what I'd do without Vi. Speaking to Bea at my breast, she teases, "Ask *her* if she wants a blanket over her head while she's trying to eat and see how she likes it!"

Bea's brown eyes are wide as she stares at Vi over my arm, and her hand is thumping the top slope of my breast animatedly. I laugh, rolling my eyes, then exhale slowly. I needed this time with Vi.

TEDDY

13

XANDER

The door of the bar swings shut with a dull clang as I walk in. Jack Taylor—our old squad leader back when my dad was still alive—had retired and he and his wife, Mae, had taken over running the pub.

Lou, our regular bartender, is off tonight. Violette Taylor, Jack and Mae's daughter and King's new lady, is standing behind the bar. Her brother, Jacob, was on my crew when my dad died, and he'd been best friends with King. Too many of us know what it's like to lose family to a fire. In the same year that I'd lost Dad, Jacob had died on a fire too. It was one of the worst years in my life and my career. King had never been the same afterward, and I don't think Violette ever fully grieved either.

Fuck, losing Jacob was tough on me too. It was my first season as sup, having stepped into the role after my dad died, and then to lose Jacob too at the end of the season was brutal. Working with Jack, I'd known Jacob and Violette since they were kids. Shit, I had practically watched them grow up. I liked to think that I was the cool uncle figure for both of them. Then I'd had to stand with Jack while he buried his son. My own guilt had eaten at me, but I know it was harder on King. He still blames himself for getting his best friend killed, even if it wasn't his fault.

When Violette sees me walking across the floor, she pulls a bottle of PBR out of the cooler, and it's waiting for me as I fold myself into one of the barstools next to Rowan Kingsley. I nod to her in thanks.

The man is dopey over his lady. She flashes me a smile and I can hear King grumble next to me, "Get your own woman." I chuckle just to get on his nerves but ignore the remark, tipping the beer up to my lips as the door opens again. Cal and Scottie walk in together, and then Cal is sitting to my other side after Scottie takes a seat too.

Violette already has a bottle of Coors opened and is setting it in front of Cal, then pours Scottie's whiskey into a highball glass. She may be twenty-eight, but it's still weird seeing the kid I knew standing behind the bar I've been coming to for too many years. She smiles at Scottie as she slides the whiskey over. I know that Violette and Scottie have become friends since Violette started dating King, and that Teddy is friends with Violette too.

My thoughts drift to the woman I can't seem to get off my mind, and I glance at the watch on my wrist, wondering briefly if she's still awake at the townhouse. I haven't seen her since this morning outside the coffee shop, and I'm half tempted to wrap up this excursion and head home early, just on the off chance I'll run into her.

It's almost as if Cal can read my damn thoughts as soon as I think them, because he braces his forearms on the ledge of the bar and leans forward so that he can look at me in profile, and says, "So are you staying at the bunkhouse tonight or are you heading home to—"

I glare at him over the edge of my beer bottle as I tip it up to my mouth again. He's grinning. The fucker is such a shit-stirrer.

XANDER

"Yeah, where the hell have you been lately?" King asks, leaning forward too. "If we're not out on a fire, you're never around. You getting tired of us young bucks, old man?"

I roll my eyes at him and try my best to change the subject. "You've got a big mouth for someone that still can't beat my mile time—"

"He's not getting tired of us, he's just found something that makes it more enjoyable to be at home," Cal mutters across me, not letting me off that easily, his grin widening.

Scottie leans forward, too, her strawberry-blond hair pulled back into a messy topknot, a shit-eating grin pulling at her lips as she looks at me.

I fix Cal with my hardest stare, but it doesn't deter him in the slightest.

"The man damn near fell all over himself today at the coffee shop when he saw—"

"Dude," I grumble, throwing myself back on my stool. Everyone thinks teen girls gossip a lot, but they've got nothing on grown fucking men, apparently. "Leave her out of this."

"Oh, there's a *her*?" King asks, his interest piqued.

I groan, rolling my head so that I'm staring up at the wood-beamed ceiling. Christ, I should have just gone home. You'd think Cal wouldn't want this to be broadcasted, since she's his sister and all. Guess payback is payback though. He's going to milk this for everything he can.

Cal takes a drink of his beer as he slaps me on the back roughly and I groan at his next words. "You think I'm going to take it easy on you just because you've got the hots for my sister? You're in for a rude awakening, Sup."

"Ooohh, I knew it!"

I bring my head back down at the excited gasp. Violette is bracing her hands on the opposite edge of the bar and her smile is wide.

My eyes narrow. "Knew what?"

Violette's smile widens. "That you're sweet on Teddy."

Scottie leans forward again to brace her elbows on the bar so she can look around Cal toward me. She winks, grinning, and I roll my eyes. "Oh, without a doubt. He's got a crush on his best friend's sister."

I groan audibly, letting my chin sink forward until it almost touches my chest. Fuck. My. Life. "I do not have a crush on Cal's sister." It's a blatant lie.

Violette taps her nail on the bar top in front of me, bringing my attention back to her. "No, sir. There's no lying in this bar. House rules."

From beneath my lowered brows, I glower at her without answering. The guys to either side of me aren't going to let me live this down. Dammit to hell. I kill the rest of my beer and set the empty bottle down on the bar between us.

"She had her hands full with all three kids—"

Violette pops the top off another PBR and sets it in front of me, swiping the empty bottle off the bar, a beaming smile on her face.

"Yeah, that's why your tongue was hanging out of the side of your head and you couldn't tear yourself away from her, *because she had her hands full with her kids*," Cal scoffs, shaking his head, then looks over at me. "You think I never noticed the way you watched her?"

"I hate you all so fucking much," I growl, wrapping both hands around the bottle of beer in front of me. My fingernail picks at the label, and I keep my eyes down.

Cal's on a roll, though. Addressing everyone but me, he continues, chuckling. "I've never seen a man fall so hard or so fast in my fucking life. Like a damn shot straight between the eyes, he was done for."

I don't fall for *anyone*. Period. As a rule of thumb for myself, I don't date. My job is the love of my life, just like it was for my dad, and I refuse to put a girlfriend or—God forbid—a wife and kids through that. And Cal knows it. They're all still cackling about Xander and Teddy sitting in a tree . . .

"That's not what this is," I mutter, raising the beer to my lips. My tone is harsher than I intend when I continue, muttering darkly, "She's a widowed mom of three; she's out here doing everything by herself, the least I can do is make sure your terror of a niece doesn't end up as roadkill or fish food because she has no sense of self-preservation yet. Besides, you all know, I don't date single moms."

I instantly regret the harshness of my words when Violette's eyes lose some of that sparkle and that smile disappears. She picks up a hand towel and fidgets with it between her fingers, her mouth tightening into a line. I sense Cal's shoulders stiffen from beside me, but don't have the guts to glance over at him.

Shit. I pinch my eyes shut and rub the back of my neck with one hand. "Fuck. That's not . . . I don't mean it like that."

Violette shrugs, tipping up one shoulder slightly. "Sounds like she's lucky to have someone watching out for her, even if it's obligatory."

Fuuuck. Now I'm sure Cal thinks I'm an asshole that's just panting after his sister with no intention of any kind of follow-through. I mean, he wouldn't be entirely wrong, because I don't even know what my intentions are with Teddy at this point. This is not going well. I should have fucking gone home.

Spanning my hands out wide, I mutter, "Wait, that's not what I said—"

"Look, she knows she's a lot to handle," Violette says, cutting me off.

I stay silent, her hazel eyes bouncing between mine. I feel like I'm being reprimanded by the principal, my chest is tight, and I feel shame burning through me. It's a weird feeling being scolded by her, having known her since she was a kid. I can feel Cal's eyes on me, burning into the side of my head. I'm too much of a coward to look at him. Violette looks over at Cal almost apologetically and then focuses her gaze back on me. "She sees herself as a hot mess on good days, and Lord knows she's doing the best she can with the shitty life hand she's been dealt in the last year . . . but you'd be damn lucky to have someone like Teddy give you any of her time or attention. Just because she's a single mom doesn't make her any less—"

"*I know that*," I murmur quietly, beseechingly, ending her heated tirade. "And I swear I didn't mean it like that." I glance over at Cal before turning back to her. "You know my dad died in a fire, the same year that Jacob did. I don't date at all. Not just 'no single moms.' Not at all. Because the thought of putting a wife and a family through what my mom went through isn't fair. All I know is that I can hear her crying through the walls at night."

Violette's eyes grow sad at that, and Cal sits straighter in his seat, but I push forward.

"And I'd rather be single forever than to hurt someone as amazing as Teddy or put any of them through losing someone like that again. That's all I can promise anyone, that I will make them worry and probably hurt them in the end. Teddy deserves better than that. And so do those kids."

"Well, okay then," she says slowly, nodding, though it's stiff and stilted. "And just so you're aware, she's not interested in dating either, anyway. So I guess you're safe, huh?"

Right. She doesn't want to date either, so this is perfect.

Cal harrumphs next to me, taking a long swallow of his beer.

That doesn't stop the ache in my chest from forming though. I rub at my sternum as if to relieve the pinch of disappointment that tightens my chest. Because even as I said the words out loud . . . I'm not entirely convinced I *meant* them. Not to mention the thought of her dating someone else. The burn of jealousy that crashes through me nearly steals my breath.

Teddy might deserve better than some washed-up, old-ass hot-shot firefighter that might not come back, but fuck if I don't want to *try*.

14

Teddy

"How are the kids? Are they sleeping? Are you sleeping? Is Bea feeding all right? How's that tongue tie?"

Balancing the phone between my ear and shoulder, I sigh as quietly as I can. "The kids are good. Dalton is ready for school to start next week, and Penny is jazzed for preschool. Dalton isn't having nightmares like he was, Penny is back to sleeping in her own bed, Bea is feeding great, and the ENT got that tie snipped weeks ago." I shudder at the memory of that tongue tie that had made breastfeeding Bea absolutely miserable for the first several weeks of her infancy.

"And you? Are you sleeping?"

"Bea is teething, which means she's not sleeping great the last couple weeks, so *I'm* not sleeping great—"

"Kent, what are we doing next weekend? We can hop over to Teddy's to take the kids for the weekend, right?" my mother-in-law calls across the room to her husband.

Colleen and Kent Hansen are the best in-laws I could have ever asked for. As I've gotten older, I've become so grateful for the fact that I don't have to suffer through having monster-in-laws. After Logan's death, they've been so incredibly supportive and helpful, and then again right after Bea was born. Colleen came to stay with us for a couple of weeks and I still maintain I don't know how I would have survived those first few weeks without her.

Our parents passed away years ago, so it's just Cal and me. But the Hansens—Logan's parents—are truly wonderful. Logan had been a late-in-life baby for them, so by the time he was grown, they had been only a few years away from retirement. They spend their time on the coast and like to golf and travel to local wineries.

I hear Kent's deep rumble through the other end of the line, though I can't quite make out what he says.

"Oh good," Colleen trills after he finishes, and I can't help the smile. "We'll be there next Friday, love. Why don't you get a hotel for the night and we'll stay with the kids and have a sleepover."

The thought is thrilling, even if I know I won't ever do it. The idea of sleeping in a bed all by myself, no baby monitor next to me or waking for middle-of-the-night feedings . . . it's like a little piece of heaven.

"I don't know if—"

"Do you have any milk in the freezer?" Colleen asks, cutting me off before I can outright say no.

I smile again. She might know me too well. I scoff silently then. She *should* know me too well; Logan and I were high school sweethearts and had been together more than fifteen years before his accident. "Well, yes—"

"Is it enough to get through one single, solitary night?" she insists.

I sigh, shaking my head in defeat. "Yes."

"And do you not trust Gram and Grampa to watch the babies?"

I roll my eyes. Now she's just being dramatic to be funny, so I play along. "Not even for a second."

"Excellent. Ice cream for breakfast, lunch, and dinner it is, then."

A laugh bubbles out of me as I sink into one corner of the couch. "Thank you. The kids will be excited to see you both. And I could use a hug."

"Oh, my sweet girl," Colleen murmurs, switching from light-hearted and teasing to sincere. "What's going on?"

I swallow past the emotion clogging my throat, laughing self-deprecatingly. "It's silly, honestly."

"If it makes you upset, it's not silly," she says gently.

Taking a deep breath in, I let it out slowly. "I got a call from the local agency. They have an opening starting in October and have my application on file from when we moved. They asked me to come in for an interview . . . but I don't know if I'm ready. If I'll ever be ready to go back to that—"

Tears burn my nose and fill my eyes. Dammit. I told myself I wouldn't get emotional over this.

"I know I should go back to work. I'm almost at the end of my four months of maternity leave that I gave myself after Bea was born . . . I can't live off the money from selling the house or-or Logan's life insurance payout forever, and I don't want you to think that that's what I'm doing—" I rush to say. "I have most of it in high-yield savings for the kids. I let myself keep out just enough to get through until after Bea was born—"

"Teddy, you don't have to explain any of this to me," Colleen says gently.

I sniffle and nod, though I know she can't see it through the phone.

"You've always been smart and responsible, and we know you will do what you think is best for you and those babies. You don't have to justify anything to me. And if you're not ready to go back to dispatch work, you can stay home for as long as you need to. Stay home until Penny goes to kindergarten. Heck, stay home until Bea starts school, for all I care. You will always have those kids and their best interest as your highest priority. We know that."

I sense a *but*, and I'm not waiting long. I smile when she continues.

"But, you need to make sure you are still finding a way to fulfill *your* best interests too, Teddy. Find something that makes you happy, because you can't pour from an empty cup."

The tears slide down my cheeks and I swipe at them, releasing a breath so that my cheeks puff out with the exhale. "I miss it," I admit quietly. "I loved my job."

"And you were great at it," Colleen says.

"Until I wasn't." The admission comes out as a whisper.

"Teddy, you have to stop blaming yourself. No one else blames you but you. How many other calls did you send Logan out on without trouble?"

Hundreds.

"You had no way of knowing what was going to happen. It was one of those horrible freak accidents. And I know that doesn't make it any easier to accept, but it was. There was nothing that you did wrong, nothing that Logan did wrong. I will miss my son for the rest of my days, and you will miss him too. Those babies will miss him. But him not being here is not your fault. Please tell me you know that. Have you been going to the grief counselor?"

"Not since Bea was born," I admit sheepishly. I twiddle the hem of my shirt between my fingers. "I just haven't had the time or energy to drive over." It's not far, barely a half-hour drive to our old hometown, where Logan's parents still live. But it seemed like a herculean effort to find a sitter for all three kids or load them up to drop them off at Colleen and Kent's home so I could continue to go to counseling.

"Don't make me move us over there so I can make sure you're taking care of yourself," she threatens gently. I know she's only half joking. "Do you think you'll at least go for the interview?"

"I don't know. Maybe. I want to. Lord knows I miss it. I'm just so scared. What if I mess up and I get someone else's spouse or child killed? I'd never forgive myself."

"You can't continue to be afraid to go out and *live*, sweet girl."

I groan in defeat. Dammit, I hate when she's right. One thing about Colleen, she doesn't rub things in, so she's quick to change the subject, for which I'm grateful.

"I'm sure we'll talk before then, but I'll see you next Friday, okay?"

"Okay, yes," I laugh, my chest feeling just a little lighter than it did before she called. "Thank you, Mom."

"You're most welcome, Teddy. I'll see you soon. Love you."

"Love you too. See you soon." I hang up the call but sit staring at my phone screen. Before I can chicken out, I dial Vi.

When she answers, she asks, "Is something wrong?"

"Does something need to be wrong for me to call you?" I ask, laughing.

"Yes. Otherwise, you'd just text me," she mumbles.

That's probably the truth, I admit. "I'm trying to live and not be scared."

"Yeah, because that's not cryptic at all," she deadpans, and I laugh again.

"My in-laws are coming next weekend to take the kids for Friday night. Are you on shift at the hospital?" I ask.

"No, but I'm supposed to bartend at Shifty's on Friday night."

"Oh. Well, crap."

"What's going on?" she asks, and I can sense she's sitting down, as if worried about what's coming next.

"They want me to go to a hotel for the night, just to get away for a few hours. I was going to see if you wanted to have a girls' sleepover with me?" I ask hurriedly. "Junk food and swoony rom-com movies and boozy drinks?" Without needing to feed Bea for a whole night,

TEDDY

I'll be able to actually indulge in an adult beverage. It's the small wins, I guess. "I'm going to drag Scottie with me too."

Vi laughs and says, "Oh, hell yes. My parents will have Hollie anyway. I'll tell Lou we need to switch one night next week. Ugh, yes. One hundred percent yes. Girls' night in," Violette sing-songs, and I grin. "No babies, no men. I'm so down."

Yep, this is going to be great. Just what the doctor—err, mother-in-law—ordered.

15

XANDER

"How's the move going?"

My brother Zach just grumbles from the other end of the line and I barely make out the words *Barbies for days*. I chuckle. He's got three daughters—my nieces—ranging in age from almost five to eleven. My brother was always the guys' guy type of dude, so having three daughters has been an adjustment for him.

Add to that the fact that their mother just up and left—the flighty bitch that she is—he's got his fucking hands full being a single dad. They just moved from their old house into a smaller apartment, something he can afford easier on his own, but that alone is another big adjustment. I feel for him, that's for damn sure.

"It's amazing how much shit accumulates over time," he grumbles. "And God forbid we get rid of any of these mismatched Barbie shoes. Chloe damn near had a meltdown when she saw a handful of them in the trash yesterday. You'd think I killed her kitten with the way she glared at me."

I laugh out loud, folding my arms over my chest and leaning back in the patio chair out back. I can only imagine the betrayed look on my youngest niece's face.

"There's just so much shit to go through." He sighs, and I hate the exhaustion that I can hear through the phone. "I did find something. I have it in the mail for you."

"Yeah? What's that?"

"It's a letter from Dad, actually," he says, and my entire body stills. "He sent both me and Joel letters years ago, and this one is addressed to you. I just never got around to sending it back to you. Sorry, brother."

A letter from my dad? A letter that he wrote and meant for me to have before he died, or after?

"When did you get those letters?" I ask, leaning forward in my chair and bracing my elbows on my widespread knees.

"Shit, it was"—he blows out a breath—"six, seven years ago? It was before we got pregnant with Chloe, I know that. I think Bailey was one, maybe? So, a while. I don't know how yours ended up in my stuff, and then it just got buried."

"Did uh—did you read it?"

"Nah," he says quietly, and I nod even though he can't see it. "If yours is as personal as mine was, I didn't think it was my place to read it. I sent it a couple days ago, so it should be to you any day now."

Fuck. A letter from my dad, written before he died. How strange will it be to read something from him, knowing he's gone now? Knowing he would be gone shortly after that letter was intended to be read?

That familiar pang of grief hits me all over again, deep and aching. The grief doesn't come as often as it used to, but time hasn't seemed to dull that pain any. My dad was a force to be reckoned with, an amazing father, fair and honorable leader and boss, and one of my best friends. Fuck, losing him was one of the hardest things I've ever had to go through. The weeks and months of emptiness just ate at me mercilessly. It took a long damn time to come out of the darkness that losing him had sent me into.

I drank too much. Fucked too much. Put myself in dangerous situations on purpose like I had some ridiculous death wish or something. And then that fog cleared and I realized what a fucking disappointment I would have been to my father if he could have seen me then.

I clawed my way out of that and haven't looked back. I still drink—probably too much on occasion—but I'm aware enough to know when I've had enough. I don't stick my dick in any willing piece of ass anymore—though I am glad even in my lowest of lows I never, not once, fucked a chick without a condom. Wrapped my shit up airtight.

I don't need any accidental kids out there in the world.

"How's Addie?" I ask gruffly, pulling myself out of the darkness my train of thought had derailed me into.

Zach sighs again, and I can just imagine the way he's rubbing at the back of his neck like he's trying to knead the stress out of his shoulders. "She's struggling," he admits quietly. "I don't blame her. She's old enough to understand that Brit left and I can only bend the truth so much for her like I can with Bails and Chloe. I think part of her blames me for her mom leaving." I hear the sadness in his voice, but he continues before I can interrupt. "Chloe is an emotional mess. I mean she's always been shy and sensitive, but fuck, man. I look at her *just* wrong and she starts crying. Asking if I'm going to leave them like Brittanee did. It breaks my fucking heart. How do you leave your kids?"

His gruff shout lands like pins. I'd never really wondered about how my dad had done it when we were kids. He'd had a good reason, from what I could see. This job, the alarming understaffing that runs rampant through this line of work . . . I understood. Zach and Joel had been younger, so they'd struggled with it more than I had. And then I'd come out here to work with Dad as soon as I was able to.

"Anyway, that letter should be to you in a day or two, I just wanted to let you know so you could keep an eye out for it. I never know when you're going to be out on a call," Zach says, clearly reigning in his own hurt and anger from his current situation. "I should get back to unpacking."

"Sure," I say into the phone, wishing like hell there was a way for me to help my brother more but knowing there's nothing I can do from half a country away. "Thanks for letting me know and for sending it my way. Take care of yourself, Z. Hug those girls for me."

"Will do, brother. Be careful out there."

"Always am," I say gravely before hanging up, the only promise I can give.

16

XANDER

I peek at the alarm clock on the nightstand next to me as I listen to the orders, phone pressed to my ear. Shit, it's early. Oh well, *rise and shine, boys.* Speaking into the phone, I say, "Thank you, we'll be on the road within the hour."

I end the call and open the text thread to Cal and King, then quickly type out the orders that I'd just received for our latest assignment. It's early as fuck, but I know they'll both get my message quickly. As captain and squad leader, they will take over sending out orders to the rest of the crew and getting them ready to leave. I hit send and stand from the bed, heading to my closet. My bag is almost always prepped and packed, ready to go. Once I grab my pack, I head out to the kitchen, where I have a pot of coffee started to brew. It's early as shit, but this fire has been burning for a solid nine hours already.

My phone buzzes and I check it, reading the responses as they come in.

KING: Copy that, Sup.
Little early for Labor Day fireworks, huh?

CAL: All of SoCal is on a fire ban. Idiots.

> **ME:** Lead says it was a non-resident
> tourist.

KING: Morons.

> **ME:** Lead also says the tourist
> perished.

CAL: Natural selection at its finest, folks.

I groan, rolling my eyes. Even though I had the same exact thought, I type out:

> **ME:** Someone died, guys.
> Get your asses moving.
> Wheels on the road in one hour.

CAL: Sorry, Sup.
Wheels in one hour.

I take a sip of the coffee as I stand at the kitchen sink, looking out over the front yard. The moon is bright, casting the yard outside in sharp relief. Teddy's lawn mower is in the middle of her side of the yard, half of the grass cut, as if she'd stopped halfway through. Setting my coffee down, I frown. If it's still there when I get back from this fire, I'll make sure to finish the lawn.

Bracing my hips against the kitchen counter, I cross my arms over my chest as I sip my coffee. That's when I hear it, the indignant wail of an infant cry. It's muffled, but I can hear it through the window at my back. I wonder if Teddy is in her own kitchen, walking around trying to soothe the squalling Bea, whose cries just get all the harder before finally ceasing abruptly.

I can hear her then, murmuring and talking to the baby, and I realize she's walked out her front door. I spot her as she steps off the covered front patio and walks toward her minivan, the headlights flashing as she unlocks it with the fob in her hand.

I'm around the kitchen and stepping out of my own front door a heartbeat later. "Teddy!" I call quietly, trying not to startle her.

She squeaks in alarm anyway, twisting around to face me, and I lose track of all thought as my brain registers what's in front of me.

"Ohmygod, Xander!" she breathes, and I can sense the mortification rolling off of her in palpable waves, her cheeks turning a vibrant, pretty shade of pink. Her hair is tied up in a messy topknot, her glasses on her nose, and her face free of makeup. She's sleep-rumpled and so fucking pretty. I can't stop staring at her, at the body that's on full display currently.

She's got Bea nursing, cradled expertly in one arm, the baby's dark head against her exposed breast. She's wearing some flimsy, comfortable-looking bralette—though one cup has been pulled down to allow access for Bea to nurse—and a pair of boy-short panties that come up just below her navel which are all she's got on her lower half. Her legs are bare from hip to ankle and her soft stomach is exposed between the edge of her panties and the bottom band of the bra. That soft, short robe that she was wearing before is on her arms, though it's been left untied so the edges hang at her sides, and one shoulder has fallen halfway down her arm. Like she just rolled out of bed and barely took the time to shove her arms into the garment. She clutches the edge of her robe in her free hand, pulling it across her body, but fuck, I wish she wouldn't. I'm utterly and completely transfixed by this woman.

"Do you need help with something?" I ask, my voice hoarse. I clear my throat. Shit.

"Umm. I think her pacifier with her stuffy attached to it fell out of my bag in the car, I was just going to go look for it," she mumbles, gesturing behind her toward her vehicle. She's still blushing a deep, rosy pink. "I'm sorry if we woke you."

I stride forward, skirting around her. She moves to take a step after me, but I say, "Stay there. You don't have shoes on. I'll find it."

Sliding the driver's side rear door open, I reach inside and flip on the overhead light. Squeezing myself in the narrow space between the bucket seats made all the narrower because of the bulky car seats is no easy feat, but I manage, and I'm back a moment later with the pacifier clipped to a tiny pink stuffed puppy.

"Oh my god, *thank you*," she whispers after I close the sliding door and walk back toward her. "I should have come back out last night to find it, but I was so tired and they were all sleeping finally and I just didn't want to get back out of bed . . ."

Bea is still suckling happily at Teddy's left breast, the slope of it bare. I stop close to her, passing the lost pacifier and stuffy to her as she reaches for it. She's somehow managed—moms never cease to amaze me at how they can do things single-handed—to pull both edges of the robe together, and has loosely tied the sash around her middle, so her body is covered now. Much to my own disappointment.

"I'm sorry if we woke you up," she says again, her chin tipping up toward me as she looks at me. There's a line across one cheek from her pillow, and it makes me smile, thinking about her sleeping so soundly.

"You didn't," I whisper back, letting my gaze trail over every inch of her face. It's warm out, despite the early hour, this record heatwave we've had not abating in the slightest. Or maybe it's just me. Maybe I'm just set ablaze from the inside out by this woman. A breeze stirs and swipes one wayward strand of hair from her messy topknot across her cheek, and I don't stop myself from reaching out to tuck it behind her ear. Her breath catches at my touch, her lips parting slightly, and fucking hell, all I want is to duck my head and see if that sound tastes good against my own lips. "I was already up. We just got a roll in Cali, so I'll be leaving in a bit."

"Oh," she breathes, her dark blond brows pulling over her eyes. Those eyes track over my face, ping-ponging between my eyes and my mouth. She licks her lips, then nods. "Well, I'm glad we didn't wake you."

"If you need anything, you call," I murmur quietly, reaching my hand out to slide my palm over her now-covered shoulder and arm. She's got my number. Not that she's ever used it. "Anytime. For anything. I mean it, Teddy."

She rolls her eyes and laughs lightly but nods again. I love the sound, so soft and husky, and the way her mouth tilts up with that smile. "Sure. While you're out on a fire call two states away, I'll make sure to call you if I lose Bea's stuffy again."

"I'll make sure my phone is charged at all times." My tone is teasing, but fuck, I'm not joking. "Come on, let me walk you girls back inside."

One corner of her lips turns up slightly, but she turns and walks back toward her front door. I can't help it, my eyes land and stay on the delectable, full curve of her ass beneath the thin material of her robe as she walks. Her body sways and jiggles with each step and goddamn, I'm practically salivating and half hard in my pants. Christ, what this woman does to me without even trying.

XANDER

Guess there's no sense in denying how fucking badly I want her.

Stepping up onto the covered patio, she turns to face me. We're closer to the same height now, though I'm still taller by an inch or two. She wrinkles her nose and smiles, and it sends a crack down my chest. "So, is this good night or good morning?"

My face splits in a grin and I chuckle. Fuck, she's cute.

"Are you going to go in and try to get a few more hours of sleep?" I ask.

"Yes, as long as this one lets me put her down," she says, wiggling Bea just the slightest in her arms.

She's stopped suckling and is back to sleep, and at the wiggle, her little mouth pops off Teddy's breast, leaving the nipple exposed. I drop my eyes as Teddy reaches down to shift the robe over herself as she laughs self-consciously. She covers her face with her free hand then and groans miserably.

"*Ohmygod.* Honestly, it's like I can't *not* embarrass myself when you're around. I swear, this type of stuff only happens when you're here to witness my humiliation. I'm so sorry. Please forget you just saw all this," she whispers, the words spilling out of her as she waves to herself as a whole.

My jaw ticks as I clench my teeth together.

Another self-deprecating laugh escapes her and her cheeks flush an even darker pink. "God, I hope I didn't just scar you for life."

Stepping forward, I crowd into her space, forcing her back a step. Her hand drops to her side as she raises her gaze to mine, mouth dropping open. "Not fucking likely, Teddy."

"What?" she whispers, the sound barely a breath between us.

"You said forget all this—" I rasp, dropping my gaze from hers to travel over her entire body and back up again. "*Not fucking likely, Teddy.* I've been dying to see more of you. And I'm not disappointed in what I've seen so far, beautiful."

Her mouth is still open, quiet, panting breaths escaping her.

Bravely, I trail just the tip of my finger along the fluttering edge of the robe that was hastily pulled over her breasts, my finger grazing her warm skin at the edge along the slope of her chest. My voice is low and gruff as I murmur, "Go inside. I'm staying until I hear the lock."

She takes a step back, then another, though her eyes don't leave mine. I nod toward the door. Turning, she opens it, then steps inside.

"Good night, Teddy."

She nods shakily. "Good night, Xander."

Before she can shut the door, I step forward until we're close again. "Oh, and Teddy?" I say, my words coming out huskily. I'm feeling ballsy, and I need her to know I meant what I said.

"Hmm?" she whispers, her eyes bouncing between mine.

Reaching out, I trail my fingers along the sash of her robe, feather-light, and she sucks in her breath, staring up at me. Whispering low, I breathe, "I really fucking like hearing you say my name when you come, Mama."

Her mouth drops open, her cheeks go red, and I can see it in those pretty gray eyes when she realizes what I mean. I let one corner of my mouth tip up before I lower my hand and step backward off the porch. "Lock the door, Teddy."

I remain where I am until I hear the lock engage from the inside, though I don't hear her steps fade away from the door. And I can't help but wonder if she's standing just on the other side, just as I am, not wanting to walk away either.

XANDER

17

XANDER

My brother Zach told me once that he'd rather fight one hundred structure fires than fight a wildfire, because with a structure fire, you know where your flames are at. But with a wildfire, it can sneak right up behind you.

I don't know if it's my own overinflated ego at having done this for nearly twenty years, but fuck that. I'd rather be out in a wildfire any day than be stuck in a burning building. I did that for years before moving out to Sky Ridge to join my dad's hotshot crew, and though firefighting is where my heart has always been, structure fires make me twitchy.

From my lookout, I know exactly where my crew is, even though I can't physically see them. They're split right now, each squad working their line. King is our lead sawyer and newly instated squaddie, so he has his team up the ridge cutting deadwood and pulling snags out of the line. Cal has the other half of the team down about a quarter mile digging the fire line out. We were fortunate enough to get a dozer hauled in for this fire, but most of the time, the lines are dug completely by hand. It's backbreaking and labor-intensive, and our days on fires start around 4:00 a.m. We're mandated to break at sixteen hours, but sometimes, I have to force my crew to stop to eat and sleep.

As superintendent, I have to have my head on a constant swivel; I'm watching wind shifts and updrafts from the head of the blaze that's getting far too close to several homes for comfort. The guys have this weird superstition that I can control the weather and make it do what I want . . . but I'm just really fucking good at reading it. Or maybe I've just been lucky as shit for most of my career. The weather plays such a pivotal role in fighting fires. If the wind changes direction and starts blowing embers into the green—the section of forests not touched by the fire—it leads to spot fires, and those can lead to crews being boxed in, or start a free burn too close to residential areas. There was a finger that snaked out a few days ago on the west flank. Mack Treynor's old Vantage Hotshot crew from Colorado was able to circumvent it before it got out of hand. My dad's old friend and colleague is retired now, but their new superintendent seems to be damn good at his job.

King and his squad had nearly been boxed in on a ridge the first day we were here, but quick thinking on King's part had gotten them all out. I'm proud as fuck; he's earned this squaddie position, and this fire has just cemented that my decision was the right one. I split my time between scouting and helping out wherever I'm needed, but I couldn't do my job without knowing I can trust my captain and squad leaders to do their jobs. I'm fortunate to have a fantastic team beneath me.

Cal and his squad have been burning out a two-mile line, boxing the blaze in after a spot fire breached our containment. With the back burn eating up as much of the fire's fuel as possible to head it off, by the time the head of the blaze meets the black, there won't be much green left for it to consume unless it throws hotspots half a mile away.

XANDER

Fuck, this fire has been a beast from start to finish.

And fuck me, but all I can think about is Teddy. Even though my focus is on this fire, she's been right there too.

I'm forty-two, almost forty-three, and not once in my adult life have I ever been so obsessed with a woman as I am with her.

I blame Violette for telling me Teddy isn't interested in dating. Because now, all I want is for her *to be* interested. Teddy has always been completely unobtainable and strictly off-limits; I knew that when I met her. I respected her marriage. But now . . .

Fuck. Now, she's *slightly less* unobtainable and not as *strictly* off-limits as before . . . and I've never stopped wanting this woman.

I've jacked off too many times to the memory of her body on display that morning we'd headed out for this fire. It's been almost two weeks and I've never wanted to get home more urgently than I do now. Her laugh, her smile—fuck, her everything—they're what're getting me through each day.

She's home alone with all three kids. I should have set up something, sent someone to check on her while I'm gone. I wonder if Violette has seen her, checked on her. I'm sure Scottie has checked in. Cell service out here is spotty at best, so it's not like we've been able to talk.

And trust me, I've checked. Numerous times. Not one call or text from her. Fuck, I hope she's doing all right.

By the end of the day, my team—alongside the other divisions and agencies transported in to help on this fire—have it controlled.

As I make my way back down the ridge to the spike camp we've been living out of for the last two weeks, my team is back. It's nearly dark already, and some of my crew are already passed out in their sacks, others chowing down on food. Everyone is dirty, sweaty, exhausted, and starving. Most of these guys will burn more calories than they'll consume out here.

King is down the trail about fifty feet, phone to his ear. He talks for just a few minutes before he hangs up, then meets up with us.

"How's Violette?" I call over.

He grins, and I realize too late that I've fucked up.

"She's great. She says to tell you Teddy and the kids are fine too."

Motherfucker.

Several of the guys turn their attention to us, some calling out razzing questions. King's grin just gets wider as he sinks onto an overturned log made into a bench. I hate the lot of them.

"Sup, you got a lady and kids we don't know about?"

"None of your business," I call out on a grumble.

"Like, Cal's sister, Teddy?" Opp asks around a bite of his food.

Cal rests his elbows on his knees, nodding, though his eyes don't leave my face.

Dammit.

Royce, our newest rookie, pipes up, sitting straighter in his seat as he calls, "Wait, Cal's sister, the woman that lives next door? The one you helped—" He stops, pantomiming delivering a baby, and I glare over at the rookie.

Opp thumps the kid on the back and mutters, "You're gonna want to stop talking right there, Roycie. He goes into papa-bear mode when you talk about that."

"Yeah, remember what happened with Morey?" King laughs, shaking his head as he digs into his food.

My jaw clenches and rage fills me all over again at the memory of what one of my douchebag crew members had muttered about Teddy's anatomy. First, his offhand comment about being licensed to lift her skirt had made me see *red*. Then, later after several drinks, he'd asked whether she'd offered up anything in "thanks" for my services. Now, I've never been one to fight, but damn, I'd been seconds away from beating that guy to a pulp. If Opp hadn't gotten me into a barrel hold, I'd have knocked the fucker's front teeth out. I'm glad Cal hadn't been around to hear it; I'm not sure we'd have stopped him from beating the guy's face in.

The trash had transferred to a crew in Arizona not long after. Good riddance.

"Oh, right," Roycie says, glancing over at me a little warily. Kid's got heart, if a little wet behind the ears still. King has really taken him under his wing. I think the kid reminds him of Jake. "I'd have done the same thing if anyone talked about someone I cared about like that too, Sup. I'm sure Cal appreciates it too."

I stay silent, and out of the corner of my eye I can see both King and Cal grinning like idiots. I can't hide much from them, not that I really ever hide anything from them at all. Cal's been my best friend for years, which makes this so much worse, and King is like my younger brother, but a whole lot less annoying than my actual youngest brother, Joel, is. Well, most of the time, anyway. Right now, I'd like to tip him backward over that log he's sitting on.

My com crackles and then the voice of the lead commanding officer comes over the static. *"Good job today, boys. Looks like this fire is cooked. You're all set to head home."*

"Copy that," I respond, clicking off the com. "Looks like we're heading home, boys. Congratulations on another successful fire."

There are whoops of excitement through the spike camp at my announcement and a shuffle of activity as they all start breaking down camp. We'll head over to the nearest tarmac and load up onto a shitty little plane that will haul us and our gear back north. And then an hour drive to Sky Ridge. But we should be home by morning.

18

Teddy

"Oh, my babies!"

I smile as Colleen sinks to her knees on the front porch, arms flung open wide as Dalton and Penny vault into her waiting arms. She kisses them a dozen times each on the cheeks and forehead, making them both giggle. Dalton makes a show of wiping her kisses off, grinning from ear to ear. Colleen narrows her eyes at him playfully, then kisses him on both cheeks again, just for good measure.

"Grampa, I swear they've grown a foot since we saw them last!" Colleen mumbles over her shoulder to her husband.

Dalton and Penny both disengage from Colleen's arms and fling themselves at Kent, who catches them both as they hug his waist.

I offer Colleen a hand and she groans dramatically as she rises from her knees.

"I'm getting too old to be getting down on the ground like that."

I laugh, but then I'm being pulled into her warm embrace, and I sink into it for a long moment. She always smells like peppermint and honey, and I take the moment to just breathe her in. Colleen has been my pillar in the last year. I don't know what I would do without her.

"Thank you for coming to see us," I whisper, squeezing her tighter for a heartbeat longer before letting her go.

Kent has Penny in his arms, and she's telling him in great detail about the blanket fort she and Dalton had constructed in the living room yesterday, and how I'd been a "mean mom" and made them take it down before bed.

Kent chuckles and winks over at me before saying, "We'll build another one tonight, how about that?"

Penny squeals in excitement and he laughs again.

Dalton does a fist pump in the air. "Are we gonna have pizza for dinner tonight?"

"Pizza? What makes you think we would have pizza for dinner tonight?" Colleen asks innocently, though she winks at me too. Pizza picnics on the floor and a pajama party are what Colleen and Kent are known for. The kids love it. They make stove-top popcorn and then build a giant blanket bed in the very center of the living room to watch movies before they camp out on the floor.

"The sheets are all switched over on my bed, so it's ready for you guys," I say, leading the group of us into the house. Bea is zonked out in her bouncy seat on the floor, the automatic bouncing mechanism keeping her slowly in motion. Colleen leans over her, just to lay eyes on her, before moving away to let her keep sleeping. "Are you sure you want me to leave? I can stay—"

"Absolutely not," Colleen murmurs, moving into the kitchen. "You get to go have a night to yourself. Like I said, you can't pour from an empty cup, sweet girl."

Though I do fully understand the sentiment, and I'm so insanely grateful for the chance to get away and just be *not Mom* for a night, the guilt and selfishness of the act are making my anxiety soar.

I have a detailed list of Bea's routine written out on a notebook. Her feeding times, how many ounces she gets, and her daytime nap schedule as well as her night schedule. The diaper station is fully stocked, and pajamas are laid out for all three kids. Dalton and Penny are easy enough, and Colleen and Kent know their routines.

"How was the first week of school?" Colleen asks, and Dalton launches into a tale about his first week in the third grade. Penny then regales her grandparents with how preschool is going, and by the time they're both done telling their stories, Bea is waking from her nap.

Colleen shoos me away and lifts my chunky almost four-month-old into her arms, nuzzling her soft cheek.

"Okay, you guys, let's give Mom hugs and kisses, and then she's going to get out of here," Colleen says to Dalton and Penny, who rush me like tiny linebackers.

My bag is ready, though it had taken me all day to convince myself to pack it at all. Just a pair of my comfiest pj's and a change of clothes for tomorrow, slippers, a smutty romance novel that I've been dying to get to, and all the fixings for pedicures and face masks. Also, two bottles of wine and enough snacks to feed an army of women.

I give them both tight squeezes and kiss them on the cheeks. Dalton doesn't wipe my kisses away, which makes me smile, and I ruffle his sandy-brown hair. "Help Gram and Grampa with Penny and Bea tonight, please? And be good. Brush your teeth before bed." I look over at Colleen then, adding, "And please, no ice cream after nine o'clock. They'll never go to sleep for you if they have that much sugar that late."

"I wouldn't dream of it," she teases, but I know she'll listen. She may be the best grandma ever and they both spoil my kids absolutely rotten, but they've always been respectful of my rules.

I hug Penny tight, then speak directly to her. "Absolutely no running away from Gram and Grampa, and no playing out in the backyard without one of them out there with you. What is the big rule?"

Penny looks up at me with her big brown doe eyes and whispers, "No running into the cweek."

I nod, tucking a stray curl behind her ear. "Right, good job."

Turning to Colleen and Kent again, I gesture over to the notepad. Colleen hands Bea over to Kent, who snuggles her close like a football.

"Everything is here. Obviously, you have my phone number, and I have my charger just in case. Phone number for the hotel is here," I say, pointing to the phone number I'd scrawled at the bottom. "I have milk thawing and there's more in the freezer. Bottles are all set up and sanitized. Don't worry about sanitizing them when you're done, I'll do that when I get back tomorrow. There are enough to not have to use any more than once. Diapers, wipes, diaper cream, pj's are all ready to go too."

Kent hands Bea over to me and I clutch her close. This is the first time I've ever been away from her and I'm starting to panic. I breathe in her baby scent. They'll be fine for one night. I get to go and be a normal woman for one single night. Nothing catastrophic is going to happen.

"If we have any issues, I will call you," Colleen says gently, sensing my rising panic. "But we'll be fine."

"I know," I whisper, my eyes meeting hers over Bea's dark head that I have pressed close to my own. I press another kiss to the top of her head, then her chubby little cheek, before handing her over. I blink the moisture from my eyes. I'm leaving for like, eighteen hours, not eighteen months, for goodness' sake! I can do this!

Grabbing my bag from beside the door, I smile at them, then blow them all kisses.

"Have a good night, Mom!" Colleen calls, holding Bea's hand and waving it, making my infant belly-laugh.

"You all have so much fun tonight! I love you," I murmur to them as a whole, and then I'm forcing myself out the front door.

My phone vibrates in my pocket and I dig it out as I walk over to my minivan. I smile shakily and lift the phone to my ear. "How'd you know I'd need you to call me?"

"Because I know how hard it is to leave them for the first time," Vi says in response. "My first overnight shift at the hospital after Hols was born, I was an absolute train wreck."

I laugh, sliding into the driver's seat and starting the engine. I blow out my breath and lean my head back against the headrest. I stare out the windshield at my little duplex, imagining all of them inside. They're going to have the best night, I know it. So why is it so hard to do something for *me*? Admittedly, I know why. "This is my first time away from Bea . . . and my first time away from any of them since Logan died."

"I get it. They'll be perfectly fine. We're going to eat trash food, drink wine, and watch the swooniest rom-coms we can find."

"You're right, this is going to be great," I murmur, glancing in the rearview mirror as I back out of the driveway. "I'll be there in about fifteen minutes, and Scottie should be there soon too."

"Awesome," Vi sing-songs. "See you soon!"

Half an hour later, Vi and I are sitting cross-legged on one of the two queen-size beds in the hotel room, sipping White Claws, a bag of Doritos propped up between us, when there's a knock on the door. Vi jumps up, the waffle weave of her jade-green lounge set hugging her Pilates-toned curves, and swings open the door.

"Hey, you found us!" she says with a smile, opening the door wider to let Scottie inside.

Scottie steps inside, an army-style canvas duffel slung over one shoulder and a grocery bag in the other hand. She understood

TEDDY

the assignment and is dressed for comfort—dark navy leggings and a plain white tank that shows off her athletic figure, and her strawberry-blond hair piled into an artfully messy topknot. I don't fully remember the first time I laid eyes on her—she was just a blur outside of Shifty's, Cal steering me past while we were both drunk. But I certainly remember him finally introducing us after they'd been rescued from Quell's Peak. It was obvious how absolutely enamored my brother was with her, even then. I'm still thankful she came into his life, as unorthodox as their beginning was.

I stand from the bed, adjusting my shirt over my middle as I do.

"Thank you for dragging me out tonight," Scottie smiles, her freckled nose and cheeks scrunching as she drops her bags at the foot of the bed. She steps over to hug me tight, just for a few seconds, and I'm reminded of just how grateful I am to have these two women in *my* life.

"I can't have a mandated girls' night out without my bonus sister and bestie. Especially since your guys are still gone. Do they have any idea of when they'll be back?"

I ask the question as nonchalantly as I can as Scottie and I pull apart, though I think they both can tell I'm fishing for information on Xander. Vi grins over at Scottie, then at me.

"Last Rowan said, probably a few more days at least," she says, grinning widely. "Are you missing your hot neighbor?"

I groan, flopping back down onto my butt on the bed. "*Violette.*"

But she laughs and waves her hand at Scottie as they both climb onto the bed too. "Oh come on, I want to hear all the gossip about you and Xander."

"Whoa, but there's no *me and Xander*—" I rush to say, sitting up straighter, my eyes ping-ponging between my two friends. "Like, we're literally just neighbors."

"Mm-hmm," Vi murmurs, though the inflection in her tone says she doesn't believe that for a millisecond.

I groan again.

"Your brother is handling this way better than I expected," Scottie laughs, grinning.

"Ohmygod, there's nothing for him to *handle*!" I exclaim, my cheeks heating. "There's nothing going on between Xander and me. *Nothing.*"

The lie makes my throat tight. They don't need to know about how he'd seen me half naked. Or what he'd said to me standing on my porch. How his eyes had taken on that dark, dangerous glint to them as he'd stared at me. They definitely don't need to know that I had given myself a self-induced orgasm once I'd gotten back into bed replaying those heated words. It had taken every ounce of self-control I had not to make any noise as I'd done it too. I take a large gulp of my drink.

"He's my neighbor and my brother's best friend. And his boss. I do not have a thing for my hot neighbor," I insist again. Even though it's a bold-faced lie.

Vi side-eyes me with a glare. "I'll say the same thing I said to him; there's no lying here."

Well, shit.

"But you do admit that he's hot."

I glare at Scottie over the rim of my seltzer.

She winks then. "Well, for the record, I think he's got a thing for his hot neighbor too."

The jealousy that flashes through me is so unexpected I jolt. I can't help it, I run through all of our nearby neighbors, trying to figure out who she's talking about, but I'm left coming up blank. Well, guess that puts an end to this stupid crush I've been fighting for months.

Vi leans over and whispers loudly, "You do realize that she's talking about *you*, Teddy. *You're* the hot neighbor."

Ohhhhhhh.

TEDDY

I flush hotly and take a gulp of my drink. The carbonation tingles my nose and I cough. *Subject change, stat.* "Do either of you have anything stronger?" I ask, wheezing.

Scottie beams, leaning over to grab the grocery bag she'd brought, then with a flourish pulls out a bottle of whiskey. "Shots, ladies?"

"We're so not setting alarms in the morning," Vi laughs, hopping off the bed to grab the little complimentary plastic cups from the bathroom. Unwrapping each one from their plastic wrap, she hands them to Scottie, who pours out two fingers' worth into each of the three cups. I swallow hard, nervousness making me giggle.

The last time I was drunk was the night I'd met Cal for drinks at Shifty's because he'd needed to talk about Scottie—not that he'd actually talked about her, he'd mostly answered in grunts and monosyllabic responses, and I think he'd even forgotten I was there at one point. I'd been giggly and drunk after three drinks thanks to my low alcohol tolerance. Logan had basically shoved me out the door to go spend time with my brother with the promise that he had Dalton and Penny handled for the evening.

Thinking about it now, I have a very fuzzy, extremely vague memory of Xander helping me with my jacket and the sensation of his fingers in my hair. And I'm pretty sure he'd driven me the half hour back home to Cedar Valley. Or maybe I dreamed that . . .

Shaking my head, I sit up straighter. Scottie holds out the plastic cup to me, one brow raised in question.

"Fuck it. Okay. I'm in," I say, reaching out for one of the cups. "To friends, no baby monitors, and sleeping in."

"To bad-ass women," Scottie says, grinning, raising her plastic cup. "And the men we bring to their knees."

"Oh, hell yes, I'll drink to that." Violette giggles, and I can't help the genuine laugh that leaves me.

I may regret this in the morning, but for now, this is exactly what I need.

19

XANDER

"Sup, that's the last of it," Opp calls out from the side of the second engine rig. They look like those animal-control trucks, with all the little doored compartments along both sides that hold all of our gear when we travel. If the fire we're called to is close enough, we just truck it. For others, like this SoCal fire, we drive to the nearest airport and are loaded onto basically a cargo plane and shipped off to wherever we need to go.

I nod over to Opp in thanks from where I'm finishing unloading the first rig. He's been with us a little under six years. He'd come in as a temp after Dixon broke his leg in the fire that killed my dad, and he fit in with the rest of the crew so well that he decided to stay. Big, burly bear of a guy, and I've never seen a man throw a fucking snag the way he does.

Curly, Gareth, and Dixon are all carrying the last of their packs into what makes up essentially our home base. It's a large, glorified metal pole barn that sits just outside of Sky Ridge. The greenish-grayish paint is worn but it's got enough space for our equipment, parking for the rigs, a decent setup for gym equipment that we utilize often to stay in shape for the job, a half-janky billiard table with scuffed-up green felt, a dart board, and a foosball table that's on its last leg. Literally. It's propped up by old phone books I'd found in the office after my dad passed.

My field office is located at the back and it's got a kitchenette that the guys are always welcome to use. Along one wall is a couple of XL twin bunks that are stacked three high for the crew members that don't live here in Sky Ridge year-round and don't want the hassle of finding living quarters. Along the other white cinder-block wall are rows of lockers where we keep our gear.

"Good work on this fire, guys," I call out to everyone. "Now, go get a fucking shower and some sleep. You're all rank as hell."

Cal waves as he climbs into his vehicle and I tip my chin to him. King's not far behind. We arrived at the airport just after six this morning. Another two hours before we pulled in here, and then the last hour has been unloading and cleaning gear before we all crash.

Most of the time, when we get back from a fire, we head over to Shifty's as a group to celebrate, but it's so damn early in the morning we're all fucking wrecked. I can't wait to eat, take a shower, and sleep.

But more than any of those things, I can't wait to see Teddy.

When I pull into the driveway on my side of the yard, I frown. Her minivan isn't in sight, and a small SUV is parked there instead. I climb out of the truck and stretch my tired, aching muscles, glancing around. Both halves of the lawn are in desperate need of a cut. Her mower has been moved out of the middle of her yard and closer to her patio, a small red gasoline can next to it.

An older gentleman steps out of the front door of Teddy's duplex, Dalton behind him. Dalton waves excitedly when he sees me and races over as I grab my pack from the passenger seat.

"Xander!"

"Hey, champ, how are you?" I ask, grinning down at the kid. His brown eyes are crinkled at the corners as he smiles widely.

"I'm great! We got to have a sleepover with Gram and Grampa and we got to stay up late watching movies and eating ice cream, and now Grampa and I are going to mow the lawn to surprise Mom, isn't that great?" His words come out fast and excited, and he's fairly bouncing on the balls of his feet.

I chuckle, then squeeze his shoulder before looking toward the man walking across the sadly neglected lawn toward us. He has kind brown eyes the same shade as Teddy's kids' and thick gray hair. I recognize him from the hospital after Teddy had Bea. Teddy's father-in-law, Kent Hansen. I've seen Colleen here a handful of times, but this is the first time I've seen Kent since Bea was born.

"Were you out on a fire? Where was it? Was it bad? Is Uncle Cal okay?" Dalton continues, firing off questions quicker than I can answer them.

I laugh again, turning my attention back to him. "Did you have ice cream for breakfast, too?" I ask, only half joking. The kid's on a sugar buzz or something.

"No, but Gram let us have extra extra syrup on our waffles. I really like syrup, but Mom doesn't let us have a lot of it."

"You're not great at keeping secrets, are you, Dalton?" the man scoffs as he stops in front of me. He extends a hand and I reach for it, shaking it firmly as the man pins me with those brown eyes. "Nice to see you again."

I smile down at Dalton and wink before turning my attention back to Kent. "Nice to see you again, Kent." I nod, then gesture toward Teddy's duplex. "Is, uh, is Teddy all right?"

"Oh, yeah, she's fine. Colleen and I came over to spend the weekend with them and sent her out for a girls' night last night."

"Did she not come home?" I ask, trying my best to keep the concern in my voice contained. The last time she was drunk, I'd had to drive her home because she was too drunk to drive. The woman has the alcohol tolerance of a damn squirrel.

Having her next to me on the bench seat that night, barely a foot separating us, her scent filling the small cab of my truck for the duration of that drive . . . it had been akin to torture. She'd been happy that night, buzzed and giggly, and her light, tinkling laughter had wound itself around the stone that has been my heart for decades. Thank God it was dark in the cab of my truck, because I'd barely been able to keep my eyes off her.

Fingers fisted tightly around the wheel, I'd reminded myself over and over again that I was driving her home—home to her *husband*. She was married, dammit; happily, blissfully married.

And not to me.

"Oh no, we sent her to a hotel to get away for the night. She just called, she and her girlfriends are heading out for breakfast before she comes home," he says, ruffling Dalton's hair, yanking me out of the memory. "I figured I'd get this lawn whipped up before she gets back. One less thing for her to worry about."

I've always liked this man, and I like him even more now. I breathe a little easier, knowing she wasn't out trying to drive drunk and had at least a few people looking out for her while I was gone. That tightness in my chest eases, though it's replaced quickly with an emotion I'm not sure I want to put a name to. An emotion I've been shoving down for years.

Shifting the pack on my shoulder, I nod over to the lawn mower. "Let me put my stuff away, and I can do that for you. I know my lawn is a mess right now too. I can just do them both at the same time, and you can spend more time with your grandkids."

"No offense, son, but you look dead on your feet," Kent mutters dryly, and I can't help the scoffing laugh that escapes me. I rub the back of my neck with one hand. I know as soon as I stop moving, I'm going to pass out hard, and my neck is sore as fuck. But I want to do this for Teddy.

"I really don't mind," I insist.

Kent nods then. "All right, lawn's all yours, son."

Dalton follows me as I walk into my duplex to set my pack down, and I make a quick walk-through to open windows. The duplex is stuffy after being closed up for two weeks in the August heat. I change hastily out of my gear and into a pair of athletic shorts and a T-shirt, sliding my feet into a pair of worn sneakers. Dalton remains by the door, waiting, and then I squeeze his shoulder as we exit. "Ready, champ?"

He beams a smile up at me and nods. And we get to work.

XANDER

20

Teddy

I may be a little hungover this morning, but the last twenty-four hours have been exactly what I needed. Nothing that a hot shower, maybe an aspirin, and the rest of this absolutely giant coffee from the Nook can't fix. Oh, and lots of water.

I'd left Vi and Scottie after hugging them both on the sidewalk outside the Nook and thanked them for an amazing girls' night. We made the promise to hang out again soon, even if it's just meeting up at one of our houses for wine and adult girl talk. I'm refreshed—despite the slight hangover—and I feel ready to take on the world.

It's really incredible what good friendships can do for your soul. And I'm so insanely blessed to get to say both of those women are my friends, but more than that, they're family. My sisters from other misters.

I'm singing along to the radio when I turn down my street, feeling lighter than I have in months. And then I spot it from halfway down the block: Xander's black pickup truck in his side of the driveway.

He's been gone two weeks.

Butterflies—or maybe they're big awkward pelicans because they seem to take up a lot of space in my chest—take flight in my middle. I haven't seen him since the morning that he'd left . . . and I'm not entirely sure I'm ready now. Nerves make me jittery.

Okay. I'm fine. I can do this. *It's just Xander.*

Xander . . . who apparently has heard my "*self-care*" and knows that I think about him when I do it.

Oh god. I'm going to die of humiliation.

Glancing at my reflection in the rearview mirror, I breathe a sigh of relief that my hair isn't a flyaway mess, and that I'd at least put on a little bit of makeup before we'd gone out for breakfast. My clothes are comfy and altogether not sexy; I'd packed my favorite pair of coral-pink bike shorts and pulled on a white, oversized tunic top where one shoulder hangs halfway down my arm, leaving my shoulder and upper arm bare.

My jaw drops open when I get closer though, and I'm not entirely sure I remain breathing.

Good Lord . . . hot neighbor is right. It really should be illegal to be that attractive.

He could cause an accident with that body on display like that.

I slowly pull into my side of the driveway, parking next to Colleen and Kent's car, if only to get a better look at what is happening in the front yard.

The majority of the front lawn is cut, just a couple strips left remain horribly overgrown as Xander pushes the mower. His shirt-less, bare upper body and torso are deeply tanned, rippling with hard muscles and dripping sweat in the late summer heat. He has a pair of black basketball shorts slung low on his hips, the band of his underwear visible just above them, and dirty, grass-stained sneakers cover his feet. His dark, thick hair is damp with sweat and keeps falling over his brow.

TEDDY

He glances over at me, those intense, ice-blue eyes meeting mine from across the yard. I can't help the blush that stains my cheeks. I drop my gaze from his quickly, my heart racing frantically in my chest, and I turn the engine off before grabbing my overnight bag from the passenger seat. Sucking in a deep, calming breath, I step out of the minivan. The sound of the mower cuts off and my gaze raises to him again. I blush hotly all over as he walks toward me.

I try—heaven above, I try—not to stare at him like I've never seen a naked man before, but good Lord, the man is just too pretty not to look at. He shoves one hand through the sweat-dampened hair at his brow, his fingers raking through it and shoving it back as he grins. That wide, white smile is like a balm to my soul after not seeing it for two weeks, and his eyes crinkle at the corners.

"Hey," he says, stopping several feet from me. His facial hair is scruffy and thicker than usual, but it only adds to that ultra-masculine, lumberjack look he's got going on. The butterflies in my stomach are loving it.

"Hey, yourself," I murmur, smiling back at him despite myself, taking in all of him. I can't help but notice the deep circles beneath his eyes. When was the last time he slept? "When did you get back?"

"A couple hours ago." His eyes drop to the overnight bag in my hand. "Can I take that for you?"

I narrow my eyes at him, forcing myself to keep my eyes on his and not letting my gaze travel over every naked inch of him that's close enough for me to touch. He's got muscles on top of muscles, and my fingers are screaming at me to touch, to let the tips of my fingers trail between the grooves of his abs. I want to take a bite out of his biceps like they're big, juicy apples.

Good grief. *Down, kitty.*

Shaking my head to clear it, I murmur slowly, "You've been gone working for two weeks and before you even go inside to sleep, you mowed my lawn."

He glances over his shoulder at the lawn that is now completely mowed, then turns back to me, a smirk tilting up one corner of his mouth. Dammit, those eyes of his are my undoing. I'm powerless under that stare.

"Uhh, yeah? What does that have to do with me offering to carry your bag?"

"*Xander . . .*" I scold lightly, shaking my head again.

"*Teddy,*" he counters in the same tone, stepping slightly closer.

I have to tilt my chin up to remain staring at his face and not at that magnificent body that's now even closer to me. All I have to do is reach my hands up and I could run my palms all over—

"Did you have a good girls' night?" he asks softly, hauling me out of my slightly pornographic daydream.

I blush scarlet. What is it about this man that just makes me lose all ability to think rationally? "Uhhh," I mumble, my brain trying to play catch-up.

Xander reaches a hand out to me and I'm so addled, I don't protest when he takes my bag off my shoulder. He just dazzles me completely. It's not fair.

"Yes. I'm a little hungover, but it was a lot of fun."

"I'm glad you got to have a little time for yourself," he murmurs, lifting the bag to his own shoulder and turning us toward the townhouse. "You deserve it, Mama."

I can't help the involuntary gasp at that huskily whispered word, nor can I stop the sharp intake of breath when the heat of his palm at the small of my back registers. It's like a branding iron, searing me. I don't even remember the last time I had a man's hands on me, even just as simple as something like this. It's . . . oh God.

"Teddy, if you keep making that sound, I'm going to embarrass myself in front of your in-laws," he whispers roughly, leaning closer so his breath fans against my ear.

Holy shit.

TEDDY

"And I rather like them, so I'd like to not make this awkward if possible. But I can't do that if I'm sporting a boner in my gym shorts."

The shocked laugh that escapes me at his boldness is more of a snort than a laugh. My hand flies over my mouth as I stare up at him in horror at the sound that I just made. It's like it's literally impossible for me to not embarrass myself to the very depths of my being whenever I'm around this man. And what he just said . . .

His chuckle is deep and low as we make our way toward the front door, and I'm painfully aware of his hand still riding low on my back, just above the slope of my ass.

Those fingers spread wide over my back, as if flexing, and then he squeezes gently. "And before you start second-guessing what I just said; yes, I fucking meant it, beautiful."

I swear my face is flaming eight shades of red as Colleen chooses that moment to open the door, Penny on her hip. "Oh, hello, my sweet girl! I thought I heard you pull in. Bea's down for her morning nap, and Grampa has Dalton down at the creek looking for crayfish. Xander, that lawn looks amazing! You must be parched, look at you sweating up a storm. Come on in, let me fetch you a drink to cool down."

"Sure, let me just go grab my T-shirt." He sets my bag down just inside the door, then dazzles my mother-in-law with a smile before jogging back down off the porch, to where he's tossed his T-shirt aside. My eyes are glued to his body as he shoves his arms and head through the holes in the shirt—sleeves cut off, as usual—and then he's jogging back over to us. I can't take my eyes off him. Colleen ushers us all inside and closes the door behind us.

Colleen sets Penny down on the ground and my preschooler launches herself at Xander, who catches her and lifts her up into his arms. She cackles shrilly, sliding her hands over his shoulders which are still damp with sweat, and then she fingers his hair. "Ewwww! You're all sweddy!"

His laugh is genuine as he stares at Penny. He shakes his head at her, making her laugh harder.

Tearing my eyes away from them, I turn to grab my bag from beside the door, if for no other reason than to give my hands something to do. This is the first time Xander has been inside my house since that day he brought me the sandwich after Bea was born.

Straightening, I turn back, just to find Colleen eyeing me knowingly. Tucking a stray strand of hair behind my ear, I put on my best smile. "I'm just going to drop this in the bedroom."

"Mm-hmm," she murmurs, her mouth quirking just the slightest with a hidden smile.

I pass by her, Xander, and Penny, slipping down the hallway. Dropping my bag inside the closet, I rush over to the full-length mirror that's propped into one corner of the room, running my hands over the brightly colored bike shorts that are clinging to my thighs. I wiggle my toes in my flip-flops, which I freshly painted last night with a new coat of polish. My shirt is hanging off one shoulder, showing off the light tan there. Reaching up, I rewind my hair up into the claw clip on the back of my head, fanning out the strands so that they lay *just so*. Then I rush into the bathroom to give my lashes another couple swipes of mascara and add a touch of blush to the apples of my cheeks.

Exiting the bathroom, I skid to a halt and backtrack, reaching into the cabinet for an almost empty perfume roller. I slide it along my collarbones and then at my wrists. I cap it, placing it back in the cabinet before my eyes drop to the flash of silver on the finger of my left hand.

Dropping my face into trembling hands, the shock of cool metal against my heated cheeks sends guilt crashing through me. *What am I even doing? Primping for a man with my wedding ring from another man on my finger? With my dead husband's parents right here? What is wrong with me?*

TEDDY

Breathing in through my nose and out through my mouth, I count to five. It's just Xander. He's my neighbor. My brother's best friend. My brother's *boss*. All he did was mow my lawn. It's not a marriage proposal, for crying out loud.

I groan into my hands, shaking my head in dismay at myself, my thoughts heading straight into the gutter. "Ohmygod," I grumble miserably, my words muffled by my hands still.

Dropping my hands and staring into the mirror over the sink, I remind myself I am a mature adult woman—a widow, for crying out loud—with three children to take care of. I can't afford distractions. Especially when they come in the form of Superintendent Xander Macomb.

When I return to the kitchen, Xander is standing at the kitchen counter with Colleen while he drinks a glass of ice water. I don't pay attention to the way his throat works with each swallow, or the way his fingers clasp around the glass, the muscles in his forearm bunching and shifting with each movement. Penny is sitting on top of the peninsula bar top, her legs crisscrossed. I focus on that instead.

"Penny, is that where bums go?" I ask, stopping at the counter.

"Ummm . . ." She giggles, glancing at Colleen, who I catch winking at my terror of a preschooler.

I shake my head as I roll my eyes where they can't see.

"No?"

"That sounds an awful lot like a question," I mutter. I glare at her playfully, making her giggle more. "Get your bum off the counter, please."

Xander sets his glass down and catches her beneath her armpits, sweeping her up and off the counter like an airplane before setting her in one of the high-back stools pulled up against the tall countertop.

"That's my bad, Mama, I set her down up here," he explains, turning his head to wink at me.

I nod, though I do my best to keep my shoulders straight and not hunch in on myself like I'm so used to doing nowadays. Especially around Xander. Especially when he uses that word. He has to know what it does to me.

Actually, I'm fairly certain he knows exactly what that does to me and does it on purpose.

That intense gaze that I swear to God can see straight into my soul pierces me, and the understanding that flashes there as he stares at me wrecks me. He's a good man, I can feel it in my soul. But . . . I can't do this. He turns back to Penny, ruffles her hair gently, then addresses Colleen.

"Thank you so much for the water. I should head next door. I don't want to stink up Teddy's house any more than I already have, and I really should get some sleep."

My mother-in-law pats his forearm and smiles at him kindly. "You don't stink, but you should definitely go get some sleep. The lawn looks perfect. And it was so nice to see you again. Teddy, be a doll and walk him to the door," Colleen insists, picking Penny up and balancing her on her hip. "I think I hear Bea waking up."

I glare at the back of her head as she walks away, knowing full well she's lying out her ass about hearing Bea. The traitor.

Clutching my arms across my waist, I smile at Xander and we head toward the door together. Stepping out onto the patio, I sigh heavily.

"I'm so sorry," I laugh, gesturing back into the house. "They mean well but they're meddlers."

"It's very apparent that they love you," he says gently, stepping down off the main porch and onto the paved walkway. "I'm glad you have them."

"Me too," I murmur, smiling. Wrapping my arms around my middle tighter, I do the thing and hunch in on myself when those eyes of his find their way back to me. His gaze unnerves me, so I babble, "I'm glad you made it back safely—"

TEDDY

"Stop doing that," he whispers roughly, those eyes boring into my own. I swear he sees too much of me.

"Stop doing what?" I ask, my throat tight. I swallow hard.

He waves at me as a whole, generalizing around my middle, where my arms are crossed. "*That*. Folding in on yourself. Like you're trying to hide or shrink or something."

I drop my arms to my sides, my heart hammering in my chest at the roughness in his voice. It's raw and dangerous and, fuck me, it's thrilling. I hate it. I don't want to like it as much as I do.

He steps up onto the patio once more, until we're close again. "I meant what I said before I left, Teddy. Don't think for one fucking minute that I haven't spent the last two weeks replaying every second of seeing your body on display like that, or remembering the way you sound . . ."

Heat creeps up my neck as he continues huskily.

"You are . . . you're fucking perfect, Teddy. I hope you know that."

Oh god. This is so bad. So dangerous. For me, my kids, my very breakable heart. Possibly his face, if Cal isn't as chill about it as Scottie seems to think. Because I'm not sure I'm ready to date again, and I can't do casual. "Xander . . ."

"Don't," he breathes, almost beseechingly. His sky-blue eyes are tortured as he stares down at me. "I know. It's okay. You don't have to say it. I just . . . I want you to know that I'm here. And I see you, sweetheart. Every fucking part of you, beautiful."

My teeth clamp over my bottom lip as he turns and strides away, disappearing out of sight.

21

XANDER

After the world's longest shower, I'm certain I fell into a coma for the next seven hours. I laid down in bed and woke up as the late afternoon sun was blazing through my bedroom window. I don't think I ever moved once I'd fallen asleep. My neck was stiff before, but now every move is like an electric shock down my spine. I do my best to stretch it out, but it doesn't do much to help. An Icy Hot patch and a beer make me feel a little better, though.

I check my phone, noting several messages from King and Cal that make me smile. It sounds like Teddy, Violette, and Scottie hung out last night at a local hotel and got drunk on whiskey and fucking hard seltzers—not my idea of a great combination, but to each their own—and they're apparently both hungover today. Violette is scheduled to work at Shifty's tonight according to King, and Scottie is on call. I almost feel bad for them, but I don't. The light that shone in Teddy's pretty gray eyes this morning when she'd gotten home had made me strangely happy too. She deserved to have that time for herself. And I'll be honest, I'm glad she was with Vi and Scottie.

Cal asks if I'm coming out to Shifty's with the crew later, but I decline. He sends me a GIF of Chandler Bing pantomiming using a whip with the caption "WHOOP-AH!" I roll my eyes, and then another GIF comes through, this one of Bugs Bunny with the heart eyes. I send back a middle finger emoji, then click my phone off.

Padding out into the kitchen, I flip through the pile of mail I'd tossed onto the table earlier, stopping at a small yellow manila envelope with my brother's handwriting across the front. I open the mailer and pull a second envelope out. It's a simple, white letter-size envelope with nothing but my name across it in my dad's untidy scrawl.

Seeing that handwriting is like a fucking kick to the chest.

It takes all the breath out of my lungs and makes my sternum ache.

I sink into one of the chairs at the table and simply stare at it for a long time, holding it between my fingers, willing myself to work up the guts to open it. To read the last thing that my dad ever left me.

I don't know how long I sit and stare at that envelope, but I shake my head and heave a frustrated sigh before pushing to my feet. I toss the envelope onto the kitchen counter and turn away, gripping the edge of the counter with tense fingers.

I glance out the front window, but neither Teddy's nor her in-laws' vehicles are in her side of the driveway. Shoving my feet into sneakers, I pull my ball cap on my head and grab my keys. It's a quick trip down the road to the nearest market, and then I'm back fifteen minutes later with the fixings for a tossed salad, a mix of fresh vegetables, and a steak.

I crack open a beer while I work, washing the veggies and setting them to marinate before spearing them onto a shish-kabob skewer. Seasoning the steak, I set that aside and work on the salad next, then take the veggie skewers, the steak, and my beer out to the back patio, where I fire up the grill. It's not often that I get to cook at home during the season, and normally I would be out with the guys tonight. Celebrating our win against that damn SoCal fire. But tonight, I'm just not feeling the crowd. Or the harassment from my crew about Teddy. None of them have let it go.

Busybodies, the lot of 'em.

My steak is about halfway done when I hear two vehicles pull into the driveway and then the commotion of Teddy and her family arriving home. The sounds comfort me. Dalton's excitable chatter, Penny's infectious laugh, shit, even the sound of Bea's occasional fussing doesn't bother me. Teddy's soothing voice as she speaks to her kids, her genuine laughter when they do something to make her smile. I admit, I enjoy the sounds of them living next door.

"Dalton, shower time, please!" I hear Teddy's voice through an open window somewhere. "But don't take too long because Penny needs a bath too."

"Only because she practically swam in her ice cream." Kent's deep rumble reaches me, and I can't help but smile. Sounds like something the tiny terror would do.

"Oooh, what smells so good?" Colleen's voice drifts out next. I hear the heavy glass slider door swish open. "Xander must be grilling out back. That smells divine. Doesn't it, Teddy? Why don't you go say hello?"

"*Colleen!*"

Teddy's horrified whisper-hiss makes me chuckle around a swallow of my beer.

"*What?*" Colleen asks, her tone anything but innocent. "It's just saying hello, Teddy."

I grin again, flipping the veggie skewers a quarter turn. The marinated mushrooms, bell peppers, onions, and summer squash do smell mouthwateringly delicious. As does the steak. Fuck, I'm starving and ready to eat real food instead of a gritty, tasteless MRE ration pack. My stomach growls impatiently. I'd been so exhausted after getting home this morning, mowing the lawn, and then my shower that I hadn't even bothered to eat before falling asleep.

"*Why are you like this?*" Teddy grumbles miserably, and Colleen's lilting laugh drifts out to me.

"Because that's what mommas do. We meddle."

I take another long pull of my beer and grin. That's exactly what Teddy had said earlier. I'm not sure if they know I'm out here, or that I can hear everything they're saying. It's not considered eavesdropping, right?

"This isn't normal. *He's my brother's boss, Colleen,*" Teddy whisper-hisses again, and then I can hear the screen slider being pushed open. "Ugh. *You're a menace.*"

"Yes, yes, all right," Colleen mutters, her voice slightly louder now. "I'll get the kids showered and bathed. Go say hi. And take him this—"

The clinking of glass bottles rattle, and then the swish of the sliding doors being shut once more. I hold my breath, remaining where I am at the grill. My back is facing the backyard, but I know the second she comes around the partition that separates my patio from hers. Like my entire body is cued to her presence.

"Um, hey," she says, her voice so timid and uncertain.

I turn my head toward her and wince at the pain that shoots up my neck and down my spine.

She stops, alarm flashing across her face before she's stepping over toward me. She sets a six-pack of beer down on the ancient milk crate turned table.

"Are you okay? *Are you hurt?*" she asks, her gray eyes flying over me, as if checking for injury.

My chest tightens at that. It's been a long time since anyone—other than my crew—has cared about my well-being.

"*Xander—*"

"I'm fine." I turn fully toward her, smiling gently, then reach up and tap the lidocaine patch that's sticking out of the back collar of my T-shirt. "Just a stiff neck, and I moved wrong."

"Oh," she whispers, taking a half step back. "I'm sorry."

I wave my hand. "Don't apologize. I kinked it a few days ago sleeping on a bedroll at spike camp. It just needs a few days to loosen up."

"Spike camp?" she asks, crossing her arms over herself.

I look down at those crossed arms pointedly and she rolls her eyes with a smirk but drops them to her sides. I turn back to the grill, flipping my steak one more time. It's done, but now I don't want to go inside and leave her.

I nod as I turn off the burners, then hunker down to make sure the propane tank is off too. "When we're out on fire calls, we set up basically like a campsite. We call them spike camps. It's our home away from home."

"You have to set up tents wherever you go?" she asks, stepping forward to peek at the steak and vegetables on the grill. She sniffs the air appreciatively.

I laugh then and shake my head. "Uh, no, not exactly. We kinda just sleep wherever we fall at night. We have sleeping bags."

"And you just sleep outside on the ground?" Her eyes shoot up to mine, her blond brows rising in surprise behind her clear-rimmed glasses. Those freckles are on display again today.

"Yeah, we just sleep outside," I answer, chuckling. Using the tongs, I pick up the steak and place it on a clean plate I'd brought out with me, then the veggie skewers. "Hasn't Cal ever told you about his work? It's not glamorous."

"I guess I've never asked the right questions," she laughs, shaking her head. "And I hate to admit that I probably have intentionally not asked too many questions. His job makes me anxious, and I

XANDER

feel like the less I know about specifics, the better I can handle it. My brain has this really great ability to imagine the worst possible scenario. When he and Scottie went missing up in the mountains last year, I was a mess. And then to lose Logan right after . . ." She stops abruptly, smiling almost sadly, like she's trying not to let the thoughts take over.

"I can understand that," I murmur gently. Her heart is just so big, she cares so deeply for everyone, and she's been hurt so much. I wish I could take all the hurt away, but I can't.

I can only make it worse.

Swallowing past the lump in my throat and pushing the thoughts aside, I turn to her, then gesture toward the open slider door that leads into my side of the duplex, because I'm nothing if not a glutton for punishment. "Would you like to come in? Are you hungry?"

"Oh, no, thank you. We just went out to dinner with Colleen and Kent and then took the kids out for ice cream. It smells delicious, though." She picks up the six-pack and extends it toward me. "I wanted to thank you for mowing the lawn. You didn't have to do that. But I appreciate it, like, a lot. Bea has been teething and neither one of us is sleeping all that great and the lawn was just one thing I didn't have the energy to do—"

Nodding down to the six-pack in her hand, I cut off her anxious rambling as I murmur, "I'll only accept that if you agree to have one with me."

Her words stop, but those gray eyes narrow on me, her lips twitching with a grin. "That's coercion," she grumbles.

"Guilty." I grin down at her, then gesture for her to go in ahead of me. "Besides," I whisper teasingly, "we can't let Colleen's meddling go to waste."

Teddy groans, shaking her head. "Oh my god, you heard that?!"

I chuckle. "Are you sure you're not hungry? This is probably more food than I can eat."

134

It's not, but I'll gladly share if she wants some. I'd love the chance to cook for her.

"No, thank you for the offer. It smells amazing, but honestly I'm so full from dinner," she laughs, following me into the kitchen that mirrors hers, though mine is depressingly empty compared to hers. She plucks two beers out of the flimsy cardboard pack and twists the tops off them before handing me one. "Thank you for the beer. Though admittedly, I probably don't need it. I'm still not entirely recovered from last night."

"Little hair of the dog," I laugh, nodding as I plate up my food and pull the premade tossed salad out of the fridge. She nods around a drink of her beer, and I can't help but stare at the way her bottom lip pillows the ridge of the beer bottle as she tips it up.

And now I'm half hard again. This damn woman has no fucking idea how enticing she is.

The white shirt she has on is falling off one shoulder still, leaving that shoulder bare halfway down her arm. One strap of her bra is showing where it crosses her shoulder to her back. I want to press my lips to that spot where her neck and shoulder meet, to sink my teeth into it, mark her up, then soothe it with my tongue and do it again.

Fuck. Now I *am* hard.

She turns to look around the living room and I take the chance to adjust myself behind the fly of my jeans. "You don't stay here very much, do you?"

"Not during the fire season," I admit, and she nods in understanding. Leading her toward the tiny table in the dining room, we sit down across from each other. I feel like an ass eating in front of her. My mom drummed manners into me, and though I'm more of a barbarian than most—living out of spike camps with half-feral beasts for men will do that—I am still a gentleman. "Are you sure I can't tempt you? I can fix you a plate—"

XANDER

She laughs, leaning her elbows on the table and wrapping both hands around the base of the bottle. My eyes track the movement, and I hate to admit that I fully imagine what those fingers would look like wrapped around my cock just like that.

"No, seriously, Xander. I'm so full. I ate my weight in pasta and breadsticks at dinner," she laughs, then wrinkles her nose, something I'm learning is a nervous habit for her, as if she's embarrassed again. She gestures to my salad. "I should have stuck with a salad, but the breadsticks smelled so good."

This woman, I swear to fucking God. I'm going to change the way she sees herself.

"After a night of drinking, I'm sure you needed it to offset that hangover," I tease instead.

She groans, laughing, as she leans back in the chair and brings the bottle to her lips for another drink. "Don't remind me. Scottie brought a bottle of whiskey. I couldn't even tell you the last time I did shots of whiskey. College, maybe? Definitely before I had Dalton."

She bites the inside of her cheek and stares at the bottle in her hands almost guiltily. I wonder if she's thinking about the night I drove her home, though I doubt it. I replay that night in my head sometimes, like some kind of masochist.

"I really shouldn't be drinking this. I'm going to have to pump and dump until tomorrow before I can feed Bea again," she murmurs, tilting her lips in a wry smile.

It's totally involuntary, the way my eyes drop to the top swell of her breasts beneath the white shirt.

"I'm sorry," I murmur, raising my eyes to hers. My voice is rougher than intended, and I clear my throat. Those damn gray eyes are like my own personal Kryptonite.

She waves one hand, shrugging. The shirt hanging off one shoulder slips just a little farther down her arm, revealing a hint of the side curve of her bra-clad breast. My fingers tighten around my own beer as I lift it to my lips.

"Gah, don't be. I wasn't comfortable feeding her yet anyway, and I have enough milk stored in the freezer to get through the apocalypse if needed."

I laugh, shaking my head. "Well, I'm glad you had fun. I'm sure you three could get into some trouble on your own."

She smiles coyly behind the beer bottle at her lips, and that mischievous grin does me in completely.

I like having her in my space. She brightens it, makes it feel warmer, almost. I need to do something to make it more welcoming in here. I want her here more often. "I've known Violette since she was a kid. Her twin brother was on my crew."

"That's right. I forget sometimes how integrated you all are as a unit," she murmurs, that smile fading. "She doesn't talk about that much, but I know Jacob and Rowan were best friends."

I nod. "We lost Jacob the same year we lost my dad," I explain around a bite of the grilled vegetables.

"Your dad was a hotshot too, right?" she asks quietly. Her fingernails pick at the label on the beer.

"Sure was. He was the superintendent before me. We worked together for almost fifteen years before we lost him." The pain and guilt that tears through me is as acute as it was six years ago. They say grief never truly fades; it just hits less often. Fuck, when it hits though, it's like a sucker punch to the center of the chest.

"I remember Cal talking about that. I'm so sorry," she whispers, her dark blond brows pulling low over her silver-gray eyes.

I nod, dropping my eyes to the food on my plate. I push the steak around with the tines of my fork. "He shouldn't have even been in that fire."

"I'm sorry, Xander. We don't have to talk about it. I know I don't like talking about the night Logan—" She cuts off her words abruptly, straightening her shoulders, then slides the beer away from her. It's only half empty. She heaves a breath in and smiles over at me, though I know it's forced. Her lower lip wobbles just the slightest, like she's trying her best to hold it together. Fuck, I just want to hold her. "There's some things in life we never really get over, huh?"

A painfully tight knot lodges itself in my chest. I don't know if it's grief or guilt or jealousy or a strange combination of all three. I feel like a dick all over again. The woman is still grieving over her dead husband, she's got her fucking hands full with three kids, and I'm sitting here ogling her with a chubby in my pants.

What would it be like to have the love of a woman like Teddy? That kind of devotion that follows even after a tragedy like what she's faced?

She rises from her seat and I push to stand, but she rushes to say, "No, don't get up. Finish your dinner, Xander. Thank you for the beer."

I sink back into my chair and watch as she flees.

But then she stops at the slider door and looks back at me, those gray eyes crinkling at the corners slightly. "I'm really glad you're back safe."

Then she's gone, slipping out of the back patio door and sliding it shut behind her. And I'm left with this ache in my chest and an empty, barely lived-in house that just for a few minutes had seemed not quite so lonely.

22

Teddy

After arguing with Colleen and Kent about sleeping arrangements, I'd finally convinced them to stay in my bedroom while I sleep on the couch. They're my guests, after all, and the sofa doesn't pull out into a bed, so it just doesn't make any sense for them to sleep anywhere else. I have Bea's bassinet set up next to me, and I'm comfortable with an extra pillow and a soft blanket. It's just for one night anyway, I'd argued.

Besides, I'm so keyed-up from my encounter with Xander I can't sleep. I've been staring at the ceiling for at least an hour. Scrolling through my phone. Listening to the sounds outside the slider door I kept cracked open.

It's late. Bea's already woken for her late feeding and is now down for the night, and I know she won't wake again until five or six in the morning. I should be sleeping. But I can't.

I'm angry at myself, at Colleen for pushing, at Xander for being so goddamn perfect and handsome and kind. I'm angry at Logan for leaving us, for putting me in this situation. And then the anger at myself starts all over again, because Logan didn't leave us . . . I sent him out on that call and he died because of it. I sent him out and he never got to come home.

But the truth of it is, the life I had imagined for myself is gone.

The most terrifying thing? Sitting there with Xander, drinking a beer and laughing and flirting—yes, I was flirting—I'd seen what a new life could look like . . . if only there weren't so many things in our way. So many obstacles that will make any kind of future together impossible.

He's a hotshot. He has one of the most dangerous jobs in the world, and he loves his job, I can tell just by the way he talks about it. It's in his blood, his soul, his heart. Every heartbeat is for his job, his crew, his passion . . .

And mine is for my kids.

How selfish would I be to put any of us through that kind of hell again? To start anything with someone who at any second may not come back to us?

Throwing my arm over my eyes, I groan as silently as possible so I don't wake Bea sleeping next to me. But God, why is he so perfect? He's thoughtful and kind and so damn good with my kids it's not fair. Why couldn't he be a boring accountant whose biggest occupational hazard is a paper cut?

My breath stalls in my chest when I hear the telltale swish of a glass slider door, followed by the slight rattle of the screen being pushed open, then closed. A creak and metallic groan drift through the darkened night beyond my own patio doors, and I can imagine him sinking into that old, weathered folding chair that looks like it's straight from the nineties. The pop of a bottle top is all that my straining ears can make out.

As silently as I can, I climb off the couch, checking to make sure Bea stays sleeping. I'm dressed in short sleeper shorts and a nursing tank top in deference to the ever-present late-summer heat that hasn't abated yet. But I pull my flimsy robe up my arms, tying it around my waist, and then slip out the patio door.

Rounding the little partition, I see Xander sitting in that chair, bare chested and wearing only a pair of gym shorts. He's got a bottle of beer in one hand, the other hand wrapped around the back of his neck, kneading the muscles there. The moon filtering through the trees above casts a silvery glow on everything, casting his face into sharp relief and deep shadows. His gaze seems nearly electric as he stares at me from where I stopped.

"Can't sleep either?" I ask quietly, my voice nearly a whisper.

He continues staring at me and I shift on my bare feet.

I nod toward where he's still massaging the muscles of his shoulder. "Is that still bothering you?"

He smiles ruefully and nods. "It'll be fine. You should go back to bed, Teddy."

But I move forward slowly, so that I can step up behind his chair. Brushing his hand aside and ignoring the zap of heat that rushes through me at just that little contact, I take a deep breath, then place both of my hands on his bare shoulders. He tenses, then grunts and twists his neck to one side. His skin is hot beneath my fingers, soft and velvety. The contrast between his darkly tanned skin and my pale fingers is thrilling. I don't remember the last time I touched a man like this.

I start slow, massaging the back of his neck at the base of his skull, and work my way down, across his impossibly wide, hard shoulders that are so beautifully made, ridged with tight muscle. He groans as I work on a particularly tight knot at the base of his neck that extends down his right shoulder blade, his head dropping forward until it nearly touches his chest. He's braced his elbows on his widespread knees, allowing me better access to the broad expanse of his back and shoulders. His body is amazing, and I'm a little embarrassed at how turned on I am just by rubbing this man's shoulders.

TEDDY

"Fucking hell, that hurts," he grunts through gritted teeth.

I chuckle lightly, backing off my touch a little.

He reaches his left hand up and covers my fingers with his, holding me there. His touch burns through me, heating me up from the inside. His hand falls away. "Don't stop. Please."

My fingers are starting to ache, but I keep going until he's a pliant, mushy pile of goo in the chair before me. I smile in the dark as I stare at the back of his head, which is tipped down low. His dark hair looks incredibly soft, and I let myself slide my fingers up the back of his neck and into the hairline at the base of his skull, using my nails to scratch lightly. The strands of dark hair are like silk against my fingertips, and I do it again. Goosebumps flash across his shoulders and he shivers, a groan escaping him. Though this time, the sound isn't one of pleasurable pain as his sore muscles release, but more guttural, more primal. Sexual.

The sound skitters through me, and I realize then that I'm damn near panting, standing behind him, my fingers shoved up through his hair. My heart is beating a frantic rhythm in my chest.

He raises his head and turns just the slightest, my hand following the movement, still threaded through his hair, until I'm staring at him in profile. The silvery, incandescent light of the moon highlights his features. He doesn't look at me as he reaches down to set the forgotten beer on the ground, then that same hand comes up and takes hold of my wrist in a firm grip.

I'm shaking, trembling where I stand behind him as his warm fingers wrap around my wrist. My hand slides out of his hair to rest on his shoulder. He tugs lightly, guiding me around the side of the chair until I'm standing directly in front of him, then pulls me forward so that I'm forced to step in between his widespread knees. The outsides of my thighs—bare to high thigh beneath the short hem of the robe and my sleep shorts—brush against the insides of his. The dusting of dark hair on his legs tickles the outsides of my thighs, a sensation I haven't felt in so long, and it's electric and thrilling. My fingers trace along the ridges of his shoulders, featherlight, as my eyes collide with the pale blue of his. His gaze is hot, so fucking hot, as he stares at me, before those eyes drop to my mouth.

From where he's sitting in the chair, the top of his head is level with the bottom of my chin. His fingers are still wrapped around my wrist, though his grip is light and tentative. Those fingers trail across the outside of my forearm from my wrist to my elbow until he's cupping the outside of my bicep in his palm.

I stop breathing altogether when he turns his head and presses his lips to the inside of my wrist, where I'm sure my pulse is practically galloping beneath my skin. He kisses the sensitive flesh, and my breath rushes in and out as heat envelops me from head to toe, and it has nothing to do with the summer temperature. His short-cropped beard tickles the inside of my wrist, and I shiver.

"Teddy," he whispers against my flesh, his lips moving almost imperceptibly, his voice coming out low and husky. Just this man's voice is an aphrodisiac to my starved libido.

His eyes meet mine again, hot and so intense it stuns me with the way he *sees* me. Like he really sees me. It's alarming and disarming and *God* I've missed being looked at like this.

At some point while I'd been massaging his shoulders, my robe shifted, and the top folds of it hang over the tie at my waist, revealing the tank top beneath that's barely covering my breasts. His other hand moves slowly, almost as if he's trying not to spook me into running, and tugs at one of the ties of the belt until it falls away, letting the sides of the robe drop open entirely. All that covers me now is the thin tank top and the barely there sleep shorts that have bunched up around the thick part of my thighs.

He groans out a quiet sigh, pressing his mouth into my wrist again while his eyes travel over me, and then the fingers that just laid me open slide over the curve of my waist beneath the robe, palming my hip. I can't help it, my eyes flutter closed and my fingers tighten where they're clutching his hard shoulders. The heat of his hand through my tank top is like an inferno, so hot it's melting me from the inside out. That same palm slides around my waist to my back, urging me closer, and I don't think . . . I just do.

I step closer, bringing my chest nearly to his cheek. I'm practically panting now, my chest rising and falling with heavy breaths, and my heart is pounding in my chest like a jackhammer. Xander turns his head, his lips leaving the sensitive flesh at my wrist and his mouth grazes the curve of my breast through my tank top. I let my head drop back so that I can stare up at the stars through the trees above us, my panting breaths the only sound in the silence of the night.

"You are so beautiful," he whispers, his voice wrapping around me at the same time his arms do, pulling me closer, until our bodies are pressed against each other. My fingers slide into his hair again, clutching his head to me as he presses kisses to the curves of my breasts, which are aching, and I so badly want to feel his mouth on me but I'm too terrified to ask. *"So fucking pretty, Teddy."*

His hands are hot as they travel down my hips and over my ass to the backs of my bare thighs. Fingers digging into the *V* between my legs, he smooths his palms up and down my legs again and again. Clamping my teeth over my bottom lip, I squeeze my eyes shut, embarrassment wracking through me as this Adonis of a man slides his hands over the softness that is everywhere on me.

I'm not fit. I'm not small. And this man is stupidly, outrageously attractive.

I gasp when those fingers dig in between my thighs, spreading them wider, and then he's pulling me forward again, spreading my legs over his to straddle his thighs. I land on him with another sharp gasp and immediately try to stand, to raise my weight off him. The chair creaks in protest of our combined weight and I'm mortified all over again. "Xander, let me up—"

But his hands are at my waist again, sliding beneath the hem of my tank top and holding me in place. "You're right where I want you, beautiful."

"But—"

"Shhh," he whispers, reaching up to thread his fingers into the back of my hair, lightly, gently. His eyes are intense on mine, his breathing ragged, chest heaving. His thigh muscles bunch and shift beneath me and I can feel just how hard his abs are. God, this man is gorgeous. "I've wanted to feel you against me. You feel fucking perfect right where you are. Fuck, Teddy, this is all I've wanted. All I've thought about."

"Xander," I whimper, my eyes bouncing between his. I don't know what I'm doing. I haven't done anything like this in so long, and not with anyone other than Logan . . . well, ever. But I want this. I'm aching between my thighs, low in my belly, and I think I'm damn near desperate to finally feel his mouth on mine, to taste him . . . The fingers in the back of my hair tighten, tilting my head toward his.

"I don't want to do something you don't want," he whispers roughly, his eyes dropping to my mouth. "But, goddamn, I want to kiss you so fucking bad right now, beautiful."

A stuttered, shaky breath escapes my parted lips, and I nod.

No part of me is prepared for Xander's mouth on mine though. He slants his mouth over mine hungrily, lips parting almost immediately, tongue darting out to tease the seam of my lips. I gasp sharply and it allows him entrance, and the first touch of his tongue to mine is like a lightning strike to my nervous system.

My entire being is on fire, and the only thing that I want right now is Xander's mouth on mine.

Holy shit, he knows how to kiss. I'm a melted puddle in his lap, and he presses me against him, gathering me close in those big, strong arms that I could get lost in. His hands are sure and steady as they roam over my body, touching me everywhere as we kiss

TEDDY

and kiss until we're both breathless. His palms slide over my biceps, urging me to wrap my arms around his neck, so I do and lean into the kiss. I've never been kissed like this before. It's like he uses his entire body, and it's the most erotic thing I've ever experienced.

Those hands slide down my back to land on the full curve of my waist, fingers digging into the fleshy part of my ass, kneading roughly, then gentling his touch to soothe the little hurt. I rock against him and he shifts beneath me, sliding down in the seat, at the same time adjusting me over him, spreading my thighs wider over his. I'm burning up, trembling against him. My desire for him is all encompassing. I'm so far out of my element, but I don't want to stop, either.

"Holy fuck," he rasps against my mouth as he digs his fingers into my hips again, grinding me over him, and with the new position, I feel him; hard and heavy between my thighs, pressing against the very center of me. Groaning roughly, he grasps my face between his hands and rolls his forehead across mine, our mouths barely brushing as we gasp together in the dark. "*Goddamn, Teddy*. You feel so fucking good. You *taste* so fucking good."

His fingers smooth across my cheeks, pushing my hair away from my face, and then he's kissing me again like he's a man on death row and I'm his last meal. I've never been so turned on by kissing. The man is incredible at this and I never want to stop. I never want this feeling to go away. I've missed this. I've missed being desired so deeply there's no stopping it, no holding it off for later.

I flit my fingers down over his shoulders, across his naked chest. There's a smattering of dark, crinkly hair across his broad chest and a strip that leads down the center of his abdomen. The ridges of his abs call for my touch, and I let myself indulge in this. Logan was a good-looking guy in that good-guy-next-door kind of way, and he took care of his body better than I do mine—he didn't carry two nine-pound babies and one seven-pound baby in a body that refuses to "bounce back"—but he wasn't nearly as cut as Xander is. Xander has muscles on top of muscles, and I desperately want to run my hands over every solid inch of him. Shit, I want to run my tongue over every inch of him. Lick him like a damn Popsicle.

I flush hot all over at that thought. Thinking about what's pressing up between us right now, about how badly I want to see it, to touch it, taste it.

He growls low in his throat as my fingertips continue to wander over his skin, the tips of my fingers acquainting myself with every dip of his ribs, the ridges of his abs, the muscled swell of his pecs. His heart is hammering beneath my right palm where it's pressed flat against him, and I revel in the knowledge that he's just as undone as I am right now. I'm still trembling, like my body is so keyed-up I physically can't contain the rioting emotions and sensations combusting inside of me.

One of his hands cups the side of my face gently, his fingers tunneling through my hair, brushing it away from my face. His eyes are so clear, burning so brightly in the moonlight that continues to filter through the trees above us.

"You are exquisite," he breathes so quietly I almost miss it. My heart nearly climbs its way out of my throat, and my nose stings with unshed tears. The sincerity in his tone nearly does me in. But I still don't entirely believe it.

"I'm not," I whisper in return, climbing my hands up to his shoulders again. A much safer spot. He's just too damn gorgeous. There's no way this is real, that he really wants me, not like this.

He shushes me with another deep kiss, those strong, capable hands bracketing my head again to hold me to him. When he breaks the kiss, he whispers, "I told you to stop doing that. You drive me absolutely crazy, Teddy. You have since the first time I saw you."

A stunned, stuttered laugh escapes me. "You can't be serious. You don't mean that."

TEDDY

Brushing my hair away from my face again, he smiles gently at me, and my heart does that flip-flop thing in my chest all over again. "I *do* mean that. I thought you were the most beautiful thing I'd ever seen."

I shake my head in awe at his words. "But I was—"

"Married. I know," he whispers, his eyes searching mine.

My face goes hot and I avoid glancing down at the silver band that still encircles that finger.

"Your hair was longer and you didn't curl it like you do now. You had different glasses back then."

I swallow hard, staring at him. I mean, I'd noticed him too—I'd been damn near struck stupid with how handsome he was. Even happily married, it had been impossible not to notice him any of the times I'd seen him when I'd been around Cal.

"Even married, even pregnant with another man's baby, I still wanted you. And, fuck, I hated myself for it," he rasps brokenly. The breath that pulls in through my lips is ragged, fraught with emotion. "You have dominated my thoughts for years, Teddy."

My head is spinning. It's all so much to take in, to process. Years. He'd noticed me for years. I let my fingers drift up the sides of his neck, lightly, just my fingernails dragging against his skin.

His eyelids flutter and he groans low in the back of his throat at the same time goosebumps break over his skin.

"I think about you a lot too."

"Yeah?" he asks, tipping his head to the side to graze his mouth along the underside of my jaw.

I can feel the small smile that tips up his lips where his mouth is pressed to my skin. I lean my head back a little, giving him better access, and it's my turn to shiver as he drags his teeth over the sensitive skin there. I nod brokenly and feel his lips grin against my skin.

"What do you think about, Teddy? Do you think about this?"

"Oh God," I whisper up to the night sky above us. "Yes."

"What else do you think about?" he murmurs, lips moving directly against me.

"How unfair it is for you to be this attractive."

He chuckles, wrapping one arm around my waist to draw me closer against him. The chair groans beneath us and I bite my lip in apprehension. I'm going to either break him or break the chair—

He stalls the worry by whispering darkly, "That thought is mutual, Teddy. What else do you think about, sweetheart? Tell me."

His mouth fastens onto my throat, just above my collarbone, and I can't help the moan that escapes me, or the roll of my hips against him. He growls against my skin, thrusting his hips up. The friction is perfect. The way he presses against me feels so damn good. God, I want to be so full of him.

"You know what I think about," I whisper breathily.

"I want your words, sweetheart. Tell me what you think about when you touch yourself," he breathes raggedly, and my eyelids flutter closed. "*Fuck*, Teddy. I need to know what you think about when you come with my name on your lips."

"You. I think about you. Like this. About what it would feel like to have your hands on me. Your mouth," I whisper into the night, keeping my eyes closed.

"Where do you want my mouth, Teddy?" he rasps, deep and growly. I clamp my teeth down on my lower lip. The dark roughness of his voice is skittering over every nerve. The man could voice audiobooks and women would swoon.

"All over."

He brushes his lips across the exposed top slopes of my breasts. My nipples are hard beneath the thin fabric, but embarrassment and nervousness won't let me say the words out loud. That was a no-touching zone for Logan after I had Dalton.

"Here?" he asks, trailing his fingers along the edge of my tank top, pulling it down slightly.

TEDDY

I nod frantically. I'm so wet I'm aching. If he touches my nipples, I just might combust. They've always been sensitive, and they're so neglected—

He flicks one through the thin material and I gasp as the sensation ripples through me, all the way to the center of me. I can feel my body clenching around nothing; I want more. I haven't had more in so long. And when his mouth closes over it through the material, laving it with his tongue, I clutch his head between my hands, my own head dropping back while I try and fail to stifle the whimpering moan that cuts through the night around us.

His other hand works its way under the fabric, pulling it down so that the material is bunched beneath my breasts now, and then his mouth is on me again while his fingers pluck at the other.

It's been so long. So damn long, and it feels so good. "Please—" I beg frantically, rocking over him, seeking more. More.

He groans against me, working me harder with his tongue while I shift against him, seeking more friction where his hardness is pressed against my aching clit. That invisible string that connects what he's doing with his mouth to the very core of me tightens, and I realize that I'm going to come. For the first time in almost a year, I'm heartbeats away from an orgasm that isn't self-induced.

This sexy-as-sin man is going to make me come with just his mouth and fingers on my nipples, and I'm begging for it to happen.

Brazenly, wantonly begging.

Shame crashes over me like a tidal wave, reminding me of what I'm doing. I pull away from him with a cry, scrambling up off his lap. My face is on fire—not to mention the rest of me that is internally screaming for stopping when I was so fucking close.

With shaking fingers, I yank my tank top up so that my breasts are covered again and back away several steps.

Xander's breathing is harsh, his chest heaving. His cock is hard and tents the front of his gym shorts as he stands. "Teddy, what—"

But I shake my head as tears well in my eyes. What am I doing? What am I thinking? Making out with my hot-as-shit neighbor while my kids and my dead husband's parents sleep just twenty feet away?

Fisting the folds of my robe in my fingers, I cross my arms over my middle, doing my best to shrink into myself. To hide. Shame burns through me relentlessly.

"I'm so sorry," I whisper miserably, raising my eyes to his. That blue is so expressive, so stunningly bright. "I shouldn't have come over here."

"Teddy," he growls, though the sound isn't threatening at all. He takes a step forward, his hands reaching for me, almost beseechingly. "Stop, please."

"This was wrong," I whisper, holding one hand up, palm out, and he halts.

He shakes his head, lips thinned into a hard line. "No, it wasn't."

His eyes blaze into mine, though there's no anger, no resentment. Just a plea, and it breaks me wide open.

Turning my hand, I show him the back of it, spreading my fingers wide. The moonlight glints off that damn ring still on my finger. The ring that still connects me to my husband. My dead husband.

"*I can't take this off*, Xander. I'm not ready to. I'm not . . . I'm not *whole* anymore." I sob once, rolling my lips in and clamping my teeth over them to keep another one from breaking out of me. "I'm so broken. I'm not ready to start anything new, and I can't do casual. I can't. You are so good and kind and perfect and I'm just *broken*—"

"Teddy, you *are not broken*," he whispers, taking another two steps toward me. I don't back up this time. He wraps his arms around me, firm but gentle, and gathers me against his chest. I let him as the tears tumble out of me. "You are not broken, sweetheart."

He holds me until the tears stop, until the shaking subsides, and I melt into his warmth, drained and exhausted.

TEDDY

"I'm sorry," he whispers against my hair, where I can feel his lips move.

My cheek is pressed flat against his chest, where I can both feel and hear his heart beating beneath his sternum. He smells amazing. Like citrus and cedar and smoke. I breathe him in, letting my body soften against his.

I don't want to want him, but God, do I want him so badly. I like Xander. Like, *really like him*.

As the panic and anxiety fade and I melt into his embrace, I let myself believe maybe . . . maybe starting something new with someone as kind and gentle as him wouldn't be the end of the world I keep thinking it will be . . .

I can be brave, right?

I nuzzle against him and take a deep, shuddering breath in at the same time he squeezes me tighter against him. All these things that I've been missing so desperately. Being held, being kissed, being wanted . . . not being alone and so damn sad all the time. He sighs above me, pressing his lips to my temple, and I squeeze my eyes shut at the way it just feels so right to be held like this.

Maybe . . . maybe it's time. With someone like him, I can be brave. We could make this work, right?

"You're right," he whispers then, and I wonder if I uttered the last part out loud. But his words are quiet, sad, and my brows knit together in confusion. "This was probably a bad idea. I don't do *more*. I *can't* do anything more than casual, Teddy. My job . . ."

He trails off, and I don't need him to finish the sentence, because I know what he's not saying, what he won't say. His job is dangerous and also the most important thing in his life. A relationship would complicate that. Something I have always known but let myself ignore.

But that doesn't stop the way my chest constricts excruciatingly at his words, making my breath stutter in my throat. He leans his cheek against the top of my head and it sends shards of agony ricocheting through me, but I'm frozen, unable to move.

He takes a deep breath in and then breathes miserably, "And I needed this reminder of why I don't get involved with single moms."

As my chest cracks open wide, I realize far, far too late, that my silly, naïve heart had already decided on wanting more. I'm not brave . . . and I was a fool for thinking I could be.

TEDDY

23

XANDER

*L*etting go of Teddy and allowing her to pull away from me just might be one of the most painful things I've had to live through.

At least, until she looks up at me with those damn silver-gray eyes that show just how betrayed she feels. And then I feel even fucking worse. The noise that escapes her, a sad, disappointed laugh, cracks my sternum open from the inside out.

"Unbelievable," she whispers, reaching up to swipe angrily at the tears that track down her cheek. "Maybe try leading with that next time." Shaking her head, she turns away from me and mutters bitterly, "Asshole."

"Teddy—"

"Go fuck yourself," she throws over her shoulder as she disappears around the partition.

I stand there and listen to the screen door slide open and shut, and then the heavier glass door as she closes that too. The flick of the lock as she engages it. It's quiet, but it echoes like a gunshot in my head. That lock sliding into place represents so much more than the simple mechanism that it is. It's closing the door—bolting it and throwing

away the key—on what could have been. What I won't ever let myself
have. Because even if she can't see it right now, it's best for her too.

And then I'm standing here in nothing but silence.

Heavy, soul-crushing silence.

My alarm blares next to me and I jolt awake, staring up through the branches of the trees, the stars obscured by the heavy smoke that blankets the area. Around me, I can hear my crew as they start to wake. Four a.m. comes early out here. Crappy instant coffee is started and we eat MREs straight out of the packages before gearing up. Half my crew heads out with King, the other half with Cal. I nod to both men as they lead their squads out into the darkness, headlamps attached to their helmets.

I work my way up a nearby ridge to the highest vantage point I can find. My mind should be on this fucking fire, but it's not. For a week all I've done is replay that moment with Teddy. When I dropped that fucking bomb on the best thing that's happened to me in, well, probably ever.

What right do I have to ask for a woman like that to sit by and wait for me while I come out here and risk my life eight months out of the year? I don't. I have no place in the life of a woman like Teddy Hansen. Or her kids. I don't deserve a woman like her.

Stomping through the dark forest, I gnash my teeth together until my jaw aches. No, Teddy deserves someone so much better than me. Someone who would be there for her. Something I can't do. Not now. Possibly not ever.

I'd gotten the call with our assignment that next afternoon. I hadn't been brave enough to venture outside, where I could hear Kent and Colleen packing their car to head home. Shame and guilt had warred inside me, battling for supremacy beneath my rib cage. I grabbed my pack and waited until Teddy and the kids had gone back inside after watching Kent and Colleen pull out of the driveway.

XANDER

Only Teddy had stepped out of her front door at the same time I did. Our eyes collided and I'd wanted nothing more than to go to her, but I didn't. I knew I couldn't. Not after what I'd said the night before.

Not when she quickly dropped her eyes from mine to turn away like I didn't exist.

So I climbed into my truck and pulled out of the driveway. That had been a week ago. And all I've been able to think about is her. About how royally I fucked up.

But I remind myself this is for the best. She'll eventually move on and be ready to date again, and I'll stand back and let it happen.

If I'm honest with myself, I don't think there's a man out there who deserves the woman that Teddy Hansen is. He'd have to be a goddamn saint to deserve everything she has to offer. To deserve to have those kids in his life.

I kick at a rotting log as I pass it, just because. I've been a mean brute all week, horrible company, and I've been reduced to communicating in grunts and snarls. Even Cal, who usually is completely unfazed by my moods, is giving me space. Though I'm not sure if it's because of the bear of a mood I've been in, or because he's pissed at me.

Not that I blame him if he is. He told me to be careful with her, for good reason. And I purposely, intentionally hurt her feelings. If I'm honest with myself, I'm a little surprised he hasn't decked me yet. I deserve it.

Thank fuck this fire is almost contained. It's relatively small and slow spreading, with weather that's worked in our favor. The ash that's filling the sky and falling everywhere is stagnant with no wind to shift it elsewhere. Which is fine by me, because that means the winds are low and not flying any embers into the green surrounding the area we've cut out.

With any luck, we'll be headed home tonight. Although I admit, the thought of home doesn't bring me that same spark of joy that it did last time.

Knowing Teddy probably hates my guts now.

XANDER

24

Teddy

"**S**hut up. He did *not* say that to you."

Curled up in one corner of my couch, I nod miserably and take a big gulp of my coffee. Vi, who is sitting cross-legged in the opposite corner, just stares at me, her jaw hanging slack.

"And this is after he kissed the daylights out of you?" she asks, raising her glass of wine to her lips.

I groan and let my head fall back against the back cushion of the couch.

"What a douche."

I snort out a laugh, closing my eyes. *My sentiments exactly.* "Yes. And I'm just the huge dumb idiot that let it happen. I was practically begging for it, Vi." I let my face fall into my free hand, rubbing my temples with my thumb and middle finger, too embarrassed to look her in the face while I confess all my dirty secrets. "I mean, I know I had just basically freaked out and said I wasn't ready for anything, but dammit, he's just *so nice* . . . I let myself think that just maybe I could try . . ."

"You're not an idiot, *he* is the idiot. And that is *not* what a nice guy does," she mutters darkly, shifting in her seat on the couch. She shakes her head and grumbles into her wine about *idiot men and their stupid penises*. I snort into my coffee.

Hollie and Penny are in Penny's room playing with Barbies, Dalton is in his room playing a video game, and Bea is lounging happily in her bouncy seat on the floor next to us. We had to forgo our usual midmorning playdate for the girls this morning due to heavy rains—good Lord, did we need it badly—and we decided to stay in and drink instead—wine for her, coffee for me, so I can nurse Bea tonight. Scottie is working, but we have plans to have coffee tomorrow morning.

All the guys have been gone since Sunday, called out on another fire. According to Vi, this one is located in Montana and was caused by a lightning strike. The news coverage is sparse and generalized, but it sounds like it's well contained by the crews on the ground.

Not that I've been watching for any particular reason. Other than to check in on my brother, of course.

No, I haven't been side-eyeing the TV anytime it pops up on the screen for any glimpse of a dark head of hair and bright blue eyes.

"You said you freaked out," Vi says, turning so she's sitting facing me fully on the couch.

I shift, angling toward her too, and nod, my cheeks heating. I'm not proud of what happened. I panicked. And cheated myself out of what felt like could have been a really good orgasm. I'm still mad at myself for that.

Staring down at my hand where it's resting on my thigh, I spread my fingers wide. I meant what I'd said. "I know I need to take it off," I whisper. "But it feels so final, Vi. Like taking it off makes it more real. That he's not coming home and then I have to do the really scary part of moving on."

TEDDY

"Whether you take it off or leave it on doesn't change that though," she says quietly, gently.

I nod again.

"That's the worst part about grieving someone who died. Learning to accept that hard truth. It doesn't matter how much we want it to be different, it's not."

"I know." My words are barely a whisper. I'm reminded of what Xander had said that night. "Xander talked about working with your brother."

Violette nods, a small smile pulling at her mouth. "Yeah, he did. Rowan and Jacob were like this"—she says, twisting her middle finger around her index—"and they did everything together. He was my twin, but they were like soulmates or something. My dad was a hotshot for years, and Jacob and Rowan always talked about joining together. That's how I know Xander, actually. His dad was the superintendent, and my dad was a squaddie for years. Our dads, Xander, my brother, Rowan, your brother. They were all on the crew at one point."

I nod, and she twists the wine goblet in her hands.

"Rowan doesn't like to talk about it, and for a long time I didn't either. They got called out to a fire on Mount Adams. Jacob went up a ridge to check on their line and fell into an ash pit. He died later due to complications with the burns he'd sustained."

Tears line my eyelids and blur my vision. I reach out a hand and cover her knee, squeezing tight. "I'm so sorry, Vi."

She nods, swiping at the tears that are tracking down her own cheeks. "I kept thinking he'd come back, if I waited long enough. If I wished for it hard enough. He'd come home and get to meet Hols, or go out hell-raising with Rowan. Show up just to give me shit and one of his squeeze-just-a-little-too-tight hugs."

I laugh at that, and she grins.

"You're the only one who will be able to know when it's the right time to take it off," she continues gently. "It's a big step. Don't rush into it . . . but don't be too afraid to let go and possibly miss out on something great."

I snort a laugh. "I hope you're not talking about Xander."

"No, fuck Xander," she mutters. Then she laughs out loud and winks. "Or, *fuck him*, if that's what you want too. Get some O's out of it. I'm not here to judge."

"*Oh my god*," I laugh, shaking my head. Wrinkling my nose, I mutter, "Yeah, that's not going to happen. He made it very clear that I'm not the kind of woman he wants. *He doesn't get involved with single moms.*"

"Well, he's an idiot, and I plan to tell him that," Vi grumbles, reaching over to grab the bottle of wine from the coffee table and topping off her glass.

I feel a little better after our talk. Even if it still stings like a motherfucker.

At first, I was hurt. Then angry. Then *really* angry. I'd bounced through so many emotions in the last week I'm not really sure where I've landed now. Betrayal. Hurt. Raging fury. Disappointment. Shame. Guilt. I've been stewing over it since it happened, letting it fester until it felt like a hot coal had been dropped into my chest. I needed to have someone tell me that my feelings are valid.

I think the one that really stings though, is the humiliation that just randomly boils up out of nowhere. The way I had so shamelessly thrown myself at the man, practically riding him, grinding my greedy ass onto his erection like a sex-starved hussy . . . I'd literally begged for it. And look where it had gotten me.

Edged like no one's fucking business and then reminded why dating is such a colossally bad idea for me. Because I'm a widowed single mom.

TEDDY

And no one wants a widowed mom of three.

Especially not Xander fucking Macomb.

He made that brutally, painfully clear. I sigh, taking another big gulp of my coffee as the humiliation of that night tightens my chest all over again.

25

XANDER

Christ, I'm bone-tired. Been up since 4:00 a.m., on the fire until 5:00 this evening, then packing up spike camp and hitting the road back home to Sky Ridge. After unpacking at base, we all agreed to head over to Shifty's to celebrate.

As badly as I want to go home and sleep, I need a fucking drink.

Cal meets me at the door, holding it open for me without a word, though we do nod our chins at each other in acknowledgment. We hardly spoke all week. I've been so lost in my own stupid head and I'm certain he's doing his best not to be that overprotective big brother I know he is.

We make our way over to the corner where our usual smattering of tables and booths are located, half our crew already here. King was the first, eager to see his lady. Violette saunters over with a tray full of beer bottles, setting several down on the chipped and cracked tabletop.

She sets the last one in front of me and I lean forward to grab it, murmuring, "Thanks, Viole—*ehhh!*"

The small, round tray she's carrying thumps me in the back of the head sharply, knocking my teeth together with a jarring click. I reach up, rubbing the tender spot on the back of my head and turn narrowed eyes onto her.

She stands over me, shoving the tray up under one arm, and then crosses both arms over her chest. She glares at me with a fire I haven't seen since she gave King a fucking run for his money. "Before you open up your mouth and ask a stupid question like 'What was that for,' you know why. *Jackass*," she snaps, her lips thinning.

Heat crawls up the back of my neck, realizing that every damn eye at our table is on us. On me. Getting scolded like a damn toddler.

"That was a real dick move, Xander. I can't believe you actually said that to her."

Fuck. These women have ganged up together. And I can feel Cal's eyes on the side of my head like a fucking laser.

"That was fucking epic, love," King laughs from where he's seated. Grabbing hold of one of her belt loops and hauling her over to him, he wraps one arm around her waist.

She's still glaring daggers at me, but her arm loops around his neck, tucking his head against her side. "You stink," she mutters, wrinkling her nose.

He chuckles again, unfazed as she ruffles his hair before bending low to kiss him. It's not a quick, chaste kiss, either. I pretend not to see the way his hand curves around her ass before she pecks one last kiss to his mouth and straightens. He watches her walk away, his gaze on her backside as she makes her way back toward the bar. He adjusts himself in his pants and I roll my eyes.

"Do you two need to disappear into the back for a few minutes?" Cal mumbles over to King, who raises a hand and flips him off without taking his eyes off Violette. Cal chuckles into his beer.

I shift in my seat, bracing my elbows on the tabletop in front of me, hands clasped tight around the bottle. I stare down at the floor between my dirty work boots. "Fucking pain-in-the-ass women," I grumble under my breath. I know she's right. Fuck, I know I was a dick to Teddy. But I did it to protect her. To protect her kids.

"*Watch it*," King mutters sharply, all levity leaving his face as he turns to glare at me too.

I sigh, nodding. Fucking hell, I'm just making a mess of everything, it seems.

I hunch my shoulders in, continuing to pick at the label on the beer bottle clasped between my hands, and then Cal is leaning forward too, so that his shoulders are only about six inches away from mine.

"I know you've been waiting for me to kick your ass all week, but I think you're doing that enough on your own," he mutters low, just between me and him.

I huff out a breath and nod solemnly.

King claps me on the shoulder from my other side. "That why you've been a grumpy motherfucker this week? Trouble in paradise?"

I shoot him a glower from beneath lowered brows.

Cal leans back in his chair again, taking a drink of his beer. He stretches his legs out beneath the table, balancing his beer on his belt buckle at his waist.

"Sup's always a grumpy motherfucker," Opp mutters, grinning over at us. "It's like his factory default setting."

"There's nothing for there to be trouble with, because there's nothing going on," I mumble, tipping my beer back. I down half of it, then nod to Violette when she raises an eyebrow at me from across the bar, a silent signal meaning *Ready for another one?* She's back a minute later with another round, placing not one, but two PBR bottles in front of me. Like she knows how much I'm fucking beating myself up over this thing with Teddy. Even if I'll never allow myself to say it out loud. Especially around these goons.

XANDER

They don't need to know that I'd almost come in my fucking shorts with Teddy grinding over me, or how incredibly soft she is beneath my hands. They definitely don't need to know I've thought of nothing but the way her mouth tastes and the way her fingers feel twining through my hair. Pretty sure Cal would gladly throat-punch me if he knew how filthy my thoughts are where his sister is involved. He doesn't need to know that. None of them do.

Or how badly I want to be the man who comes home to her every fucking night.

Well, I've made sure that's never going to happen. My chest tightens again, like it always does, when I think about the way she'd stared at me like I'd just kicked her puppy.

The door opens and Cal's head swivels, a smile breaking out across his face, and I know without turning that Scottie has just walked in. Placing his beer on the table in front of us, he rises from his seat and takes several steps toward her. I glance over my shoulder at them just as he wraps one arm around her waist and lifts her clear off the floor, their mouths meeting.

She's still wearing her EMT uniform, like she came straight over after her shift ended without taking the time to change. Like she couldn't bear to be away from him a second longer than necessary. My chest tightens painfully. Why now, after all this time, do I want that?

"Glad to see you in one piece," she whispers as he sets her back down on her feet. She runs her hands over his chest as if assessing for any hidden injuries.

He grins and kisses her once more.

"There's this lady, she's kinda scary. She made me promise I had to, so I try to do my best," he teases lightly, quietly. Then, his voice dips lower, softer. "Still with me?"

She smiles up at him. "Always."

His fingers flit over a faint scar at her hairline above her right eye, his eyes going soft for a heartbeat before dropping his hand and turning back toward the table. He shoves Roycie's booted feet off an empty chair at the table next to us and pulls it over to our table, then sits down. Scottie takes the seat Cal had previously been sitting in as Violette shows back up with a highball tumbler of brown liquor for her.

"Thank you, Vi," Scottie says, smiling up at her.

Violette smiles back and I grit my teeth until my jaw aches. Everyone else gets a friendly hello but me, apparently.

Cal's arm settles across the back of Scottie's chair, his fingers trailing along her neck beneath her hair that's pulled up into a sleek bun, and her hand finds its way to Cal's thigh.

Those little, mindless touches between lovers that speak volumes. Not wanting to be apart, even just for a moment.

I finish the second beer and reach for the third. Before she can walk away, I ask Violette, "Can I get a whiskey? Make it a double, please."

Fuck it. I might just get drunk tonight.

XANDER

26

XANDER

"Come on, you heavy bastard," Cal mutters, slinging my arm over his shoulder and heaving me out of the passenger seat of his truck. "Let's get you into bed."

My feet are moving along the dark walkway that leads to my side of the duplex in stumbling, unsteady steps. Fuck, I haven't been drunk like this in years. Possibly since my dad died. That was a rough night. This might turn out to be a rough night too. I'm already dreading the morning. I don't bounce back from hangovers the way I used to in my twenties.

"Thanksh for driving," I hear myself say, then lick my parched lips.

"No problem, you idiot," he mutters again, leading me toward my front door.

It's dark. My house is dark and I don't want to go inside because it's fucking empty and lonely as fuck. I want to go into Teddy's.

I want to see her, see that sunshine that just pours out of her when she smiles. I want to hold her. Fuck, I miss her. And I have no right to. I drop my head until my chin nearly touches my chest.

"Oh my god, is he okay?"

My head snaps up at the sound of her voice. She's turned her porch light on and is standing in the halo of light as it spills out onto the walkway in front of her duplex. She's barefoot—why is this woman always fucking barefoot? Doesn't she know how dangerous it is out here at night with no fucking shoes on—and she's wearing that damn robe again. She's got it clutched closed over herself, her arms wrapped around that curvy body that's haunted my every fucking waking thought and dream at night. Her golden-blond hair is piled high on her head in an adorably messy topknot, tendrils framing that face that I've missed so fucking much.

"Yeah, he's okay," Cal chuckles then, continuing to lead me toward my front door.

I don't want to go, and I stop my feet from moving just so I can continue to stare at her for a little longer.

"He's going to feel like hell in the morning, though."

"Is he drunk?" she asks, taking a step toward us.

They're talking about me like I'm not right fucking here, like I can't hear them.

"Oh yeah," Cal laughs then, squeezing me around the rib cage to try to get me moving again. "He's fucking hammered."

But I keep my feet planted, eyes on Teddy as she moves closer, stepping out of the light filtering from her door into the shadows where we're currently standing. She tilts her head sideways slightly, as if assessing me, and then steps to my other side and slides her arm around my waist too.

And suddenly I'm home.

I let my head tilt down to rest against the top of hers, and I feel her deep inhale against my side.

"Come on, let's keep moving," Cal mumbles, getting me in motion again. "Keys?"

"Left pocket," I whisper between dry lips.

XANDER

Cal digs into my pocket, producing my key ring that has my truck key and the key to my house. He gets the door unlocked and then we're moving inside the dark entryway. Teddy flips a light switch and the living room lights up, highlighting the hallway too.

"I can get him down the hall," Cal says over me to Teddy, who nods and lets her arm fall away from my back.

I can't help it; I reach back with my other hand for hers. I breathe easier once her fingers slide between mine, twining and squeezing, and she follows us down the hallway to my bedroom. God, I wish I wasn't so drunk right now. I have so much I want to say to her. So much I want to apologize for. Tell her how I'm an idiot and I didn't mean what I said. That I don't care about any of it. I want her. I want her in whatever way I can have her, and her kids. But it's like my brain and my mouth have stopped all communications through my neural system and my mouth stays resolutely shut.

"You're going to need to change these sheets tomorrow since you haven't showered yet," Cal grumbles as we make it to my room. He deposits me on the bed, reaching over to flip on the small, dim lamp that sits beside my bed. I have a moment of panic as Teddy sees my room, my bed, for the first time. The light is dim, casting a low ring of light across the floor and onto the bed. I don't have much and I'm kind of a neat freak, so my room is clean and my bed is made, even if there's a fine layer of dust across most surfaces from neglect. "And I'm *not* getting you in the shower."

"Ish fine," I manage to mumble, sinking onto the edge of the bed. My eyes find Teddy's face again. She's so damn beautiful it hurts.

Cal drops to his knees and unlaces my boots, pulling them off one by one and tossing them aside. I realize I should be embarrassed at having Teddy see me like this, but my brain can't seem to focus on anything other than the fact that she's here. Watching me.

She disappears out the door with a quiet, "I'll be right back," and Cal nods to her over his shoulder.

"Pants on or off?" he asks.

"Off."

I manage to help get my Nomex pants down my legs and wrestle my black undershirt off over my head, tossing both toward the clothes hamper in the corner. I miss, but I don't care, because then Teddy is back with a tall glass of water and a couple of Tylenol cupped in her palm.

I'm sitting on the edge of the bed in nothing but my boxer briefs, but her eyes don't leave mine as she steps forward, holding out her hand. I cup my palm and she drops the capsules into it, then hands me the glass. I swallow down the capsules and drink half the glass of water in one long swallow.

"If your drunk ass is good now, I'm going to go home to my woman," Cal mutters from the doorway.

I nod, and he slaps the doorjamb lightly. "You're lucky I love you, man." His gaze slices to his sister, who still has her back to him. "Ted, do you want me to walk you back?"

She glances at him over her shoulder, and I watch, mesmerized, as a small smile pulls at one corner of her mouth. "I'll be okay. Thank you, Cal."

Cal stares at her for a long moment, then turns his eyes to me. His face is mostly blank, but I don't miss the tightness of his mouth or the concern that darkens his eyes. Then he sighs, nods, and lumbers out of the room, leaving us alone together. My brain still isn't functioning at full capacity and I'm unable to articulate anything coherent as she turns back to face me. Instead, I just reach out my hand and wrap my fingers around the belt of her robe that's tied at her waist, pulling her slowly toward me.

She doesn't fight it, just steps closer until she's standing between my spread knees. Just like we were a week ago, before I fucked everything up.

XANDER

My hands are still dirty and soot-stained, my fingernails need a deep scrubbing, and the sight of my fingers wrapped around the clean softness of the belt isn't lost on me. I let my head drop forward until my forehead is resting against her sternum and let my eyes close as I breathe her in.

She takes the water glass out of my hand and sets it down on the bedside table before sliding her arms around my head. I breathe out, swallowing hard around the emotion that clogs my throat at having her so close. I drop my hold on the belt of her robe and slide my hands over her hips, down the outside of her thighs. And then I'm curling both arms around her hips, holding her to me like she's my own personal lifeline. When I feel the press of her cheek against the top of my head, I take a shuddering breath in.

We stay like that for a long time, or maybe it just feels like a long time to my inebriated brain.

"I need to go home, Xander," she whispers slowly, softly. Her fingers have been trailing through the too-long hair at the back of my head and I nuzzle into her touch, not wanting her to let go. Not wanting to let go myself.

There's still so much I want to say. So much I need to say. I don't want her to go even though I know she needs to. Her kids are alone, sleeping, while she's over here taking care of my drunk ass.

God, I'm pathetic.

I take a deep, steadying breath, absorbing her scent and wishing I could just live in it and never come out. But I nod, then untwine my arms from around her hips and raise my head from the pillow of her breasts.

"Go to sleep," she whispers gently, her fingers sliding through my hair—which I know is dirty and dusty and probably grimy—and I nod again, my eyes bouncing between her gray ones. They look almost silver in the low light, and her freckles seem darker across the bridge of her nose from the glow of the lamp beside us.

And then she stuns me completely by leaning down to press her lips to my forehead softly, lingeringly. Her hands cupping either side of my face, fingernails scraping against the overgrown scruff across my cheeks and jaw. It's heaven and hell all rolled into one.

Her lips move against my forehead as she says so softly I almost think I imagine it, "Good night, Xander."

She reaches out and flips off the bedside lamp, dousing us both in darkness, and then she's slipping away, out the bedroom door and down the hall. I swallow hard as the light from the living room goes dark too, and then I hear the soft click of my front door as she lets herself out.

XANDER

27

Teddy

ME: Any idea why I had to help put a VERY inebriated Xander to bed last night after Cal brought him home?

VI: Ummm. I plead the fifth.

ME: 😒
Of course you do.

VI: Wait, it was after two am when I sent him and Cal out. Why were you even awake?

ME: I heard a strange truck in the driveway. I was getting Bea back to sleep after her middle of the night feeding. Got up to see who it was and saw Cal trying to manhandle Xander out of his truck and up the sidewalk.

VI: Oof. He did seem a little rough around the edges last night. Like he's been beating himself up like crazy. I didn't think I served him that much.

> **ME:** The man could barely walk, Vi. He looked tortured. I've never seen him look so . . . I don't know. Morose?

VI: Well, realizing you messed up a great thing with an amazing woman will do that to you. According to Rowan, he was a mess all week. Grumpy as a bear.

> **ME:** You think I'm amazing? Awwww. Will you marry me?

VI: You're not really my type, babe.

> **ME:** Damn. Figures. It's because I don't have a dick, right? I can get a strap-on, if that's your thing.

VI: Woman, I just spit out my coffee all over myself. Now I have to go change before rounds.

> **ME:** . . . So that wasn't a no . . .

VI: [selfie of Violette dressed in nurse scrubs covered in coffee stains and a scowl on her face]
You're ridiculous. You're spending too much time with me and Scottie. We're corrupting you.

TEDDY

ME: Yes, but you love me anyway. You did say I was amazing, after all.

VI: I have work to do, you crazy person lol. Go check on your sexy, tortured, hungover neighbor.

ME: [GIF of soldier saluting]
Ok. Going in. Wish me luck.

VI: You don't need luck. You've got boobs. Works better than luck.

I click out of the text thread, shaking my head. Standing at the kitchen sink, I take another long drink of my coffee. Dalton and Penny are off to school, so it's just Bea and me this morning. She was up way too early so she's already zonked out for her morning nap in her crib.

Taking a deep, steadying breath, I pour a second cup of coffee and then clip the baby monitor onto the back pocket of my cutoff jean shorts. My T-shirt is oversized and the V-neck dips low over my cleavage. I step out the front door and around to Xander's, sucking in another deep breath, and then I raise my hand and knock lightly.

Thirty seconds later, I'm beginning to second-guess my decision when it opens.

My jaw drops and I fully realize that I am staring but unable to stop myself.

A towel is slung around his hips, his torso and upper body blessedly, wonderfully naked. Water runs down the broad expanse of his chest and down the valley between his abs. His hair is wet and strands stick to the side of his face and neck, but his scruffy beard has been trimmed.

"Hey," he says, those eyes wreaking even more havoc on my system than the sight of his wet, naked body already has.

"*Hey,*" I respond lamely, my voice coming out high and squeaky. *Ohmygod, am I drooling?* I snap my mouth closed and shove the cup of coffee forward, though I temper the movement so the hot liquid doesn't slosh out over the rim. "I, uhh . . . I wanted to check on you. And bring you coffee. Here."

"Thank you," he murmurs, that deep rasp making my stomach do somersaults. He takes the cup of coffee from me and our fingers brush, sending jolts of electricity up through my fingers and straight to my heart.

I lift my cup to my lips, just for something to do with my hands, which are trembling.

"And uh, thanks for last night. I'm sorry. I don't usually let myself drink like that."

"Don't apologize for that," I whisper, swallowing hard. "It's no big deal."

"I do need to apologize for what I said before though," he says softly, his brows lowering over his eyes sadly.

"Please don't," is all I manage, clutching my cup of coffee between my fingers. "I understand. You don't have to explain—"

"Yes, I do," he insists, his eyes tracking over every inch of my face, like he's trying to memorize it. Like he missed me. "Teddy . . . Fuck." He looks down at himself, a soft, self-deprecating laugh tumbling from him. "Let me get dressed, and then can we talk? Please?"

I must be a glutton for punishment, because I find myself nodding slowly, and then my traitorous mouth opens and says, "Okay."

"Great," he says on a breath, like a weight has just been lifted off him. His eyes brighten, and that stunningly white smile sends me even more off-kilter. "Give me like, three minutes. Do you want to come in? Is Bea sleeping?"

TEDDY

"Umm, sure," I murmur. "And yes, she's sleeping. I have the baby monitor in my pocket, just in case."

He steps aside, letting me step in over the threshold, and then he's closing the door behind us. He walks ahead of me, and I can't help but stare at the broad, tanned expanse of his back, the way the muscles shift and contract with each move he makes. Or the round firmness of his butt beneath the towel. His feet are bare and I laugh lightly when I realize he has left a trail of water through the hallway to the door.

"I'm sorry, I didn't mean to interrupt your shower. I didn't even know if you'd be awake yet."

"I woke up hungover as fuck," he chuckles, talking to me over his shoulder. He stops at the kitchen island and takes a drink of the coffee. He hums appreciatively. "Thank you for this. And for the water and Tylenol last night. It helped a lot."

I lift my coffee to my lips and take a drink as he skirts around the counter.

"I'll be right back," he says quietly, and I nod. He disappears down the hallway and into the bedroom, the door closing.

Cup clutched in my hands, I wander around the living room, though there isn't much to look at. A few pictures of what appears to be his brothers, his mom, and his dad are on the wall, but that's it. His house is clean and well-kept, but it's just . . . empty. And it hits me all over again that he's rarely here.

The door at the end of the hallway opens and he steps out in a pair of jeans and a black T-shirt that clings to his shoulders and biceps like paid actors. His chest fills out the shirt in a way that makes my mouth go dry. He's using the towel to scrub at his still-wet hair with one hand, leaving it tousled and messy, and, dammit, now I just want to run my fingers through it too.

He tosses the towel over the back of one of the dining table chairs as he walks over to where I'm standing. Picking up his coffee cup, he takes another drink. "Seriously, thank you for this." When I nod, he gestures to the couch. "Will you sit with me?"

This feels dangerous. A couch is far more intimate than the dining table, where the table itself would separate us. We've already established that I can't keep my hands off this man when he's around.

Sitting next to him on a couch?

Dangerous. So, so dangerous.

Leading me over to the couch that looks like it's straight out of the nineties, I take the baby monitor out of my back pocket and set it on the coffee table. Actually, most of the furniture and what little décor is around looks outdated, like he never bothered to update anything after taking over the house after his father died.

He angles his body into the opposite corner, spreading his knees, and then balances his left arm along the back of the couch. I lower my body into the other corner, folding one leg beneath me and cradling my coffee between my hands in my lap.

"How are you?" he asks, breaking the silence, and I swallow around another gulp of coffee.

I shrug one shoulder awkwardly. "I'm fine," I manage to whisper, darting my eyes up to his for just a brief moment before slicing them away again. Last night messed with my head. Like, a lot. Shit, the last week has messed with my head more than I'd like to admit. The hot and cold, back-and-forth of everything is exhausting and so confusing. But the way he'd held on to me last night, like he never wanted to let go . . . like he needed it as much as I did . . . it did something to me. To my heart. Cracked it open and, dammit, but that little fissure is widening and letting him back in. "You?"

He shrugs one shoulder, lifting his coffee to his lips. He watches me so closely. It makes me nervous, the way he stares at me so intensely. "Teddy."

Ugh, but the way he says my name . . . it's like a balm to my nerves and an electric shock to my system all at once.

TEDDY

"You really don't have to say anything," I whisper, dropping my eyes to the coffee swirling in the cup balanced between my palms. "I understand, Xander."

Setting his coffee cup aside, he reaches over to where I'm sitting and plucks my cup out of my hands. I watch with wide eyes as he sets it down on the coffee table in front of us, and then he's sliding his arms around me and hauling me to him.

One heavy, muscular arm is banded around my ass, the other around my back, moving me into position until I'm once again straddling him with one knee on either side of his hips. My shins are flush against the couch cushion beneath us, my thighs spreading over his, and I flush hot all over when my shorts ride up high on the inside part of my thighs.

My hands land on his chest, spreading wide as I balance myself and keep him somewhat at arm's length, but he's having none of it.

What is it with this man and wanting me on top of him?

"I'm going to crush you—"

"Teddy, if you say one more word, I'll turn this ass pink," he rasps, spreading his hand wide on one of my ass cheeks, the heat of his palm hot even through the jean shorts. "I want you right here, okay? *This*"—he groans, urging me closer—"is right where I want you."

He smells so good, fresh out of the shower, skin and hair still damp, and I so badly want to sink into him, to get lost in him for just a little while. I want to believe every word he says, want to believe what I can feel pressing up between my thighs. I push against his chest with my hands, angling my chest away from him so I can stare into his sky-blue eyes.

"Xander . . . what are you doing?" I search his eyes, terrified of what I see and what he's going to say.

"I'm trying to apologize, but you won't sit still," he grumbles, tightening his hands on my waist.

I go still. God, this is so confusing. "You said you don't get involved with single moms. I haven't magically gone from a single mom of three to not having kids in a week—"

"*Stop*," he whispers earnestly, and I do. His hands come to rest on the wide slope of my hips, fingers digging into the meaty part of my ass. Those eyes that I know I could get lost in if I let myself are so deep and infinitely sad as he murmurs quietly, "I know what I said. My biggest rule for myself since joining a hotshot crew has always been that I don't date period, Teddy. It's not fair to ask someone, anyone, *especially* someone with kids, to be with me. Knowing how dangerous my job is. My parents' marriage dissolved in front of me and my brothers because of this profession. My dad was a career hotshot; it was the love of his life. And it broke my mother's heart to watch him walk away from us every spring to come out here, never knowing if he was going to come home. So, she finally gave him an ultimatum; it was her and us or the job. He chose the job. She never forgave him and she never got over him. And then she lost him all over again when we lost him six years ago."

"Xander . . ."

"Let me finish, please," he whispers, swallowing hard.

I nod for him to continue, though I have to concentrate really hard on not letting my eyes fill with tears. My nose is stinging with them.

"You know my dad died in a fire. He was set to retire at the end of that season, and he never made it to retirement."

The sadness in his voice, that quiet hurt that drops his deep voice into a rasp has my heart clenching in my chest.

"He saved our entire crew from that fire. We came too close to not making it out . . ."

I can't help it then as the tears I'd been fighting fill my eyes. I remember the fear, the panic, that had raced through me when I'd learned how close Cal had come to being taken too. Cal had only ever told me the basics, but I know he had been close enough to see Xander's dad's final moments, that he hadn't been able to help him, and it's haunted him for years. Probably still does, though he doesn't talk to me about it much.

Xander smiles tenderly, sadness still clouding his eyes, as he reaches up and swipes a thumb across my cheek as one of those tears slips past my lids. My throat closes around the tears and the fear that shivers down my spine.

"He fought like hell to get his team out, and it cost him his life. I made a promise then that I would honor that sacrifice. And I've done my best to do so. That's why this is so fucking hard for me, beautiful. Because I've never been committed to anything in my life other than fighting fires. *This is all I know*. I know that all I could promise you is a life full of worry and fear, and that's not fair to you. Not fair to your kids, who have already lost so much and have been through so much hurt. You already have your brother to worry about. I hate the thought of you being worried for me too. I'm so sorry that I hurt you, sweetheart. I thought I was doing the right thing. I can't tell you enough how sorry I am for causing you pain because I'm an emotionally stunted idiot."

I can't help the little laugh that escapes me. He presses his forehead to mine and rolls it, and I squeeze my eyes shut. My heart is cracked wide open, painfully so. And it's leaving me so achingly vulnerable. It's truly terrifying.

"I swear I didn't mean it the way you took it, beautiful. And fuck, I know it's not fair to ask this of you. To ask you to forgive me for being a jackass, and for asking you to open up to me. I know that," he whispers brokenly, clasping my jaw with both hands to tilt my face away from his. To pull back far enough to force me to look him in the eyes.

And then I'm lost, irretrievably, in his gaze. I never want to find my way back out again either. Because this man . . . this man is ruining my heart in ways that I am wholly unprepared for.

Dragging his mouth across mine lightly, he breathes raggedly, "But I'm so tired of fighting this. *I'm crazy about you, Teddy.* You're all I think about anymore. Every waking thought and every dream at night . . . it's all you. It's only been you."

TEDDY

28

XANDER

"Light it up, boys!" I call out to my crew.

Some nod, some call out affirmatives, and others simply shout back, "Yes, Sup!"

We're doing a burnout on a section of property that surrounds a local historic site to protect the building. In reality, it's a dilapidated barn-turned-museum that in my opinion could use a good torch, but the local council has deemed it a historic landmark for Sky Ridge. With the heat wave we've been dealing with since July and next to no rain, we were assigned to come out and clear out snags, thin the brush, and back-burn the surrounding acreage to prevent any fires from getting too close, if there happens to be any that flare up in the area.

King and his squad are digging line around the west side of the property. He's in his element; the bastard gets to direct the use of a Bobcat to clear a lot of the thistly brush while Cal and his team are using their drip torches to scour a defensive line.

It's easy, fairly mindless work. Weather conditions are pristine for this kind of job, and it gives us something to do between long-haul fire assignments. We prefer to work at night since it's easier to see where our flames are, and we have the added bonus of not baking beneath the hot sun all day. It's not that much cooler, but with no sun beating down on us, it's almost enjoyable.

We'll be here until late as fuck—more like early as fuck. We might be lucky to get out of here by the time the sun is coming up tomorrow, but none of us mind.

I miss the days that I could work a drip torch alongside Cal. Normally I'd be out keeping an eye on my squads, but this prescribed burn is a cinch, and I need the exhaustive manual labor of digging tonight.

Anything to keep my mind from Teddy and the conversation from the other morning. How I'd opened myself up in a way that I've never done before, to a woman that in her right mind would tell me to take a fucking hike . . .

But she hadn't. She hadn't pushed me away or rejected me like I'd thought she would. No, this woman had simply kissed me back, so gently, just a whisper of our lips against the other's, and then she'd said, "I don't think I want to fight this anymore either, Xander."

Before either of us could say anything else though, Bea's little cries had come through the baby monitor sitting on my coffee table, the lights flashing from green to red as her volume went up. Teddy had scrambled from my lap, straightening her shorts and blushing furiously— fuck, I love the way her skin flushes pink all over when she looks at me, when she catches me watching her—and I desperately want to see that color all over her body, with nothing between us. My need for her is ravenous, and I can't wait to be granted more of her.

I'd let her go after she picked up her coffee cup and the baby monitor, but I'd followed her to the door, sliding my hand around the front of her throat just as she'd made to escape, and I'd kissed her again. Just once. Just a mostly chaste kiss to her delectable, delicious mouth. And a promise to see her later, to which she'd nodded.

XANDER

Going more than twenty-four hours without laying eyes on her is akin to torture, and I'm not too proud to admit that the thought of leaving her to come out for this fire assignment *really fucking sucked*.

I'm not getting any younger. I may not be entirely past my prime, but I can admit that my body is slowing. Not by much, but I can tell the difference. My joints ache, my back is stiff most mornings, I've got more fucking gray hairs threading through my hair and beard than I'd like . . . and all I have to show for almost forty-three years on this Earth is a hand-me-down house with furniture that is all vintage from the eighties and nineties, several undoubtedly unhealthy coping mechanisms for grief, and a career that's kept me from having that white picket fence and a family.

Which I was fine with, I remind myself as I slice my Pulaski through the foliage and dirt, ripping up a line. The ache in my muscles is a welcome relief. Sweat beads and slides down my forehead and cheeks as I push harder, losing myself in the work. I never wanted a family. I didn't need it. I didn't need anything but this, day in and day out, and my crew. My friends, my brothers, this family I've found along the way.

Straightening, I heave out a breath and glance around. The low-lying fire is spreading slowly, just like we want it to, burning up all the dead and dry foliage, turning all this green to black that will protect the area and allow new growth to come through in the spring.

It's something to see, truly moving and almost magical, the way the earth breathes new life into itself after decimating everything. I've traveled to old wildfire sites years after the burn, and I'm always awed at what I see. New green, young trees sprouting from the ashes and thick, healthy foliage coming back strong even after so much devastation.

"She's a beaut," Cal pants as he steps up beside me, his drip torch hung low at his side and the flame extinguished. We watch our guys as they work the low blaze up a slow rolling hill, to where King has directed a dozer to push the line about a half mile away surrounding the entire property. The reds, oranges, and yellows of the flames are brilliant in the darkness. Truly a sight to behold.

"That she is," I agree. There's never been a sight that I've loved more than a blaze eating up a hillside. That is, until now.

Until Teddy.

God, I can't wait to get home. To see her tomorrow. For the first time in my entire life, I'm dreading waking up alone. For the first time in my almost forty-three years, I want nothing more than to wake up next to a woman after having fallen asleep next to her. No, not just a woman. *My* woman.

My fucking woman. Teddy. I want to go to sleep every single night and wake up every goddamn morning next to *Teddy*.

She may not be mine yet, but I have every intention of making sure that is exactly where we end up.

I clap Cal on the back and grin over at him. "Let's burn this bitch so we can go home."

"Fuck yeah," Cal grunts on a chuckle, and then we dig into the line.

Because I have somewhere to be in the morning.

XANDER

29

Teddy

"Oh thank god," I mumble as I open the door, letting both Violette and Scottie in. I'm bouncing Bea in one arm, keeping my four-month-old moving. She's cranky tonight and doesn't want to be put down.

Hollie says a quiet hello and then beelines for Penny's room. Over Scottie's shoulder as she stops on the patio, I spot Dalton in the front yard playing catch with Xander, and when Cal and Rowan step into the middle of the yard, Dalton's face lights up like Rockefeller Center at Christmas. That barbed-wire-guarded, concrete-slab fortress built around my heart crumbles a little more. *Dammit*, I'm so screwed.

Scottie looks over her shoulder at what's caught my attention, then turns back and grins widely. "Oh, so you've got it *bad*-bad, huh?"

"*Shut up!*" I whisper-hiss, shooing them both inside so I can close the door. I lean against it, my body sagging, Bea facing outward where I have her clutched to my chest. They both laugh their asses off at me, and I try to give them my best glare, but I know it falls flat. "*Bad-bad* isn't even close. This is catastrophic. It's a calamity.

A disaster in the form of one sexy-as-hell neighbor *slash* my older brother's boss and best friend. *What is wrong with me?*"

"Ummm . . . I brought wine!" Vi giggles, holding up not one but two bottles of wine by the necks like she's showing off a prize fish catch.

I can't help but laugh at her attempt to curb my rising panic.

We make our way into the kitchen, where Violette makes herself at home by uncorking the first bottle of wine while I grab two stemless wineglasses and a crystal tumbler for Scottie's whiskey from an overhead cabinet. These girls' nights have become a weekly ritual, and I live for these few hours of adult girl time, even if that means we're still fielding a barrage of *Mom!* from all directions and I'm sporting an ornery infant as a body accessory.

"Okay, so please explain to me—*in extreme detail*—why that absolute moony expression on your face is such a calamity. Because from where I'm sitting, it looks like a damn good problem to have"— Scottie chuckles, pouring herself out a couple inches of the whiskey she brought and taking a sip—"and I know that that hunk of man out there gets the same dopey look whenever he talks about you."

I'm swaying in one spot, twisting my body this way and that to keep Bea moving. She's tired but won't go down for her nap, and she's been a terror all day because of it. I almost canceled on the girls tonight—because who wants to listen to a fussy baby while hanging out with your friends—but I'd needed them too badly. I have to talk this thing with Xander out or I'm liable to combust.

Vi reaches for Bea and I sag with relief at the momentary reprieve.

"Thank you," I whisper, taking a drink of my wine while I have two free hands.

"Okay, so I'm still waiting for this explanation," Scottie grumbles, pulling herself up to sit cross-legged on top of my counter. I narrow my eyes at her. If Penny sees her sitting on the counter . . .

"I'm a single mom."

TEDDY

"*You are?!*" she exclaims, feigning shock.

I roll my eyes at her and she laughs.

Pointing out the window, she mutters, "Doesn't seem to be an issue anymore. Next."

"I'm a widow. It hasn't even been a year since my husband died," I say, taking another gulp of my wine. Liquid courage.

"There's no timeline on grief or how you choose to live your life," Scottie counters. "And if anyone has a problem with that, send them my way."

Violette nods, swaying with Bea cradled in both of her arms. "Healing isn't linear, Teddy. There will be good days and there will still be really hard days too. He seems to want to be here for both."

"He's a hotshot," I whisper, letting my shoulders sag a little more.

Scottie and Vi look at each other and then back to me, and Scottie says, "Yeah? And? So are Cal and Rowan."

I wave my hand between them and sigh sadly. "But you're both so much stronger than I am. How do you do it? How do you let them leave knowing they're walking into *a wildfire*? I mean I know Cal has been a hotshot for as long as I can remember, like since I was a teenager, but it's . . . I don't know. This *feels different*. The worry I feel for Cal is so vastly different than the worry that I feel for Xander now . . ." I glance between them, my shoulders sagging. "Doesn't that terrify you?"

"Of course it does," Vi says softly, still rocking with Bea. "And the fear you have for Cal is *going* to be different than the kind you feel for Xander." She shrugs. "I used to worry about my dad every time he was gone. I would do obsessive things when he would leave: eat his favorite dinner the first night he was gone, place his slippers in a certain spot beside his bed. He always came home."

I nod, taking a deep breath.

"When Jacob joined the crew, I did the same things. And then he died," she continues softly, still swaying with Bea. She looks down at my daughter, then presses her cheek to the top of Bea's head. Raising her eyes to mine, she says quietly, "I realized we never really have control over what happens. We just have to appreciate the moments we have and hope they walk back through that door to us. I have to believe that Rowan is always going to come back. I can't let myself think otherwise, or I would be a mess."

Tears sting my eyes. "But I already am a mess and we're not even *a thing* yet," I whisper miserably. "I already lost the love of my life and it nearly killed me. I don't want to do that again. What if I can't handle it? What if I'm not strong enough?"

"Just so you know," Vi says, bouncing Bea in her arms still, "you are without a doubt the strongest woman I know. You lost your husband; you had a baby—*an emergency home birth with no medication*, mind you—and you're raising three amazing kids. You're doing it by yourself *and* you're fucking killing it, Teddy. You're like an OG badass."

I laugh, then swipe at the tears that have pooled in my eyes and are threatening to spill down my cheeks.

"Teddy, if I told your brother to quit, he would turn in his resignation today, but fighting fire is what makes him feel alive, and taking that away from him would be losing a part of who he is. And maybe it's because I haven't lost like you have, but . . . I couldn't do that to him. It wouldn't be fair to ask him to quit to make me happy," Scottie says gently.

I take a shuddering breath in and blink away more tears.

"Cal's smart, I trust him to come home to me when he's done. Therapy helps. Actually, we're both in therapy for different reasons. It doesn't always make it easier, but you'll drive yourself crazy if you don't have an outlet. Weren't you doing grief counseling before you had Bea?"

I nod while Vi bounces Bea gently. "Yes, I was, but it's so exhausting trying to find a babysitter for the kids so I can drive over. I mean it's not that far, but it's a solid two, two-and-a-half-hour venture having to drive back to Cedar Valley—"

"*Moooom!*" Penny screeches as she and Hollie come barreling out of her bedroom.

Scottie hastily hops off the counter as Penny rounds the corner, and I can't help the snort that escapes me.

Penny's loud shriek sends Bea into a fit, and she starts crying loudly, so I take her from Vi and try to soothe her, rocking her close. Her little face is scrunched up. She's so tired; if only she would go down for her nap.

"Penny," I sigh, looking down at my four-year-old, her brown eyes wide. "I know I've asked you not to scream like that, especially in the house—"

The front door opens and I glance over as Xander steps inside, his intense gaze zeroing in on me and Bea and the contrite-looking Penny standing in front of me. He steps over toward me, his eyes slicing over to the other two women, nodding in acknowledgment.

Dropping into a crouch in front of Penny, he turns her toward him, then winks over at Hollie too. "Why don't you girls come outside with us? We're playing catch with Dalton, and I think it would be even more fun if you two came out to play with us too. I'm sure Uncle Cal would love to have you come outside. What do you think?"

Penny is jumping in place, excitement leaving her body through wiggles. "Let's go, Hollie!"

"Shoes!" I call to her as she and Hollie race for the door. They slip their shoes on and race out the door, leaving Xander in their dust. Through the door we can see Hollie as she crashes into Rowan's legs, and then he sweeps her up into the air over his head, making her laugh out loud.

I'm still bouncing Bea in my arms as Xander pushes his hands on his knees to stand, rising until he stands directly in front of me and I'm forced to look up into his face. I can feel Vi and Scottie's eyes on us and I blush hard.

"Let me help you, Mama," he murmurs quietly, reaching for my squalling infant. My eyes bounce between his before I nod and let him take her from me.

There's something about this man that causes the women in my family to just swoon over him, and my four-month-old isn't immune to his charms either, apparently, as she stops fussing almost immediately. She nuzzles into his chest, his large hands looking even more impressive spanned across my infant's back and cupping her diapered bottom. She yawns broadly and I can't help the half-hearted scowl that I send her way, the little traitor.

"Ooooh, Xander has the magic baby touch," Vi teases from where she's standing at the counter, her glass of wine suspended in one hand. She winks.

He rubs Bea's back soothingly, his bearded jaw resting against the top of her head as he stares down at me, those eyes of his so hot I feel like I'm overheating from the inside out. My belly does flip-flops and cartwheels and handstands. Those butterflies in my stomach have a whole-ass gymnastics routine, it seems.

Then, surprising me even further, he dips his head and presses a kiss to the corner of my mouth. I forget how to breathe normally.

"I've got her, Mama," he whispers against my skin, making me shiver, before he leans away and addresses Scottie and Violette. "We'll be outside. Enjoy your wine, ladies."

And then he's heading back out the front door, closing it behind him. We can hear the kids laughing and playing and the deeper timbre of the men's voices through the opened windows.

"Dear Lord, did your ovaries just explode? Because that was like *top-tier*-level dad hotness," Vi laughs, fanning herself.

I blush scarlet and cover my cheeks with my palms.

"Good for Xander."

TEDDY

I laugh out loud, stunned and embarrassed and possibly a little manic. "You guys. I can't with this man."

"I see what you mean when he calls you 'mama'. *That's hot*," Vi says, and winks again.

Scottie laughs.

"Ugh, it just does something to me"—I whine, using my hands to gesture to my middle-ish area—"down here."

"That would be your ovaries saying, *come to mama*," Violette sing-songs on a laugh as she does a little shimmy-shake, and I can't help the awkward-as-hell snorting laugh that escapes me. Good God, the things these women say.

"Oh God, no," I laugh, shaking my head and waving my hands across my body in a giant *X*. "Absolutely not. I'm barely four months postpartum from my last baby. And that's skipping like, a hundred steps, Vi. We haven't even had sex."

"But you want to."

I glare over at Scottie, who is once again perched on the counter-top, grinning as she swirls the whiskey in her glass. I groan and let my head fall back so that I'm staring at the ceiling before I nod pathetically. "God, so bad."

"Get some, Mama," Scottie chuckles, winking. "I'll even make sure to distract Cal—"

"Oh God, stop," I moan, clapping my hands over my ears. "I don't want to hear about any of the kinky shit you do with my brother."

Scottie laughs out loud, her eyes twinkling with mischief. "It's no fun if it's not kinky."

I groan, dropping my head back to stare at the ceiling again. "I need more wine for this conversation."

Vi holds up the bottle with a wide grin. "You know Daddy-Xander has got some kinks hidden up those sleeves of his. I can't wait to hear about it."

"What sleeves?" Scottie chortles, tipping back her whiskey before pouring out another couple inches. "He's always in cutoff shirts. He has nowhere to hide those kinks. I'll bet he's"—she ticks off on her fingers—"gonna be dominant, but like a *soft dom*. You're kinda sweet, so he's not gonna want to scare you off, but watch out, because it'll be coming. You're going to come so many times you can't breathe. He's an ass man, so you've got that going for you—"

I choke on a drink of my wine, spluttering on a half laugh, half cough. "I can't—*the what*—wait—What makes you say he's an ass man?"

She stares at me like I'm an idiot and points out the window to where the men are, muttering, "The man can barely tear his eyes off your ass whenever you're around, my dear sis. That man is obsessed with your fanny."

"And her boobs," Vi laughs, nodding at my chest.

I'm blushing ten shades of red.

"Don't forget her boobs. I already told you once, I'd motorboat the shit out of your tits."

"I cannot handle you guys," I laugh, shaking my head again. "But at least we're done talking about Scottie and Cal's sex life."

"Oh no, we're circling back to that," Vi giggles, waggling her eyebrows. "I want to know the kinky stuff. Just in case Rowan doesn't know a new trick. *Not* that he is short on any number of kinky tricks," she whispers, grinning, making me laugh and roll my eyes again. "But I'm always down to try new things."

Scottie laughs and glances out the window. "Vi, don't look now, but your man has the tiny human."

Violette moves closer to the window and groans, her body going soft.

I peek over Vi's shoulder to see that Rowan is taking a turn holding Bea, who seems to be fast asleep. He's holding her in a football hold in one arm, but he's gazing down at her adoringly.

TEDDY

"Gahh, why is that so hot?" Vi whispers with a moan. "Lord, he looks good with a baby."

He must notice us staring out the window, because his gaze lifts from Bea's face to the window. When he sees Violette, he grins, holding Bea a little closer. Pointing down to the baby asleep in his arm, he then points to himself, and then at Violette. Then the guy winks.

"Yup, that man is so getting me pregnant," Violette mutters almost wistfully. I laugh out loud.

"Better you than me," Scottie chuckles, taking another drink of her whiskey.

"You don't want kids?" I ask, glancing over at her.

"Uhh, no," she laughs, shaking her head. "For various reasons, I don't think we'll be having kids. And baby poop makes my eggs *schloop* right back up my fallopian tubes." She shudders violently, and both Vi and I laugh so hard I'm wheezing. I have to agree with her on that one. "I'm perfectly fine staying the awesomely cool Aunt Scottie."

I walk over and hug her hard. "I'm so glad my kids have you as their awesomely cool Aunt Scottie. And baby poop *is* the worst."

"How did we go from talking about orgasms to baby poop?" Scottie asks, leaning back.

"Isn't this how all friends' conversations go?" Vi teases, and I grin.

I slip one arm around Scottie and the other around Violette, hugging them both at the same time. "I love you, crazies. Thanks for being my squad."

"You're stuck with us," Scottie says, and I smile. Thank God for small miracles.

30

XANDER

Cal has Penny on his shoulders, her fingers fisted like a death grip in his hair. Hollie had wanted King's attention, so he'd handed the baby off to me so he could pick up his soon-to-be step-daughter, if he has anything to do with it. He's obsessed with Violette, and I'd be shocked if they're not engaged within the next year. He's practically chomping at the bit to marry her and give her more kids.

Bea is zonked out, happily snoozing away in the crook of my arm. I'd heard her fussing from inside, could see each of the girls taking turns trying to soothe her, and then when little miss feisty pants had screeched like a banshee inside, I'd taken the situation into my own hands.

Giving Teddy and the girls a little kid-free time is the least I can do. We're three grown men, we can handle a couple kids, right? Dalton has been a huge help too. What a kid he is. So mature, although I sometimes think I can see a hint of sadness in his brown eyes. I can only imagine how much he's missing his dad.

Cal steps up next to me, Penny's feet kicking at his chest. He gestures down at the sleeping infant in my arm. "If you're trying to win brownie points, I think it's working."

Raising one brow, I shrug. "Just trying to give them some kid-free time."

"Mm-hmm," he mutters, his tone indicating he doesn't believe a word I said. "Don't fuck this up, man. If I have to hear about how you hurt her feelings again, I'm gonna have to hit you."

"I'd expect nothing less." And it's the truth. I sigh, shifting the sleeping baby closer to my chest. She makes a little noise and I can't help the grin that cracks over my face. Fuck, she's cute.

I'm crazy about these kids. I'm crazy about their mom. Totally enamored. But I'm not ready to tell Cal that, not yet, anyway.

I had admitted as much to Teddy that morning in my apartment, but it's different coming clean about my feelings to my best friend. To her brother. The guy that's always had her back, watched out for her, and just wants what's best for her and her kids.

We both know that might not be me.

"This"—he says roughly, gesturing to the baby I'm holding, squeezing his arms around his nieces' legs, and then to his nephew in the middle of the yard—"is her world. If she's letting you into this part of her life . . . fuck, man, just be careful with her. Please."

I nod sagely. There's nothing else I can say in the moment.

"Hey, who's in charge of manning the grill?" King asks then, jogging over to us. Cal swings Penny off his shoulders, making her shriek again, startling Bea in my arms. I rock her gently until she's back to sleep, then glance over at both of them.

"Grill is around the back, I can get it lit if one of you wants to patty up the burgers." I hitch my chin toward the side of the house.

"Kids, who wants to learn how to make hamburgers with your hands?" King asks over his shoulder, to which Dalton and both girls shout yesses into the evening air. "Lead the way, Sup."

Ten minutes later, we've got all three of the big kids in the kitchen with freshly washed hands. Standing on chairs at the kitchen counter, Penny and Hollie are helping smash the burger meat into oblong-shaped patties, which King is secretly reshaping into circular disks where they can't see, and Dalton is helping Cal mix together a salad.

I've got the grill heating but with Bea still asleep in my arms, I'm learning it's quite difficult to do anything one-handed. I'm gaining a new respect for how Teddy manages to do absolutely everything and making it seem effortless in the process.

A soft knock on the slider door pulls my attention, and then I smile when all three women enter, glasses of wine or whiskey in their hands. Cal pecks a kiss on Scottie's mouth as she sidles up to him and Dalton to peek in on their progress with the salad, and Violette steps over to King and Hollie.

"You've been holding her for a while, do you want me to take her?" Teddy asks as she comes to stand in front of me, her eyes soft as she gazes at her baby in my arms. I like the look on her face. Soft and serene and relaxed. Happy.

"Nah," I murmur quietly, letting my own gaze drift over her face. Her hair looks so soft, piled into a claw clip on the back of her head, while little tendrils frame her face. Just the hint of makeup across her cheeks, which are flushed pink from the wine she's consumed. Her lashes look long and soft behind the lenses of her clear-rimmed glasses. "I got her, Mama."

"Xander," she whispers, raising her eyes to mine, and I'm drawn inescapably into her silver-gray gaze. "You have to stop saying it like that."

I grin, ducking my head closer to hers. "Like what? *Mama?*" I rasp the word the way I know makes her knees weak.

Her pupils blow wide, her mouth parting.

Goddamn, I want to kiss her.

XANDER

"Yes," she breathes almost raggedly, and I let my eyes drop to her mouth.

"Why?" I murmur. "You don't like it?"

She huffs a breathy laugh, her tongue darting out to wet her lower lip.

The sight of her tongue flicking over that bottom lip, the one that I want to nip at sharply and hear her gasp out my fucking name, makes my dick throb in my jeans.

"You know I do," she whispers, raising her eyes to mine again.

"Teddy."

"Yeah?" she asks, her voice high-pitched and breathy again. Pink tinges her cheeks. So fucking pretty.

"I'm going to kiss you," I breathe.

It's not a question. I'm warning her.

Her eyes dart to my mouth and then slowly, so fucking slowly, climb back to mine. And then she nods. "Okay . . ."

Holding her baby in one arm, I slide my free hand up until I can clasp the back of her neck in my palm, angling her head up toward mine as I drop my mouth to hers. Sipping at her lips gently, repeatedly, I finally linger, pressing until I feel her lips open beneath mine. Darting my tongue into her mouth, I taste her. Just for a moment. Just long enough to give myself a raging hard-on at the feel of her mouth and the taste of her lips.

Reluctantly, I pull away. Damn, I could kiss her forever and not get tired of it. Dragging the backs of my fingers along her cheek, I smile when she opens her eyes. That same look from earlier is on her face. Soft and serene. Happy.

It's like a drug, one I know I'm absolutely powerless against now that I've gotten a taste of it. I want to be the one that makes her happy like this.

And I'll do whatever it takes to make sure that I do just that.

31

Teddy

The guys shoved us girls out of Xander's duplex as soon as dinner was over, refusing to let us do the dishes—and who am I to argue with that?—so we'd allowed ourselves to be shooed out to enjoy the last of our wine and quiet girl time. Sitting around the little patio table out the back sliding door of my duplex, we're laughing and chatting and I'm so blissfully content it's a little disconcerting. I haven't felt like this in so long, it's almost foreign.

A citronella candle is lit on the small glass tabletop between us, the flame flickering in the light breeze that just barely stirs the evening air.

Leaning back in my chair, I sigh and close my eyes. "I should really get my kids to bed, but I'm so comfortable I don't want to get up."

Violette hums in agreement, though none of us make any move. "I know, I should be getting Hols home to bed too. But this is nice. Relaxing."

We can hear the guys talking and the kids laughing from inside Xander's house as they clean up the dinner dishes.

"It's nice to not have to do it all alone," I admit quietly, my eyes still closed, head tipped back. "Does that make me a terrible person to say that out loud?"

"Not at all," Scottie says softly, and then I feel her hand squeeze mine gently. "You've been doing all of this alone for months, Teddy. It's okay to let someone else help you. Especially if they look that hot doing it."

"Are we talking about Xander or my brother?" I ask, cracking open one eye to look at her.

She laughs, tipping her head back. "Pfft, I was talking about us," she laughs, shrugging her shoulders.

I grin, then let my eyelid drop closed again.

"Cal adores your kids, by the way."

"I would hope so," I laugh lightly, rolling the back of my head along the back of the chair. "He's the one that was begging me to give him nieces and nephews. He just likes that he can spoil them absolutely rotten and then send them back home all cracked out on sugar."

Scottie snorts a laugh, nodding. "Isn't that the truth."

We're quiet for a time, listening to the guys and kids inside. This weird, patchwork family that seems to have been stitched together at random but feels so right, somehow.

I roll the pad of my thumb over the smooth underside of my wedding band on my finger, then look down at it. Taking a deep, steadying breath in, I whisper into the fading twilight to the two women that have become like sisters to me, "Thank you for letting me be a mess, you guys. This has all been so confusing. Both in my head and my heart. Thanks for allowing me to try and talk it through without judgment."

"You're not a mess, you're a human," Vi says gently, reaching out to squeeze my hand. "And this is a judgment-free zone. You know that."

Before any of us can say anything else, an indignant cry reaches us from inside Xander's house and I sigh. "Well, that's my Mom-cue."

The slider door opens and closes next door and then Cal appears around the walled partition with a now fully awake and hangry Bea in his arms. I silently thank myself for switching to water after my second tiny glass of wine earlier.

"Okay, okay, little miss crabby pants," he mumbles, bringing her to me. "I get it, I'm your least favorite person right now."

"Only because you don't have working nipples," I laugh, teasing lightly.

His nose wrinkles and he makes a disturbed sound in the back of his throat, which makes Vi and Scottie laugh.

I take hold of her and she cries all the harder for a handful of seconds while I adjust my top in the dark. Cal averts his gaze and then a second later Bea's angry fussing cuts off abruptly as she latches on. I adjust the loose-flowing shirt over the both of us, and by some miracle, she doesn't try to shove it off her head.

Cal places his hands on Scottie's shoulders, massaging them, and she groans, tipping her head forward until her chin nearly touches her chest. He chuckles. Dusk is fully settled around us, the only light the single citronella candle that sits in the middle of the table, though it does little to break up the darkness, shrouding each of us in deep shadows.

My brother motions toward Xander's side of the townhouse, then asks, "Are you ready for them to come home for bed? Penny is sacked out on the couch."

"Probably should," I say, resting my head on the back of the chair. "Just give me a couple minutes to finish here and get her changed for the night, and then I can come get them."

"We've got it," Cal says, leaning over to squeeze my shoulder before dropping a kiss to the top of Scottie's head. He disappears around the corner.

TEDDY

"This is amazing," Vi mutters, sinking lower in her chair, her eyes closed. "I could definitely get used to them taking over kid duty."

My chest twinges with a hit of envy. She gets to go home with her man, as a family, the three of them. In an hour, I'll be alone again. Putting my kids to bed and then going to bed alone. Just like every night. Switching Bea from one side to the other, I sigh, closing my eyes. It was fun to think about while it lasted, anyway.

When she's finally had her fill, I lift her up to my shoulder and rub her back gently until her tummy settles, and then I heave to my feet. Both women follow suit, and I hug Violette with one arm and say goodbye with a promise to meet up for coffee later in the week, before they head over to Xander's. I slip inside my own house to change the baby and get her into a set of footed pj's. Carrying her with me back to the living room, I smile when Dalton comes in through the sliding door in front of Cal and Scottie. Xander has a sleeping Penny cradled in his arms.

"Tiny terror just couldn't hang with the big dogs," he chuckles, shrugging those muscular shoulders, then winks at me. "Where would you like her?"

"In her bed," I say, gesturing own the hall. Xander's heavy footfalls sound behind me as I lead the way, turning on the hall light as he enters her bedroom. "She can sleep in those clothes. If I try to change her out of them, she'll wake up and then be up all night."

He lowers her to the bed and then covers her with the comforter, tucking her in gently. I flip on the nightlight beside her bed, and then we exit her room as quietly as we can.

"Dalton, brush your teeth and head to bed, please."

He nods, turning to Cal and Scottie. Scottie ruffles his hair gently and Cal holds out his fist, which Dalton bumps with his own.

"Good night, dude," Cal and Scottie say.

"Good night, Uncle Cal, good night, Aunt Scottie." Dalton grins, then glances over at Xander, who holds out his fist too.

My chest cracks when Dalton's grin widens farther before he fist-bumps Xander.

"Good night, Xander. Thanks for showing me that trick with the bat."

"Of course. You'll be killing it next year if you keep practicing. We'll try and catch a spring game next season when Detroit comes out to play Seattle," he says, tucking his hands into his front pockets.

Ugh, my heart . . .

Dalton's brown eyes go wide and they bounce between Xander's and mine in awe. "Seriously? That would be so cool!"

Xander grins, shrugging. "As long as it's okay with your mom, sure. Maybe your uncle can come with us."

Dalton does a jump and punches his fist into the air in excitement. "Yeah, Uncle Cal! Come with us!"

"Let's just get through fall and winter before we start worrying about spring sports," I laugh, laying my arm across my son's shoulder and squeezing. "All right, big man, it's really time for bed." He squeezes me around the middle before skipping down the hallway to the bathroom. I roll my eyes and glance between Xander and Cal. "You don't know what you just started."

Both men chuckle. Bea is wide awake now and much happier than before, but I'm already regretting allowing her to nap as long as I did. She'll be up for hours now. She's waving her little arms like crazy at Cal.

"Oh, *now* you're happy to see me," he mutters sourly, though his eyes twinkle as he takes her out of my arm.

Dalton pops his head out of the hallway. "Good night, everybody. Good night, Mom."

"Good night, bud, I love you," I murmur, smiling over at him. He waves, and then his door closes. I turn back to Xander, Cal, and Scottie. Scottie leans in for a quick hug, then I slip one arm around

Cal's waist, hugging him too. He squeezes me gently. "Good night, you guys. Thanks for coming over."

"Coffee with Vi later this week?" Scottie asks, and I nod with a smile before leading them to the front door.

"Good night, you guys!"

Cal finally hands Bea back as we reach the door after giving her a dozen kisses to each cheek. The big softie is wrapped around her tiny finger. "See you soon, sis," he says, leaning down to whisper, "I can kick his ass if you want."

"That's not necessary," I whisper back, rolling my eyes. Squeezing his bicep, I murmur, "Love you."

"Ditto."

Xander exits with them, turning to give me one last look.

"Thanks again for tonight. Good night, Xander."

"Good night, Teddy." His voice wraps around my middle, making my fingers tremble where I'm clutching the edge of the door. Those eyes are laser-focused on my face.

I'm too chicken to ask for a kiss in front of my brother and Scottie, so I just smile and then close the door. I blow out a long exhale, puffing out my cheeks as I sag against the closed door. I can hear their murmured words beyond the door, but the sound fades as they walk away.

Glancing down at my infant, I murmur, "Come on, chicklet, it's time for Mom to get ready for bed too."

Taking Bea with me, I get her situated in her bouncy seat on the floor in the bathroom as I wash my face, brush my teeth, then change out of my clothes and into a pair of matching boy-short underwear, along with my favorite nursing bralette. Pulling my robe on, I tie it at my waist and then we settle into bed. I read on my Kindle while she nurses one more time, and then she's out like a light. Carrying her into the room she shares with Penny, I lay her down as gently as I can, and sneak back out of the room. With a sigh of relief, I pad to the kitchen.

A light tap on the sliding patio door turns my head with a startled gasp. On the other side of the glass, Xander stands in the darkness beyond, but the light from the lamp across the room highlights his features. He holds up one hand, a little pink puppy attached to a pacifier suspended there.

I roll my eyes and smile, heading over to the door. Pulling it open, I laugh. "This damn puppy. I swear we lose it at least once a day."

"I'm just glad I spotted it," he chuckles, handing Bea's comfort item over to me.

"Thank you for tonight," I murmur quietly. "You didn't have to do all that, but I appreciate it nonetheless."

Leaning one shoulder against the doorjamb, he folds his arms over his chest, and I'm acutely aware of the way his eyes travel over my face, then lower, before climbing back up to mine. I swallow hard, my fingers shaking slightly as I clutch the pink stuffy between my hands.

"I had a good time," he says quietly, that deep, husky timbre of his voice sending the butterflies in my belly to fluttering like crazy. "Your kids are great, Teddy. You've done such an amazing job with them."

"Thanks for, uh, for offering to take Dalton to a game," I murmur, wringing the plushy between my fingers. I try to smile, but it's wobbly. "Logan was supposed to take him this year, but . . ." I shake my head, forcing the smile back on my face. "I understand your schedule is crazy, but I appreciate you offering, even if it doesn't happen—"

"Why wouldn't it happen?" he asks, those dark brows pulling low over his eyes.

I stand a little straighter, taken off guard by the sharpness in his tone.

TEDDY

"I just meant—it's still a long way out, Xander," I whisper, worrying my bottom lip with my teeth. "That's seven, eight months from now."

"And?" he asks, shifting his feet, though his arms are still crossed over his chest. The muscles in his upper arms are bunched and I can't help but wish I could drag my fingers along those deeply tanned muscles.

"Xander," I laugh hesitantly, blowing out a sigh.

"I'm crazy about you," he continues. "That means every part of you, Mama, and your kids are a part of you. It might have to happen before the fire season starts, but we'll go to a game. I keep my word."

"Oh," I whisper, the word escaping me in a puff of breath.

One corner of his mouth tilts up in a smirk.

"*Oh*," he repeats, eyes twinkling. Pushing away from the doorjamb, he takes a step toward me, forcing me to look up into his face as he draws near. His hands bracket the sides of my face, his thumbs stroking along my cheeks.

I'm trembling, shaking where I stand.

"I told you I'm tired of fighting this, Teddy. I tried to. *Goddamn, I tried*," he breathes, shaking his head. "I know you deserve so much more, but I'd like to try to give you the world, beautiful. If you'll let me."

32

XANDER

Reaching behind me, I slide the patio door closed. Her pupils are blown wide, those pretty pink lips parted. Goddamn, she's so fucking pretty like this. And that damn robe that lets me see just enough to drive me fucking wild imagining her body beneath it.

Palm flat, I slip my hand along her hip and around to her back, applying pressure and urging her closer. Until every inch of this glorious body is pressed flush against mine, all of her softness to my hardness. She gasps sharply, her eyes going wide. Stroking my thumb along her full lower lip, I groan and dip my head, taking her mouth with my own.

Fucking Christ. The way I want this woman . . . no, the way I *need* this woman. It consumes me. Every part of me craves her in a way I can't explain.

Her arms twine around my neck, pulling me closer, and I'm fucking done for. I grab handfuls of her ass in my palms, squeezing tightly, kneading, stroking. I want my hands on her bare skin.

We kiss until we're breathless, panting into the semidarkness of the room that surrounds us. One dim lamp is on across the room and the light over the stove is on too. But the rest of the room is shrouded in shadows, including us.

Turning her so that she's facing away from me, I lower my hands to the tie at her waist and slowly loosen the knot. I give her plenty of time to stop me if she wants to, but she doesn't. Her chest is rising and falling rapidly, her back pressed tight to my chest. My heart is hammering wildly beneath my ribs and my cock is so hard I ache with my need for her. Spreading the thin robe wide, I cup her breasts in my palms, squeezing and kneading, then pinching her nipples between my fingers. Her back arches as she lets out a soft cry.

"Shhh," I whisper raggedly, raising one hand to her mouth and covering it lightly. I chuckle against the skin of her neck, where I plant my mouth. "You're going to have to be quiet, Teddy."

She nods against my hand, and I lower it, sliding my hands along the bare skin of her waist between her underwear and bra.

"Fuck, you're so soft," I groan, squeezing my fingers around her waist, the pads of my fingers digging into the soft flesh of her middle. Grinding my hips against her ass, I relish the quiet gasp as she feels how hard I am against her. "Goddamn, Teddy. You drive me crazy, sweetheart. Can I touch you?" I slide my right hand lower, to the band of her underwear. My fingers tease the elastic. "Can I make you come?"

She nods desperately against my chest, her head twisting so she can reach for my mouth with hers. Such a greedy thing.

Sliding my hand beneath the band of her panties, I sink my teeth into her bottom lip when my fingers encounter what I've been fucking dreaming about. I tease my fingertips along her lips, circle her clit lightly. She cries out against my mouth and I grin darkly. My beautiful little Teddy is loud. This is going to be fun.

Sinking first one finger inside, I pant against her mouth. "Fuck, Teddy, you're so wet. Is this all for me, Mama?"

"Yes," she cries on a breath, her eyes hazy and heavy lidded as she stares up at me. "Yes, Xander."

Pushing a second finger deep, she whimpers and her knees shake. I band my other arm around her waist, holding her steady as I pump my fingers inside her hot channel, her inner muscles clenching around me. Goddamn, she's fucking perfect. I push deep, flicking my fingers over her G-spot, and she shudders against me, a sharp cry escaping her. Naughty thing.

"Shhh," I breathe against her temple, my eyes flicking to the hallway and the closed doors beyond it. I slide my hand up from her middle to cover her mouth lightly, but the fingers of my other hand never cease. I'm so hard it hurts, and I'm sure I'm leaking in my boxer briefs. The walls of her pussy are squeezing my fingers, little fluttering convulsions that tell me she's close, and when she goes over, it's going to be hard. She pants through her nose, her body curving in on itself as I draw her closer against my chest, and I can feel her heart hammering through her back. Fuck, I want to feel her come on my fingers, my tongue, my dick. "I'm going to make you come, Teddy, but you need to be quiet, beautiful. Can you do that for me? Or do I need to keep my hand here?"

She nods against my hand, then shakes it, mumbling something unintelligible. I grin against her temple before ducking my head and pressing my open mouth to the curve of her neck, where it meets with her shoulder. I pump my fingers inside her, flicking the pad of my middle finger on that spot, and then her body bows in on itself again as she detonates on my hand. Her knees start to buckle and I tighten my arms around her, holding her up against me, my hand still clamped over her mouth as she lets loose a raw cry of pleasure.

The muffled sound is nearly my undoing; I will remember the sound of her coming for the rest of my days. Her inner walls are pulsing, squeezing my fingers so tightly I groan against her neck. Fucking hell, she feels so good.

XANDER

"Such a good girl," I breathe against the skin of her neck, continuing to pump my fingers inside her, slow and deep, drawing out her orgasm and prolonging it. She shudders against my chest, her own chest heaving. I release her mouth when I'm sure she's done being loud—God forbid one of her kids wakes up and walk in on *this*—and she pants raggedly into the fragile darkness of the room that surrounds us.

I can smell her, feel her drenching my hand that's still stuffed inside her panties and lazily stroking inside her. I'm hard as stone pressed against the soft roundness of her ass and she grinds back against me. I bite down on her neck, scraping my teeth against her skin, and she gasps sharply, her walls tightening around my fingers in reaction. I growl against her neck. "Fuck. *Teddy.*"

I pull my fingers out of her, and she watches, her eyes impossibly wide, as I bring those fingers to my mouth and suck. Her taste is like heaven and hell all rolled into one. I want to taste her from the source.

Dropping my other hand from her mouth, I collar her throat with my palm, holding her against me as I kiss her like a man possessed.

"Xander," she pants raggedly. "Fuck me. Please."

I've waited years to have this woman, and I have her in my arms, begging for me. How am I supposed to tell her no when she asks so nicely?

"Bedroom," I rasp against her mouth. "I want you naked on the bed with these thighs spread open for me so I can eat this pretty pink pussy. Can you do that for me, Mama?"

33

Teddy

I can't believe I'm doing this.

I can't believe how hard I just came on this man's fingers. My brain is still half addled, I think. As we make our way down the darkened hallway, nerves take hold of me, though I'm not sure if the trembling is from nerves or the intensity of that orgasm.

As soon as the door to my bedroom closes behind us, his hands are on me again. Touching and gripping everywhere, like he can't get enough of the feel of me beneath his hands. My robe is shoved off my shoulders, letting it pool around my feet, then he's flicking the front clasp of my bralette open and shoving the straps down my arms.

His mouth falls open as my breasts spill out of the bra, and then he breathes, "Fuck, Teddy. You're so fucking pretty."

Kneeling in front of me, he drags my panties down my thighs and I place my hands on his shoulders for balance as he helps me step out of them. Until I'm completely naked in front of him. His mouth presses into my stomach and I squeeze my eyes shut tight, embarrassment heating my skin.

His hand cracks down on one of my ass cheeks in a sharp slap, making me gasp, my eyes flying open to stare down at him where he's still kneeling in front of me. The sight of him on his knees in front of me is thrilling, he's so darkly handsome.

His voice is raspy as he demands, "Get out of your head, Mama. Tonight, all you're allowed to think about is how amazing we feel together. Got it? How many times can you come before you're begging for mercy, Teddy?"

He stands, pushing his hands into my hair and angling my head up so he can crush his mouth to mine, kissing me thoroughly, until I'm a melted mess of a puddle in his hands.

"Get on that bed. Spread these thighs for me and let me see what I've been dying to taste."

I stare up at him, dumbfounded at the filthy words, a nervous laugh escaping me, but I do as instructed.

Reaching up, his shirt is pulled over his head to be tossed aside, and I'm afforded an unrestricted view of his chest, abdomen, and shoulders. I watch as his strong fingers work quickly at his jeans, shoving them down his thighs, until he's in nothing but a pair of tight, sharply tented black boxer briefs. I can't wait to see him. His thighs are long and thickly muscled, dusted with dark hair, though I can't see as much as I'd like to with the lights off. The moon is filtering through the window, highlighting us in a faint silver glow. He looks dark and dangerous standing at the foot of my bed, naked except for the black underwear, one hand gripping his cock beneath the fabric.

I'm naked on the bed, just like he asked, and I'm grateful for the darkness. I know my body is soft and round in all the places I wish it wasn't, and I'm glad that at least for this first time—assuming there will be more of this to come—some of my imperfections are somewhat shadowed.

"Please, go slow," I whisper then, my words barely a breath in the dark, nervousness making my throat tight. He kneels on the bed, lowering his beautiful, strong body over mine until he's pressed fully against me. His brow furrows with worry as he cups my cheek. "It's just . . . been a long time, Xander. And obviously not since Bea was born . . . Sometimes it can be a little painful, at-at first . . ."

His brow smooths out and then he's ducking his head and kissing me fiercely.

I moan, fisting his hair in my hands, and then his mouth is moving down my neck. He presses kisses to my throat, and I can feel his lips moving as he speaks. "Then I guess I just need to do my job and make sure it's not."

"It's okay, it's normal," I assure him, but he shakes his head.

"I would never forgive myself if I caused you any pain, Teddy. Let me get you ready for me, please," he rasps against my skin.

I shiver, digging my fingers into his hair and holding him to me.

His mouth is moving lower again and I tug on his hair between my fingers, pulling his mouth up before his lips close over the tips of my breasts. I let go of his hair once he's looking at me, sliding my hands down to cover my breasts. "Xander . . ."

"Why can't I taste these, Teddy?" he asks, swiping his lips over the backs of my fingers.

A bewildered, terrified laugh bubbles out of me. "B-because."

His gaze is heated as he stares up my body at me, his lips still trailing over the back of my hand that's covering my left breast. His beard tickles the back of my hand. "Because why? You let me before. That night. Sitting in that chair outside. You let me taste you through your shirt, and then you let me put my mouth on them too. Why not now?"

I sigh brokenly. I'm terrified of what will happen if he plays with my nipples again. I leaked through my tank top after the last time, and I'll die of shame if it happens again.

"I know . . . but . . . I don't want you to be—" Squeezing my eyes shut, I groan when he lifts my left hand away from my body. His tongue is there then, circling my nipple, before his lips close over it. "Oh shit."

The sensation zaps all the way to the center of me. Logan never played with my nipples after I had Dalton. He always said it was weird, and I hadn't pushed him about it. But God, I've missed this.

His deep, tortured groan rumbles up through his chest and I can feel it around my nipple as he sucks it, laves it with his tongue, effectively cutting off my anxious thoughts. It's impossible to focus on anything else as his hand moves my other hand away, and his fingertips pluck at my other breast. My back arches off the bed and an agonized moan leaves my throat as my fingers dive back into his hair, holding his head to me.

"I can't tell you how often I've thought about this," he groans around the bud in his mouth.

"Seriously?" I ask, laughing, then groan again when he flicks his tongue rapidly.

He raises his head and those eyes pierce mine. "We will circle back to this conversation later, beautiful, but right now, I want to enjoy every delicious part of my meal. This is just the appetizer." One of his hands slides down my body and parts my thighs, his fingers finding my aching center like a magnet. Two fingers slide deep and my back arches off the bed, my eyes rolling into the back of my head as he flicks those fingers deep. "This is my entrée, pretty girl. And I intend to feast. I didn't get nearly enough of a taste earlier."

"Holy shit," I breathe raggedly, sinking my fingers back into his hair, holding on tight as he flicks his tongue over my left nipple again and again at the same time his fingers are doing wonderful, magical things inside me.

"Goddamn," he groans, lifting his head and switching to my other breast, giving it the same adoring attention as the first before he slides down my body.

I squeeze my eyes shut, too embarrassed to watch as he sinks to his knees on the floor at the edge of the bed, slinging my thighs over his shoulders. And then his mouth is right there, tongue darting out to lap at my clit in quick, rapid flicks before settling in to devour me whole.

My entire body is shaking. It feels so good, his fingers inside me, his tongue and lips and teeth on my clit. I open my eyes just to find him watching me from between my thighs. The sight is so filthy and erotic, I moan out his name.

"Fuck, you taste so fucking good," he groans low, leaning away to sink his teeth into the softness of my inner thigh.

I gasp sharply at the spasm that rockets through my core at the shock of pain.

He growls in approval, kissing the hurt gently. His eyes are on me as he rasps, "Are you going to come on my fingers, Teddy? I can feel it—"

He fucks me with his fingers, flicking with each deep thrust until I'm a writhing, panting mess as he replaces his mouth on my oversensitive clit, and then I'm coming. My legs shake where they're slung over his shoulders and my body curls up on itself, my abs contracting almost painfully with the intensity of my orgasm. One hand fists in his hair, the other clamping down on the bed sheet next to me as I try not to scream.

"Shhh," he groans from between my thighs as I sob brokenly, still shaking uncontrollably. "*God*, Teddy. You come so good for me. You soaked my hand; what a good fucking girl you are."

Embarrassment flushes my skin, making me hot all over as I come down from that high. "Ohmygod."

His fingers slide out of me and I gasp loudly when he flattens his tongue and drags it along my pussy before sinking inside. He groans gutturally, his arms wrapping around the thickest part of my thighs to hold me to him. The man said he wanted to feast, and he does.

TEDDY

Good God, am I happy to be his meal. Especially when he makes me come harder than I've ever come before.

"Mm-hmm," he hums against me. Leaning away for a half a heartbeat, he demands, "Come on my face. I want to feel this pussy come on my tongue, Teddy."

There's no denying the man what he wants. I couldn't if I tried. I come again, shattering with a muffled cry aimed at the ceiling as he wrings every drop of pleasure out of me like I'm the most delicious thing he's ever tasted.

I'm incoherent at this point. I'm dotted with sweat, the back of my head is thrashing on the bedsheets beneath me, and all I can manage to say is, "Ohmygod, ohmygod."

He lifts my hips up off the bed, shoving a pillow beneath my ass, and then he's kneeling between my thighs, rising up like a dark statue. God, this man is so pretty to look at. And damn, he's gloriously naked. I get my first look at his cock, hard and long and so much bigger than I'd expected.

Pressing two fingers deep inside me again, he stretches his fingers wide and I whimper, aftershocks still fluttering through me. "Are you ready for me, Mama?" he asks from above me. His other hand grips his cock in his fist, pumping slowly.

My mouth goes dry. I nod. "I can put a condom on, Teddy, but I'd really love to feel this bare pussy around my cock. I've never gone bare with anyone else before."

"I've never been with anyone else," I whisper, licking my lips. "Only ever . . ."

He nods, and I don't finish the sentence. I don't want to speak his name right now. Not in this moment with Xander.

"We don't have to do this, Teddy," he whispers through the dark, his voice low and pained but so understanding.

"I want you," I breathe, reaching for him. "I want you, Xander. Please. Fuck me bare. I want to feel all of you."

He drags the head of his cock along my lips, soaking himself in my wetness. Notching himself at my entrance, he pushes forward, just a little. Bracing one hand against the bed next to me, he lowers his upper body until he can capture my mouth with his in a searing kiss.

"Tell me to stop if it's too much, Teddy," he murmurs.

I nod frantically, my hands scrabbling at his waist as he rocks his hips against mine, sinking a little farther inside.

My mouth drops open on a quiet whine, the stretch more than I expected. His other hand curves around the back of my neck, angling my mouth against his. I'm lost in the kiss, the taste of him, the feeling of being so incredibly full.

"Goddamn, Teddy, tell me this is okay," he rasps against my lips. "You're so tight, sweetheart. Am I hurting you—"

"No, no, no," I chant, smoothing my hands over his back. "Xander—"

"Say it again," he groans, rolling his forehead against mine.

My eyes are locked on his. We're connected from head to toe, but more than that, I can feel his heart beating so close to my own. "*Xander*," I whisper, my lips dragging against his as he pushes the rest of the way inside. Our mutual groans of pleasure echo around the quiet room. I flit my fingers along his bearded jaw, before drawing his mouth back to mine. The rise of my hips propped up on the pillow allows him a deeper angle, making me tremble beneath him. "Ohmygod."

Pushing himself up, Xander kneels between my thighs, then drapes my thighs over his. Smoothing his palms over every inch of me he can reach, he finally settles his hands on the curve of my waist where my hips flare out, fingers digging in sharply. Pulling out slowly, he sinks back in, repeating the move several times. The slow, deep thrusts allow my body time to adjust to his intrusion and drive me crazy with each one.

TEDDY

My eyes are caught on his; I can't look away. His fingers tighten around my waist, his hands trembling lightly.

"Fuck, you feel amazing. So fucking tight. Like you were made for me, Teddy."

His dark, whispered words send flutters through me, and his mouth drops open as I squeeze around him. His thumbs dig into my stomach and then he pulls out, slamming back in hard. My tits bounce with the force of his thrust and I slap a hand over my mouth to muffle the cry that breaks free.

"Ohmygod, yes," I pant from behind my hand, my vision going hazy. "Please. Just like that—"

He does it again and then holds, pulsing inside me. He's pressing against that magical spot deep inside and I sob brokenly. Then he's moving. Deep, quick thrusts, his hard, muscular thighs bunching and shifting beneath mine as he fucks me, his hips slapping into mine fiercely. Our bodies move in unison, already attuned to the other, as if anticipating what the other needs before we can even vocalize it.

It's an intimacy I hadn't expected and it catches me off guard, making my chest tighten. Oh, but this is so much more than sex. So much more, and I know without a doubt that my heart is in very real danger of being lost to this man. The way he is healing the broken pieces of me one by one, stitching me back together piece by piece . . .

He moves one of his hands from my hip, smoothing the flat of his palm against the lower part of my abdomen. I have only a second to allow embarrassment to rush through me before he's pressing his palm down against me, between my hip bones.

"*Oh*," I gasp sharply, my thighs shaking as an orgasm barrels down on me, the pressure of his hand on my stomach and the way he's hitting that spot deep inside combining into a maelstrom for my overstimulated body. "Oh, Xander, I'm going to—"

"Yes," he grunts, thrusting faster, harder, depressing his hand a little harder on my abdomen.

The sensation does me in.

"*Come on, Mama.* Give it to me. Fuck, please, Teddy, let me feel this pussy squeeze my cock—"

I shatter, my back arching off the bed, thighs shaking violently.

His movements slow slightly and I watch as he shudders too, his head tipping back as his mouth drops open. "Goddamn, such a good girl coming on my cock, Teddy. *Good fucking girl.*"

He rocks his hips against mine in shallow, slow thrusts. I'm seeing stars and panting like I've just run a damn marathon. The magic this man wields over me . . .

He drops onto his elbows and slides his arms beneath my shoulders, his mouth crashing into mine. This kiss is almost brutal in its ferocity, like we can't get close enough.

"Please," I pant brokenly, burying my fingers in his hair. "Please."

"Please what, beautiful?" he rasps against my mouth. "What do you need? Soft and slow?"

I shake my head and he grins against me.

"Hard and fast?"

I nod frantically, my lips dragging across his.

He nips at my lip and sucks it between his teeth, then kisses me again. "Hold on to me, Mama. Don't you fucking let go."

Clasping him close, I sob as he unleashes, pounding into me hard and deep and fast, our bodies slapping against each other. Sweat makes our bodies slick as we move together, and when I'm about to go over that edge again, he pins my throat with one hand, tipping my face up to his.

"I'm going to come, Teddy. Where do you want it?"

Delirious and seconds away from coming myself, all I can do is sob. "Don't stop," I beg raggedly.

TEDDY

"*Teddy*," he demands sharply, his fingers tightening around my throat.

My body is tightening and I can feel my orgasm building. Yes, yes, yes . . .

"Where. Do. You. Want. My. Cum?"

"On me. In me. I don't care, just don't stop!" I sob, and then I drop my forehead to his shoulder as I come again, harder than before. My entire body shakes, my inner muscles spasming around the hardness of him pressed so deep inside.

"Shhh," he groans raggedly, pushing my face into his shoulder as I come apart. I sink my teeth into his shoulder to muffle the noises that are being pulled from me as he fucks me into oblivion, and he grunts with the sting of pain but I can't help it. "Oh fuck, yes, Mama—"

He slams in again, all the way to the hilt, then holds. His body above me goes taut and then shudders, his deep groan low and guttural, and I can feel it as he comes too. His forehead drops to the mattress next to my shoulder, his lips parted as he heaves heavy, gasping breaths.

"Holy shit," I pant against the skin of his throat, kissing away the hurt. "That was . . ."

He leans up to press a kiss to my temple, then smooths my hair away from my sweat-dampened face. "I know," he whispers roughly, his touch tender. "*You are amazing*, Teddy. So fucking perfect."

Cradled in his arms with our hearts beating together, I let myself believe his words.

Because here in the darkness, in the quiet aftermath, I can admit to myself that I'm falling for Xander Macomb, and I so desperately want to believe that he is falling for me too.

34

XANDER

"Stay here," I tell Teddy, pulling out of her and climbing off the bed. I disappear into the en-suite bathroom, then find a clean washcloth and turn the water on to warm. I clean myself up, then take the warm, wet cloth back to the bedroom. Teddy has pulled the sheet up to completely cover her body, but she's unaware yet that that's just not going to fly with me. It's something we'll work on.

Tugging the sheet from near her feet, she gasps when I yank it down her body, uncovering what I'm not yet done admiring.

"What are you doing?" she whispers, her voice husky.

It sends a jolt through me, and I will my dick not to respond. Down boy.

"Taking care of you," I tell her simply before kneeling beside her on the bed. My hand drifts up her thigh, urging them to part.

Lying back against the pillows, she rolls her lips in and stares up at me, that same nervousness back in her eyes again. When she finally lets her legs fall open, I take my time cleaning her up from the mess I'd made of her.

"I didn't hurt you, did I?"

Her eyes soften then, that mouth that I could spend the rest of my life tasting tilting up at the corners. "No."

"Good," I breathe, smoothing my palm over her hip and up to her waist. I can't stop touching her. It physically pains me to stop running my fingers along every bare, soft inch of her body. She's my worst addiction, and I have no chance in hell of kicking it. Leaning down, I kiss her, slowly, deeply.

I'm a goner for this woman. Mind, body, soul. It's all hers. Even if she doesn't know it yet.

Sighing against her lips, I peck one more kiss to her mouth and then stand, rounding the bed to bend low and grab my underwear, jeans, and T-shirt.

Sitting upright in bed, she pulls the sheet back up until it covers her breasts, her eyes wide as she watches me. "Are you leaving?"

"I figured you wouldn't want me to stick around, with the kids here."

I stop what I'm doing to face her as she nods stiffly, then drops her eyes to her fingers, which are twined together in her lap. The sheet is tucked beneath her arms over her chest.

"Right. Sure," she whispers. "Will you, um, can you hand me my robe, please?"

Dammit. She's doing that shoulder-hunch thing where she curls in on herself, making herself shrink. I hate when she does this, like she doesn't understand how fucking amazing she is. I sit back on the edge of the bed, gripping her chin between my finger and thumb and force her face up so that she's looking at me again.

"Hey. Don't do that," I whisper, my gaze flitting over her face. She swallows hard and a fissure opens in my chest. I realize then what my swift departure must look like to her. Swiping my thumb over the curve of her bottom lip, I tell her, "I didn't think you would want the kids to see me here . . . but I would much rather stay here and hold you, if that's what you want. I'm not ready to let go of you yet."

Her lower lip trembles and I lean forward to kiss her gently. She nods just the slightest. "Yes, please."

"Come here," I whisper against her mouth, pulling that damn sheet away from her body again and dragging her into my lap. Sliding the fingers of one hand up through her now tousled blond waves, I curl my fingers into the strands and pull taut, limiting her range of motion. Her mouth falls open beneath mine in a soft, breathy gasp, and the sound goes straight to my dick. I sip at her lips. "I will do whatever makes you happy, Teddy. If that means sleeping in this bed holding you all night and sneaking out early as fuck so Dalton doesn't catch us, that's what I'll do."

She laughs lightly, almost hesitantly, her lips pecking at mine, like she can't fathom ending the embrace either. Her fingernails scratch lightly at my beard. It sends goosebumps down my arms.

"I'm really mad at you," she whispers, though her tone says the opposite.

I chuckle, tightening my arms around her. She feels so good in my arms. "Yeah? Why's that?" I tease.

"Because those were some of the best orgasms I've ever had," she laughs, dropping her face into the curve of my neck.

"And that's a bad thing?" I ask, laughing too.

"No," she teases quietly, "but it's going to make me want to keep you around."

Pressing a kiss to her forehead, I repeat with a whisper, "And that's a bad thing?"

Teddy inhales slowly, her rib cage expanding with the breath, then lets it out slowly, her lips trailing against the side of my neck. My heart thuds heavily in my chest. Even though she hasn't said the words, I know what she's not saying.

That she and I both know that there is a very real possibility that we are both going to want something that I can't guarantee.

XANDER

35

Teddy

Buzzing wakes me up, and I groan, reaching over to turn my alarm off.

Swiping up my phone, I glare at it, my vision blurry without my glasses, because it won't shut off. What the hell? Squinting at the brightness of my phone screen, I realize it's only 4:00 a.m. Why the hell is my alarm going off at 4:00 a.m.?

A heavy, deep sigh from behind me makes me go still, my heart pounding in my ears. Oh shit. Xander . . .

The mattress shifts beneath his weight as he rolls over to the other side and then the light of his phone screen glows as he lies back down behind me, and I realize it was Xander's phone ringing, not my alarm.

"Yeah?" is his only answer as he picks up the call. His voice is rough and husky from sleep, and he doesn't try to hide the fact that he just woke up to whoever is calling at this ungodly hour. I lower myself back to my pillow and half turn onto my back, glancing at him over my shoulder. "Oregon? How many acres? Shit. Okay."

Leaning up onto his elbow, he rolls toward me, planting a kiss to the tip of my bare shoulder. It sends my heart skittering in my chest, and those butterflies in my belly are currently at a rave. He's listening to whoever is on the other end of the phone, but his lips are dragging along the back of my bicep and my shoulder.

He nips at the tip of my shoulder, making me gasp into the darkness of the room. "I'll let the crew know. Thanks, Marty. We'll be on the road in a few hours."

My heart sinks. I don't want him to go. I like having him here, and now I have to let him leave. How do Scottie and Vi do it? I thought I'd have a few more days to come to terms with all of this before the inevitable happened. I know he has this job, I know he *loves* this job. But I'm selfish and I want him safe. Here. With me.

The call is disconnected and he tosses his phone away a second before his hand slides beneath the covers and across my naked body. Curving his arm around my waist, he pulls my back against his chest, his mouth dipping low to settle on the crook of my neck and shoulder. I sigh, settling against him, though my heart is hammering in my chest at the feel of his hard length against my ass. He grinds against me, groaning into the curve of my neck.

"I'm not going to lie, I like waking up like this," he whispers against my skin, tightening his arm around my waist. He palms my breast, squeezing lightly.

"Yeah?" I ask breathily. "Like what?"

"With you," he rasps. "Naked."

"So if I were wearing clothes, you wouldn't like it?" I tease, my voice reedy and thin as he plucks at my nipple.

"Not at all, it would just take longer to get to this—" he murmurs, sliding his hand down my body until he's cupping my pussy. He groans low, the sound rumbling against my back and in my ear. His fingers slide inside easily. My back arches and my thighs fall apart,

TEDDY

giving him better access. "You were fucking made for me, Teddy. So wet. So soft. So tight."

Rolling us until I'm flat on my stomach, he stretches out over my back, his knees digging into the mattress on either side of mine. Reaching between us, he slides his hand across the curve of my ass, then slips his fingers between my thighs. Stacking my arms beneath my head, I press my cheek to them.

"Can I fuck you like this?" he asks against my temple.

I nod, shifting my hips and then I moan as the broad, blunt head of his cock is pressing at the entrance of my pussy.

"Are you sore? I don't want to hurt you—"

"No," I whisper, turning my head so I can look at him over my shoulder. "Please, Xander. Stop treating me like I'm breakable."

"As you wish, Mama," he groans darkly just before his teeth sink into the meaty part of my shoulder.

I muffle the cry of pain into the mattress and then an ecstasy-filled moan is torn from my lips as he slams inside, all the way to the hilt. He gives me just a moment to adjust before he's hammering into me with deep, hard thrusts.

"Holy fuck, Teddy. Goddamn, you're so fucking perfect. You take my cock so good, beautiful. So fucking good."

One of his hands slides beneath me to grip the front of my throat in his palm.

As his fingers tighten just a little, I moan again at the wickedness of it all. So vastly different than anything I've ever experienced. Not to say that sex with my husband was bad, but it was nothing like this. It's so entirely consuming, and dear God the man knows what he's doing. The angle at which he's fucking me is hitting that spot that makes my legs shake and my toes curl.

"I need you to come. Soak my cock with your cum so I can paint you with mine," he rasps harshly, his hips never relenting in the pace he's set.

My fingers are fisted in the sheet beneath us. His filthy words send me over the edge.

"Xander," I pant, my voice muffled by the hand still wrapped around my throat. I'm so close.

"Yes, beautiful?" he asks, pressing his mouth to my jaw. His chest is pressed tight to my back and I can feel every ripple of muscle that bunches and strains with each of his powerful movements. He groans, low and primal.

Squeezing my eyes shut tight, I cry out, my body hurtling toward release.

"Oh fuck, I can feel you, Mama. You're doing so good, taking my cock so deep. Good girl. Good fucking girl, Teddy."

Burying my face in the mattress, I try not to scream, but the orgasm that rips through me is so intense I'm afraid I might pass out. Stars burst behind my tightly closed eyelids and then his hand disappears from my throat. Panting brokenly, I sob as my body shakes and trembles, toes curling.

Arms rigid as he holds himself over my back, his hips slap into mine once, twice more, before he stills with a groan that's more of a growl in the back of his throat. He comes in long spurts, filling me, and I shudder at the feel of him pulsing inside of me.

"Ohmygod. Ohmygod, *Xander . . .*"

Lowering until his chest is pressed to my back once more, he sucks in heaving breaths behind me, wrapping his arms around my body, sliding them beneath my chest to hold me close. His lips trail across the back of my neck, my shoulder. My face is still buried in the sheet and I'm a panting, trembling mess.

"Goddamn, Teddy. You're so perfect, sweetheart. *So fucking perfect.*"

I start to laugh, then groan, as the motion squeezes my inner walls around his length that's still buried inside me. A blush spreads across my cheeks. "I've made a mess on my sheets."

TEDDY

"I think that's a joint effort on the mess," he chuckles, then kisses the back of my neck again before sliding out of me.

I blush again.

"No, not that," I whisper, shifting onto my elbows before sitting up. I roll my lips between my teeth. Bea slept through the night and the intense orgasm triggered a letdown . . . Twin wet spots have bloomed on the sheet beneath me where my breasts had been pressed into the mattress. I groan, the ache in my breasts almost painful. I can only hope Bea wakes soon.

He chuckles lightly before dropping his gaze to my chest. Trailing his fingers down between my breasts, he then circles one nipple that's currently leaking. My face is hot with embarrassment, but the hunger and intensity in his gaze stuns me. Using his finger and thumb, he plucks at the hard bud and a growl rumbles out of his throat as droplets wet his fingers. "Goddamn, this is so fucking sexy."

I laugh hesitantly, biting my lip even as he continues to stroke my breasts, staring at me like he can't get enough.

Raising his eyes to mine, he points to the baby monitor on the other side of the bed where the night vision camera is pointed at her crib in Penny's room. "She just started wiggling. Do you want me to go get her?"

"Um, not yet," I whisper, blushing again. "I need to clean up first."

Xander hands me my robe that he'd tossed to the floor the night before, and I pull it on my arms as I slide out of the bed. I grimace lightly, squeezing my thighs together.

Stepping in front of me, he frames my face with his hands and tips my face up toward his so he can peck light, sipping kisses to my lips. "I'm probably a caveman for saying this, but I very much like the idea of my cum dripping out of you right now."

I roll my eyes, splaying my hands wide on his still bare chest. He's pulled his boxer briefs on, but that's all. He drops his hands to the curve of my ass, squeezing and kneading.

"Go get yourself cleaned up," he whispers.

I nod, blushing again, then sidestep around him and head out the bedroom door to the bathroom. By the time I'm done and washing my hands, I can hear Bea fussing lightly. I rush out of the bathroom to get to her before she wakes Penny, but I'm brought up short when Xander quietly exits Penny's room and closes the door almost silently. Bea is cradled against his chest. He smiles over at me as I come to stand in front of him, and the sight does something to my heart. Dammit, I'm in so much trouble.

"There's Mama," he whispers softly to my infant, who has now seen me and is seconds away from full meltdown mode.

I take her quickly, then shrug one shoulder of my robe down. It snags on my arm, so Xander tugs it the rest of the way down until one breast is bare. Settling Bea in the crook of my arm, her little mouth is searching, and Xander surprises me further by reaching out his hand and lifting my breast gently, guiding the nipple to Bea's waiting mouth. When she latches on, I sigh and he trails his fingertips down Bea's soft cheek almost reverently. The look of pure adoration on his face is nearly my undoing. I'm so screwed.

"Are you going to be okay while I'm gone?" he asks quietly, raising that hand to tuck a strand of hair behind my ear.

I rest my cheek in his palm and nod.

"I've never not wanted to go out for a fire call, Teddy. You're making this really fucking difficult."

My heart sinks again and I close my eyes as he strokes my cheek with his thumb. I don't know what we're doing. How either of us are going to make this work seems impossible to me. I'm trying not to sink into a panic attack at the thought of him leaving. Scottie is right: Asking him to give up something that makes him happy, something that he loves, simply because I'm a coward, isn't fair.

"I'm sorry," I whisper, opening my eyes and raising them to his.

TEDDY

"Don't apologize," he murmurs, ducking his head to kiss me. "It just means that I'm going to do everything in my power to get back here as quickly as I can. Because now I've got you here waiting for me."

36

XANDER

"So," Cal huffs from several feet away, straightening and leaning against his Pulaski, "is this thing with you and Teddy like an *actual thing*?"

Glancing over at him from where I'm hunched over digging my way through our line, I mutter, "Is this really what we need to talk about right now?"

We're in the thick of Mount Defiance near the south trailhead. A couple of novice adventure hikers had let a campfire get out of hand, spreading to the nearby forest. Lucky for us, it's a fairly small blaze, and we should be done in a couple of days. It's another easy job.

That doesn't mean I necessarily want to be having this conversation with my best friend though.

Opp, Caleb, Sam, and a few others are all farther down the trail, about fifty feet away. I glance over at them, though none of them seem to be paying us any attention.

"I'm just watching out for my sister," Cal says, his tone clipped and terse. "She's not like the women you're used to—"

"Christ, Cal," I snap, straightening and leaning against my Pulaski too. I stare over at him. "And what kind of women am I used to?"

Cal's lips thin. He swipes his safety glasses off and scrubs at his jaw, leaving a trail of soot and dirt down both sides of his face. "I just mean she's not the love-'em-and-leave-'em type."

I bark out a harsh laugh, shaking my head. "You think I don't know that?"

"I just know how you are with women—"

"You know how I *was* with women," I correct, turning back to my line and picking up my ax.

He snorts. "You've always been so goddamn vocal about not dating beyond hookups and casual flings. Forgive me if I'm concerned because—I can only assume you're now fucking my sister—and let's be fucking real here for a second, Sup. She's not really your type."

I point one finger at him, my eyes narrowing behind my own safety glasses. "I highly suggest you think real hard about the next words that come out of your mouth, Cal. Your sister is beautiful."

"I never said she isn't," he snaps, tossing his ax to the ground and bracing his feet wide on the rocky terrain we're standing on.

I sigh. Goddammit, I really don't want to fight this motherfucker. Opp stops digging and straightens, turning to face us. Fuck, now we've got an audience, though I'm not sure any of them can hear what we're saying.

"But you can't pretend that you haven't had a 'type' for the years that I've known you. And Teddy isn't it."

My blood is boiling beneath my skin and I straighten again, tossing my own ax to the ground as I spread my arms wide. "What do you want me to say, Cal? Huh? I chose women that were the opposite of her on purpose. Because then there was no fucking confusing them for who I really wanted. I've been crazy about your sister for years, man. *But she was married.* Married to the perfect fucking husband that gave her three incredible kids that I'm just as crazy about. And then he died and I know I'm not worthy of her, dammit. I'm not worthy of those kids." Blowing out a heavy exhale, I drop my arms. "I convinced myself that I didn't want a relationship because of this job, because of the way my parents' marriage failed. Because it was easier finding women that were nothing like what I wanted than having to admit to myself that I was in love with another man's wife." I suck in a sharp breath at what I'd just admitted out loud for the first time.

Cal's dark brows shoot up, his face going blank as we stare at each other. "You're in love with Teddy?"

I exhale sharply, bending low to swipe my Pulaski off the ground, keeping my eyes averted. "Yeah."

"Does she know that?" he asks, shifting his weight from one foot to the other. I can just see him out of the corner of my eye, hear the crunch of loose rocks beneath his booted feet as he moves.

I shake my head. "No. She's . . . she's not ready to hear that yet."

"Why didn't you tell me?" he asks quietly.

I bark out another harsh laugh. "Tell you what, and when, Cal? While she was happily married? You'd have kicked my ass. After her husband died? Yeah, hard no. While she was in labor? Fuck, I'd have kicked my own ass."

He snorts a laugh, nodding. "I guess you're right." Bending low, he picks up his ax, twisting it between his gloved hands. "What are you going to do?"

"Fuck if I know," I mutter, digging in again. "She's still messed up over Logan's death, and I don't blame her. She shouldn't be with someone that heads out and puts themselves in danger for a fucking living. She deserves to have someone there with her, someone to take care of her and those kids, someone she doesn't have to worry about."

"And that's not you?"

XANDER

"That's a version of me that I'm not sure I'm ready for yet," I answer honestly, grunting as I work around a particularly heavy rock. "Hanging up my helmet and putting this down?" I gesture to my ax, then shake my head. "This is all I know. I can't make her any promises because we all know how quickly this job can turn. I made my dad a promise and I'm bound to honor that first."

"But for how long?" Cal asks. "How long until you feel that you've sacrificed enough of yourself to this career before you can walk away and not feel guilty about it?"

"I can't walk away," I mutter. "That's what makes this so damn hard, Cal. I can't walk away from this, no matter how much she might want me to. I love her . . . but I love this too. I'm not ready to walk away. Not yet. My dad gave up his family to make sure he was here to do this job. I can't just walk away from this when he gave his life to make sure we got out of that fire. To make sure *you* got out of that fire."

He nods solemnly. It's been six years since my dad died, but those wounds live deep. I think Cal suffered worse than I did after his death, having watched it happen. I'd probably have nightmares too, if it had been me. Instead, I'd been halfway down that fucking mountain with the first half of my crew, with the assumption that Cal and my dad would be right behind me.

But only Cal had come back down off that mountain. He'd had to break the news to me, to tell me what had happened, his eyes haunted and his voice breaking with emotion.

We both understand the dangers of this job and go in each time with the knowledge that no matter how well trained we are, anything can happen. But that's a risk we all understand and have accepted as part of the job.

That doesn't change the fact that I will move heaven and earth to make sure I get back to her. I will claw my way through hell to make it back to her every time. To make sure I get to hold her in my arms for another day, another night. Now that I've had a taste of what life is like with her in it, I'll fight tooth and nail to keep it.

As if reading my thoughts, Cal sighs and looks over at me.

"Teddy is probably the strongest woman I know . . . but I don't know that she's strong enough to handle this," he says quietly, sadly, shaking his head.

It's a fear I've had myself. She's this incredible mix of strength and fragility. That sense of protectiveness that I've felt for her for so long has only multiplied.

Cal claps me on the shoulder, squeezing tightly as he says roughly, "So you better make sure you know what you're doing, Sup. Make it home to her every fucking time, because I can't watch her go through that again."

Emotion tightens my throat, and all I can do is nod, a silent promise to do my best.

XANDER

37

Teddy

Checking my reflection in the full-length mirror in the corner of my bedroom one more time, I squeeze my eyes shut and take several slow, long breaths in and out. My heart feels like it's choking me, it's climbed so high in my throat. Nervous energy races through me like I've just shotgunned several Red Bull cans back-to-back. I'm twitchy and anxious.

Opening my eyes, I smooth my hands over my body. A soft, fluttery black blouse is buttoned over my breasts and tucked into high waisted, wide-legged black slacks that hug my hips and make my butt look good. I have a body slimmer beneath it, smoothing out my mom-tummy and keeping all my wobbly bits in check. A light, dusty blue blazer covers my arms and highlights my waist, though I leave it unbuttoned due to the heat. I'm starting to think this heatwave will never cease.

I pulled my hair up into a clip on the back of my head, face-framing tendrils left to flutter against my cheeks. My makeup is simple and chic. A pair of pointed-toe suede flats in a color that perfectly matches my blazer are on my feet. I'm probably overdressed, but an interview is an interview, and I desperately want to make sure I make a good impression.

I nod at my reflection and mutter to myself, "It's an interview, Teddy, not your execution."

It doesn't help, but at least I tried.

Leaving the safety of my bedroom, the hard soles of my shoes click on the linoleum in the kitchen as I enter. Colleen looks up from the bag of groceries she's unloading on my counter and smiles wide, then holds up one hand and circles her finger.

I laugh, doing a slow spin to show her the entire outfit.

"That color blue is just stunning on you," she says, beaming. Penny and Dalton are at school, and Bea is currently rolling around on the floor for some tummy time with several toys.

"Thank you," I murmur, blushing. I pick up my purse and sling it over my shoulder, then sigh and put it back down. "I don't think I need my giant diaper bag purse to go to an interview."

"Just take your wallet and your keys. That's all you need. And I better not see you back here for at least three hours."

"What? Why? If an interview lasts that long, there's something fishy going on, Colleen," I mutter, laughing.

"Go get your nails done, go to lunch, go to the bookstore and get yourself a new book or two," Colleen says, waving her hand dismissively. "I don't care what you do. Just don't come back right away."

I hug her tightly. "You really are the best," I whisper, then pull back, holding her by the shoulders. "But you know better than that."

"I'll kick your fine-looking rear right back out of this house," she teases lightly, pushing me away. "Now get, go get a coffee before you have to be there."

I laugh out loud, shaking my head. "I definitely don't need a coffee. I already feel like I'm going to buzz right out of my skin as it is."

"Well, nonetheless, get out of here. I'm going to teach Bea how to make a lasagna."

TEDDY

Snorting a laugh, I roll my eyes, but give her a salute and say, "Yes, ma'am."

I grab my wallet and my keys out of my big purse and then I cross the living room to where Bea has just rolled from her tummy to her back. She's got a crinkly baby book clutched between her tiny hands and she's kicking her legs in baby excitement at her conquest. I lower my body to my hands and knees over her and smooch her all over her face and neck, avoiding her grabby little hands before she can either make a mess of my hair or swipe baby drool over my jacket or shirt.

"I'll be back in a bit, bug," I whisper, then heave myself to my feet, and then I'm out the door.

Climbing into my minivan, I start it and reverse out of the driveway before I can convince myself that this is a colossally bad idea.

It doesn't take long to drive across town to the local county police department, but then I sit in the parking lot for a long time, staring at the brick building.

Grief, guilt, sadness, and anger all cascade through me like a kaleidoscope on an endless cycle as I sit and stare at the building, the people and deputies coming and going. I'd had to move away from Cedar Valley, a slightly larger city than Sky Ridge that's located a couple towns over, to get away from the life Logan and I had shared. I'd moved a whole county over to escape the people who I had let down in so many ways. As a 911 dispatcher for Cedar Valley, I'd known all the emergency personnel in my district, all the police officers, deputies, firefighters, and EMTs. We'd been family for ten years . . . and after Logan's accident, I just . . . couldn't. The pain and grief and pitying looks from those that we'd worked with for so long ate at me.

It's why I quit the department, why I took an early maternity leave and then moved away. I couldn't stay and be around all the people

I'd let down. All the people that miss Logan as much as I do. Even if they don't blame me for what happened, I do.

I know a handful of the surrounding counties' officers and EMTs through my old department, but thankfully not many. It's one of the reasons I said yes to Sky Ridge when Cal suggested the move. A fresh start, while being closer to Cal and Scottie and still being close enough to Logan's parents that they can see the kids a few times a month.

Taking a deep breath, I force myself to exit the car and walk inside.

Forty-five minutes later, I'm sliding back into the minivan feeling both lighter and heavier at the same time. The interview went great. It wasn't even a real interview; they knew they wanted me. It was more just an informal onboarding meeting to go over scheduling availability and salary and to meet the deputies and the other dispatchers. They're all friendly, and it felt good to be back in the familiar atmosphere of the station.

I wasn't surprised at the mandatory counseling and the psych evaluation criteria they'd requested before I begin, but I won't lie and say it didn't sting, at least a little bit. I know it's standard procedure, a way to protect me and my new team, to make sure I am mentally capable of handling this job, especially after everything. But I'm just sensitive enough for it to bother me, even if I know it's for the best. Even if I know that it would be mandatory even *without* my past.

Now that the adrenaline and anxiety coursing through my system have started to wane, I'm drained and exhausted. So I decide on a small pick-me-up and drive over to the Nook. I order myself my iced coffee with caramel sweet cream and a lemon blueberry muffin, then park myself in a booth along the wall.

My mind is a maelstrom, anxiety crashing through me anew as I pick at the crinkly paper wrapper that surrounds my muffin.

TEDDY

My stomach is in knots and I honestly don't think I can take a bite without making a mad dash to the bathroom to empty my stomach of its contents. Fingers shaking, I lift my coffee to my lips and take a tiny sip, then set it back down with a thunk on the table in front of me. Burying my face in my trembling hands, I focus on slowing my agitated breathing. Squeezing my eyes shut behind my hands, I try not to focus on how frantically my heart is beating in my chest, making me lightheaded. God, I haven't had a panic attack in so long.

I'd been doing so good.

And one little interview sends me spiraling.

I snort a derisive, self-deprecating laugh. Why they would feel fit to hire a mess like me is worrisome. Maybe I'm not ready for this after all.

The noise inside the coffee shop is loud. It's busy and customers are chatting over the sound of the music system piping a Taylor Swift song through the building.

I'm still focusing on slowing my breathing when the booth seat directly next to me dips with the weight of someone else sitting down and I startle. Before I can drop my hands though, an arm is draped over my shoulders, squeezing me into a muscular, hard side.

The smell of diesel fuel, smoke, and pine reach my nose instantly and a soft, almost silent sob escapes me.

Xander.

Eyes still covered by my hands, I lean into him as his hand smooths up and down my arm, his other hand cupping my face and turning me into him. His fingers trail over my face, my hair, and his lips press into my temple as he whispers quiet, nonsensical words into my hair.

"Hey," he murmurs quietly, that deep, soothing timbre of his voice lulling me. "What's going on, Mama?"

I laugh hesitantly, embarrassed to be seen like this. So, changing the subject, I whisper, "I didn't even know you were back in town."

"We just got back." His quiet, husky words are partly muffled against my hair, where I can feel his lips moving as he speaks. "I got home and Colleen came out, said you had an interview and she'd told you to take an hour for yourself. I know your addiction to coffee, so this was the first place I looked."

Leaning away slightly, I lower my hands after swiping beneath my lashes for any escaped tears, then look up at him. "You came to find me?"

"You're the first person I want to see when I come back," he rasps, stroking his fingers along my cheek.

His gaze is tender, shining with honesty. He's filthy, soot and dirt hastily scrubbed off his face, but he's the most beautiful thing I've ever seen. Leaning down, he presses a kiss to my mouth, a chaste, unhurried kiss. One laced with a promise of more later.

"Now," he murmurs gently, tucking that strand of hair behind my ear, his eyes tracking over every inch of my face as if trying to catalogue each feature. "Want to tell me why my girl is sitting alone in a coffee shop clearly having an anxiety attack?"

My heart does this ridiculous pitter-patter thing in my chest at his words. *My girl.*

Fucking swoon.

I sigh, pursing my lips and leaning into him again, burying my head in the crook of his neck beneath his jaw.

"I had an interview today."

"That's what Colleen said," he says gently, rubbing his hand down my arm again. "What was it for?"

"A job."

"Teddy," he growls low, tilting his head down toward mine.

I let out a small huff of a laugh. It's kind of fun annoying this man.

I inhale deeply, taking in his scent that is becoming achingly familiar to me. "It's a job with Sky Ridge as a dispatcher."

"And that is cause for an anxiety attack?" he asks gently.

TEDDY

I groan lightly, doing a weird yes-no bobble thing with my head. "Do I have to start at the beginning, or just a quick run-through?"

"You tell me whatever you're comfortable telling me," Xander says quietly, squeezing me close again. "If you want to skim, that's okay. If you want to talk it out, that's okay too. I'll listen."

I nod, the top of my head shifting beneath his chin. "Even if I have to talk about Logan?"

He squeezes me tighter, nodding. "Even then."

Sighing heavily, I whisper, "You know Logan and I worked together?"

He nods against the top of my head, so I continue.

"I'm sure you know he was an EMT, and I worked as a dispatcher in the same district. We worked side by side for a decade, and I loved my job." I squeeze my eyes shut tight, holding on to him even tighter.

He must sense the shift in me, because he wraps both arms around me. We're cocooned together in this little booth, the coffee shop around us disappearing.

"What do you know about Logan's accident?"

"I know the basics, just what Cal shared. He was an EMT. Sent out on a call in the middle of winter and got struck by a passing vehicle while trying to load into the ambulance."

Pain slices through me all over again, like it happened yesterday and not almost a year ago. Throat tight with emotion, I manage to whisper, "I was the dispatcher that sent him out on that call."

"Fuck," he whispers on a groan, holding me closer. "Teddy . . ."

"I shouldn't have been working that night. Penny had been fighting a double ear infection all week, and I'd barely slept. On top of that, we'd just found out I was pregnant with Bea—morning sickness had me hunched over a trash can between calls. I should've swapped shifts. I should've been at home." I shake my head, the memories assaulting me all over again. "It was snowing, and an older gentleman had slid off the road into a ditch and hit his head. It should have been a minor call, quick in-and-out. I remember wondering why it was taking so long to hear back from them, annoyed, even, that he hadn't called to say they were back at the station." I take a deep, steadying breath in and let it out slowly. Then I whisper, "And then I answered the call and found out my husband was dead at an accident I'd sent him to."

Xander's arms are like vices around me and I realize then that I'm shaking from head to toe. Tears rim my eyes and make my vision blurry as he rocks me against him. I haven't talked about this with anyone outside of grief counseling. It's not something I've been able to vocalize to anyone.

I don't know what it is about this man that makes me drop all of my shields. All these carefully crafted concrete walls with steel reinforcements and barbed wire turn to dust around him.

It's a terrifying revelation.

Something about him makes me want to open up, makes me want to try. Being around Xander reminds me what it's like to not be so goddamn alone all the time, to not have to suffer through everything on my own. Reminds me what it's like to have a partner to share things with, all the good and the bad and the ugly.

"I felt responsible for sending him out to that accident. I got my husband killed," I whisper, my nose stinging with more tears. "I was given bereavement leave, and then never went back. I couldn't walk into that station, take calls, and send other people's loved ones out. I couldn't stand the thought of getting someone else killed the way I had gotten Logan killed."

"That wasn't your fault," Xander rasps, his lips moving against my temple. I breathe him in, and then nod slowly. "Please tell me you haven't gone this whole time blaming yourself for what happened."

"I could say that, but I'd be lying," I laugh lightly, settling into his embrace. "Logically I know it was a freak accident. One of those perfect-storm situations that none of us could have seen coming. But yes, I still blame myself. So going to this interview today just . . . brought everything back. I loved my job. I was good at my job," I huff, shaking my head. "But the idea of sending those deputies, EMTs, and firemen out on calls knowing I could very well be the reason they don't get to go home to their families . . . It's debilitating."

"You would not be the reason they don't come home," he whispers, rocking me gently. "Every person in this profession knows the risks and are willing to take those risks to help others. A freak accident, a fireman not making it out of a structure fire, an officer being injured: None of those things would ever amount to being your fault, Teddy. It's . . ." He sighs heavily, pressing his cheek to the top of my head. "It's the reality of the job, and even though it's not fair, we know what we're getting ourselves into."

I swallow around more tears. Hearing him lumped into that is terrifying too. Because he's right; he's right there along with them, running headfirst into danger without a glance back. Same as Cal. Same as Scottie, my—hopefully—soon-to-be sister-in-law. I would be working directly with Scottie, since she works for Sky Ridge EMS.

"I couldn't forgive myself if I sent Scottie out to a call and she didn't make it home to Cal," I croak, tears strangling me. I shake my head then, rolling my eyes at how ridiculous I'm being, but I can't help it. "I don't know that I'm ready for this. God, I'm such a baby."

"How many people did you help in your decade at Cedar Valley, Teddy?" he asks, tilting my chin up.

Embarrassed at the tears streaking my cheeks, I try to lower my face from him, but he's having none of it.

"How many times did you answer that phone and you were the person on the other end of the line, helping a total stranger through the worst time in their lives? How many people did you save, sweetheart?" He strokes my cheek gently, reverently, as he stares down at me, and more tears slip down my cheeks. "You can't let the absolute worst-case scenario be your measure of normal, or let that keep you from doing a job that you know you can do. A job you know you are great at."

God, this man. If he were any more perfect, he'd be a unicorn.

"Do you miss it?" he asks then, smoothing my hair away from my face and swiping his thumb across my cheek, wiping away the tears that I'm almost positive have smudged the little bit of makeup I had on.

"So much," I answer honestly, my lip wobbling.

He kisses me lightly, tenderly. "Then don't let the exception to the rule scare you away from helping those that need it, beautiful." He squeezes me close again, then whispers, "Can I take you home?"

I nod, sighing. "Yes."

He stands, pulling me up with him. He swipes under my lashes again, smiling down at me as he does, then kisses my forehead before leading us out the door. When we get to the sidewalk, he leans in close and lets his hand rest on the top curve of my ass, his fingers flexing. And then he's glaring down at me.

I blink up at him, confused by the sudden change.

"Whatever torture device you have on under these clothes that you think you need to keep all of this contained"—he bends low to whisper in my ear, making me shiver—"take it off and throw it away."

I blush furiously, laughing up at him. "Xander, I'm not throwing away my Spanx, they smooth everything out—"

He shakes his head as we stop at my minivan. He opens the door and I slide in, but he doesn't shut the door right away. Instead, he leans in and kisses me deeply, his tongue swirling into my mouth, and I can't help the moan that rumbles out of me.

"You don't need smoothing out," he growls low, lips moving directly against mine. "And I want to be able to feel my girl's body when I touch her."

TEDDY

I blush all over again. He sips at my lips, then drags his mouth along my jaw and down the side of my neck. He reaches over my left shoulder and pulls the seat belt across my body, buckling me in, before leaning away. His gaze is hot as he stares at me, making my heart trip all over itself in my chest. He winks, and I swoon.

"I'll see you at home, *Mama*."

38

XANDER

Colleen is outside with Bea in her arms when I pull into the driveway, just shortly after Teddy.

"Oh good, you're home," Colleen says to Teddy, hugging her when she climbs out of the minivan. "I was wondering if you'd let me pick up Penny and Dalton from school today and take them to get a treat." The older woman gestures over to where I'm just climbing out of my truck and winks. "Let you two kids have a proper 'welcome home.'"

"*Colleen!*" Teddy whisper-hisses, and I grin widely as Teddy blushes furiously.

Colleen winks and I huff out a low chuckle as I cross the yard to where both women are standing.

Bea waves her chubby arms at me and I let her grab hold of my index finger in hello. I beam down at the tiny thing that has me so thoroughly wrapped around her little finger. All of Teddy's kids do, to be honest. I'm crazy about all of them.

"That's very generous of you, Colleen," I murmur, just a hint of teasing in my tone.

"I'm just glad my meddling worked," the older woman says, and I smile at Teddy while the blush staining her cheeks spreads to her chest.

"You're the worst," Teddy whispers, hiding her face behind her hand and shaking her head. "This isn't normal, Colleen."

"Pfft." Colleen waves one hand and laughs, then winks at me again.

God, I adore this woman. So off-the-wall and not at all what I would expect.

"Since when have I ever done anything considered to be *normal*? Go on, I'm going to get little miss loaded up and then we're going to head out. You two have fun. We'll be back in a few hours."

"Ohmygod," Teddy moans, burying her face in both hands as her shoulders shake with laughter.

Colleen heads back into the house with Bea, leaving us out in the yard.

Dropping her hands, she huffs out an embarrassed little laugh as she looks up at me. "I'm so sorry."

"Don't apologize." Ducking low, I set my lips against the shell of her ear and breathe huskily, "I'm going to use every second of those few hours to worship this body, Teddy."

"Holy shit," she whispers, swaying into me slightly.

I chuckle, planting my mouth against the underside of her jaw. "I need to shower."

"Okay," she breathes, her lids fluttering closed.

I groan, settling my body against her side, pressing my hips into her. I'm already hard, erection straining behind the fly of my Nomex pants.

"Don't take too long."

I kiss her fiercely, just for a second, sending my tongue into her mouth. Fuck, I was only gone a few days and I'm fucking starving for her. I release her and step away, chuckling darkly as she sways where she stands. "I'll only be a few, Teddy."

She nods, biting her lower lip, and I force myself to walk away.

I strip as soon as I'm in the bathroom, then shower as quickly as I can while being as thorough as possible. I ignore my raging hard-on, more than happy to wait for this time with my girl. God bless Colleen.

I'm stepping out of the bathroom when I hear Colleen call to Teddy from the driveway that they'll be back later, and then Teddy's front door closes.

I barely take the time to pull a pair of basketball shorts and a T-shirt on before I'm padding over to Teddy's house. She blushes that pretty pink I like so much as she sees me standing outside the back patio door, and then she's pulling the door open to let me in. My hands are on her in an instant. She's taken her pretty blue jacket off but is still wearing the same pair of cock-teasing, wide-legged pants and buttery-soft black shirt she was earlier. My fingers dive into her hair and I release the tresses from the clip at the back of her head, sending her hair in waves around her shoulders and over my hands. We kiss like teenagers, hungry and desperate.

"Bedroom," I rasp raggedly, pulling my lips from hers.

She pants against my mouth but nods.

"I want you naked, Teddy. Fuck, I've missed you."

"I missed you," she whispers earnestly, and I don't doubt the words for a second.

Turning her by the shoulders, I give her round, full ass a sharp slap through the material of her slacks.

She gasps, then giggles as we make our way to the bedroom.

As soon as the door closes, I reach for her again. Tugging the soft blouse out of the waistband of her slacks, I haul it over her head and toss it to the floor. Her upper body is covered in a black bodysuit that is also tucked into her pants. I reach for it, but she slaps my hands away.

"The pants have to come off first," she says with another one of those embarrassed little giggles. "It's a full-body shaper."

I glare down at the tight contraption, sliding my fingers beneath one of the straps that's digging into her shoulder. "This looks painful, Teddy."

She shrugs while my fingers go for the button and zipper of her slacks. I smooth my hands over her hips, inside the material of the pants, and with a whisper of fabric, the pants fall to her ankles. She blushes, smoothing her hands over her body in the tight spandex, almost as if trying to cover herself from me. This woman, I swear. I'm going to show her how fucking beautiful she is to me.

Fingers once again digging beneath the straps at her shoulders, I waste no time dragging it down her arms. Her breasts are released first, falling free of the tight material, and I groan because this goddess is braless beneath it. Ducking my head, I suck one nipple into my mouth, nipping lightly with my teeth. She gasps, her fingers sliding into my still-wet hair. But I'm not done yet. I sink to my knees as I pull this damn contraption off my girl, her soft, glorious body being revealed inch by inch.

I lean away and growl up at her. Goddamn, the things I could do down here on my knees to this woman. She finally steps out of the tight black Spanx and I hold it up in my fist, then toss it across the room.

"I will slice this damn thing to shreds if I see you wearing it again," I warn before rising to stand.

She blushes again, her tongue darting out to wet her lips nervously as I reach behind me and pull my shirt off over my head, letting it drop to the floor too. And then I'm shoving my shorts down my thighs until I'm as naked as she is. I can't stop staring at her. She's just so fucking pretty. Dragging my knuckles along the slope of one breast, I groan at the softness.

"Goddamn," I rasp, my eyes eating up every glorious inch of her. The early-afternoon sun is filtering through the windows, making her skin glow warmly and turning her hair to gold.

"Please close the curtains," she whimpers, her hands coming up to cover herself shyly.

I growl at her, and she halts. "No."

"Please, Xander—"

Grasping her wrists, I pull her hands away from the body that she's trying desperately to hide from me, and I shake my head. "I want to see you, Teddy. Every fucking glorious inch of you. And I can't do that if I shut out all the light."

"But—"

"No *buts*," I murmur darkly, and then my eyes track over the curves displayed in the tall mirror across the room. Forcing her back several steps so that we are directly in front of that mirror, I cup her jaw in both of my hands. "I'm going to sit in front of this mirror, and you're going to turn around and face it too. Then, you're going to spread these legs and sit on my cock."

Her lips part, and I rub my thumb across the full, kiss-swollen bottom one. "I can't do that."

"Yes, you can, beautiful."

Her throat works as she swallows, her eyes wide and wary. "But I'm all—"

"Oh, sweetheart, I know. And it drives me fucking wild."

My hands slide down her throat and over her shoulders, then down to settle on the plump curve of her waist, where her wide hips flare out. Her pale skin looks creamy and velvety in the mirror behind her, and I let my gaze drift from hers to marvel at the sight before me. Her ass is what dreams are made of, so I curve my hands over the delicious roundness, the difference of the rough darkness of my hands against her smooth, pale flesh a heady sight. I grab handfuls, squeezing and kneading, spreading her cheeks lightly.

Her hands grab hold of my waist, fingers flexing against my ribs as I continue to pet and stroke along every inch of her that I can reach. I'm powerless against her, this hold she has on me, on my heart. Pressing my hips into the softness of her belly, she gasps, and the sound does wonderful, awful things to my already rock-hard dick. It jumps between us.

The midafternoon sunlight filtering in through the window across the room sends rays of light dancing across the bed, the floor, over Teddy's skin. She's fucking perfect. Goddamn ethereal in her beauty. I'm going to worship every single inch of her.

I sink to my knees again, dragging my hands along the exaggerated hourglass of her ribs, waist, and hips, at the same time pressing my mouth to the cushion of her stomach. There's no part of her that is toned; she's all curvy, grabbable softness and I can't fucking get enough of her. This body drives me crazy.

Her hands sink into my hair, grabbing handholds, and I grin against the softness of her belly, pressing my open mouth to the cushiness of it, letting my tongue flick out and trace several faint stretch marks. One of her hands slides down and tries to cover where my mouth is, but I grunt at her, and then my palm is cracking across one plump ass cheek in warning. She gasps again, and the sound sends me over the edge.

I sit back so that I'm sitting on my heels, my thighs spread just slightly. I stare up her body, and I realize that I never want to be anywhere else. I want to spend the rest of my days worshiping this goddess in front of me, and I'll make her see it too.

Grabbing the slopes of her hips, I turn her to face the mirror. She turns her eyes away from her reflection, but that's okay for now. By the time we're done, she's going to know just how fucking beautiful she is.

I glide my hand from her right hip, down over her ass cheek, and press it between her thick thighs. She shifts, allowing her thighs to part enough for me to get my hand where I want it most, and I groan against the softness of her backside when I feel just how wet she already is.

"Oh, fuck," I groan again, taking a love bite out of her left ass cheek. "You're so wet for me."

From my seated position on my knees, I grab hold of her hips again and draw her to the floor as well. When her knees hit the floor in front of me, I grin at her in the mirror and let my eyes track over the globes of her breasts, the dark nipples already peaked and begging for attention.

"Spread your legs for me, beautiful," I breathe against the soft skin behind her ear.

She hesitates just a moment before shifting, spreading her knees. I'm so hard it's fucking painful.

"Now, straddle my legs and sit on my cock until you take every inch, Teddy."

Her eyes are trained on mine as she does as I say, shifting backward until her thighs have straddled mine. Her knees are on the floor on either side of mine, and she's spread wide as she moves into position. It's filthy and erotic and it takes every considerable ounce of my self-control not to come already. Reaching between us, I position myself at her entrance, dragging the tip over that pretty pink pussy that is on full display for me in the mirror.

"Sit."

She heeds the command, doing as I say. The curves of her ass are against my abs, her shoulders level with my mouth, and I lean in and press hot, open-mouthed kisses along the ridge of her shoulder as she settles on me, drawing me into her with aching slowness. I watch over her shoulder in the mirror as her body takes all of me. I've never seen anything as sexy as watching her take my cock inside her. Banding my arm around her middle, I hold her back flush against my chest and my mouth drops open at the sheer euphoria of being so deep. Fuck, she's tight. So fucking tight. Her head tips back as she settles on me fully, and I can feel those inner muscles twitching around my cock. I see stars.

"Fucking Christ, Teddy," I whisper out a groan against her neck. "Do you see that? Do you see how fucking beautiful that is?"

She drops her chin, her eyes meeting mine in the mirror. I cup her pussy in my other hand, spreading her wider so we can both see the way she takes me, all the way to the hilt.

"Oh my god," she moans, and my cock twitches inside, making me grunt in agreement.

"Fuck, this is beautiful," I groan, spreading her with my fingers. The sight of my cock disappearing into her is heady and thrilling and so fucking erotic, and whether she knows it yet or not, she's all fucking mine. I stroke the pad of my thumb across the tight bundle of nerves at the apex of her thighs and she gasps, grinding down onto me. "Mm-hmm. Just like that, pretty girl."

"Xander."

Her eyes are on mine in the mirror, her lids heavy, lips parted. One of her hands is clutching my forearm that I have banded across her middle, holding her to me. The other hand is covering the back of mine where it's buried between her legs.

Using the arm around her waist to lift her, she accommodates, her thighs shifting slightly, and then I slam my hips upward as I haul her back down to my thighs. Her fingers scrabble against my skin, her mouth dropping open with a silent cry. Fuck, this is everything. *She* is everything.

She does it on her own this time, rising up until my tip is all that's left, and then she's dropping down, sinking me back inside to the hilt. I grab a handful of the flesh at her middle, dropping my mouth to the curve of her neck, where I let my teeth sink in for a bite before soothing the hurt with my tongue.

Her inner muscles clench around me and I grin against her neck. "Oh, you naughty thing. You like the pain?"

She nods, the movement stilted and jerky, while she continues to ride my cock. Her thick, creamy thighs are spread wide over mine and I release my hold around her torso and her pussy to grab soft handfuls of her thick hips. I guide her, using the downward motion of her body to thrust up hard. Her hands land on the planes of her thighs, using them for leverage. I slam upward again, letting my fingers bite into the cushiness of her hips. Taking another love bite out of her shoulder, she moans and drops her chin forward.

"So fucking pretty," I groan from behind her, never faltering in the hard, deep thrusts upward. "Such a pretty girl, spreading wide for me. You take me so well, beautiful."

Her eyes find mine in the mirror again. I drag my hands over her hips, up the wide slope of them, to the narrow softness of her waist. Cupping her breasts in my hands, I squeeze them, kneading them, and then I roll each nipple between my fingers and her body bows against me, her pussy tightening around my dick.

"Oh fuck, Teddy," I rasp, pressing my mouth to her shoulder again. I roll her nipples again and she bites her lip, mewling lightly.

"Oh God, Xander, that's going to make my—"

I feel it then, the warm wetness that dribbles between my fingers and I watch our reflections, enraptured, as rivulets of white trickle out of the nipples I have pinched between them. I can't help it, I pound upward into her fiercely, the sight of her leaking between my fingers driving me wild. Her hands cover mine and I see the heavy stain of a blush that covers her chest and cheeks.

XANDER

"Lower your hands," I command darkly.

She stares at me, her lips parted, her breaths sawing in and out of them.

"*Teddy*. Drop your hands so I can see."

She does as she's told and I grin darkly at her.

"Good girl. You will not cover one inch of your body from me, do you understand?"

She hesitates and I thrust up again, earning another cock-twitching gasp from her.

"You are the most exquisite woman I've ever seen, sweetheart. Every part of you. Even the parts you don't think are beautiful."

I let my palms cup her tits again, pushing them together. "These tits? Fucking gorgeous. See how well they fit in my hands? Like you were made for me."

I slide my palms down, until I can grab hold of her waist, my fingers digging into the softness of her stomach. "Do you know how many times I've jerked off to the memory of you pregnant? This body rounded and full . . . fuck, I felt like an asshole, like a fucking pervert. But goddamn, you pregnant is one of the prettiest things I've ever seen, Teddy. I've never wanted kids, but fuck me if I haven't thought about what it might be like to watch you grow with my baby inside you."

Her mouth drops open again, shock entering her features. "Xander . . ."

Fuck it, I'm all in, anyway. About time she realizes it too.

I grab handholds on her heavy, wide hips, pushing up inside her, my cock pulsing with the need to come. "These hips; I've thought of nothing else but holding on to these while I fuck you from behind. Christ, the thought of watching my cock pound into you, your ass in the air and head buried in the sheets . . ." I curve my hands around the fullness of her ass, where it jiggles with every hard thrust, every move she makes as she rides me. I give her ass cheek a hard slap and she whimpers again as her pussy pulses around me. I groan, gritting my teeth, running my palms from her hips to her tits and back, reveling in the way her softness gives way to my fingers. "If all of this isn't bouncing and jiggling around, I'm not fucking you hard enough."

"Oh God," she cries, and I know she's seconds away from coming.

I drop my hands to curve them around her heavy, soft inner thighs, spreading her wider over me. I let my fingers circle her clit, and she sobs as she undulates her hips against me.

"Xander, please!"

"You're right there, pretty girl," I breathe into her neck. "Ride my cock, come all over it. God, I want to feel you—"

She sobs as her body bows in on itself and I feel it as she comes hard. She squeezes her eyes closed and tilts her face away, but I'm not about to let her miss this.

"Eyes on the mirror, Teddy. Watch how beautiful you are when you come for me," I grit out, and she opens those gray eyes, finding mine in the mirror. Fuck, she's stunning as she shakes and trembles against me, around me, and I wrap both of my arms around her torso as she rides out that high. Her inner muscles are squeezing the life out of me, but I hold back, because this is about her. Her eyes never leave mine.

When she slumps back against my chest, her breaths heaving in and out of her, I nuzzle her neck with my nose, my lips.

"So. Fucking. Beautiful." I punctuate every word with a hot, open-mouthed kiss to her skin, working my way up the side of her neck, to her jaw.

She twists her head toward me, staring wide-eyed, still panting those uneven breaths. And then I crush my mouth to hers, kissing her deeply, fiercely.

Our lips and teeth and tongues tangle, we kiss until we're both breathless, and I feel the last of her climax ripple away, until the shaking turns into a new kind of trembling.

XANDER

Releasing the hold I have around her middle, I nip at her lower lip, then soothe it with my tongue. "On your hands and knees."

She moans lightly as she rises off me, her limbs shaking as she settles on her hands, her round ass splayed for me like my own personal feast. I can't help myself; I lean forward and sink my teeth into one supple cheek before rising onto my knees behind her. Her eyes are on me in the mirror as I position myself at her entrance again, pushing the broad head of my cock into her wet and glistening folds, just an inch. I settle my palms over the heavy curves before me, over her back, the soft roundness of her hips and ass, letting my fingers trail lightly over the sensitive flesh at the back of her thighs. She trembles beneath my touch, goosebumps flashing across her skin.

"Do you understand yet how unbelievably stunning you are?" I ask her reflection.

She bites down on her lower lip, uncertainty flashing in her eyes.

"Do you understand how impossible it was for me to stay away from you? *You own me*, Teddy. My body." Curving my hands around the meaty part of her hips, I haul her back toward my waiting cock, burying myself as deep as I can go in one long, hard thrust. I'm so hard it hurts. I know I won't last much longer; the tightness, the sensation of her gripping me is hurtling me toward my own orgasm. "My heart." I pound into her, hard enough to make her tits sway with the thrust, and she whines, the sound ricocheting through me like a wrecking ball. I'm fucking done for. She's everything. *My everything.* "My fucking soul, Teddy."

Her mouth drops open, her eyes wide on mine in the mirror.

"Do you feel how badly I want you, Teddy?" I glide my hands over her possessively. I'm fucking feral for her at this point. "You do this to me. Drive me fucking crazy."

She nods, her eyes luminous as she watches me.

I let my own gaze drop to where we're connected, her ass resting against my thighs, my abs, and I smooth my hands over her gently, lovingly. Pulling back, I groan through tightly clenched teeth at the sight of her body swallowing me whole as I push back in. Her back arches, granting me better access, and I slide deeper. She sinks down onto her forearms, her forehead thumping into the carpeted floor, and her hands spread wide on the floor above her head.

I slap her ass, earning another clench around my dick and a breathy gasp from her lips.

"*Eyes*, Teddy. I need those eyes, beautiful."

She raises her head, shifting back up onto her palms, pushing back against me. But her eyes find mine, as always, and I let loose. Gripping these soft, grabbable hips in a tight hold, I slam into her, over and over again. Her mouth opens on a silent cry, her brows pulled tightly together. Her tits sway with every hard thrust, and I'm torn between watching her beautiful face and watching this glorious body taking everything I'm giving to her. Her inner walls pulse around me, and I know she's close. I recognize the fluttering. She's going to come again.

"*Xander*." It's a soft, keening sound. So desperate. So needy. So fucking *mine*.

Fuck, *my* name on her lips, a prayer, a plea. My goddamn ruin. I'm undone.

"*That's my beautiful girl*," I rasp, hips snapping into hers again and again. My balls are drawing tight, my release converging at my spine. "Come for me, pretty girl."

And she does. Her back bows, her thighs quake, her pussy clenches around me, and my vision goes hazy as my own climax roars through me, scorching me from the inside out. My hips snap into hers once, twice more, all finesse fleeing as I spill inside her with hot, long spurts, my cock pulsing as she draws every drop from me. The groan that tears out of my throat is almost a roar.

I'm panting raggedly, my heart a hammering cadence in my chest. God above, I haven't come that hard . . . ever.

XANDER

Her head drops forward between her bridged arms, shaking as she holds herself off the floor. I trail my fingers from her bottom up her back, then back down the indent of her spine. She shivers, letting out a breathy moan.

"My beautiful fucking girl."

"I didn't believe you," she whispers, her head still bowed toward the floor. Then she raises her head, meeting my gaze in the mirror again. Her eyes glisten with tears, but a soft, radiant smile pulls at her lips, and it sends fissures through my chest. "But I do now. You make me feel beautiful, and sexy, and desirable."

"You are all those things," I whisper in return, unable to keep the shakiness from my voice. "All of it, and so much more, sweetheart."

I pull out of her, groaning as I push to my feet. My legs shake—fuck, she made me come so hard I saw stars—and offer my hand to her to help her stand. She wobbles too, and I can't resist the urge to wrap her in my arms and hold her against my chest, tucking her head beneath my chin. Her arms slide around my waist, her fingers trailing along my spine as we stand that way for a long moment, enjoying the peace only lovers feel.

And then she squirms against me and looks up, her nose wrinkling adorably. I peck a kiss to her lips, a soft, chaste kiss, and ask, "What is it?"

"You certainly like to make a mess of me . . ." She blushes prettily, and I grin, that age-old, primal urge to beat my chest with my fists rising in me. *Mine*.

"I wasn't lying when I said I do very much like the sight of my cum dripping out of you," I rasp against her mouth.

She bites her lip and that blush deepens.

"It's a reminder of where I've been, what you do to me, and what I do to you. I like marking you as mine, Teddy."

A soft inhale of breath. Her eyes raise to mine. "Is that what I am? Yours?"

Grabbing handfuls of her backside in my palms, I nuzzle her neck before kissing my way back up to her mouth. "If you'll have me, yes."

"Are you sure?" she asks against my mouth. "I come with a lot of baggage, Xander, and I can't do casual. I have kids—"

"You're a package deal, and one I understood before this ever started, Teddy," I whisper gently, stroking her hair away from her face before cupping her jaw in my palms. I let my thumbs rub along her cheekbones as I stare down into those beautiful eyes. "There's no amount of 'baggage' that could make me not want this. But I don't want you saying yes to something you're not sure about. My job . . . I know the risks. And that's why I fought against this so fucking hard."

"Because of Logan," she whispers, and I nod solemnly.

"Because the thought of causing you or these kids any pain is abhorrent to me." Taking her hand in mine, I drag it to my mouth and press a kiss to the center of her palm. "I love you, Teddy. I think I have for a while, sweetheart."

"Xander . . ." she breathes reverently, her eyes shimmering as she stares up at me. I know she's not ready to say it back, and that's okay. As long as she doesn't push me away.

I kiss her palm again, then whisper against her skin, "It's okay. I just need you to know. I told you I was done fighting this, and I meant it. You and these kids mean the world to me. I don't want just casual with you. I want everything, beautiful."

XANDER

39

Teddy

"What on earth is all this?" I ask, laughing, as I open the door to Xander.

He grins, winking at me, and it sends my heart fluttering wildly in my chest. He steps inside, leaning down to kiss me quickly.

"I'm cooking us dinner to celebrate your new job starting tomorrow."

"You're cooking dinner? Here?"

He nods as he straightens, though he drags his mouth along my cheek. The rasp of his beard tickles, sending shivers down my entire body. "Mm-hmm."

Stepping into the kitchen, he sets the two paper grocery sacks on the counter and reaches into one and then pulls out a bottle of wine. He digs into his pocket, producing a wine key, and proceeds to open the bottle. "I'm on food, dishes, and kid duty. Pour a glass of wine and go take a bath while I get dinner ready, okay?"

"Xander, this is too much," I breathe as he starts pulling groceries out of the bags. He nods to the cupboard, and I dutifully pull down a wineglass. He takes it, our fingers grazing, then pours out a small amount of wine before handing it back to me. I'm staring at the back of his dark head like he's some kind of mythical being.

"I should have asked first, do Dalton and Penny like spaghetti?" he asks, turning to me as I stare at him. His eyes soften, like he can see the awe on my face, but continues like this isn't out of the ordinary for us. "If not, I can make something else."

"We love s'ketti!" Penny exclaims from the other side of the couch, where she'd been lying on the floor playing. She jumps over the back of the couch, ignoring my warning scowl, and launches herself at Xander's legs as she barrels into the kitchen. He scoops her up into his arms, placing her on his hip. Her little face scrunches up then, pointing to a produce container sitting on the counter. "I *don'* like muh'rooms though."

Xander laughs, bouncing her in his arms to get a better hold on her. "That's okay. These are for me and Mom."

"Do you have garlic bread too?" Dalton asks, climbing into one of the barstools on the opposite side of the counter. He leans on his forearms across the space, peering into the bags and at the items Xander has already fished out of them.

Xander reaches into the bag and pulls out a loaf of French bread. "Homemade is the only way to go. Do you want to help me mash the garlic and mix it into the butter?"

"Yeah!" Dalton says, bobbing his head.

Xander turns to me then, grimacing slightly. "You do have a garlic press, right? My dad wasn't big on home cooking, so he didn't leave me with much in the way of homewares."

"Yes, I have a garlic press," I laugh, skirting around him and Penny to fetch it out of one of the drawers. "Xander. This is a lot."

Spreading his hand wide across my lower back, he urges me closer so that I'm tucked against his other side. "I'll be the judge of that. Come on, take that wine and go take a bath. Has Bea eaten?"

I blush and nod. "Yes, but she'll be hungry again before bed."

TEDDY

"So just one small glass," he whispers, and winks. "Gotta keep my little one fed too."

"Xander . . ."

"You keep saying my name like it's going to change the outcome of this evening," he laughs, dropping a kiss to my lips.

Penny snickers behind her hand.

He twists his head to look at her. "What's so funny?"

"You kissed Mommy." She giggles behind her hand.

"I did," he says, nodding. Looking at her and then over to Dalton, he asks gently, "Is that okay with you guys?"

Dalton shrugs his shoulders from where he's still leaning on the counter, watching us. "Yeah, I think so. You make Mom smile, so it makes me happy."

My heart squeezes in my chest, and my nose stings with unshed tears.

Xander's arm tightens around my waist and he turns his head to look at me. "She makes me happy, too, champ."

I blink rapidly to dispel the tears lining my eyes, and I avoid looking directly at Xander. His lips press into my temple and I sigh. I'm so screwed.

"Go on, Mama. I've got things handled out here," he whispers against my temple, and I nod.

"Okay," I whisper hesitantly. Picking up the glass of wine, I head down the hall.

Shutting the bathroom door, I turn the taps on to start filling the bathtub and even squeeze in a little bubble bath I find under the sink.

I don't remember the last time I indulged in an actual bubble bath or even had time to consider one.

I strip out of my shorts but hesitate before I pull my shirt off over my head. Padding out of the bathroom, I grab a couple of candles and bring them back with me. Lighting them, I turn the overhead light off, and the candle flames flicker across the walls and cast just enough light to see. It's quiet and cozy. God, what a luxury this is.

Sinking into the warm water, I sip my wine, reveling in the moment. I never get to do this.

Xander is spoiling me, and if he's not careful, I could get used to it.

I must languish in the warm water for close to half an hour before a soft knock sounds on the door. "Come in," I call quietly, and then Xander appears around the door. He has a glass of water in one hand, and he swaps out my empty wineglass for the water.

I have barely a second to be embarrassed, very aware that the only thing keeping him from seeing all of me is the thin layer of bubbles clinging to the surface of the water before he leans over the tub. Bracing those sexy, strong arms on the rim of the basin to leverage himself over me, he drops his mouth onto mine in a soul-stealing kiss. One hand disappears beneath the surface of the water, slipping between my thighs. I moan into his mouth, my entire body heating as his fingers find what he's looking for.

"Are you enjoying your bath?" he husks against my mouth.

I nod, my eyelids fluttering closed as those fingers slide inside me, slow and deep. "Good. Dinner should be ready in about ten minutes. Come join us when you're dressed."

And then the bastard leaves me practically panting in the dim light of the room and ridiculously turned on. Holy shit.

Stepping out of the tub, I dry off and then wrap the fluffy towel around my body before padding into the bedroom. I move to grab my go-to outfit of biker shorts and a loose tunic top, but stop myself. Instead, I step over to the closet and thumb through the hangers, my fingers sliding over a simple, dusty-blue maxi sundress with a built-in shelf bra, so I don't have to put a nursing bra on beneath it. It has thin straps that cross over my shoulders, a V neckline, and a slit clear up the thigh. I haven't worn it since last summer, before I was pregnant with Bea. It's flowy and comfortable and casual enough

TEDDY

for a simple dinner with Xander and the kids, while just provocative enough to drive this man a little crazy.

God, I hope it still fits.

I pull on a pair of cheeky panties and then slide the maxi dress over my curves. I'd piled my hair up in a claw clip while I'd lounged in the warm bath, and stray tendrils are curling against my neck and temples. Brushing just a touch of blush to my cheeks and refreshing my mascara, I stare at myself in the mirror for a long second, running my palms over the dip of my waist and down the wide fullness of my hips. My right thigh peeks out of the high slit of the dress, my feet bare where the hem brushes my ankles.

Garnering my courage, I open the bedroom door and step out, releasing a long breath. It smells divine, but it's the music drifting to me from down the short hallway that steals my breath. I can't help but laugh as I enter the living room.

Lifelong hotshot bachelor Xander Macomb is currently listening to Disney sing-along songs playing from the Bluetooth stereo. Penny is singing loudly along with Elsa, her arms thrown wide as Xander spins her in the center of the kitchen by one hand. Bea is cradled in his other arm facing outward, her little back tucked into his chest, her arms and legs kicking and waving like crazy. A wide, mostly toothless grin stretches across her face. Dalton is sprawled out on his back on the couch, his head propped up on the arm and a chapter book resting on his chest, but he grins up at me as I walk through.

My heart cracks wide open in my chest at the scene before me.

Oh God, I missed this. My kids missed this. These moments that mean so damn much but seem so little in the grand scheme of things. Something as simple as making dinner together as a family and dancing in the kitchen. Tears sting my nose, but the smile that pulls at my lips is one of pure happiness.

Dalton is right. Xander makes me smile. He makes me happy.

I never thought I'd have this again. I was so sure that I would never *want* to have this again.

Xander's eyes find mine then as I come into the kitchen, and his gaze travels from the top of my head down to my toes and back. The heat in that gaze when it finds mine again is scorching. He licks his lips, then bites the bottom one between his straight, white teeth. I swear I hear a deep growl rumble out of his chest a second before he steps over to me.

Clasping the back of my neck in his palm, he angles my head up and back so that I'm looking up at him. My breathing stutters as he brushes his lips across the corner of my mouth.

"Fuck, Teddy," he whispers beneath his breath, that low rumble for my ears only.

I'm practically panting.

"You are stunning. So fucking pretty, Mama. Goddamn, the things I want to do to you . . ."

Penny chooses that moment to interrupt us, wrapping her arms around my thighs as she bounces in place. "Mommy, dance with me!"

Xander kisses me swiftly, then backs away. I don't miss the way the back of his hand passes over the fly of his jeans, making me blush as I turn toward Penny.

"Last song and then dinner," Xander says, stepping around the kitchen counter to set Bea in her Pack 'n Play in the living room. He makes sure she has several toys within reach, and then he's back to the kitchen. He dishes up everyone's plates, asking me about portion sizes for Dalton and Penny while Dalton helps set the table with silverware and napkins.

Once I have both kids settled at the table, Xander stops me with his hands on my waist and his mouth on the curve of my neck. "This may be dinner, but I know what I want for dessert."

I giggle, shaking my head. "Xander."

TEDDY

"Sit down and eat while it's hot. Would you like a little more wine with dinner?" he asks, stepping away.

I shake my head, and he refills my water instead, placing it on the table. Once we're all seated, he leans on his elbows and looks over at Dalton. "How was school today, champ?"

Again, my heart cracks open. Dalton launches into a tale about what they'd learned in science, and then Penny gets a turn to regale us with her knowledge of the full alphabet. Sitting kitty-corner to one another at the table, Xander looks over at me and winks before sliding his left hand over the bare skin of my thigh that's peeking out of the slit in my dress.

The heat of his palm on my skin burns through me, his fingers squeezing around my thigh, just above my knee. I can't deny that I love having his attention, his open affection, like this. It's like a balm to my soul, and to my heart.

It's a little ridiculous how truly crazy I am about this man. He hasn't said he loves me again since that first time, but his actions say it for him. I can see it in his eyes as he watches me.

I want this. I want this so bad I ache with it. It's so damn easy with him. And he's so good with my kids it's unfair.

Dinner is always a little chaotic, and Penny manages to spill her milk on the table. Before I can stand to grab a towel, Xander is pushing to his feet. He leans down and pecks a quick kiss to my mouth, surprising me. "I've got it. Stay here."

Once dinner is done, he sends both big kids to the bathroom to wash their hands and faces and to change into pajamas just as Bea starts to fuss in the Pack 'n Play. He takes my empty plate to the sink while I grab her. Glancing over at him almost shyly—how this man can still make me blush after everything is beyond me—I slip one strap of my dress down my arm and settle the baby in to nurse.

Bea cradled in one arm, I wander around the dining space, picking up plates and bringing them to the sink. Xander rinses them before putting them in the dishwasher, and then dries his hands. Turning, he leans his hips against the counter, legs crossed at the ankles. Crossing his arms over his chest, he drags one hand down his lower face, staring raptly as I shift Bea from one breast to the other with practiced ease, righting my dress single-handedly.

"You amaze me, you know that?" he asks, raising his eyes to mine. The awe, the wonder, the pure adoration on his face as he watches me steals my breath entirely.

I blush again and lower my eyes, letting my fingers trail over Bea's soft cheek to avoid the intensity in his gaze.

"Thank you for tonight." My words are quiet and earnest. I don't have the courage to look him in the eyes as I say it, so I keep my eyes trained on Bea's face. "This was . . . I really liked having you here with us like this, Xander."

"I'd like to spend all of my nights with you like this, Teddy. When I'm home. I want to be with you and the kids," he says quietly, and I can sense that he's still staring at me. "If that's what you want."

I nod slowly, raising my eyes to his. A tentative, hesitant smile tugs at my lips, and they wobble just the slightest. "Yeah, I think I do."

"Good," he whispers, one corner of his mouth tilting up in that adorable grin that I've come to love so much.

Shit. Do I love Xander? Could it be possible that I've fallen for him this quickly?

Later, after we've tucked all three kids into bed—together— he draws me into his arms in the darkness of the kitchen and slow-dances with me to the quiet stillness of the house around us. And I admit that, yes, it's very possible that I've already fallen for Xander.

40

Teddy

"How is the new job going?"

I puff out a long exhale, trying to blow the strand of hair out of my face as I finish piping the frosting letters onto the sheet cake in front of me. Well, I'm not a professional, that's for damn sure.

I sigh, glaring down at the *D* of Dalton's name that I've scraped off and redone three times already.

"It's good. It's been an adjustment," I say, shrugging as I glance over at Violette and Scottie. "I'm only doing two shifts a week for now. Colleen is staying with us two days a week to watch the kids for me. I don't know if I'd be able to do these hours without her help."

Scottie is currently slicing cucumbers and bell peppers for the veggie tray, and Vi is mixing together a dip. The guys are on kid duty again, keeping them all entertained out in the front yard, along with Colleen and Kent, who came for the day to celebrate Dalton's birthday.

Turning, Scottie waves the knife around a little wildly, making me laugh nervously as she says, "Well, you should know, everyone really likes you. I can't tell you how many times the other paramedics

272

have said they love when you're on the line. You really know what you're doing, sis."

"Thanks," I mutter, still laughing and eyeballing that knife she's wielding. "Let's not have to call for any chopped-off fingers tonight, though, yeah?"

She chuckles and turns back to the veggies in front of her. "You never let me have any fun."

Xander comes in through the front door and stops beside me, pressing a kiss to my temple. "Birthday boy is asking when he can open presents. I told him I'd ask the boss lady."

Rolling my eyes, I smile up at him. "The birthday boy knows he can't open presents until after we eat. He's trying to con you, sir."

His chest rumbles with a deep laugh and he shakes his head. "Makes sense why he'd ask me and not Cal. Bet he knows the rules."

The two women behind me laugh at the same time I do. I nod, grinning up at him. He kisses my lips and I sigh happily. "That he does. Food is just about ready. How's Bea?"

"Getting hungry."

I drop my voice and breathe, "And how are you?"

His eyes sparkle as he rakes his gaze over my face, then down my body.

Heat rushes up between my legs. Heaven above, will I never get enough of this man?

"Getting hungry," he repeats, barely making a sound, his gaze returning to mine.

"*Groossss*," Scottie whines, then looks over her shoulder and winks. "Get a room, you two horndogs."

Grinning over at her, he grabs me around the waist, making me squeak in surprise as he lifts me. The frosting bag falls from my hands onto the counter, and then his thick, muscular arms forces my legs to wrap around his waist. I open my mouth to protest, but

TEDDY

he just grins at me wolfishly, making me laugh again instead. "That is a great idea, Scottie."

"*Xander!*" I shriek, laughing, as he carries me down the hall.

His chest is shaking with laughter as he sets me down at the door, but the laughter ends abruptly when his hands capture my face between his palms and he kisses the daylights out of me. Pressing my body up against the doorframe, he leans into the kiss, effectively turning me into an absolute puddle in my panties.

When Xander isn't off on a fire, he's with us, just like he said he wanted to be. It's a little terrifying how easily he's slipped into our normal routine, how well he handles the daily ups and downs of having three kids. He helps Dalton with his homework, puts Penny to bed, spends his evenings with us and eats meals at our place.

He also spends most nights in my bed.

Doing deliciously, wickedly amazing things. With his tongue. His fingers. His cock.

"You're a beast," I whisper against his mouth when he releases me from the kiss.

"I couldn't wait another second to kiss my girl," he rumbles back, using his thumbs beneath my jaw to tilt my head up farther, stretching my neck so he can bury his mouth there. Nipping, kissing, licking.

The man can't keep his hands off me.

It makes me feel beautiful, desired. Sexy. And cherished, in a way I don't think I've ever felt. Even with Logan. I made the decision to go back to grief counseling, and talking through things with her has been both cathartic and emotionally exhausting.

Whatever this is with Xander . . . it's intense and all-consuming, but talking it out in therapy makes it a little less terrifying. I haven't been able to say it out loud yet, but I can admit to myself that I think I'm in love with Xander. It's helped so that I can enjoy the moments we have together without the guilt completely consuming me. I still carry that grief, but it's not quite as debilitating as it was.

It certainly helps that this man is positively crazy about me, and I can't seem to get enough of him either. Like now.

I shove at his chest, panting. "Get back outside to watch the kids. I have a cake to finish."

"Yes, boss lady," he rasps, winking, before leaving me pressed up against the doorjamb.

When I make it back out to the kitchen, Vi mimes fanning herself and swooning comically.

I blush. Dammit, these women are going to torment me endlessly.

"Goddamn, get it, Momma," Scottie laughs, piling the veggies on the platter in a colorful array. "Safe to say things are going well?"

"Ohmygod, are they ever," I laugh, returning to the cake. I fix the *D* on the cake one last time and then give up. It is what it is. It might not look the greatest, but I'm happy to say it'll taste just fine, thank you very much. "I keep waiting for the other shoe to drop, like there's no way this is real. Am I allowed to be this happy again? To . . . *to fall*"—I whisper the word, biting my lip before continuing. "I'm terrified it's going to be taken away from me at any second."

"I think we all feel like that from time to time," Vi says, placing the dip in the center of the veggies, then dusts her hands off. "But that man is nuts about you, that's obvious. Pretty sure it would take a Cat-5 hurricane to tear that man from you at this point."

"Or a wildfire," I quip dryly, only half joking. I squeeze my eyes shut and berate myself. *Don't do this now. Don't ruin this. This is Dalton's day.*

Before either of them can say anything, I grab several platters of food and head out the front door. The guys have laid out several queen-size flat sheets on the grass as picnic blankets, and I force a smile onto my face as I get closer. Vi and Scottie exit behind me, both carrying food too. I avoid their prying gazes as best I can.

We eat, laugh, play, and then sing Dalton a rather loud and off-tune rendition of "Happy Birthday" before allowing Dalton

TEDDY

to open his presents. Cal is lying on his side, head propped up in his hand as he leans on his elbow, with Scottie stretched out in front of him. His other hand is idly stroking her side, almost absent-mindedly, like it pains him to lose that physical contact with her. Rowan is sitting up, knees raised, with Vi sitting between them with her back to his chest. Hollie and Penny are lying on their bellies on a sheet next to us, and when I look over, they're playing with a grasshopper that they've managed to catch. I grin and roll my eyes.

Kent and Colleen took their leave as soon as presents were done, but Colleen will be back in a few days to watch the kids for me while I work.

I stand, handing Bea over to Vi, who snuggles her close while I gather the discarded wrapping paper and a few of the leftover dinner items. Cal pushes to his feet and picks up several of Dalton's new gifts, then follows me into the house.

"So . . . this thing with Xander."

My brother is awkward as hell sometimes. I blow out a heavy exhale and turn, leaning my hips against the kitchen counter. He's staring at me, though his expression is guarded, worried almost.

"Are you mad about it?" The words come out hesitantly, so quiet I'm not sure he even heard them.

"No," he says slowly, shaking his head. "I'm not mad about it. I just . . . I don't want to see you get hurt again. I worry about you more than you know I do, Ted. You're my little sister."

I smile gently over at him. "I know you do. That's what makes you the best big brother."

He shakes his head, rolling his eyes. "Don't be a sap."

"You started it," I tease, shifting my weight from one foot to the other. Crossing my arms over my stomach, I ask timidly, "Did you know how he felt? Before, I mean?"

He bobbles his head side to side, his mouth pulling up into a sort of half grimace, half smirk. "Yes and no. I didn't know the extent of how he felt necessarily, but I noticed things. Like the way he always watched you. I didn't really put it together until recently. He's pretty crazy about you, Ted."

My face heats and I drop my gaze to stare at my toes. "I think I really like him, Cal."

"I know," he says gently. "That's what scares me."

I nod, still staring at my toes. "It scares me too."

He crosses the space between us and leans his hips against the counter beside me, draping his arm across my shoulders and tugging me into his side. I slip my arm around his waist, leaning my head against him for a long minute. He squeezes my shoulder. "He might be my boss, but I'll kick his ass if he hurts you. I'll take the write-up."

I bark out a laugh, shaking my head as I look up at him from where we're standing side by side. "Thanks."

"Come on, let's go back out," he mutters, winking. "That's enough mushy love shit for one night."

When we wander back outside, Xander is kneeling in the grass in the middle of the yard with Dalton, working to put together the automatic football-throwing machine he'd gotten from his grand-parents. It moves side to side and up and down before launching the football into the sky. Dalton runs halfway across the yard, spinning as the ball is launched, and he almost has his hands on it, but misses, rolling into the grass with a laugh.

"This thing is so cool!" Dalton exclaims, throwing the football back to Xander, who gets it ready again. This time, when the ball is launched, Dalton is ready for it, making a spectacular running catch.

He runs up to Xander, who ruffles his hair and holds out his fist. Dalton bumps it, grinning up at him.

"Way to go, champ. That was a great catch!"

"Thanks! Can we do it again?"

Xander glances over at me and winks. "We'll stay out as late as your mom will let us, champ."

TEDDY

Ugh. My heart. I look down at my left hand, the wedding ring I've been avoiding taking off, because in a way, it protects me from admitting what I've known for a while. At least, that's what the grief counselor told me at this week's session. And it makes so much sense . . .

I twist the ring on my finger and then sigh. It's time to be brave and take it off. To put it away and turn the page on that wonderful chapter of my life . . . to start a new one.

With Xander.

41

XANDER

I'm too old for this shit.

We're a town over from Sky Ridge helping the local fire department contain a blaze that jumped from a barn fire to the surrounding wildland. We were quick on the scene and there isn't much damage, but goddamn, this was not the way I wanted to end my night.

No, I wanted to end my night buried balls-deep in my beautiful woman, wrapped up in her bed like we have been for the last several weeks.

I'm a wreck. Utterly and hopelessly enamored with Teddy and her kids. For the first time in my life, I hated leaving to head into a fire. Even knowing it's a simple job and I'll be back home to her within a few hours, considering that we can keep this from spreading. Which my crew is doing pretty fucking well.

I'm on a quad, the small headlights showing my way through the forested area as I scout. The boys are working fast and hard to head this thing off so we can all go the fuck home.

Picking my way carefully over dead logs, rocks, and up a steep embankment, I'm able to find a good spot to watch the blaze. I breathe a sigh of relief seeing that my team has it covered. Only one small section still blooms red in the dark.

So, down I head, back toward the action.

I find a narrow strip of mostly flat land with little to no obstructions running along a long line of fencing and hit the throttle, the headlight beams bouncing in the night and illuminating the smoke that's drifting everywhere.

I can hear my crew on the other side of the tree line as I get closer, and then I'm airborne as the back end of the quad flips up on the right front wheel. I have a heartbeat to register what's happening before I'm tossed into the fencing that I've been zipping along.

And as the bite of the razor wire registers as it catches my fall, I know this isn't going to be pretty.

42

Teddy

"Nine-one-one, what's the location of your emergency?"

After a long day, I'm ready to be heading home. I'm a half-hour away from being done and I cannot wait to get home to Xander and the kids.

"Uh, yeah, I've got a guy out here that's caught in some razor wire. We've almost got him cut out, but he's in pretty rough shape."

"What's the location?" I ask again, keeping my voice neutral as I type.

"We're down here at a structural fire on Clemmons."

I continue typing. I was the one that had responded to the original call for the barn fire, sending out the local fire department to handle it. "Is the victim conscious?"

"Yeah, poor bastard," the guy says, and I press my lips together.

I send the codes and immediately get a response from EMS that they are en route. "I have EMS on the way. How badly is he bleeding?"

"Hard to tell in the dark. Hey, Opp, how bad is Sup bleeding?"

My fingers stall on the keyboard in front of me and my back straightens as if a string attached to my head has just been yanked. "Sir, who is the victim?"

"Sup. Superintendent Xander Macomb from the Sky Ridge Hotshot crew," the man says distractedly.

I feel the blood rush from my head and I feel faint.

"We had them called in to help after it spread to the surrounding forest area."

I'm barely listening. I try to keep typing, but my brain has given up all functioning. And then my phone is buzzing next to me, Cal's name scrolling across the screen.

"Sir, hold on one moment," I manage to whisper, and then I call over to Laurel, who just walked in. "Laurel, I need you to take over."

"Teddy, you look like you've just seen a ghost! Are you all right? Is it your kids?" she asks, striding over to me. She yanks the headset off my head and places it on her own, then pushes my chair aside. "Go. Whatever it is, I've got this."

I swipe my phone off the desk and stand, stumbling as I answer my brother's call. "Cal?"

"He's fine," my brother says, though it doesn't calm me in the slightest.

Panic is coursing through me, making my limbs feel both like they weigh a million pounds and like they're filled with helium at the same time. I'm outside and rushing to my car.

"He's ornery as fuck and that mug looks a little less handsome than it did this morning—"

"Callahan Woods, don't you make this into a joke right now," I snap, my throat closing as tears well in my eyes. "How bad?"

He sighs, and I can only imagine the way he's rubbing the back of his neck right now. There's a lot of noise in the background. "It's not great. His right forearm got tangled pretty bad when he landed

282

along with his side. His face got a couple decent slices. Ambulance just got here, but he's crotchety as hell and is refusing to get in."

"You tell that man to get into that fucking ambulance and that I'll meet him at the hospital," I whisper-hiss, making Cal chuckle.

"Hey, your woman says get your ass in the ambulance," he calls over.

To which I then hear over the din of other voices, "Teddy? Sweetheart, I'm okay!"

I fight back the sob that is pushing at my throat as I drive toward Bakersfield Hospital. "Tell him I will believe that when I see it for myself."

"She says you're a lying sack of shit."

I hear Xander's answering laugh, but then it's choked off by a pained groan. "Cal," I choke out.

"I know," he whispers, and I let the tears slip down my cheeks. "I know, Ted."

"Tell him I'm on my way and that he better be too."

"I will," he says gently, and then we hang up.

I'm a nervous wreck waiting in the parking lot of the hospital's emergency department, and when I see the flash of the ambulance lights pulling in, I'm out of the car and sprinting across the parking lot before it's even stopped. The doors open and I see Scottie and Matthew before my eyes fall on Xander on the stretcher inside.

His shirt has been cut off him and his upper body is bare, but white bandages crisscross over his abdomen and completely cover his right forearm and hand, and in one spot it's blooming red with blood as it seeps through. White butterfly bandages are keeping several cuts on his face closed.

"Ohmygod," I whimper, my fingers flying to cover my lips. "Xander."

"Hey, beautiful," he says, smiling over at me as they unload him from the back of the ambulance. His face is taut with pain, his lips thin. He's paler than ever, which worries me. They start wheeling him inside the doors, and I follow, my hand finding his unbandaged left hand. I squeeze so tightly I worry belatedly I'm going to hurt him, but then he squeezes back. He grins wryly, bringing my fingers to his lips as we walk. "This isn't the date night I had planned for us later."

I can't stop the choking laugh that escapes me as I look over him entirely. "You're incorrigible."

"I really didn't need all this fanfare," he quips lightly. "I could have just wrapped it and got back to work."

Scottie blows out a snorting laugh, rolling her eyes. "That flap of skin hanging off your arm says otherwise."

"It's fine," he mutters, though his lips thin again as they transfer him from the stretcher to a freshly made hospital bed in the emergency room. "No big deal. Just superglue it and send me back out."

"You're not funny," I whisper, tracing my eyes over every inch of him, dragging his dirty, soot-stained hand to my lips. His skin smells like soil, smoke, and diesel fuel, a combination of scents that will more than likely forever link my brain to Xander.

"Rookie mistake is all," he mutters, though his eyes are soft as they meet mine. I know he's trying to play this down like it's no big deal, to comfort me. "I promise you, sweetheart, this is nothing. I'm fine."

"Well, just humor me, please," I whisper against the backs of his fingers. I fight against the tears; he doesn't need to see me be a complete basket case over something that probably isn't that big of a deal.

"Yes, Mama," he murmurs back, uncurling his fingers so he can cup my jaw in his palm, his thumb strumming along my cheek.

I close my eyes for just a second, taking a long, steady breath in.

I'm ushered out of the room then with the promise that I can come back to see him shortly. Scottie walks me back out to the waiting room. "They'll probably stitch him up, give him an antibiotic shot, and then send him on his way. I know it looked like a lot of blood, but his gear kept it from being worse."

She hugs me tightly and then she and Matthew are gone, heading back out. I sit in one of the uncomfortable vinyl teal chairs and bounce my leg nervously. I call Colleen to tell her what happened, and that I'll be home shortly. She assures me that she can put the kids to bed and she'll be waiting for me when I can get back.

Head propped in my hand, I have my eyes closed when the sound of the automatic door swishes open and then, "Hey, beautiful. Ready to go?"

My eyes fly open and I jump out of my chair, rushing toward him. He's got a hospital-issued scrub shirt pulled on to cover his previously naked torso. White gauze is wrapped around his entire right arm from fingers to bicep, and I can see the bulky wrap that encircles his torso and chest beneath the fabric of the scrub shirt. A sheaf of papers is folded in half and clutched in his left hand, hanging at his side.

"Any discharge instructions?" I ask, stopping in front of him.

I'm scared to touch him, anxious that I'll somehow hurt him, making me a nervous wreck. He drapes his left arm over my shoulder and pulls me into his body, dropping his mouth to my forehead in a kiss. Tears burn my nose again. God, I hate this.

"Just to keep everything bandaged for two days before taking any of the wrappings off, and to redress it every few days for a couple weeks. Stitches can come out in two weeks. Guess I'm taking a sponge bath at home," he grumbles, earning a side-eye glare from an older woman sitting in a chair by the door as we make our way toward it.

Out in the dark parking lot, his arm still slung over my shoulders, I lean into his side. "You scared the shit out of me," I whisper into the darkness as we make our way toward my car.

TEDDY

His mouth presses to the top of my head again, and I hear him murmur quietly, almost sadly, "I know, sweetheart. I'm sorry. I'd love to promise you it's the last time, but we both know that's probably a lie, and I don't want to lie to you, Teddy."

43

Teddy

"Everything okay?" Colleen asks as soon as I'm through the door.

I set my purse down on the counter and sigh, nodding. I'm exhausted. The last few hours were emotionally taxing, and I'm trying hard not to spiral.

"Xander had an accident out on a fire," I say quietly, unsure how to organize my thoughts into any semblance of calm.

"Come sit," Colleen says, pulling out one of the barstools at the kitchen counter.

I do, sinking into it gratefully. She moves around my kitchen, pulling a small pot out of the cupboard and filling it with water. She sets it on the stove to warm, and then plucks a mug out of the cabinet as well as a bag of tea. We're quiet while she works, and then a few minutes later, she sets a steaming cup of tea in front of me.

"Chamomile," is all she says, then sits down next to me.

"Thank you," I whisper before cradling the mug between my fingers, warming them. I hadn't realized how chilled I'd gotten sitting in the emergency department waiting room. The fear, the worry about Xander, comes crashing through me all over again, followed by such intense guilt that it seizes my breaths. Tears well in my eyes and I blink rapidly to dispel them.

"I always knew you and Logan would end up where you did," my mother-in-law says into the quiet of the room. "It was like we just knew as soon as he brought you home that first time this was it. There was never going to be anyone else that fit him better than you did. Through every stage of your lives, you two were always constant. Not to say you were both always sunshine and roses," she smiles, teasing lightly.

I smile into my tea, tears filling my eyes.

"But there was just this rightness between you. You made my son the happiest man, Teddy. You gave him a wonderful life and three beautiful children. He loved you with everything he had in him. You always had this warmth, this glow, whenever you looked at him. You loved him so well, sweet girl."

Grief tightens my throat. I did love Logan. So, so much. And part of me still does. For most of my life, he was my only love. My great love. But now, with Xander . . .

She reaches out and takes one of my hands in both of hers, squeezing it tightly. I glance up at her, my vision blurry.

"I see that warmth in you now, Teddy. I see the glow coming back to your eyes, whenever you look at Xander. I hated seeing that light leave you after Logan died," she whispers earnestly, tears shimmering in her own brown eyes. "You already love him."

I open my mouth to say something, though nothing comes out. I don't know that I'm ready to admit it, but denying it feels wrong too. "I don't want you to be upset with me," I finally manage to whisper, my voice breaking around the words. "Because Logan was your son."

"Teddy," Colleen murmurs, gathering me into her arms for a tight hug. "You are just as much mine as he was. Part of you will always love him and will always grieve for the love and the life that was stolen from you . . . just like I will always miss my son. I might meddle more than I should, and I might push harder than what is conventional; but I love you and I want to see you happy again. Take this chance. As scary as it is, take it. How could I say that I love you and be upset with you because you're finding joy again? That's not what love is," she whispers so gently, cupping my cheeks, her eyes shining.

I'm crying fully now.

"I love you enough to want to see you be *you again*, my sweet girl."

Who gets this lucky with a mother-in-law? There's no judgment in her eyes, her tone, her words. Just simple, undiluted, unconditional love.

"I'm so grateful for you," I whisper, smiling, before leaning in to hug her tightly again. "You are the best bonus mom I could have asked for."

"Kent's mother wasn't quite as fond of me," she says, laughing, waving one hand. "I promised that I would never be that way if I was fortunate enough to be blessed with a daughter-in-law. It helps that you're pretty fantastic."

I laugh out loud, leaning away to swipe at my eyes. "I love you."

"As you should," she teases.

I smile gratefully over at her, and she says, "I love you, Teddy. It's okay to be happy again. I promise."

44

XANDER

I made Teddy go inside her house to tuck her kids into bed while I headed into mine. I'm a filthy, bloodstained mess and need to clean myself up.

Stripping out of the hospital scrub top, my boots, and my now-bloodstained Nomex pants, I do the best I can to wash my body without getting the bandages taped to my right side and wrapped around my right arm wet. I use the handheld showerhead to wash the rest of my body, and then bend over the best I can inside the tub to wash my dirty hair and scrub the dirt and soot off my face and neck. Toweling dry, I sling the towel around my neck and venture into the bedroom to find a pair of sweats that are easy to pull on and a clean T-shirt. The burning pain from the cuts is dull and aches even through the meds they'd given me in the hospital.

Walking barefoot back to the kitchen, I see out the window as Colleen pulls out of the driveway to head home for the night. Teddy's two work shifts are over for the week, so Colleen won't be back until next week.

I grab a beer out of the fridge and pop it open, lifting it to my lips and downing half of it before I cringe and set it down. I'd forgotten about the pain meds. Shit.

Sinking into one of the chairs at the dining table, I pick up the yet unopened envelope that I've been staring at for weeks now. I pick it up and carry it with me through the house. Sit and stare at it some more. Now, I pick it up and tap one corner of it on the table in front of me.

I just can't bring myself to open it. To read it. I don't want to know what my dad's last words are to me. I'd almost thrown it away without opening it but then had sworn viciously and dug it back out, slapping it down on the counter and stalking off. Leaving it for another day.

I keep telling myself I'll read it when I get back from the next fire.

And then I get back from the fire and I do this all over again, just staring at it. Just to toss it aside and tell myself *after the next fire, I'll open it*.

A soft, timid knock on the glass patio door turns my head, and I smile before standing. Teddy is there, waiting for me to let her in. My beautiful girl.

She's got the baby monitor clutched in one hand as she steps inside. I curl my arms around her at the same time she twines hers around my waist gently. We stand like that for a long time, simply breathing each other in, reveling in the closeness. I can feel her heart beating against my chest, the little way her lips flit over my pecs as she presses kisses to where I know she can feel my own heart beating.

"What's this?" she asks, gesturing to the table where the envelope sits.

I sigh, tightening my arms around her shoulders and pressing my cheek to the top of her head. "It's a letter from my dad."

XANDER

"Your dad?" she whispers, surprise lifting her tone.

I nod. "My brother is moving and found it stuck in with some of his stuff. He sent it back to me, but I haven't been able to read it."

"I had a voicemail from Logan that I refused to listen to after he died," she whispers, spreading her fingers wide across my back. She scoffs lightly. "Once I finally convinced myself to listen to it, I was so mad."

"What did he say?" I ask, rubbing my uninjured cheek against her head.

She shakes her head, another scoffing laugh escaping her. "Just that he loved me and that he would see me after his shift."

I squeeze my arms around her.

"I was so angry at him for leaving. For not coming home after the end of that shift. Leaving me alone with our two kids and pregnant with another baby. I deleted it and then cried because I wanted it back."

I chuckle lightly, rocking us together gently. "You're not really selling me on reading this letter, sweetheart."

She shrugs. "You'll never know until you do." She tips her chin up so she can look up at me then. "Are you coming to bed?"

Smoothing the fingers of my left hand over her hair, I kiss her chastely. "Probably not tonight, Mama. I'm going to be tossing and turning all night and I don't want to keep you up."

"I don't mind," she whispers against my lips, and I smile. "Please don't make me sleep without you tonight. I need to know you're okay, that you're here."

I hate that she worries about me, but I know there's no point in telling her not to. "Okay."

"No funny business," she warns, glaring at me adorably.

I laugh, reaching around her to turn off the lights.

"If you think a couple cuts will keep me from fucking you tonight, you're sorely mistaken, beautiful."

"Xander . . ."

"Yes, Mama?" I murmur, dragging her into my arms once again. Dropping my mouth to hers, I kiss her thoroughly.

She sighs, her eyelids fluttering open to stare up at me. "That's not fair."

"What's not fair?"

"Kissing me to distract me."

"Is that what I'm doing?" I ask, nipping at her lower lip.

She moans, and I smile.

That's what I thought.

She tugs me by my left hand through the patio door and over to hers. Honestly, her duplex is more my place than my own is at this point. I haven't slept in my own bed in weeks, and I can't even lie, I don't really want to. Wherever she is, is where I want to be too.

A dim lamp has been kept on in the corner of her bedroom, softly illuminating the room. She sets the baby monitor on the bedside table and then turns toward me, her hands reaching for me.

"I have another idea that will be a little . . . less exertive . . . for you," she whispers, tilting up on her tiptoes to press her mouth to mine.

Her fingers are playing with the bottom hem of my T-shirt, the backs of her fingers teasing the flesh of my abdomen. She raises the T-shirt slowly, drawing her hands along every inch of my abdomen, my ribs, my chest, until I can yank it over my head, letting it fall to the floor. I suck in a breath when those fingers slide back down my abdomen to slip into the waistband of my sweats. I was already half hard—simply kissing her does that to me—but all the blood in my head rushes south at her tentative, teasing touches.

My left hand slides up the side of her neck, thumb wrapping around to collar it from the front, and the little moaning sigh that escapes her lips drives me a little crazy. She's so fucking receptive, so trusting. I love watching her come to life beneath my fingers, my mouth.

"What did you have in mind, Mama?" I breathe, dragging my mouth across hers over and over.

Her hands flatten on the sides of my waist, fingers sliding inside the waistband of my sweats until her palms are flat against my ass, and then she's dragging the pants down. I'd forgone underwear because they were too much of a bitch to get on one-handed, so as the sweatpants lower, my cock bobs out between us, hard and heavy.

"I want your cock in my mouth," she whispers, her lips moving against my own.

Goddamn. This woman.

"Yeah?" I ask, the single word ripping out of my throat in a growl. My fingers tighten around her neck, just slightly, at the same time tilting her face up toward mine.

She nods, those gray eyes limpid and silver in the dim light. I can feel her pulse thrumming beneath my fingers.

"You want to suck my cock, Teddy?"

She nods again.

Fuckkk. "On your knees. Show me how bad you want it."

I thought I was prepared for the sight of Teddy on her knees in front of me, but nothing could have prepared me for this. Goddamn, this woman is incredible. So fucking beautiful. Her golden-blond hair is twisted up into a clip, so I reach out and release it, tossing the clip onto the floor as her hair tumbles down around her shoulders. The only thing that will be holding this hair back are my own hands. Running my fingers along her jaw reverently, I sweep her hair away from her face.

"Open your mouth," I rasp, taking my cock in my fist and stroking it slowly.

She licks her lips and then she does as I ask, sticking her tongue out.

I grin wolfishly down at her. "Greedy girl. You want this so bad, don't you?"

She nods again, and I guide the tip of my shaft to her lips. Her jaw opens wider and I groan as she closes her lips around the tip, her tongue swirling over the head, and then she brushes my hand aside so she can take me deeper.

"Oh fuck," I rasp, my eyes sliding shut when the tip of my dick reaches the back of her throat. I gather her hair in my left hand, holding it back, twisting my fingers into it and gripping the back of her head as she works me inside her mouth. She's fucking glorious. My chest heaves with panting, heavy breaths, and I watch her, this woman that I'm fucking crazy about.

My hips rock of their own volition, my dick sliding in and out of her mouth. What a fucking sight. I go deep again and she gags around my length, but she doesn't pull back.

No, this incredible fucking woman just slides her hands around the backs of my thighs and pulls me closer, and then she swallows, the muscles of her throat closing around me.

I see fucking stars.

"Fuck!" I hiss, my mouth falling open. "Holy shit, Teddy. You're doing so fucking good, Mama. *So good.*"

She hums around my length and it sends shivers up my spine. She pops off my dick and looks up at me. "Fuck my mouth, Xander. Come on my tongue. Please."

Fucking marry me.

Gripping the back of her head roughly, I bend low and ignore the sharp twinge in my side so that I can take her mouth in a hard, searing kiss. Her lips are puffy and soft and I taste myself on her. I fight the urge to beat my chest like a Neanderthal.

"You want me to fuck this mouth, Teddy?" I growl, nipping her swollen bottom lip between my teeth sharply.

She gasps, and then nods frantically.

I grin against her mouth. Goddamn, I can't get enough of this woman. Like she was fucking made for me. "You want my cum?"

"Yes," she gasps, her breathing ragged. She's so beautiful it hurts. She shifts on her knees, pressing her thighs together. Oh, my little Mama likes this a lot. "Please."

"How can I tell my girl no when she asks so nicely?" I breathe on a dark growl. Straightening, I gather her hair back in my hand again, holding tighter than before. "You keep your eyes on me, Teddy, understand? Do not close your eyes. I want you to watch what you do to me, sweetheart. And when I come down your throat, you better be coming on your fingers."

Her lips drop open in shock, a blush staining her cheeks prettily. "You want me to . . ."

"Play with your pussy, Teddy," I groan, tapping the head of my cock against her lips. She opens for me. "Play with that pretty pink pussy until you come all over your fingers. But do not close your eyes. Eyes on me."

She nods, her hand disappearing between her thighs and into the sleep shorts she'd already changed into before coming over to my house to find me.

"Now open this mouth and take every inch," I whisper. I slide myself back between her lips and she hollows her cheeks, sucking me in. "Fucking Christ, Teddy, I'm not going to last with you doing shit like that—"

She does it again and I growl out a warning. Her silver eyes are twinkling, the little brat. And then she starts circling her clit and I love the way she moans around me at her own pleasure. My grip on the back of her head tightens.

"Ready, Mama?" I ask, and she nods. I unleash, pistoning my hips in short, deep thrusts. She gags again but I don't stop. Her eyes are on mine, and the sight does me in. She's just so goddamn beautiful. Every fucking part of her is made for me. She's shuddering against me, her eyes fluttering closed as she moans, and I know she's close. Fuck. "I'm going to come, Teddy. Don't you dare close your eyes.

You look at me when you come. You look at me when I give you every last fucking drop—"

She cries out around my cock, her shoulders trembling as she comes, her thighs shaking where she's kneeling.

"Yes, Teddy, come on your fingers for me." I groan at the sight of her coming with my cock in her mouth. She moans, her eyes on mine, glassy and heavy lidded, and then I'm coming with a guttural growl, my vision going dark at the edges with the intensity of my release. Long, hot ropes of cum paint the back of her throat and she swallows every drop like the good girl she is. I shudder, fingers clenching in her hair before sliding out to smooth tenderly over her cheek and jaw as I slide out of her mouth. "Goddamn, my beautiful girl. You did so fucking good."

I chuckle then, swiping at the corner of her mouth. Her lips are puffy. She's never looked more beautiful.

"Are you laughing at me?" she asks breathlessly, her voice husky, eyes teasing. "You could damage a girl's confidence doing something like that—"

"Fucking brat," I growl in warning, grinning as I shake my head at her. Leaning down, I kiss her again slowly. "That was the best fucking blowjob I've ever gotten. I was just thinking that that was not any less exertive . . . And now all I want to do is taste this wet pussy and make you come again."

"Xander—" she moans, protesting, but it's weak. We both know the night isn't over yet. Not even close.

XANDER

45

Teddy

"What happened to Xander's arm?" Dalton asks from the back seat.

I look in the rearview mirror and my heartstrings tug at the way he's fiddling with a baseball between his hands. I smile as brightly as I can muster, doing my best to ease the worry etched into his young face. "He flipped his ATV last night on a call, kind of cut up his arm a bit. But he's okay."

Turning my attention back to the road, I follow traffic and head in the direction of Dalton's school. Penny is always our first drop-off. Once I'd walked her inside and then climbed back into the driver's seat, he'd asked about Xander.

"Mom," he says quietly, and I look up into the rearview mirror again. "Is Xander going to die too? Like Dad?"

"Oh, sweetheart, no," I murmur, my heart cracking for this sweet, sensitive boy.

"His job is dangerous, right? More dangerous than Dad's was," he continues, and I hate the shimmer of tears that fill his brown eyes.

My chest is cleaving in two.

"What if he dies, too?"

Flipping my blinker on, I turn onto a side street and then pull over onto the shoulder. I climb out and open the slider door so I can climb in. Tears sting the bridge of my nose, but I push them back. Right now, my big little man needs his momma.

"Come here, sweetheart," I whisper, and he unbuckles, climbing between the seats so I can wrap him up in my arms.

This sweet boy. He's at the age where he's starting to want more independence, but at the same time, he's still a boy that needs extra snuggles sometimes. He's going to get embarrassed in a couple of minutes at the show of emotion, but I want him to know it's okay to have these big feelings. Especially for people we care so deeply about.

"Some people have big, dangerous jobs, but those people are highly trained. Xander has been doing this job for so long he could probably do it with his eyes closed," I whisper, rocking him gently. I swallow hard. "What happened with Dad was an awful accident, bud. Something none of us could see coming. But the people that do these jobs, Dalton, they know that sometimes bad things might happen. They know that they're saving people that need help. And that's a really amazing thing. To be so selfless that they want to do a scary job because they know that other people might be too scared to do it. But there's always going to be people that need helping and saving."

"I really miss Dad," he whispers, his little voice breaking, and then his shoulders are shaking.

I hold him tightly, tears leaking out of my own eyes at the heartbreak causing my son pain.

"I don't want Xander to die too."

"Oh, buddy," I murmur, clutching him close. "You're not going to lose him, okay?"

"I made a wish on my birthday, but now I'm scared for it to come true."

TEDDY

"What wish, sweetheart?" I ask gently, rubbing his back.

He takes a deep breath in. "Don't be mad . . . I figured since you two like each other a lot and we like him too that it wouldn't be too bad. But I wished for Xander to be my new dad, since I don't have one anymore, and I think he likes me and Penny. And baby Bea never got to have a dad . . . But I'm scared that if he does get to be my new dad, that he'll die like Dad did. And then I'll have lost two dads."

I'm stunned, lost for words as what little bit of my heart that had been left unshattered crumbles into dust at my feet.

And I realize that I'm not the only one that's in love with Xander. My kids love him too.

By the time I get Dalton calmed down, we're late for drop-off, but I don't care. I call the school and inform them that he will be a little late, and we go out for breakfast, just us and Bea. Once he's back to his usual self, I take him to school, walking him into the office to sign him in. He hugs me tightly around the middle, and then he's off.

Driving back home, I'm a wreck. Tears won't stop flowing from my eyes, and it feels like my chest is caving in on itself. What am I supposed to do? I have no idea how to traverse this. My children are so head over heels for this man . . . how am I supposed to promise my son that Xander isn't going to get hurt, or worse? I can't make that promise. No one can.

Unloading Bea from the back seat, I carry her inside. Xander's truck is in the driveway, but he's not inside my house, so I'm assuming he headed over to his side of the duplex while we were gone. I nurse Bea and she goes down for her midmorning nap easily. Tucking her in, I grab the baby monitor and slide open the back patio door, stepping over to Xander's.

I knock lightly, though I know he sees me approach from where he's standing in the kitchen. His phone is to his ear, but he steps over and slides open the patio door, allowing me inside.

"Yeah," he says, turning back to the coffee cup sitting on the counter. He goes to lift it but realizes he can't with his right hand bandaged the way it is and swears under his breath before shifting the phone so it's tucked between his shoulder and ear. He picks up the coffee cup with his left hand, raising it to his lips. "How many acres?" He listens, his lips pulling into a grimace. "Vantage crew is missing? Fuck." He's quiet again, listening to whoever is on the other end of the line, his eyes finding mine, and I know what's coming next. My heart breaks all over again. "How many are missing? How long?"

I clutch the back of one of the dining chairs, my knuckles turning white with how tightly I'm gripping it to keep myself upright.

"We'll be on the road in an hour," he says, and I squeeze my eyes shut, my body sagging.

He hangs up but immediately dials another number. When it's answered, he says quietly, "Wheels in one hour." He's quiet for a second, and then I recognize my brother's voice on the other end of the line. "Vantage crew is missing." My brother's gruff expletive hangs in the silence. "Okay. Round up the boys. We leave in one hour."

He hangs up a second time, and the silence between us is deafening.

"I've got to go, Teddy," he finally whispers, and I open my eyes.

Damn this man for stealing my heart. For making me fall in love with him, for making my kids fall in love with him. Damn my own weakness for doing exactly what I've been saying I won't do . . .

How do I protect my heart—and my kids' hearts—when he's taking them all with him when he walks out that door?

TEDDY

46

XANDER

"What about your arm?" she asks, gesturing to my right side. Her words are brittle and they slice through me. I hate seeing her upset like this.

I glance down at the bandages and flex my fingers as much as I can inside the gauze. It's going to be a bitch working one-handed, that's for sure. Or I'll just cut the damn stuff off and hope the stitches hold.

"I'll be fine," I murmur, stepping toward her to pull her against me.

She's stiff, holding herself rigid.

I exhale heavily, leaning my cheek against the top of her head. "I need to go grab my pack."

I release her and head down the hall to my bedroom. She follows, slowly, her arms crossed over her middle as if trying to hold herself together.

"I don't know how long we'll be gone," I tell her while grabbing my pack from the closet. I set it on the bed and start rifling through it, making sure everything is ready to go.

"I don't want you to go," she whispers, and I look at her from where I'm going through my things on the bed.

I straighten. "I know, but I have to, you know that," I murmur gently. Fuck, she's making this really fucking hard. "This fire . . . it's bad. An entire crew is missing, I have to go help—"

"You're injured, Xander! Still healing, and yet you're *jumping* to head back out into another fire? A fire that you just admitted to being extremely dangerous—" Her words cut off abruptly as she shakes her head in disbelief, tears shimmering in her eyes, making them look like liquid silver.

Dammit. This is why I don't date. Because this, the moments before I'm supposed to walk out the door and head into a fire, are always the worst. And I can't blame her for any of it. "That is exactly why I have to go, Teddy," I say, forcing my voice to remain even as I continue readying my pack. "There are teams out there that need help. I cannot sit here and send my crew out there without me. I can't stay here and wait while other teams battle this blaze, knowing I should be out there helping—"

"*You're hurt!*" she cries again, gesturing to my right arm again. "What good are you out there if you're hurt? Other than raising the risk of you yourself getting hurt even worse—"

"Believe it or not, I know what I'm doing," I mutter, my tone harsher than intended.

She reels back, her brows drawing together.

I exhale a heavy breath, scrubbing my hand over my face. "I have been fighting fires since you were in grade school, Teddy."

"I don't want you to go." Her words are quiet, desperate. She's curving in on herself, like she always does, and I fucking hate that I'm the cause of it. A tear slides down her cheek and she reaches up to swipe at it quickly, but not before it seizes my own heart in my chest. "Please, Xander. I can't watch you walk out that door. Stay. Stay for me, *please*."

XANDER

"You know I can't do that." The words physically pain me to whisper.

Her lips wobble and she wraps her arms around her middle the way I hate.

"Teddy, if I could stay, I would. *For you*, I would if I could, but I can't—"

"*You can!*" she cries, more tears slipping down her cheeks. "You said you love me . . . You just have to choose me. Choose *us*." Her voice breaks on the last word and she dips her chin as she cries.

I ache to hold her, but I know if I do, I won't have the strength to walk out the door, to meet my team and do the job I know I have to do.

The job I am honor bound to do.

"I told Scottie I wouldn't beg you to stay, but I'm not brave like she is, Xander. I can't watch you walk away from me, knowing you're willingly walking into something as dangerous as this. *Please*," she begs quietly, raising those eyes to mine, and I almost break.

Fuck, I almost say yes to her, just to erase that pain from her face.

"Please, don't go. Don't make me worry about losing you. I'm not strong enough to do this again."

"You lost your husband, Teddy, and I understand how scary this is for you. But you're asking me to give up something *I love*," I whisper, shaking my head. "Something I am good at, something that lets me help people. You're asking me to give up what I love because you're too scared to try—"

"*Yes!*" she sobs, spreading her fingers out wide across her chest as if trying to contain the hurt. "Yes, I am scared! I'm terrified! I had a great love and I lost it, but why am I the bad guy because I'm not jumping at the chance to go through that again? Losing him nearly killed me, Xander. Not to mention my kids . . ."

That stings more than I expected it to. Makes my heart feel like it's being trampled inside my chest.

I've suspected she's not over her husband, but hearing the words come out of her mouth, that he is her great love . . . it hurts far more than I want it to. My own walls go up as hurt and anger and bitterness take over. Jaw hardening, I point to her left hand, still splayed wide across her chest. I'm not proud of what comes out of my mouth next. "When do you plan on taking that ring off your finger, Teddy?"

She swallows hard, her face paling slightly in the dim light, her fingers twitching where they rest. "Xander . . ."

I shake my head, just once, and she presses her lips together, more tears filling her eyes. "You're asking me to give up the love of my life, while you're still wearing another man's ring."

Tears spill over her lids and she blinks rapidly, though her eyes never leave mine. "He was my *husband*, Xander . . ." Her whispered words are nearly deafening in the quiet of the room, ringing like death knells in my head.

"I love you, Teddy. But do you love me?" I ask, my voice sounding hollow to my ears.

Tears shimmer in her eyes again, her chest and shoulders shaking, but she stays resolutely silent.

The pain in my chest is nearly debilitating. Why do people do this to themselves? This fucking sucks.

Backing away, I lower my eyes from hers. I need to get out of here. I'm late as it is. My team is waiting for me.

"*Xander—*" she cries brokenly, taking a stumbling step toward me, reaching out one hand. I shrug away from her touch and she sobs, her shoulders shaking as she stops in the middle of my bedroom. "He was my husband—"

"*Was!*" I exclaim with a shout, spreading my arms wide.

Tears slide down her cheeks unchecked, her lower lip wobbling precariously.

The agony in her eyes is nearly my undoing. My breathing is ragged, chest heaving, heart fucking breaking. I know I'm not being fair, but cornered animals rarely fight fair. "*Was*, Teddy. He's gone. He's gone, and I'm *right fucking here!*" I slap my hand to my chest, where my own heart is threatening to end me. *"I'm right here, dammit!"*

She sobs, her body shaking with her tears. "Xander, you have to understand this isn't easy for me—"

A derisive, cold snort escapes me, and another broken sob from her tears my heart clear out of my chest. She wants me, but not enough to let me have a place in her heart. I was a fool to think I could win her heart when it still belongs to someone else.

And because I'm a heartbroken, mean bastard, I lash out the only way I know how.

"Oh, I understand perfectly," I mutter, snatching up my pack and turning toward her, but I refuse to let her tears sway me. I can't keep doing this. Pining for a woman that will never want me the way I want her. "When you're ready to move on from that ghost in your bed, let me know, Teddy. Because I can't keep competing with a dead man's ghost for your heart, and I sure as hell won't be a placeholder in your bed for him either."

Her shoulders shake with her tears, her lips pressed tightly together to silence the sobs wracking her body.

"I need you to go," I growl through the ache in my throat. My jaw twinges with how hard I'm grinding my molars together, and I gesture toward the door behind her. "I'm late, and my crew is waiting for me."

47

Teddy

I've never been one to follow the news on forest fires.

It only ever added to my anxiety, knowing my brother was out there. So I avoided them for the most part. I would wait until I heard from him, because no news was good news in my head. If he's not messaging that he's okay, he's just busy and I can't worry about him while he's risking his life.

Now, though?

I've been glued to the TV for over two weeks. Any and every mention of this fire in the mountains of Arizona has only fueled my anxiety and panic, but I'm simply a glutton for punishment and can't stay away. My brother has messaged that they're all safe, but it's been days since either Scottie or I have heard from him. Violette said yesterday she'd gotten a brief video call with Rowan, but that was it. He was mildly injured, just a twisted ankle, but I know the fear she is struggling with after his accident earlier this year, when he'd been burned badly.

I haven't heard from Xander, though I'm grateful for Cal, Scottie, and Vi for keeping me up-to-date on him. Even if every mention of him tears a little more at my soul. I don't blame him for not reaching out to me.

Scottie and Vi are sitting on my couch with me. A pizza box is opened on the coffee table in front of us, though none of us have eaten much. This fire has been brutal, an absolute beast. The Vantage crew that Xander had mentioned lost three of their hotshots before teams could get them out. High winds, unpredictable hotspots, and treacherous terrain have made it obvious this fire is not going down without a fight. It consumed everything in its path, and several small mountain towns were evacuated.

Camera footage from above the fire, either by drone or helicopter, makes my throat close. It's massive, the destruction. Never-ending scorched earth and flames shooting high into the sky, curling like a forked tongue in the high winds. I'm sick to my stomach.

The camera footage switches to coverage of a ground crew, and I hold my breath for a sight of Xander, though I know it's a slim chance with the number of crews they have on the ground for this blaze.

"Hey, there's Cal!" Vi exclaims, pointing to the television.

Scottie sits up straighter, her eyes widening on the screen. She blows out a heavy breath and smiles weakly.

I squeeze her hand tight in my own.

"And Rowan, oh thank god!"

Then there's Xander, facing the camera from several yards away, his face nearly black with soot. His eyes flashing that intense sky blue from behind his safety glasses. The clothes he's wearing are dirty and soot stained, and I can just make out the bandage on his right hand, now nearly black with grime.

He looks exhausted—they all do—but the grin on his face as he looks around at his crew . . . he's out there doing what he loves, what he was born to do. The man was born to be a hero.

My fingers tighten around Scottie's again, and I focus so hard on his face that I don't even realize that I'm crying.

"See?" Scottie says, squeezing my hand back. "They're all okay."

I laugh, and then I'm sobbing, dropping my face into my hands as my shoulders shake with the tears that pour out of me.

I was so scared to tell him I love him that I let him walk out without telling him. I let him walk into that fire thinking I don't love him, when that's not even close to the truth.

I love Xander with every breath in my lungs, every beat of my heart. He told me he wants everything, and I let him walk away thinking I didn't want that too. Because I was too scared to try again.

"I was so selfish," I mumble through my tears, finally raising my head enough to swipe at my face. "Ohmygod," I groan, tipping my head back to stare at the ceiling. "He must hate me."

"I doubt that's true," Vi says gently, patting my shoulder. "They all know we get emotional and scared. It's normal."

"But I doubt either of you basically begged Cal or Rowan to stay," I whisper brokenly, heaving a shuddering breath to steady myself. "I begged, you guys. I would have gotten down on my knees. I was so incredibly selfish to ask him to give this up because I'm not strong enough to handle it."

"Rowan got the call for a fire once right as I was starting my period," Violette mumbles, grimacing slightly. "I might have thrown a fork at him when he said he had to go and I cried because I didn't want him to leave."

I snort out a startled laugh, looking over at her incredulously.

Her eyes go wide and she holds her hands out. "*What?!*" she exclaims, laughing too. "I wasn't *aiming* at him. It was just in his general direction!"

"Oh my god," I laugh, shaking my head. "That's hilarious. And a little terrifying."

TEDDY

"Shut up," she laughs, shoving my shoulder gently before reaching out to snag a piece of the pizza.

The news footage has since moved on from the ground crew, leaving me feeling bereft. I could have stared at Xander's dirty, stupidly handsome face forever.

I desperately need him to come home safely.

Looking down at my left hand, I spread my fingers wide on my thigh.

The nakedness of my finger is still something I'm getting used to, but it doesn't hurt the way I expected it to. The small indent and pale strip where my wedding band had sat for over a decade will take time to fade, but . . . it somehow doesn't feel wrong.

It feels like spring, like the beginning of something fresh and new. I just need Xander to come home so I can tell him everything.

48

XANDER

It's been a month of fighting this fucking bitch of a fire and I'm exhausted. Ready to go home.

It's been a fucking month since I've talked to Teddy, heard her voice. That morning that I'd left had nearly fucking killed me. But being without her . . . fuck. I can't keep doing this. I need her so fucking fiercely, every damn part of her. Her worry, her fears, her laughter, her love. I want it all.

Cal and Rowan have kept me in the loop about what Scottie and Violette have told them, but that's about it. Just that she's okay, that the kids are okay.

Nothing else.

This Geronimo fire in Arizona is just about toast, and I can't fucking wait to get our orders to go home.

Sitting on an overturned log, I sip a cup of steaming-hot, shitty campfire coffee and stare down at the envelope that I'd stuffed in my pack before I left that morning. It came with me, remaining inside one of the interior pockets throughout the entire fight.

But now, with this fire's end on the horizon, I pull it out and stare at the handwriting scrawled across the front.

"You ever gonna read that?" Cal asks, sitting down next to me, a plate of food in each hand. He hands me one and I take it with a gruff thanks. "You've been staring at it for an hour."

I huff out a derisive laugh, shaking my head. "Fuck, I've been staring at this for two months."

"What is it?" he asks around a mouthful of food. His legs are spread wide, elbows braced on his knees, his plate suspended in front of him.

I fold the envelope and tuck it into the front pocket of my shirt for safekeeping, then dig into my own food before answering.

"It's a letter from my dad."

"No shit?"

I nod, taking another bite of food. Fuck, I'm starving. "Zach found it in his shit when he was moving. Sent it back to me. I just haven't had the balls to open it."

"Are you scared of what it says?" Cal asks.

Shrugging, I huff out another sigh. "I don't know. Maybe?"

Cal has already scarfed down his plate, and he sits up straighter, then stands, clamping one hand on my shoulder. "Read it, you pussy."

And then he's gone, striding away into the deepening twilight. I finish my plate, then set it aside. I rub my palms together. Anxiety is coursing through me like I've been zapped by a live wire.

"Fuck it," I huff, taking the envelope out of my pocket and ripping the seal open. I hate how much my hands are trembling as I pull the letter out and unfold it. My heart beats triple time as I see my dad's handwriting filling the page. There's no date on it. Scrubbing one hand over my heavily bewhiskered jaw, I start to read.

Son,

There comes a time in every man's life where he starts to reflect on the choices he's made and what path those choices led him down. After thinking on this for several months, I figured it's high time to put my rambling old man thoughts down in the hopes that maybe my choices can help you along the way.

I don't worry about Zach or Joel the way I worry about you. Zach has Brittanee and the babies to round his life out, and Joel is still young. He might be kind of a loose cannon, but I think he'll be figuring out his own ways soon enough. Although, don't tell Zach I say so, I've never really been a fan of that wife of his. Or maybe I just don't know her all that well and she'll prove me wrong.

I can't tell you how proud I am of you boys following in my boots in your own ways. Fighting fire is in our blood, it's in our hearts. It's who we are. And I'm damn proud of all of my boys for making the decision to be a part of this profession. You've proven yourself these last years as a 'shot, and this old man can admit to getting emotional when I think about you taking over as sup here soon. You've made one helluva squaddie and a cap, and I can't wait to see what you can do with this crew as sup leading them. You're fair, honest, a damn hard worker, as well as a good man. You've always had a level head on your shoulders, son. Thinking ahead, planning. Watching.

But that brings me to what I really want to talk to you about, and as you well know, I've never been a man big on sharing feelings and all that mushy shit. I can only hope you boys always knew how much I loved you and always will. I might not have said it often enough, but I hope you knew anyway. I didn't take the time or the effort necessary to love your momma the way she needed, and it cost me the love of my life. Walking away from her, losing her, is my only regret in this life. I let the love I have for this job, the duty I feel to keep going, overshadow the love I have for her and it cost me in spades, son. She asked me to stay and I walked away because I was too fucking proud to admit I needed her more than I needed to breathe, and that scared the hell out of me.

Now, I see the way you watch someone, and it reminds me a lot of the way I imagine I used to look at your mom. Like she was the sun and I was the fool that couldn't stop staring at her even if it killed me. I see it, even if no one else does.

So, if there is only one piece of advice you ever take from your old man, let it be this, Xander: If you have the chance to have that kind of love in your life, hold on to it. Hold on to it with both hands, fiercely, and don't let your pride or some misplaced sense of duty to this job keep you from it. You choose her, every time, son. Don't make the same mistakes as your old man. I found the love of my life and I squandered it to chase fire. And I've lived the last thirty years knowing my heart was beating halfway across the country with a woman that I didn't cherish the way I promised to.

Don't lose that, if you get the chance to have it. Promise me you won't let that kind of love slip through your hands. We're never really worthy of women like that, but we can try with every damn breath in our lungs to love them the way they deserve. So if she ever comes to you and asks you to choose her, and she will, if she loves you like I'm sure she will, you do it. Without question. Without hesitation. Because I promise you, you don't want to get to be my age and realize you lost the best thing in your life.

Don't let yourself get so comfortable in this life that you miss out on something great, son.

—Dad

I must read through it three times from start to finish before letting my hand drop between my knees. I squeeze my eyes shut, fighting like hell to keep the sting of tears at bay.

Pinching the bridge of my nose, I swipe at the tears that gather at the corner of my eyes. Fuck, I miss this man.

But as I sit here, I realize I miss someone else far more. I miss Teddy with every fiber of my being. I'm not whole without her. Without Dalton and Penny and Bea. I need them so fucking much. I love them, fiercely.

Pushing to my feet, I stride over to Cal and clap him on the back. I know what I need to do, and for the first time, I have not one single fucking doubt in my mind that I'm doing the right thing.

"We need to talk," I say gruffly, and he nods.

Because I'm going to choose that woman every damn time.

XANDER

49

Teddy

The leaves have already started to turn colors, and Xander still isn't back.

They've been gone over a month, and I'm going crazy waiting for him to come home. I have so much to tell him. I've considered reaching out to him, to call or text, but fear that I ruined everything by not telling him how I feel keeps me from doing it. Besides, he deserves to hear it in person.

The kids miss him terribly, and I keep telling them that he will be home soon, before they even know it. I just hope that I'm right. I know normally they get mandated breaks from these big fires, but I also know Xander and his team; they will have not followed those orders and stayed to help.

Because these men are some of the bravest and most honorable that I know.

When my phone rings, I pick it up off the counter and answer Scottie's call. "Hey—"

"They're home. They just got back to base and are unloading," she says in a rush, and my entire body goes still. "I'm sorry, Cal told me not to tell you until they were back—"

"That's okay, thank you for telling me," I whisper, spinning in a circle. I laugh, the sound coming out slightly more hysterical than intended, and I slap my hand to my mouth before saying, "I'll see you there."

"Yeah, I'm not waiting for him to get his ass home before I say hello," Scottie chuckles on a grumble. I know she's missed my brother fiercely. "I'll meet you there."

We hang up, and I shout, "Guys, get your shoes on! Xander is home, let's go!"

Dalton vaults over the back of the couch with an excited shout, racing for his bedroom to pull on a sweatshirt and to put on his shoes. Penny is bouncing excitedly in place, her little pigtails lop-sided and waving crazily. I point her in the direction of her shoes, and she slides them on as I rush to buckle Bea into her car seat.

I take half a second to run into the bathroom, just to check that I'm not a total hot mess, and then we're out the door. My jeans hug my curves perfectly, and the long-sleeved top I'm wearing highlights the fullness of my breasts and the narrowness of my waist. My hair is clipped up in a half ponytail at the back of my head, and I push my glasses back up the bridge of my nose.

I manage to get the kids all buckled in and then we're pulling out of the driveway. I know where their base is, having gone there with Cal a handful of times throughout the years. The late-afternoon sun is filtering through the colorful leaves as we drive.

God, I hope I didn't mess this all up completely. Or that he changed his mind about me . . . about all of us. I can only pray that he still loves me.

TEDDY

I see Violette's car parked ahead as we pull into the parking lot, and across the way she and Rowan embrace tightly. He's got her lifted, one arm wrapped beneath her bottom and the other around her back as they kiss. My brother and Scottie are hugging, their foreheads pressed together as they talk and kiss.

As Dalton helps Penny unbuckle, I lift Bea out of the car seat and hold her to my chest, my eyes scanning the people milling around before I take hold of Penny's hand, and the four of us start across the dirt parking lot. I'm sure we're a sight.

I still don't see him, my neck swiveling from side to side, my eyes scanning every face. Where is he?

"Xander!" Penny shouts, startling me, and then both my son and daughter take off at a sprint toward the man that just exited the base building.

Emotion tightens my throat as I take him in. A grin flashes across his face and then he's dropping to his knees, spreading his arms wide as they crash into him hard enough to knock him off balance. He wraps them both in his arms and tugs them close, hugging them tightly. He raises those blue eyes to mine as I reach them, and then he's standing.

I launch myself at him, Bea still clutched in one arm, and I laugh and cry when my other arm curls around his strong, steady frame, those arms curving around me too. It's like coming home.

"Hey, Mama," he whispers, and I can't help the tears that fall when I hear the hitch in his own voice. "Fuck, it's good to see you, beautiful."

I lean away, just slightly, not willing to lose my hold on him just yet, but I have to say what I need to say.

"I'm so sorry," I stammer, my eyes flitting over every inch of his face. My fingers curl into the fabric of his shirt. I don't care that he's filthy, I just need him close. "Xander. I was so selfish, and I'm so sorry. You are the most incredible man I've ever met and I was

318

so wrong to ask you to give something like this up. Something that makes you the man that I love."

His eyes crinkle at the corners when a smile slowly pulls at his lips. One hand comes up and cups my cheek, his thumb caressing gently. I sniffle, but taking my eyes off of his is impossible.

"You love me?" he asks quietly.

"So much," I sob, nodding as I tilt my cheek into his palm. I'm vaguely aware of Violette stepping up beside us to take a wriggling Bea from my arm. "So, so much. I love you. I want everything too, Xander. If you can be brave enough to walk into fires, I can be brave enough to stand beside you while you do it. And we'll be here waiting for you every time."

Xander stares at me as he brackets my face with his strong hands, and with both of my arms free, I close my fingers over the backs of his, holding him close.

"I was a coward. I was terrified of how much I loved you, of how much my kids love you. I should have told you I love you so many times. I should never have let you go thinking you weren't the love of my life." He swipes at the tears tracking my cheeks, a gentle, loving smile on his lips. But he lets me continue, though my voice is broken with the emotions rolling through me. I lick my lips and forge on, my lips wobbling. "I loved Logan. And there's a part of me that will always love him. I will always cherish the time that we had together, and the life I had with him. But there's no ghost, Xander. Because I love you for the days we have ahead of us. I want everything with you, this future we've been given. Only you. I want this, whatever it takes, no matter what it is, or how far away it takes you from us. I want to be brave for you. To take this chance with you."

His eyes drop to my left hand and I swear I can see the tension leave his body as he sees my bare finger. He drops his forehead to mine, rolling it there, our noses bumping, lips barely dragging across the other.

TEDDY

"I love you so much," he whispers, pressing sweet, sipping kisses to my lips. Then he laughs, his breath puffing against my face. "But, sweetheart . . ."

Oh god. My heart cleaves in two. He's going to tell me he can't do this. I ruined everything by taking too long.

"You're going to be stuck with me a lot more than usual," he continues, his eyes shining down at me. "Because I just handed in my resignation. Effective immediately."

I'm struck completely motionless. My brain is moving slowly, as if it's trying to wade through molasses.

"What?" I whisper breathlessly, stunned.

He strokes his fingers over my cheeks, then smooths my hair back away from my face. His eyes rove over all of me before returning to my own. He smiles, so tenderly it makes my heart ache. "I'm getting ahead of myself, sweetheart. First, I need to tell you that I am so sorry, Teddy. For what I said before I left, for being a giant dickhead. I knew I was being unfair to you, and because my pride was stung, I lashed out at you. I had a really smart man give me some big advice. And I'm going to get a lot wrong, and I'm never going to be perfect, but I want all of our days together, Teddy. The beautiful, the mundane, the scary, and the ugly ones too. But I want you with me for all of them. I want this family. I realized that I can't walk away from you again. I can't walk away from these kids. Even if it's temporary. *I love you more than fighting fire, Teddy*," he breathes reverently, pressing his forehead to mine.

My fingers fist tightly in his shirt, clutching him to me as tears slip down my cheeks.

"I need you like I need air, and I'll do whatever it takes to make sure we have everything in this life that I can. I want every fucking day with you. You are my forever, sweetheart. And I'm not waiting for that to start."

"But you love this," I whisper against his mouth. "I can't ask you to give that life up."

"I do love this, and I love you all the more for being willing to stand by me . . . but I know that this is what I need to do. To stay with you. To live *this* life. Maybe put my own ring on that finger and do my best to put a baby in you—"

Grinning, I shake my head, our lips rubbing together as I huff out a laugh. "You're insane. And just what are we going to do with four kids?"

"I'll give you as many babies as you'll let me," he whispers, curving his body over mine. "I think we'd make some damn cute kids together. Promote Bea to big sister."

"Get a room."

Xander flips my brother off over my shoulder and I laugh again. My heart is so unbelievably full.

"What do you say, Mama?" he asks, kissing me again. "Be my girl?"

I sigh, looping my arms around his neck, a smile pulling at my lips.

"I suppose so . . ." I whisper teasingly, and he growls, his eyes narrowing. "Guess it's only fair of you to make an honest woman out of me. Since you already did the baby part . . ."

His head snaps up, eyes wide. His arms tighten around me as he growls low, *"Teddy . . ."*

I tug on the back of his neck until his mouth is once again on mine, and I breathe, "Welcome home, Daddy."

TEDDY

50

Teddy

"I've got to help get these rigs unloaded and cleaned. It might be another hour before we're ready to leave," Xander says, squeezing his arm around my waist. Dalton stands at his side; Penny is in Xander's other arm, braced on his hip; and I once again have Bea cradled against my chest. I tip my head up to look at him from where I'm standing beside him, and his eyes soften as he looks at me.

Like I hung the moon or something. I'm certainly not complaining.

After my surprise announcement, the entire crew erupted with cheers. Scottie and Vi scolded me for not telling them, but I know they won't stay upset with me for long. Cal hugged me tight, lifting me off the ground. When he turned to Xander, he extended his right hand, which Xander took in a firm shake. Cal clapped him on the back with his other hand before pulling him in for the manliest "bro hug" I've ever seen. My brother's eyes were suspiciously wet when they pulled back, and Xander's gaze was adoring as his eyes found mine again, though I'm not sure what had been said between them where no one else could hear.

"Why don't you take the kids home, and I'll be there shortly? I want to shower before I come over," he says.

I shake my head. "Come shower at my place. I'll join you."

His eyes darken with lust as he captures his bottom lip between his teeth, a low growl emanating from his chest, but he shakes his head. "I'm filthy, Teddy."

"I'm aware. Please. I don't want to be away from you longer than I have to be. Let me take care of you for a change," I whisper, my eyes searching his. When he smiles, it crinkles his eyes at the corners, just the way I love, and I smile too.

"Okay, Mama. I'll meet you at home," he says softly, kissing me again.

I nod against his mouth.

"I love you, Teddy. So damn much it makes it hard for me to breathe."

"That might be a heart attack, you old ass," King chuckles as he passes, heading back to the rig, having sent Vi and Hollie back home too. "Might want to get that checked out, Sup."

"I'm not your sup anymore," he calls back, grinning.

It sends my own heart to tripping in my chest. Holy shit. He really retired. King turns, walking backward, his head tilted to the side in question.

Xander nods his chin toward Cal and says, "That title belongs to him now."

Tears prick my eyes and I smile at my brother, who smirks just a little and shrugs.

"Yeah, well, someone's got to keep these hooligans in line now that you're leaving to be all family man and shit."

King claps Cal on the back as he passes, and I watch as the two of them head toward the doors of the base building.

TEDDY

Xander walks us back to my minivan and helps buckle Bea and Penny into their car seats, double-checking them, just like I always do. My heart melts.

"Will you be here when we get up tomorrow?" Dalton asks from the back seat as he buckles too.

"I sure will, champ," Xander says from the open slider door. A beaming smile lights up my son's face, and he nods, satisfied. "Come on, Mama. Climb in."

He holds my door for me as I slide in behind the wheel, and he leans in over me to fasten my seat belt. I laugh, eyeing him like he's a lunatic. "What are you doing?"

He tests the belt, and then lets his hand rest on my stomach. Butterflies erupt in my midsection when I realize what he's doing. Kissing me gently, he says, "Just making sure you're all safe. My entire heart is in this vehicle, Teddy."

Ugh, this man is so fucking swoony.

"I'll see you at home in an hour, okay?" he asks, rubbing his thumb back and forth, where it's still pressed to my abdomen.

I nod.

"I love you."

"I love you, too," I whisper, loving the way the words feel on my tongue. "Don't take too long."

He nods, and then he's ducking out of the door and closing it gently. By the time I get us home and do dinner and bed routines for all three kids, Xander's truck rumbles into the driveway. He doesn't bother going into his side of the duplex, he just walks into mine, like we both know this is where he belongs.

Circling my arms around his neck at the same time his arms go around my waist, I lean up and press my mouth to his in a long, thorough kiss that leaves me aching. "Let's get you cleaned up."

He lets me go so I can turn around and head toward the hallway, but he keeps one of my hands clasped tightly in his own, like he can't bear to lose contact. In the bathroom, I lean into the bathtub and turn on the shower taps to warm. He strips off his dirt- and soot-stained Nomex gear as I set out fresh towels and grab bottles of his favorite body wash and shampoo from below the sink. I'd gotten them as a surprise for him before his accident, so he could shower here, but then he was gone.

Once he's naked, I gesture for him to step into the shower. He does without argument, and when I've set my glasses on the bathroom sink and stripped as well, I step in behind him, pulling the shower curtain closed. He's fully submerged beneath the spray, scrubbing both hands over his face and shoving the wet strands of his hair back. The darkly tanned muscles of his back, shoulders, and arms ripple with each move he makes.

I can't help myself; I step forward and lay my hands flat along his rib cage at his sides before sliding them around to his abdomen, leaning close to press my lips to the center of his spine. God, this man is so beautiful. And he somehow wants me, loves me.

He covers the backs of my hands with his own, holding me in place, and turns his head to look at me over his shoulder. "Fuck, I missed you, sweetheart."

Pressing another kiss to his spine, I murmur back, "I missed you too. I'm glad you're home."

His fingers smooth up and down my arms for a moment before I pull back, reaching around him for the bottle of shampoo. He turns as I squirt some into my cupped palm, then replace the bottle on the shelf.

"Get down here so I can wash your hair," I tell him, my tone gentle but leaving little room for argument.

He grins, the flash of his dimple appearing beneath his thick beard. It's possibly the longest I've ever seen it, and I'm not mad about it. It's sexy as hell.

TEDDY

He lowers to one knee and grasps my hips in his hands, his thumbs digging into the flesh of my stomach. Xander leans close and presses his mouth to my sternum, just between my breasts, his breaths sawing in and out heavily. And with him on his knee before me, I work my fingers through his hair, sudsing the strands thoroughly. I scratch his scalp with my fingernails and he groans, tipping his head back slightly, his eyelids fluttering closed. I grin impishly, happy that I can make him feel good too.

Reaching above us, I take down the handheld shower head and rinse his hair of the shampoo. His hands don't stray from my hips, though his fingers flex against me as I work.

I suds up his hair once more with shampoo to get any residual dirt and grime out of it, rinse it again, and then he stands. His cock bobs, hard and heavy, between us. Those incredible blue eyes of his are hungry and he reaches for me, but I tsk him lightly, shaking my head.

His dark brows lower over his eyes and he groans in misery. "Please, sweetheart. I want to touch you. I need to touch you."

"I'm not done taking care of you yet," I murmur, reaching around him for the bottle of bodywash and a loofa I have hanging against the wall. His heated gaze watches as I pour out some of the cedar-wood and citrus–scented body wash and work it into a lather. "Turn around, please."

"You're teasing me, you naughty fucking thing," he growls low, but does as I say. I grin from behind him, loving that I can drive him crazy like this.

I start at his shoulders, working the loofah over every inch of his skin. Down his back, over each taut butt cheek, each arm from shoulder to wrist, and then I kneel, working the suds over the backs of his thighs and calves. Standing, I turn him to face me.

His chest is damn near heaving with each breath, his gaze hot and hungry as he takes me in. I roll my lips in between my teeth to hide my smile and raise my arm, starting the process over at his shoulders and moving across his chest and abdomen, down his hips, circling dangerously close to the rock-hard erection he's sporting. He growls low, the sound making me shiver, but I keep going.

Kneeling once again, I lather each thigh and work down his shins to his feet. Then, and only then, do I look up at him. His chest heaves, his hands curling and uncurling into fists at his sides, like it's taking every bit of his self-control not to touch me. Biting my lip, I smile coyly up at him and he shakes his head, chuckling.

"You wicked, wicked thing," he rasps darkly.

I drop the loofah but raise my soapy hand, circling his hardness in my fingers and sliding from base to tip and back. I make sure to soap every inch of him, slowly.

"Fucking goddamn, Teddy," he chokes out, his control breaking as he slides his hands around the back of my head. "Please, Mama. I need to be inside you."

Standing again, I push him backward with my hand in the center of his chest into the spray of water, the suds sluicing down his body. He reaches behind him, twisting the handle of the water and turning it off. His hands are on me an instant later, hauling me to him. One hand tangles in the back of my hair, tied up in a bun, forcing my mouth up to his. His kiss is fierce, hungry. Like a man starved, he devours my mouth, until we're both panting and breathless.

With a groan, he grabs the towels I left beside the shower and wraps me in one, then steps out, taking my hand and assisting me out as well. Haphazardly drying his own body, he tosses the towel over the curtain bar before reaching for me again, but I'm already working on drying myself off. Xander tears the towel from my hands and tosses it too, and a laugh bursts out of me when he wraps both arms around my hips and lifts me off my feet, carrying me out of the bathroom and into the bedroom. One lamp is dimly lit in the corner and casts the room in soft light and stark shadows.

TEDDY

I half expect him to drop me into the center of the bed, but of course he doesn't; he sets me down gently, then pushes me onto my back, spreading my thighs as he settles over me. But he doesn't kiss me again. Instead, he sinks down and presses his mouth to my abdomen, his hands spanning wide on my hips, framing my lower stomach. My fingers glide into his hair as he presses sweet, tender kisses to where our baby is currently growing. Once again, tears prick my nose, and I have to blink rapidly to dispel them from my eyes.

"Hi in there," he whispers reverently to my stomach. I smooth the wet strands of his hair back away from his forehead. He looks up my body at me and smiles, his own eyes misting. "My baby is really in here?"

"Your baby is really in here," I whisper back, nodding. My lips wobble as I smile. "The doctor confirmed I'm six weeks. So it's still very early, Xander, but yes. We're having a baby."

Crawling up my body, he wraps one arm beneath my shoulders and the other cradles the back of my head as he kisses me, slow and thorough.

"I fucking love you so much," he rasps against my mouth.

Shifting my hips, I circle against him, where I can feel his hardness at my hip. He's keeping his weight off of me, but I need to feel it. I need his weight on top of me, I need him to fill me. "Please, Xander . . ."

He chuckles lightly, his teeth nipping at my lip, making me gasp. He moves so that his hips are between my spread thighs. Where I want him the most. "Who's the one begging now?"

"Shamelessly," I pant raggedly, sliding my hands down his back to clutch his perfect ass. "I've waited so long for you, please. Fill me up. Remind me I'm yours, Xander."

"You're all mine," he groans, lining himself up against my pussy. I'm soaked already, all the teasing in the shower turning me on just as much as it had him. Leveraging himself up on his hands, he raises his chest off mine and drops his chin to look between our bodies. "Watch how well this pussy takes my cock, Teddy. Watch how greedy it is for me."

He pushes inside, inch by inch, and our matching moans are a dirty, needy melody in the semidarkness of the room around us.

"Fuck, Teddy. Oh shit, am I going to hurt you or—"

"No, no," I pant raggedly, shaking my head against the pillow.

"Good," he grunts, his jaw clenching tight as he sinks inside me slowly, working in and out in shallow thrusts. "I'm going to take my time with you tonight, Mama, but right now I want to fuck you. Fast and hard, Teddy. And then I'll take my time."

"Ohmygod," I breathe, nodding frantically, watching as his thickness disappears inside me. Until he's buried to the hilt and circling his hips against mine. When he does, it hits that special spot and I can't help the moan that leaves my lips. He grins from above me, that wicked, mischievous smirk, his long, damp hair falling forward over his brow. Sliding out all the way to the tip, he slams back in, hard. Clasping his jaw in both of my hands, I drag his mouth down to mine, his beard tickling my palms and my lips as he kisses me. His thrusts are long, deep, and fierce, and it's not long before I'm starting to shake as my climax bears down on me. A tear slips down my cheek and I sob as I shatter in his arms, "I love you."

"That's it, that's it," he groans, pistoning his hips into mine, his mouth dragging against my own as I continue to come, shuddering against him. My inner muscles are convulsing wildly around his hardness and he hisses, "Goddamn, you come so good for me. I love you so fucking much, Teddy. Did this sweet pussy miss my cock, sweetheart?"

TEDDY

"Oh god, yes, Xander," I cry out, but his mouth muffles the sound with a kiss.

"Say it again," he rasps out the demand against my mouth.

Shoving my fingers up through the hair falling over his brow, I whisper breathlessly, "I love you, Xander."

Dropping his forehead to mine, he groans, then his hips stutter in their thrusts as he comes too. My fingers are tangled in his still-damp hair and I hold him to me as he shudders against me, filling me.

His chest heaving, he falls to my side, dragging me with him and drawing me against his body. He smooths his hands over my hair as we work to slow our breaths and hammering hearts.

Drawing my thigh up over his hip, he smooths his palm from my thigh all the way to my waist and back before settling his hand against my abdomen between us.

"Thank you," he whispers above me, his lips moving against my forehead.

I raise my chin, my eyes finding his. "For what?" I breathe, smoothing my fingers over his brow and then down his cheek, cupping his jaw tenderly. I can't stop touching him.

He turns his head, kissing the center of my palm before returning his cheek to it. "For giving me everything I didn't know I wanted and needed. For loving me," he murmurs quietly, his fingers flexing against my stomach.

"Thank you for loving us," I whisper back, those damn tears filling my eyes again. "Thank you for always seeing me, even when I didn't see you."

He turns his head again, pressing his lips to my palm once more, and then whispers reverently, "You always saw me, Teddy. We just had to wait our turn. But I'm never letting you go, and I'm not wasting a second of this life with you, Mama. *Marry me*," he breathes, and my heart trips over itself with incandescent happiness. "Don't make me wait to call you my wife. Please, Teddy."

"Okay," I whisper, nodding, my eyes on his, my lips wobbling again. "Yes. Yes, Xander."

I can be brave, with Xander by my side, loving me. I can't wait for that either. Our future together, this life, this chance. Our new forever.

TEDDY

EPILOGUE

XANDER

SEVEN MONTHS LATER

"Look who I brought," I say quietly, pushing the heavy door open slowly. The hospital room is quiet, early-afternoon sunlight filtering through the half-closed blinds across the room.

My beautiful wife is sitting up in the bed, and she smiles wide as the four of us trek inside. Dalton has a bouquet of flowers in his hands, and he sets them on the wide window ledge like I'd instructed before we came in. Penny is tiptoeing across the polished tile floor, being as quiet as she can, just like we'd rehearsed. The little hellion has chilled out—if only mildly—in the last year.

Thirteen-month-old Bea is in my arm, her short brown curls tied up into my best attempt at pigtails. Kent and Colleen follow us in, shrinking the room and filling it with a lot of whispered chatter. Before the door closes behind them, Scottie and Cal enter. I shake my head. I think we're at capacity for this tiny room.

I step over to the side of the bed and lean down to press a tender kiss to my wife's forehead. She tips her face up to me, a serene, content smile pulling at her lips. Goddamn, I have the most beautiful wife.

Bea reaches for her and I slide her off my arm slowly. "Okay, remember, we have to be very careful," I whisper to the toddler. She settles against Teddy's side, resting her head against the slope of her breast. "How are you feeling? I wasn't gone for too long, was I?"

"Xander, you were gone for less than an hour. I'm okay," she laughs lightly, reaching out to stroke my cheek, her fingernails rasping against the thick stubble of my beard. I clasp her hand in mine and bring her fingers to my lips, kissing them tenderly. Fuck, I love this woman. "Rowan and Vi came up while you were gone to sit with me and meet the baby."

We both peer down at our newborn daughter, Spencer Leigh Macomb, swaddled and happily sleeping in my wife's other arm. Penny tugs at my shirt and I bend over to lift her up gently, setting her on the edge of the hospital bed. She leans over the baby, oohing almost silently.

My heart is so fucking full. Dalton hangs back, and I step over to him. "Do you want to go look?"

"Can I hold her?" he asks, looking up at me.

I look over at Teddy, who nods with a smile.

"Okay, champ, in that chair. Let me grab this pillow—" I say, swiping the pillow I'd used the night before off the little foldaway bed in the corner of the room. I get him situated, and then move to lift my newborn daughter out of Teddy's arm. I press a kiss to the pink hat that covers her dark head of hair—for which we can thank all of Teddy's hellacious heartburn the last few months—and then carefully lower her into the cradle of Dalton's arm, supported by the pillow. "Good job, man. Such a natural."

He rolls his eyes. "I've done this before."

I chuckle lightly, nodding as I sink into a crouch beside him. Kent, Colleen, Cal, and Scottie have convened on Teddy, leaving just Dalton and me with the baby. I watch my stepson as his brown eyes move over his new little sister reverently.

XANDER

"She's cute," he says, and I have to agree. Teddy did a damn good job.

And we didn't have to have an emergency home birth, thank God, though all the guys had made sure to text me to remind me of my alternate career now that I've retired from being a hotshot. This birth was completely uneventful, for which I'm eternally grateful. I'm not entirely sure I could have been quite so calm and collected this go-around.

Cal had more than earned his place as superintendent and proved to be just as fair and demanding a leader as I'd hoped he would. He made Rowan captain shortly after, and I can't pretend I'm not damn proud of both of them. Forever my brothers.

The part of me that had struggled with feeling duty-bound to the job has faded over the last year. I guess because now I've got something that I view as the most important job I'll ever have in my life. Something I feel fucking honored to have been given the chance to do.

Being a husband and a father. Watching all of my kids grow—because Teddy's are just as much mine now—is the best thing ever. Spending every single day with the love of my life and knowing she's the one I get to climb into bed with every night. The one I get to make love to and prove that my love for her and this family is steadfast and unwavering.

We moved out of the duplex—both apartments—and found a home down the street from Cal and Scottie. We have a yard big enough for the kids to play in—with no creek running behind it, thank God—and room for our growing family. Glancing over at Teddy, I'm not at all ashamed to admit I'd love nothing more than to add at least one more to our family . . . when she's ready, of course.

While we were unpacking at the new house, Teddy had quietly offered to leave the photos of Logan boxed up, but I pulled her into my arms and told her no. Dalton and Penny—and someday

Bea too—need to have those reminders of where they came from. The love Teddy and I have, this life we've taken the chance on, isn't threatened or diminished by the life she had with Logan. I know that, now. And they deserve to know who he was and how loved they were by both of them. Our wedding picture now sits side by side with the one of a very young Teddy and Logan from so long ago. These kids will always know how much they're loved by us too.

"Xander?" Dalton whispers, catching my attention.

I shift on my haunches and look up at him. "Yeah, champ?"

"Will this baby get to call you Dad?" he asks, his voice quiet so that no one else can hear.

I nod, placing my hand on his shoulder and squeezing lightly. "Yeah, she will."

"Oh," he says, nodding, looking back down at the baby before raising his eyes to mine. "Do you think it would be okay if we call you Dad, too?"

I glance over the arm of the chair, where I can see Teddy. Her focus is on us, and I have a feeling she heard the conversation, because her eyes are shining with tears. My chest seizes as I return my gaze to Dalton.

"You know, champ, I would be honored if you wanted to call me Dad," I somehow manage to whisper around the lump that's lodged in my throat.

As I look over at my wife again, I think back to that letter from my dad, and I like to think that he'd be damn proud of the life that I've got now.

Because I found that once-in-a-lifetime love . . . and I'm holding on fiercely with both hands.

**KEEP READING FOR AN
EXCLUSIVE BONUS CHAPTER . . .**

Teddy

FOUR MONTHS LATER

"We're certifiably insane, right? This is insane. What were we even thinking when we said yes to this? Is it too late to tell your mom we can't make it?"

My mind is running a million miles a minute, mentally going over our packing list for each kid, myself, Xander, the baby . . .

Xander steps up behind me, wrapping those big, strong arms around me, clasping me close. His chin drops to my right shoulder, leaning his temple against mine. I melt into his embrace, the tension and anxiety disappearing—at least momentarily—while in his arms. I cover his arms with my own where they're wrapped around my middle.

"Everything we do is probably certifiably insane," he chuckles, lips moving against my cheek as he squeezes me tighter. "Traveling across the country with three kids and a newborn? That's nothing. We've done crazier shit, Teddy. Like getting married two weeks after I retired."

"That wasn't crazy," I whisper, turning my head to peck a kiss to his lips. "That was perfect."

"That it was," he breathes against my lips, and my entire body lights up.

God, the way this man still makes those butterflies in my middle take flight with the simplest things.

"And to answer your last question, yes, it is far too late to tell my mother we're not coming," he laughs then, nuzzling my neck again. "She'd probably riot and then fly out here to get our asses moving herself."

"You're probably right," I laugh, sighing. "And I know you're looking forward to seeing Zach and Joel."

"I honestly don't remember the last time I was back in Petoskey," he admits, once again hooking his chin on my shoulder. "It will be nice to spend some time with both of them. And my mom. I know she deserves more visits. Thank you for saying yes when she invited us, Teddy."

"Of course," I whisper, squeezing his arms. "I adore your mom."

The house is quiet around us, all the kids tucked into bed for the night. Spencer is sleeping in her crib in the nursery, at least for now. She will end up in the bassinet next to our bed at some point tonight, as usual. Xander had insisted she start in the crib tonight though so my frantic late-night packing and repacking wouldn't disturb her. He's gone over the checklist with me a dozen times, and I'm grateful as always for the man that he is. Always our provider, protector, and hero. Spencer is one thousand percent a daddy's girl and has him wrapped around her little finger. Honestly, it's no different than the other three either. You'd think these kids hung the moon with how much he adores them. And vice versa.

I'm reminded again of just how lucky we all are to have him.

The baby monitor perched on the kitchen counter next to us chirps, just once, and Xander chuckles against my neck. "Noisy little sleeper she is."

"Right?" I laugh, and then I sag against his chest and let my head drop back to his shoulder and groan. "She's only four months old, Xander. Don't you think she's too young to travel this far?"

"The flight will be a piece of cake, and we fly in as close to Petoskey as I could get us. Spence will sleep most of it anyway, I'll handle Bea and Penny, and Dalton will help if we need it. We've got this, beautiful."

My mind goes back to the mile-long packing list. What if I forget something important and we suffer a meltdown of epic proportions mid-flight?

"Do you need a distraction to get you out of your head, Mama?" he whispers against my ear, dragging his mouth across my temple and cheek. One of his hands slides down my front, lingering over every curve—this once-again postpartum body is soft as always—before dipping below the waistband of my leggings, his palm cupping my pussy before sliding a finger through my folds. He groans against my neck and I rock back against his hips, feeling him grow hard against me. "Goddamn, Teddy. You're always so wet. So ready. Like you can't get enough of your husband."

I nod, my knees growing weak when he slips two fingers inside. He knows just how that word drives me wild. The first time he'd growled the word *wife* in my ear, I'd come almost instantaneously.

The eight weeks of healing after Spencer's birth were the longest and most miserable of my life . . . but God, had he made the wait worth it. He'd been so patient after my six-week checkup, and I hadn't gotten the all-clear like we'd hoped. The final two weeks had been *hell*. We'd teased each other to the point of insanity, driving each other wild with repressed need.

"Yes," I whisper, nodding. "I love the way my husband fucks me."

He sinks his teeth into the meaty part of my shoulder and I moan, grinding my hips against his erection.

TEDDY

His fingers slide out of me and I whimper—I fucking *whimper*—and then he's spinning me to face him, his hands diving into my hair as he hauls me up and against him, mouth crashing to mine. He kisses me until I'm breathless, a trembling, melting mess of a woman. Those hands leave my hair, trailing down my body until he's gripping handfuls of my ass in both his palms, grinding me against him like he can't get enough either.

And then he reaches down and grasps me beneath my ass, picking me up. I don't bother arguing or protesting; it never does any good. The man does what he wants, and if he wants to pick my ass up and carry me, I'll let him.

He crosses the room to the big L-shaped couch in the living room and sits, sinking into the soft cushions, my knees landing on either side of his hips. He never stops kissing me, hands roaming over me as I settle on his lap, the *V* of my thighs cradling his hardness.

I love this part; the frenzied, passionate make outs. His kisses drive me wild, the way his hands don't stop moving, petting and stroking every inch of me.

"If you don't take these off in the next ten seconds, I'll rip them off you," he warns gruffly, voice rough and low.

I laugh, then scramble up, peeling the leggings and my panties down my thighs and tossing them away. I know the threat isn't idle; he's ripped several already.

By the time I'm climbing back onto his lap, he's yanked his sweatpants down his hips, hard cock bobbing up against his abdomen, tip leaking. Using my thighs, I lift myself over him as he grips his cock in his hand, positioning the head at my entrance.

He doesn't thrust up, but lets me take over as I sink down onto him. "Such a good wife, Teddy," he breathes roughly as I take all of him, settling my hips against his fully. He stretches me so deliciously. He groans when I spasm around him, his hands sliding over the curve of my hips, holding me still. "Fuck, sweetheart. You're so

342

tight. So fucking tight for me. I'm never going to get enough of you, Teddy. Never."

"Never," I agree on a whimper as I start to move.

His head falls back against the cushion of the couch behind him, his mouth dropping open with a groan.

"Do you love your wife's pussy, husband?"

"Fuck yes," he groans raggedly, thrusting upward as I come back on a downward stroke. "Like it was made for me."

One hand slides down until it's between us, his thumb finding my clit and stroking in quick circles. My rhythm falters as I cry out at the added stimulation, my inner muscles tightening around him. "Xander. Ohmygod."

"Ride me, Mama. I want you to come on your husband's cock at least twice," he demands quietly, his fingers never ceasing their movement. "Make a mess of me, Teddy, and then I'm going to fill you up."

"Yes," I whine, doing exactly as he instructed. My thighs shake, head tossed back as my orgasm begins to build deep inside. "Don't— don't stop, Xander. I'm so close—"

"That's it, Mama," he growls, and I let out a soft cry as I come around him, my chest seizing as I shake uncontrollably. His other hand grips my left hip hard, grinding me against him as I shatter. "*Atta girl, Teddy*. Do it again. *Fuck*, I love feeling you come."

The thumb against my clit never ceases, and I know it won't be long before I'm coming again, one on top of the other, as overstimulated as I am. On the edge, I sob brokenly, grinding my hips in a circle, unable to lift off him. "Oh fuck, oh fuck, *please*—"

"Give it to me, *wife*," Xander demands, releasing his grip on my hip and collaring my throat instead.

Both of my hands wrap around his forearm and wrist, holding on as I come again, harder this time. Squeezing my eyes shut tight, my mouth opens in a silent cry into the darkness of the room cloaking us.

TEDDY

"Yes, yes, Teddy—*good fucking girl*—"

He spins us, tossing me onto my back on the couch, and then he's moving. Hips shunting forward hard as he fucks me into the cushions. With one hand braced on the cushion above my shoulder, he uses the other to shove my shirt and bra up, baring my breasts. And then his mouth is there, sucking first one nipple into his mouth before switching to the other.

"Fuck," he groans around my nipple, his hips driving faster, harder against mine. "Fuck, Teddy, I'm going to come, sweetheart—"

Wrapping my legs around the backs of his, I hold him close as he swells inside of me, and then I feel every pulse as he empties inside me. A shudder wracks his body as he comes, his forehead falling to rest against my shoulder.

Enclosing him in my arms, I pull him closer until he relents and settles his body over mine. Stroking his dark locks away from his forehead, I press a kiss to his temple as our frantically beating hearts and ragged breathing settle.

"I love you," I whisper against his temple, smoothing my fingers over his hair, his cheek, down over his shoulders and back. "So much, Xander."

Raising himself onto his elbows, he captures my mouth with his own.

This kiss is gentle, tempered, and languid. His voice is low, reverent, when he whispers back, "*I love you, Teddy*. I have for so long, I don't remember a time I didn't."

I believe him.

GLOSSARY

ANCHOR POINT: a strategic location from which to start building a fire line, starting at a natural unburnable area, such as rock scree, creeks, or trails. The goal of an anchor point is to prevent the fire from burning around the fire line, pinning firefighters from behind.

ASH PIT: a hole in the ground filled with hot ash and embers.

BACKBURN, BACKFIRE, OR BURNOUT: terms for intentionally putting fire on the ground and burning vegetation against an active flame front to deprive it of fuel.

BLACK: the area that is already burnt.

BUGGY: a transportation vehicle consisting of seating with no water supply. It has a total of eight seats, allowing for a large number of crew to be transported to the fire.

CHAIN: a unit of measurement, commonly used in wildland fires. Eighty chains equal one mile, so one chain is sixty-six feet long.

CONTROL OR CONTAINMENT LINE: any constructed or natural barrier used to impede a fire's progress.

CRAMPONS: a metal plate with spikes fixed to a boot for walking on ice or rock climbing.

CROWN FIRES: when canopies of trees light with flame. These are often the largest, hardest to contain, and fastest-moving fires. When one canopy ignites, that fire can begin jumping from tree to tree.

DIVISION: the person who implements an assigned portion of the incident action plan (IAP) and is responsible for all operations conducted in the division/group on wildland fire incidents.

DRIP TORCH: a handheld tool used to set controlled fires, or prescribed burns, by intentionally igniting fires by dripping flaming fuel onto the ground.

EMBER WASH: a shower of hot embers, carried by the wind, often enabling the fire to "jump" over control lines and spread by creating spot fires. Embers can travel over a mile before falling.

ENGINE: a truck or other ground vehicle that can transport and pump water, via hoses, onto a fire.

ENGINE CREW: a team of up to ten firefighters attached to an engine, tasked with initial, direct engagement of a wildfire. They use a variety of tools, primarily relying on hoses and water.

ESCAPE ROUTE: a predetermined route to allow firefighters to get to safety, should the situation become unsafe on the ground.

FIRE-CHASING BEETLES OR MELANOPHILA BEETLES: insects attracted to forest fires because they use freshly burnt (and sometimes still-smoldering) wood to lay their eggs. They gather near the fire and have a vicious bite, often attacking wildland firefighters working on a fire line.

FIRE LINE: a line of ground without vegetation that will presumably stop or direct a fire's progress. Firefighters dig line by hand, using Pulaskis and other tools.

GREEN: fuel-laden area that hasn't yet burned.

HAND CREW: general-purpose wildland firefighters. Hand crews are typically eighteen to twenty people and work on digging line, clearing trees and brush with chainsaws, and setting controlled burns with drip torches.

HELIBUCKET OR BUCKET WORK: a bucket that hangs from a helicopter by a cable and is used to transport and apply water or retardant directly onto a fire. Helibuckets can be dropped into a lake or river to refill with water, holding as much as 2,600 gallons.

HELITACK CREW: a team of firefighters trained and certified to support helicopters to fight fires.

HOTSHOTS: an intensively trained team of wildland firefighters primarily tasked with directly engaging a fire and digging hand lines.

IMET: the incident meteorologist.

INCIDENT COMMANDER: the leader on a fire and one of as many as dozens of people managing the complex planning, safety, strategy, and operations on a conflagration.

LADDER FUELS: flammable materials, like small trees or low limbs, that allow a fire to move from the forest floor up into the canopy, increasing the intensity and potential growth of a fire. When those fires grow larger and "ladder" up trees, they can ignite crown fires.

MRE: meals ready-to-eat. A self-contained, lightweight ration that provides a full meal for an individual.

NOMEX OR YELLOWS: the yellow shirt worn by wildland firefighters. Nomex is a trademarked term for a flame-resistant fabric widely used for industrial applications and fire protection equipment.

OSBORNE FIRE FINDER: a device used by fire lookouts to locate directional bearing of smoke in order to alert fire crews to a wildland fire.

PRESCRIBED OR CONTROLLED BURN: a planned fire that is intentionally set to achieve specific management goals such as to reduce wildfire risk and restore natural ecosystems.

PULASKI: a tool with a head that has an ax blade on one side and an adze on the other.

ROLL: a fire assignment.

SCREE: a mass of small loose stones that form or cover a slope on a mountain.

SHIP: a helicopter.

SNAG: a dead, often fire-killed, standing tree that presents a hazard for firefighters on the ground.

SPOT FIRE: an occurrence when embers drift across control lines and settle on vegetation or other flammable material, igniting new flames.

STIHL: a brand of chainsaw, used by wildland firefighters to cut brush, snags, and debris.

TORCHING: when one or more trees goes up in flames.

UTV: a utility terrain vehicle. A motor vehicle designed for off-road use that's typically larger than an all-terrain vehicle (ATV) and is often used for work rather than recreation.

VOLLY FIREFIGHTER: a volunteer (wildland) firefighter.

ACKNOWLEDGMENTS

I honestly don't even know where to begin on this one, guys. I have so many people to thank for helping make this book and this series not only possible but the absolute powerhouse that it's turned into.

First and foremost, to Sloane and Paisley. I can't say enough thank-yous to the two of you for believing in this absolutely batshit crazy idea I had and for running with it. This series wouldn't have come to life without both of you working on this with me, and I'm so incredibly grateful for getting to be not only author friends but real-life friends too. I couldn't have done this without you.

Sloane, woman. Honestly, a billion thank-yous will never suffice. Thank you from the bottom of my heart for believing in me and in this collaboration, and for your unwavering and selfless friendship. I'm looking forward to our champagne celebration together. You are my author bestie, my heart friend. I love you, sis!

Paisley, we made it to the other side! This series wouldn't be complete without you as a part of it, and I am so grateful that you said yes to us! Thank you for the encouragement, the ideas, the endless group chats to get everything perfect! Cheers to us, babe!

Mom, as always, my number-one fan, my biggest cheerleader, and the best proofreader around. You told me my idea wasn't completely insane—not sure yet if that was true or not—but you believed in it and in me. Thank you for loving me and believing that that fifteen-year-old with the reams of notebooks would be here one day. You knew it all along.

Kara, my work bestie, my bookish bestie, my ride-or-die for all things bookish events, and the best PA an author girlie could ask for. Thank you for keeping me on track even when my little author heart wants to deviate from my writing schedule and work on nineteen different things all at once . . . you keep me down to, like, three. Thank you for your unfiltered and honest feedback and telling me when I've got something gold and when I don't. You're always right, dammit, lol. Thank you for believing in this switch and not letting me sink into that self-doubt I'm so great at. You knew this was it. I love you!

Rachel, thank you for taking this series and making sure we weren't off on different planets in our plots and timelines. Your dev edits were impeccable. You took the chaos of three authors and three separate novels and harnessed it into this polished series. Like Thanos with the Infinity Stones. You're a badass!

Whiskey Ginger. Ma'am. These covers. I'm still not over how incredibly beautiful they are. Thank you for taking our half-baked ideas and turning them into these amazing covers!

Cathryn, thank you for making the insides of these books just as stunning as the outside! From cover to cover, these books are simply incredible to look at. Thank you!!

Shannon, the woman that kept all of us on a leash and on a schedule . . . I can't imagine how stressful we made it for you! Thank you for every damn thing you did to make sure we knew what the hell we were doing at any given point, lol.

Betas/ARC readers/Hype Squad. Holy crap, you guys, thank you for all the feedback, for loving this series and these characters as much as we do and for being unabashedly vocal in your praise and promotion of these books!

S. Our very own hotshot extraordinaire. Thank you for every single text message, screenshot, fire map, and info link you sent to us. Thank you so much for entertaining three crazy-ass women with absolutely no idea what we were doing and for being determined to make sure we held strong to the authenticity of this profession that deserves so much more praise than it gets. You were incredible, sir. Thank you!

T. Thank you for being my rock and my friend through this last year, for the boundless "I'm so f*cking proud of you's" you've lavished me with when I needed them most, and for being the giver of the best hugs ever.

My agent, Nikki at SBR Media, thank you for rallying behind us and making things happen! I look forward to the future with you on my team!

To the entire Slowburn team, thank you for seeing the life in this series and running with it! I cannot wait to see where this series goes with your team at the helm!

Last but not least, you. The readers. A million and one thank-yous to all my readers, whether you've been with me since the beginning or if you're just discovering me . . . **Thank you**. I can't believe I get to do this for a living, and it's all because of every single one of you. I am so incredibly grateful.

I hope you love Xander and Teddy as much as I do.

ABOUT THE AUTHOR

DANIELLE BAKER is a romance author whose books include the Petoskey Stone Series, Holiday Novella Collection and *Honor*, the third book the Sky Ridge Hotshots series. She was born and raised in the beautiful city of Petoskey, Michigan. When Danielle isn't writing or spending time with her family, she can be found with a cup of coffee in one hand and a book in the other.

Instagram @author_daniellebaker

TikTok @author.danielle.baker

MORE BOOKS BY DANIELLE BAKER

PETOSKEY STONE SERIES

Love Unbound

Best Kept Secrets

A Heart So Wild

When Hearts Collide

Lessons in Love

HOLIDAY NOVELLA COLLECTION

Be Mine, Valentine

Lucky in Love

Birthday Wishes

Halloween Night

Meet Me Under the Mistletoe

Midnight Kiss